THE SENTIENT

A NOVEL BY
LUCAS GORTON MCINTIRE

THE SENTIENT

Lucas Gorton McIntire

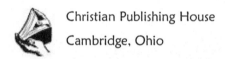

Christian Publishing House
Cambridge, Ohio

Christian Publishing House
Professional Conservative Christian
Publishing of the Good News!

CPH Since 2005

ISBN-13: **978-1-949586-04-6**

ISBN-10: **1-949586-04-9**

Table of Contents

CHAPTER I

NIGHT TERRORS

"Aauugghhh!!" Tabatha releases a chilling, blood-curdling scream as she wakens from a deep sleep. She sits up on her couch, exhaling heavily as if she just finished a triathlon. She reaches over and grabs a syringe filled with a special medication out of a brown pouch off the coffee table. The medicine helps to stabilize her metabolism, which already burns twice as fast compared to the average person but increases several times more than that during what she calls – a night terror. 'Night terrors' seem to be affiliated with her telepathic abilities. They began about two years ago, and though were random events, they were very rare. Now they seem to happen far more frequently and sometimes even occur during the day. She calls those, 'daydreams.' She wipes the sweat off her forehead and runs her fingers through her matted strawberry blond hair, about shoulder blade length, slightly damp from sweat, attempting to untangle it.

Naomi, Tabatha's aunt/godmother, adopted her after she was born. Tabatha's mother died during childbirth due to complications of having twins, which Tabatha is the oldest. Her twin sister, Sarah, reportedly died hours after taken to the N.I.C.U. The two of them visit the gravesites of Martha and Sarah regularly.

Naomi was startled awake from the sound of Tabatha's scream and rushed from her bed to the living room, where Tabatha normally sleeps, even though she has a king-size bed that takes up nearly her entire bedroom.

"Tab!" Naomi shouts.

"I just had a dream," Tabatha responds before Naomi asks, shoving M&M's in her mouth as fast as she can swallow them, to help replenish her strength.

"What happened?"

"I'm fine mom," again responds before Naomi asks.

"Are you....ok?" Naomi stands next to the couch, staring critically at Tabatha. "Tabatha, please stop using your telepathy on me. We can hardly ever have a conversation when you do that."

Tabatha puts the bowl of m&m's back on the coffee table and leans back into the arm of the couch. She puts her hand on her forehead; her flesh is burning up – another symptom of her hyper telepathic activity that will soon return to normal after injecting herself with the medication. A little grin appears on Tabatha's face in response to Naomi's comment. "I know mom, I'm sorry."

Naomi smiles, "so, another dream, huh. They're becoming a little more frequent, aren't they?"

"They're becoming more vivid." Tabatha sits up, swings her legs off the couch and rests her elbows on her knees and her face in her hands.

"Oh sweetheart, tell me about it."

Tabatha takes a breath. "Well, it was pretty much the same, maybe a little clearer. I'm in a dark room strapped to the same table. Two individuals dressed like doctors were sticking me with I.V. A power cable of some kind was plugged into an implanted outlet in the back of my skull – like it's going into the base of my brain. It's just, eeeee," Tabatha cringes at the image and the feeling.

"Oh-my-goodness!! Tabatha!!" Naomi likewise cringes at the thought, then feels the back of her head for an outlet.

"In your other dreams, you said you couldn't read minds, but you were projecting thoughts into the minds of the people trying to harm you, and that made them go kind of crazy, right?" Naomi reminds Tabatha and walks into the kitchen.

"Yeah, I wasn't able to do it this time. I got the impression that I was sedated. Very weird. The craziest part of it is that I could feel it this time. When I felt like I was being electrocuted, I woke up." Tabatha leans back into the couch and gazes intently at Naomi standing in front of the fridge on the other side of the kitchen island – which was the only divider between the kitchen and living room.

"Yes, please."

"Would you like some – tea – TABATHA – STOP IT!!" Naomi lectures Tabatha, who chuckles under her breath, grinning nearly from ear to ear.

"Ok-ok, I'm sorry mom." Tabatha apologizes.

"Ever since you were a child, your *gift* has both amazed me and drove me crazy. However, I'm proud of how you've disciplined yourself to use it without taking advantage of others with it."

"*Gift?! HA!!*" Tabatha gets up, goes to the kitchen, leans against the island, and looks toward the ceiling. "I work in a department of mostly men, need I say more. I'd rather *not* be able to see *or* hear most of what the human psyche can produce." The two of them chuckle. "And, admittedly, I can't say I *never* took advantage of someone with it. If it weren't for a particular numerically intellectual chick in my college math class, I would never have passed calculus." Tabatha admits.

"Well, if that's the worst you've done, I can't complain." Naomi smiles. As far as the boys you work with – I *believe* you *can* turn it off," Naomi reminds Tabatha. "Ya, you're not as innocent in that area as you let on, dear child."

"Touché," Tabatha responds in admittance. "However, it's not as easy as you think – to, as you put it, 'turn it off." She corrects Naomi.

"You're a gorgeous young lady Tabatha. Maybe you can drag one of them, boys, you work with down the aisle at least," Naomi winks.

"Hahaha!! Right – I'm thirty-six moms...not that young anymore. Most of them would *have* to be drug down the aisle, that's for sure. But, they're just acquaintances. And, *definitely* not the 'bring home to your parent's type either.' Although there is one guy who works in decrypting digital threats – he has some fun thoughts." Tabatha smiles.

"So, you're lusting over another mans' lustful thoughts of you?"

"Mom!!" Tabatha retaliates,

"That's just..."Naomi begins.

"...Weird?" Tabatha finishes her sentence again.

"Well, yeah, it is honestly."

The tea kettle whistles. Naomi grabs a cup from a cupboard, pours some tea in it, and hands it to Tabatha.

"Actually, he's married." Tabatha blows on her tea.

"He's married and thinking about kinky stuff with you?" Naomi inquires.

"Ha-Ha! First off, mom, it's just weird hearing you use the word *kinky*. And, he thinks about his *wife*, not me." Tabatha takes a sip of her tea.

"Well," Naomi puts her hands on her hips in sarcasm. "First off, I'm sixty-five, not dead...and now you're saying you dwell over the thoughts another man has for his wife?" Naomi laughs, "That's even worse."

Tabatha stares at Naomi, holding her tea with both hands, with a scolding look on her face which quickly melts away to laughter. "Hahaha! Yeah, it is worse, isn't it," Tabatha says, with a slightly guilty conscience. "Gosh, I'm horrible."

"You're not horrible, sweetheart. I'm just giving you a hard time," Naomi admits. "You just need to find a nice handsome young man."

"More like a middle-aged man." Tabatha adds.

"At my age, you're all young."

"The first man I meet whose mind I *can't* read, will be the guy I drag down the aisle, ok mom?"

"Ha. Ok, Tabatha." Naomi kisses her on the cheek. "I need to go back to sleep. It's three a.m., and we have church in about six hours." Naomi walks out of the kitchen.

"I know, thanks mom, good night, or morning, or whatever." Tabatha leans on the island with her tea in front of her.

"Oh! And he has to be at least six feet tall! Black hair! Clean-shaven! Athletic! And..." Tabatha adds to her list of qualities in her imaginary future spouse before Naomi interrupts her.

".....Sure sweetheart! I'll make sure I sign you up for the single seniors' bible study I go to on Tuesday evenings before my funeral," Naomi shouts from down the hall.

"Seriously, mom!?"

Naomi closes her bedroom door.

"Seriously, Tabatha," she says to herself. "I can sign yourself up for the single seniors' bible study." Tabatha walks to the picture window in the kitchen, looking over Washington D.C. from her top floor condo, attempting to view amidst the city's light pollution.

"Have the Bible study here and become a hermit. Maybe buy a bunch of cats too." Tabatha continues the depressing rambling to herself. "Yeah. That could work."

Lucas Gorton McIntire

CHAPTER II

DAYDREAMS

"Good morning…"

"Good morning, Pastor."

"Welcome, & good morning," Pastor Reed greets the guests and attendees entering Prince Community Church in Bowie Maryland.

Pastor Reed is the third generation of pastors to lead this same church, started by his grandfather Billy Joseph Reed sometime in the mid-1930s. Naomi had grown up in Bowie, Maryland and attended Prince Community Church since her youth. Naomi and her late husband raised Tabatha as best they could in the same manner, and for the most part, succeeded, even with her, *gift.*

Tabatha left Bowie, Maryland, when she was 19 to attend college in Cambridge Maryland to study criminal justice. She later moved to Washington D.C. To work for the Federal Bureau of Investigation. Tabatha's unique Telepathic ability was a huge advantage to the organizations' interrogation practices. However, the question of legality arose during a federal drug trafficking trial about eight years earlier, regarding the use of telepathy to obtain information against the will of a defendant, which could (and did) compromise the defendants' rights to plead the fifth amendment in some cases, regardless of actual guilt.

As a result, the justice department developed regulatory requirements that would allow Tabatha to retrieve information from a defendant telepathically. Also, the question of where best telepathic intelligence gathering would be most applicable was considered. The obvious answer was national-defense. Therefore a special arm of the anti-terrorist segment of the F.B.I. that works in conjunction with homeland security, was created – T.I.D. ('tide'), or 'Telepathic Intelligence Division.' The department was also classified above top secret – like Area 51, if Area 51 existed, however, if we knew Area 51 existed, it wouldn't be classified, if it is classified, anyway – I digress. To satisfy the government watchdogs who spend their time calculating where taxpayer dollars go, the 'Terrorist Intercept Division' was the public terminology for the acronym T.I.D. It's a good thing a lot of big and important-sounding words begin with the letter 'T'...like *transference*, or *tergiversation* – say that ten times fast.

Regulations surrounding the secret department were many. Restrictions on research dealing with Tabatha's' genetics were on the top of the list. These were to keep at bay unethical practices that could arise by manipulating her DNA or expose her to inhumane treatment. However, general blood work was acceptable for the monitoring of her health and related purposes.

Only select government officials have access to this classified division – the President, Vice President, Joint Chiefs, and the Joint Chiefs Chairman and Vice-Chairman. The secretary of state, secretary of defense, as well as the directors of both the F.B.I. and the C.I.A. A small selection of senators who reside on the U.S. Senate Armed services committee and the Senate Select Committee on Intelligence created a T.I.D. oversight committee. However, some have still expressed more intense interest in *studying* Tabatha's biology than protecting her identity or continued concealment of her potential from the public at large. The one who pushed heavily for the government to conduct studies on her in recent years was the current secretary of defense, Allen Terrence.

Secretary Terrence spent most of his adult life in the military. Having shown an aptitude for science in the engineering field, he helped develop new military hardware. After several tours in the military and making his way up the ranks to a five-star general he eventually landed in the statutory office of the chief of staff and held that position through two administrations. During that time, his primary investment was the Defense Advanced Research Projects Agency or D.A.R.P.A. He was eventually tapped and confirmed as the Secretary of Defense for the current administration. Since then, funding for secret defense projects has risen astronomically.

However, very few within Tabatha's own private social circle, as small as it is, even know her gift. And those who do go thru great strides to keep it secret.

A roaring engine grabs pastor Reeds' attention slightly. Pastor Reed turns to see a 4x4 truck with metallic green paint, black trim, and with the largest tires that can legally be driven on a U.S. road, pulls into the parking lot. The pastor walks up to the truck as the engine rived up and died.

Pastor Reed opens the driver's side door to greet the individual. "Good morning Ms. Tabatha Johnson," he looks past Tabatha, "good morning Ms. Naomi."

"Good morning, pastor." They both replied. Tabatha unbuckles her seat belt swings her legs over the side of her seat, pulls up her ankle-length skirt and jumps out of the truck.

"You look nice today, Tabatha." The pastor compliments

"Thanks, pastor." Tabatha tucks in her white dress shirt and straightens out her pitch-black business skirt then shakes her head to flip her permed hair.

"Tabatha! Get me out of this thing!" Naomi shouts, unable to get down from the passenger side of the truck.

Pastor Reed runs over to Naomi with Tabatha walking behind pressing down her skirt still. "Let me help you out there, Naomi." Pastor Reed manages to get Naomi in his arms and carries her down.

"You can carry me into the church if you want, Pastor," Naomi says, flirtatiously with a grin and flashing eyes.

"I'm sure I could," he responds, laughing then stands her up.

"Ok, mom, quit flirting with a man of God. I'm sure you'll call down lightning on yourself or something." Tabatha opens the back seat passenger door and grabs a crockpot of chili for the fellowship meal after the service.

"Well, that would be quicker than falling to my death from out of your truck," Naomi responds.

"Why do you have to have such a gigantic truck anyways?" Naomi complains like she does every time she rides in Tabatha's truck.

"I thought you wanted to see the world."

"Yes, *see it*, not look down at it from outer space."

"Hahaha!! You two crack me up." The pastor interjects, laughing. "Let's go inside, ladies."

"If you think that's funny, wait till you hear about what she *listens* to at work," Naomi divulges to the pastor,

"Seriously, mom?!" Tabatha responds as they walk inside the church.

The customary Worship aspect of the church service ends after the singing of Amazing Grace. The pastor dismisses the ten-member quire and the few musicians that lead the congregation through the worship. The pastor opens his Bible on the oak podium at the top of the three-step altar and asks the congregation to stand. "If you would stand with me out of respect for Gods' Word."

The congregation stands, many with their Bibles in hand. "Please turn with me to second Corinthians, chapter ten and verse five." The ruffling of pages could be heard as the congregants find the passage of scripture.

"We demolish arguments and every pretension that sets itself up against the knowledge of God, and we take captive every thought to make it obedient to Christ. Let's pray together," the pastor then leads the congregation in prayer.

Tabatha's attention, however, is diverted to the pew next to hers. She looks over, and among the individuals standing with their heads lowered in prayer was a very well dressed young black lady in her mid to late-twenties. With her were three children – two boys and a girl. The oldest, around nine years old, was standing with her mother praying as well. The other two, who were much younger, were sitting coloring on the blank side of the church bulletin. All three children were very well dressed – the boys in black suits and ties, and the girl in a little white dress with her hair in braids with white bows in them.

Then another individual also catches Tabatha's attention. In the back pew, sat a middle-aged unshaven black man, whose clothes looked as if they were discovered in a dumpster or possibly during an archeological dig. Neither individual had been to the church before.

"Tabatha!" Naomi whispers frantically. "Sit down! Sit down!" Naomi tugs on her shirt. Then Tabatha notices that she's the only one standing, and nearly the whole congregation is watching her stare at the man in the back of the church. Embarrassed, she quickly sits down.

The service ends with a concluding prayer in Jesus' name, and the pastor dismisses the congregation to the activity center where a fellowship chili lunch is waiting. Naomi and Tabatha exit the pew.

"I'll meet you in the activity center. I need to talk to the pastor about something real quick," Tabatha says to Naomi.

"Ok...see ya in a minute."

"Pastor!" Tabatha shouts to get his attention. "Hey, pastor..." she continues attempting to jog in her high heels up to the podium.

"Tabatha," the pastor steps down from the podium to meet her. "A little lost in *thought* today, are we? Pun included," the pastor responds, attempting to make light humor out of her embarrassing episode earlier in the service.

"Ha-ha, funny. I got something just a *little* important to tell you," Tabatha adds, using her fingers to illustrate 'little.'

"What is it?" The pastor asks.

Tabatha looks around to make sure no one is listening to them, then in a soft voice says: "I just wanted to let you know that the man, who is still sitting in the back row, is waiting for everyone to leave and he's going to ask you for monetary assistance..."

"Tabatha...you can't just...."

"Just listen. He has two homes, a fifty thousand dollar truck, and six kids from two women. He doesn't need anything, and if you want to see for yourself, you can go for a quick pre-church lunch snack at the burger joint down the road. Just make sure you sit by the window facing south."

"Tabatha. Our conversation about *free-will?*"

"Yes, I know, but this is important and I'm almost done. The black woman that came in with three kids that looks all bubbly as if life is perfect for her – her husband died a few months ago, her house got foreclosed on and all four of them are living in her car at a truck stop." Tabatha pulls two one-hundred-dollar bills out of her purse and puts it in pastor Reeds' hands. "Give this to her anonymously, please. She's the one who could *really* use the help," Tabatha concludes.

"Tabatha...!" Cindy, Pastor Reed's wife, who is also Tabatha's best friend, exclaims with a smile and opens her arms to embrace Tabatha.

"Cindy...!" Tabatha responds in the same way. "Oh my goodness, you had to put your dog to sleep, I'm so sorry."

"Oh, yeah, we did. My husband wasn't supposed to tell you that," Cindy responds with a slightly disappointing glance toward her husband, the pastor, who in turn, made a similar look to Tabatha. "It was sad, I miss her so much, but she was so sick,"

"I bet it was sad," Tabatha says with her eyes widened, realizing she shouldn't have brought up the topic.

"Well, Cindy, the pastor has a meeting with someone real quick, so why don't we head to the activity center." Tabatha locks her arm into Cindy's arm and pulls her down the aisle while looking back at the pastor, mouthing; "I'm sorry."

As Tabatha and Cindy left the sanctuary, the poorly dressed, homeless-looking man then limps his way to meet with the pastor.

"Past'a..." the man says in a soft, sad voice in a slight southern accent.

"Yes sir, can I help you?" Pastor Reed responds.

"I hope so. I have just been down on my luck the last few months, and was wondering if there is anything you and your congregation can do to help me out at all."

"What do you need help with?" The pastor inquires.

"I just need some money for some food and to help pay for a place to stay. You see, I – I've been sleep'n in parks and under overpasses. I'm just tired and my luck's all ran out. I figured that a man of God such as yourself would have compassion for someone in my current position," the dirty old man answers.

"Well, if you are hungry, I can pay for some food for you to eat. There is also a homeless shelter not too far from here. I can take you there, as well," The pastor responds.

"Well, I don't want to trouble you by having to take me to get some food, if you just had a few dolla's, then I can go and get somet'n. And, plus, that shelt'a, well, it's full. They turned me away," the man continued.

"You mean the shelter that's on 47th and Cleveland Street turned you away?" The pastor asked knowing full well that there was no shelter on 47th and Cleveland; in fact, there was no 47th and Cleveland anywhere.

"Yes, Sir Past'a. That's the one."

"Well, sir, I'm sorry I can't help you right now. But if you give me your name and contact info, if you have contact information, I can have our trustees get in touch with you to see how we can better assist you."

"Honestly, Past'a, my names not in the system anywhere, and I don't have any way for anyone to getta hold of me. I'm kind of a drift'a. I'm on disability, for my back pain, from a job, so I can't work...." The man is interrupted by the pastor.

"Ok, that's enough, I'm not an idiot sir. I offered what I can, and if you don't like what I have to offer, then you can *attempt* to rip off some other charity," the pastor firmly concluded.

The man tilted his back and tensed up. "You all are nut'n but bunch hypocrites; stuck up rich snob folk. Don't care about anyone but themselves!!" The man started shouting.

"Kyle?" Cindy walked into the sanctuary. "Is everything alright?"

"Yes, Cindy," the pastor responded. "This gentleman was just leaving.

The man nodded his head lightly, "yeah, I see how it is." He turns and struts down the aisle past Cindy, who backed up slightly in intimidation of the man. He walked out of the sanctuary and out the front doors of the church toward the street.

The pastor followed him out of the sanctuary, stopping next to Cindy and watched the man through the glass doors for a minute.

"Let's go eat babe," Cindy suggests.

"Yeah, let's do that." They start down the hall. "Actually, Cindy, I just remembered that I need to check something out down the street for a moment. I'll be back shortly ok."

"Oh, well, ok. See you in a few." Cindy heads down the hall to the activity room.

"Oh, and if you wouldn't mind letting the council members know that we might want to bump up security for a little while around here as well!"

"Sure thing!" She responds.

"Thanks, Cindy!" He shouts as he jogs out the front doors to his 1989 white Honda accord.

He backs out of the driveway and races down the street to the fast-food burger joint. He runs inside and finds a seat by a window facing south. The customers and order-takers watched him momentarily as he made a b-line to his seat. Slightly embarrassed at making a seen the pastor politely nods to those watching and smiles than turns his attention toward the restaurant's parking lot. There were two trucks and a compact car parked right outside the window.

A few minutes later, Pastor Reed notices a man walking into the parking lot toward the vehicles in front of the window. He quickly pulls his iPhone out of his pocket. Sure enough, it was the man from the church. The man opened the door to a big red truck that looked as though it had just recently been driven off of a dealership lot. For it still had a ninety-day temporary tag in the license plate holder. The man hopped in the truck, closed the door, and started the engine. He then looked up through the windshield and saw the pastor waving and taking a picture of him in the truck. Alarmed, he peeled out in reverse and hit a police car that just happened to be passing behind him heading for the drive-through lane.

The pastor ran outside to see if everyone was ok. As he ran up to the police car, the man in the truck jumped out and sprinted down the street. The cop on the passenger side called for help over his two-way radio then checked on his partner whose side of the vehicle had been struck. He was dazed but ok, so the passenger cop hopped out to chase the man. However, by then, he couldn't see him. Pastor Reed talked to the cop and showed him the picture of the man. The cop instructed the pastor to email the picture to an address at the station. Then the pastor told the cop everything that had happened. After the conversation between the pastor and the cop, an ambulance drove up, along with two more police cars. Pastor Reed walked back to his car and started back toward the church before deciding to take a detour that just so happens to pass by a truck stop.

Back at the church, while pastor Reed was having an adventure verifying Tabatha's claims, much of the congregation stayed for the fellowship luncheon. Though a few left directly after the service. The young black lady, whose name was Molly, and her three children were invited to stay and eat. However, since she didn't know anyone at the church personally, they left.

The activity center had several tables with four to six individuals at each. The room was alive with conversations. The dialogue varied from table to table. Some, politics were the topic, another was family or family matters, for the youth it was a more diverse array of subjects from the latest and greatest gadgets, to movies, and of course boys/girls. Yet other tables found themselves critiquing the morning's sermon.

Tabatha sat with Cindy and a few other women. They were hysterical with laughter. Tabatha had a sarcastic sense of humor and a talent to make any situation into a comedy. Most of her one-liners revolved around her singleness or imaginary romance. Occasionally she targeted her married friends with her sarcasm.

In the middle of their hyperventilating laughter, Tabatha noticed a man simply standing in the middle of the room staring back at her. He was large in stature and his face was slightly unclear.

"Who's that?" Tabatha asked.

The other women at the table looked to see who she was talking about.

"Who's who Tab?' Cindy inquired.

"That guy, standing there in the middle of the room." Tabatha attempted to deduce the psychic stream from his mind but it resembled irrational chatter, and the vague images she perceived were incomprehensible – kind of like watching television ladened with static.

The ladies were all starring in the middle of the room in confusion. Naomi, sitting at a table with some older ladies, happened to glance at Tabatha's table and saw them all looking at the middle of the room in confusion. Immediately Naomi got from her chair.

"Excuse me. I'll be right back," Naomi, excused herself in a rush.

"Is everything alright," one of the ladies asked, sensing an anxiousness in Naomi.

"I'm not sure. Hopefully, everything's fine." Naomi walked quickly but not so fast as to cause a scene. Naomi was confident that she knew exactly what was happening at Tabatha's table.

"It was probably the chili," one of the older ladies said, attempting to explain Naomi's sudden departure.

"Tabatha," Cindy says, "there's no one over there."

The congregation started disappearing like smoke along with all the tables. The walls began closing in all around her. Then the individual whose face was unclear walked toward her. A square opening began cutting out of the wall behind him and a dark piece of glass formed in the opening. Tabatha understood was she was experiencing now – a daydream.

"Cindy! Are you there?"

"Tabatha, I'm right here. What's going on?" Cindy looks directly into Tabatha's face, but Tabatha could not see her.

"Go find Naomi, please! I'm, uhhh, having an episode," Tabatha explains in a way as to not expose her ability.

"Yeah, ok," Cindy gets up quickly to find Naomi. The ladies at Naomi's table directed her to the bathroom, thinking that's where she had gone.

"Twenty four." The man spoke directly at her in a Russian accent. "Nod, if you can hear me?" Tabatha responds with a nod.

"Good." The strange man moves out of her center of vision, exposing a horrifying reflection in the glass.

She saw herself strapped to a vertical platform with tubes protruded from her nostrils. A feeding tube hung out of her mouth. A large power cable ran from the back of her head down to the floor and plugged into some a power source like a small generator. Tubes of liquid were attached to her arms intravenously. She was covered by a hospital gown. Splotches of blood were present on the gown, and her hair looked as if it hadn't been cut or cleaned in years as it was matted beyond belief and fell down to her legs. An area on her neck was sunk in with a noticeably brutal scar. It appeared to have been healed for quite some time.

The visual caused Tabatha to fall out of her chair onto the floor. At this, the attention of everyone in the activity center tuned into what's taking place at Tabatha's table. One of the other ladies at the table laid her flat on the floor. "Oh-my-gosh!!! She's burning up!!!"

"Do we need to call 9-11!!" one member of the congregation frantically remarked.

"Cindy went to get her mother. I think she suffers from seizures or something." Another one responded.

"Your performance was flawless," the stranger in Tabatha's vision continued.

As her daydream continued, she could see monitors behind her in the reflection of the glass. They depicted digital images of x-rays of the human skull and M.R.I. images of a brain. Additional video feeds of burnt villages and deceased bodies that portrayed what looked like a post-military strike somewhere in the Middle East.

Cindy had rushed to the bathroom where Naomi was *not* found. Then after leaving the bathroom, she saw, through the glass doors of the church, her husband pulling back up in the parking lot and ran outside. As she approached her husbands' car, she spotted Naomi trying to get into Tabatha's truck so Cindy ran to Naomi instead.

"Naomi!"

"Yes, I know, Cindy. I'm trying to get her medicine but I can't reach the glove box!!" Naomi complained about Tabatha's truck being too high again.

"What's going on?" Pastor Reed guessing a problem is present the way Cindy ran outside and how frantic Naomi was, trying to get into the truck.

"Tabatha is having a pretty severe episode, pastor!!" Naomi yells. Pastor Reed knew exactly what that meant and rushed inside.

"Here, let me get it, Naomi." Cindy, who was 5'7, a whole 7 inches taller than Naomi, and not to mention her ability to jump, unlike Naomi, allowed her to climb up in the truck more easily. Cindy opened the glove compartment. "What does it look like?"

"The brown pouch! It has a syringe with a needle and a little bottle of liquid," Naomi explains.

"Here it is! I got it." Cindy jumps out of the truck.

"Run and give it to the pastor, he'll know how to do it – you're faster than me."

Cindy obeys and takes off to the activity center, followed slowly by Naomi. Cindy finds Pastor Reed and hands him the pouch. Suddenly a small vibration is felt by the congregation in the room.

"Is there a little earthquake going on here?" Someone randomly asks.

"Yep, that's just an earthquake," the pastor responds without missing a beat. He plunges the needle in the bottle and fills up the syringe, then finds a vein in Tabatha's arm and pushes the needle in it. Tabatha's eyes are slightly rolled back into her head, but a few seconds after the injection, her eyes came back, and her breathing slowed as the activity center returns to her vision. At this point, Naomi made it back into the activity center.

"Mom?" Tabatha lets out as her eyes dim, and her head falls to one side in sleep.

"Naomi," the pastor says, pulling the needle out of Tabatha's arm, "I think you need to call her doctor again."

Lucas Gorton McIntire

CHAPTER III

REASONING

"Good morning, who are you here to see today?" The Dr. Office registration associate asks.

"Good morning. I'm Tabatha. I have an appointment to see Dr. Glessinjer at nine o'clock." Tabatha sets her wallet on the counter, opens it and pulls out her insurance card.

"Date of birth, please."

"One-twenty-nineteen eighty-one."

"It looks like there's a fifteen dollar co-pay." Tabatha then hands the associate her debit card.

"You know Tabatha, Dr. Glessinjer is single," Naomi blurts out once again, always attempting to solve Tabatha's romance issues...or the lack thereof.

"*Mom!*" Tabatha criticizes in a whisper and embarrassment. "Wait. Actually, mom, he's...."

"Oh, no. He's engaged now," the office associate interrupts. "If you could just sign this please." She hands Tabatha a copy of a receipt to sign.

"Well, that's too bad for you two," Naomi comments, attempting to make humor out of the topic. Tabatha signs her name and hands the paperback.

"Oh, I *know!*" The associate whispers. "He's *a hottie.*"

"Yeah, he's..." Tabatha begins to speak before the associate interrupts again.

"Oh, I've had some thoughts...." The associate begins to divulge.

"*Wow!* Yeah you do. Might want to keep those to yourself. You could go to prison for that," Tabatha interrupts, getting a glimpse of *those thoughts.*

"I could go to jail for what?" The associate asks with a smirk on her face, obviously unaware can deduct what she was thinking.

"Oohhh, nothing. Thanks," Tabatha grabs her copy of the receipt, then she and Naomi go find a seat in the waiting room.

Tabatha leans toward Naomi and whispers her opinion of the office associate, "freak-ooo,"

"What was it?" Naomi asks out of curiosity.

"Trust me, mom, you would have a heart attack if I told you," Tabatha answers as they take seats.

The waiting room was pretty empty. An elderly couple was a few chairs down. A lady and her child were in a glass room that was soundproof playing with toys. Next to Tabatha, separated by an end table and sitting diagonally from her was an ordinary-looking man probably in his thirties, seem to be well built. He was reading a home and garden magazine. Their eyes met momentarily, and they smiled at each other.

"Peculiar," Tabatha says softly.

"What is?" Naomi asks nosily.

"That guy right there," Tabatha whispers.

Naomi looks over. "Yeah, well, he is reading a home and garden magazine."

"What? That's not what I was talking about." Tabatha continues in whispers. "He's not thinking...I think."

"Are you serious?" Naomi responds with a great idea.

"No, mom, don't even think about that."

"Too late. He doesn't have a ring on his finger, he's handsome and you can't read his mind...that's the one!"

"Mom, he can probably hear you." Tabatha glances over and notices a little bit of a smile on his face...he was eavesdropping just slightly.

"I'm sooo sorry, sir. My mom, she's just..." Tabatha scrambles find an appropriate word to describe Naomi as for the moment. "...She's got dementia – slightly."

"Oh, I do not, Tabatha." Naomi faces the young man. "What do you think of my niece? She is ultra-single."

"Oh-my-gosh!!" Tabatha puts her face in her hands, attempting to hide.

"Ha-ha. Well, ma'am, you're niece seems very nice and she is very attractive," he says then goes back to reading the home and garden magazine.

At hearing that response, Tabatha lifted her face and was about to speak when.

"Tabatha Johnson! The doctor will see you now," a medical assistant shouts across the room.

Tabatha and Naomi stand up, but before heading toward the medical assistant, Tabatha gets the courage to ask a burning question to the guy. "Are you a human?"

"Ha-ha," the guy chuckles. "Well, we'll find out for sure after my appointment," he jokes. "Good luck, hope everything turns out ok."

"Yeah, me too, thanks," Tabatha responds.

"Are you human? Really, Tabatha? That's a pick-up line if I ever heard one," Naomi lectures.

"Yeah, whatever." The guy follows Tabatha with his eyes until she's out of the room, then goes back to reading his home and garden magazine.

The medical assistant takes Tabatha and Naomi behind the registration office. She weighs Tabatha and checks her height. She then leads them into a small examination room, where she takes Tabatha's blood pressure and all the usual vitals before the doctor comes in.

"Alright, the doctor will be in shortly," the medical assistant says after typing Tabatha's vitals into her tablet then leaves' the room.

Tabatha, sit's in one of the two chairs against the wall just inside the door. She pulls out her phone to check her social media and her text messages.   "You better move mom, he's about to plow through the door," Tabatha warns Naomi, standing just behind the door.

Naomi quickly moves over, and the door flies open as Dr. Glessinjer plows into the room. "Oh wow, Sorry, Naomi, I almost got you good," the doctor apologizes.

"That's ok Dr. You can knock me over any time," Naomi winks at the Dr.

"Holy infatuations batman!!" Tabatha responds to Naomi. "Do you have to flirt with every guy that you come across?"

"Well, if you don't, I might as well. Besides, it's funny and cute when little old ladies hit on young guys," Naomi defends herself and sits down in the empty chair.

"You too should be a comedic team," Dr. Glessinjer says, laughing. "Hop on the exam table for me." Tabatha obeys.

"I'd tell you to keep your thoughts to yourself, mom, but I know you wouldn't. Plus, it still wouldn't help *me* any," Tabatha says with her head tilted so the Dr. can check her lymph nodes.

The Dr. puts his stethoscope on and places the end of it on her back, "deep breaths." Then he moves it to her chest to check her heartbeat.

"You can keep that there as long as you want – *doctor*," Tabatha flirtatiously said.

"Now she flirts with a guy," Naomi says, sitting on a chair and reading a truck magazine of all things that were lying in the stack of magazines. "Of course she has to pick the one that's about to get married."

Tabatha glances at Naomi with an evil eye.

"Oh, that's right! Congratulations!" Tabatha says with enthusiasm for the doctor. "Oh, and she is really pretty too, you stud," she lightly slaps his chest. "Oh, I love her hair. And she has silver eyes? What? That's awesome. Oh and she's your pastors' daughter? Whoa! Talk about accountability."

"Tabatha, you know better than that. Just because you *can* do something, in your case, read minds, doesn't mean you should dispense that information." He reminds her

"Yeah, I know. Like that line: 'with great responsibility...' from that movie where some kid got bit by a spider, right?"

"Yeah, something like that. But even more, you're accountable to God for what you do with it."

"You tell her, doctor." Naomi had to add her two cents in, continuing to read the truck magazine.

"As far as accountability, there's someone else that holds me accountable."

"Yeah, I guess it helps to have someone around who can read your mind, huh," Tabatha responds with a little conceit.

The doctor looks sternly at her, "you really think that *you* are the one who holds me accountable?"

Tabatha looks toward the ground with guilt.

"I will admit Tabatha, what you can do is amazing, and as a scientist in the medical field, you fascinate me. And, true, you do make 'accountability' for how I think more tangible, but keep in mind that *you too* are held accountable for what *you think* as well." Dr. Glessinjer pulls his stool underneath him and sits in front of Tabatha pulling her knees toward him. "The Bible says that man looks on the outward appearance and in your case, I would add the mind, but the Lord looks on the heart. And the *heart* is something that even *you* cannot see into." The Dr. continues as he takes his little rubber mallet and strikes the top of her knees, checking her reflexes.

"You're right, doctor. I feel like total yuck now."

"I'm sorry, that wasn't my intention," the doctor says comfortingly. "Open wide," the doctor shines a light in her mouth to exam it. "I can only imagine the things you see, especially in your line of work. I mean the evil that's out there. And yet, you manage to put your faith in God over your ability. That has to be hard, and I'm sure tempting at times," he says encouragingly. Tabatha smiles.

"So, my mom set up the appointment. Did she tell you what happened?"

"She told she witnessed." He then pulls out two brown Velcro pouches out of his jacket. In one was a syringe, a needle, and two little bottles of liquid and the other pouch were two additional bottles of the same fluid. "Here you go." He hands her both pouches. "I have to say that I'm getting a little concerned about these episodes, or dreams, as you put it. Especially now that they're taking place while you're awake – and more frequently." The doctor sits back down on the stool.

"I know!" Tabatha hops off the examination table and starts pacing. "What's going on with me, doctor?" She says in frustration.

"I'm not a hundred percent sure Tabatha. However, I don't think these are merely dreams."

"I agree. I'm thinking that I might be seeing the future. Maybe, the way I die or something? What do you think?"

"Ha. Your ability is hard enough to explain as it is, but I'm not ready to make that kind of hypothetical leap into the unknown," he responds, highly skeptical of the idea.

"I'm not talking hypothetically. In the last couple of dreams, including the ones I've had while I was awake, I'm being dissected or experimented on. In fact, two days ago, I woke up from a dream..."

"...Naomi told me about that one, too," he interjects.

"Did she tell you that I could even feel it this time? Oh, that was creepy or at least creepier than normal anyway." She stops and takes a breath to calm her anxiety. She looks toward the floor, puts a hand on one hip, and massages the middle of her forehead. "I don't know, but as you said, it's happening more often and in less than twenty-four hours, I had that night terror and then that daydream yesterday at church. Thank God for Pastor Reed and mom."

"I understand your frustration, and yes, fast-acting on their parts. Believe it or not, I spend more time researching everything I can to make sense of this for you, than I do working on anything else..."

"Seriously, mom?" Tabatha picks up on Naomi thinking about the guy in the waiting room. "Aren't you supposed to be a super godly, modest little old lady?"

"I'm human, get over it, sweetheart," Naomi responds without missing a beat and without lifting her eyes off of the truck magazine. She turns the page.

The doctor gives Tabatha a confused look.

"Oh, sorry, she has a crush on some guy in the waiting room," Tabatha divulges.

"Ha-ha. Oh really?" the doctor says with a chuckle.

"Yeah, and trust me, you don't want to know."

"I believe you." The doctor then walks over to the counter, where a flat-screen T.V. monitor is hanging above the sink. "I want to show you something." He picks up his tablet from off the counter and pulls a stylus out of his pocket and begins moving it around the tablet screen syncing it to the T.V. monitor.

"Ok, so you know that your metabolism burns higher than normal and...."

"Aaaand, yes – as a result, my body produces more energy..." she interjects in a way that says, get on with the point.'

"Right. The average person generates around one hundred watts or so, give-or-take, of power."

"...And I generate way more than that. That's why I eat like thirty times a day and never get fat – that's the part of my weirdness, admittedly, I do love."

"Ha-ha-ha. Yeah, I can believe that." Dr. Glessinjer taps the stylus on the tablet a couple of times and a 3D image of a brain showing neurons flashing and other animated activity in the image appears on the monitor.

"You generate nearly *two hundred* watts of power. Frankly, it's literally by the grace of God that you're alive."

"That's the definition of a miracle I'd say," she says fascinated.

"To say the least. This is your brain from your M.R.I. a couple of months ago." He taps his stylus on his tablet again, which brings up an additional brain image next hers. "This is a normal human's brain. Do you see the differences?"

"Whoa, my brain looks like it's on *fire*."

"I determined that your brain requires more power because of your telepathy, which is pretty much always turned on, so to speak, right?"

"She can turn it off. She told me that," Naomi interjects still starring at her magazine.

"Mom! I can't always do that," Tabatha corrects Naomi.

"David, it's more like turning the volume down – sort of. I guess you can kind of think of it as being in a room, where there are different groups of people, and each group is having a different conversation. You know how you can hone in on one conversation that catches your attention, so you automatically filter out the other conversing groups? That's an easy way to explain it. If that makes any kind of sense."

"That does make some sense." He responds, fascinated. "Now, you've mentioned previously that your telepathy has advanced fairly significantly if I remember correctly," he confirms.

"Yes, I've been able to interpret audio and visual information since I was a child. Accessing and retrieving short term memories since I was a teenager and later long term memories as well as suppressed memories. But in the last couple of years, I've been able to use the telepathic information from one individual to access information of associated individuals elsewhere and interpret all that information simultaneously," Tabatha further explains.

"That sounds impressive. I would probably equate this advancement in your telepathy to the continuous development of your frontal cortex. The average individual's frontal lobe doesn't reach maturity until somewhere in their mid-twenties. But in your case, it's taken longer due to the extra complexity of your neurological network."

"Uh-hu," Tabatha responds to the information with a blank stare. "Anyways, the bad thing about all this is that it completely wipes me out if I push it hard. Especially when it involves digging through suppressed memories. Unless I gorge myself on like twenty thousand calories right before performing that trick," Tabatha further explains.

"And that's also what I wanted to talk to you about. The last time that you were in here, you told me you started having these episodes, or-dreams as you put it, about a year ago at the time, right?

"Yeah, maybe just under."

"Ok, now check this out under magnification." The doctor, again, taps his stylus on the tablet which zooms in on the image of her brain. "This is your cerebrum under high magnification. Look at these lines. You said your brain looked like it was on fire, right?"

"Yeah."

"These are follicles waiving around on your cerebrum. They move in sync with each other from what I can see, which means they are working together. You know what those remind me of?"

"I do now, but I'll just let you tell me – since you're the doctor."

"Yeah, humor me would you,"

"Sorry."

"They remind me of miniature receiver needles like a radio dial. You continue moving it until you get a radio signal that comes in. My first theory is that these follicles receive whatever signals the human mind produces. Which of course, we don't know what kind of signal the human mind emits."

"Ok, that's just weird-looking," Tabatha leans over the counter to look at the image even closer. "They look like little worms moving around."

"Yeah, kind of."

"Ewe. What about the sleep study test from last month?"

"Right." He taps his tablet again and yet another image of her brain appears.

"Whoa!"

"I know. This is what your brain was doing while you were having that big bad dream that night. We were lucky that you had one of those dreams while we were doing this test."

"I don't know about lucky, but this is crazy. What does all the back and forth between red and blue mean?"

"Well, remember the E.K.G. I had you hooked up to while we were doing this at the same time? It recorded how much energy your brain was using. Tabatha, your cerebrum is consuming between two hundred watts of power when it's lit up in red and four hundred watts of power when it's lit up in blue. While you were having your *dream*, your brain was sucking up five hundred to six hundred watts of energy. Your metabolism does seem to increase slightly to compensate for your brain using so much energy during these moments. However, your metabolism seems to burn out real fast. It would be like a big truck if you stick a little battery in it. It might start the engine. But, once all the fancy electronics and so forth are turned on, that battery will be out of juice in no time," he further explains.

"Are you hearing this mom?"

"Yep, E.K.G.'s, M.R.I.'s, watts, worms, and other things I never learned in grammar school," Naomi responds, still reading the truck magazine, to which Tabatha rolls her eyes.

"That does explain why you nearly become paralyzed after most of your so-called night terrors. And more so your daydreams, because you're already using more energy as your body is being active. The problem that you face when your body starts burning up like that is the probability of slowly cooking your insides."

Tabatha gives the doctor a nauseating look. "But then that's what the medicine is to help prevent, right?"

"Well, it can't prevent any of those episodes; it helps to stop it. Though we could hook you up to a generator and then when you have an episode, your brain would use the energy from the generator so your body wouldn't be affected – ha-ha," David jokingly responds.

"I suppose it would have to be hooked directly into the base of my brain, right?" Tabatha asks.

"Well, I wasn't realistic, but, yeah. I suppose it would be, in real life, a pretty nasty procedure. You're not really considering…"

"No-no-no. Absolutely not. It's just that in my dreams, a cable is plugged into the base of my skull. I think it's hooked up to a generator."

"You know, I have asked some of the top neurosurgeons' in the country that if a person's brain had to absorb like six hundred watts of energy if it could be done using an external source."

"And?"

"Most just laughed at me, rightfully so. However, a few said that it could *theoretically* be done. But, no neurosurgeons that they knew of would even attempt something like that in his or her right mind."

"Unless there's a mad scientist out there without a conscience. But I digress. So, this is all, like, super fascinating, but it doesn't answer the question about what these dreams represent."

"True. Based on this new information I have, I do have a theory about this as well. I don't have the resources to test this theory for sure at this point, but it's more logical than you seeing your future death or whatnot."

Tabatha folds her arms and rolls her eyes. "I bet I know more about terrorists than you," she says, feeling intellectually insulted.

"I believe you."

"So?" Tabatha takes a seat next to Naomi and faces Dr. Glessinjer.

"I think you are receiving *and* sending information during these periods."

"Really? Sending information? But I can't send information. I've honestly tried to do that before. I once thought that if I can read and see thoughts that maybe I can also project thoughts. Maybe even get control of someone's mind. That would be helpful in my line of work for sure."

"That would also be *completely* subverting the free will of another person, Tabatha," the Doctor remarks.

"I'm talking about stopping some horrible things from happening though," Tabatha defends herself.

"Yes, I know, though, I'm sure that would become a slippery slope. But let's get back on the topic at hand."

"Right, ok, so how would I be *sending* information?"

"I don't know for sure, but I think you are, in fact, communicating with someone else's mind. Perhaps someone who has similar functionality that your mind has. Or, at the very least, someone who can *send* a signal, or images. Maybe they can, as you stated, project thoughts. I don't know for sure yet, but that's the best-educated answer I can conclude at this point." The doctor stands up and scratches his head, "and even that theory is hard to wrap *my own* mind around."

"Whoa! Someone else like me? I wouldn't be the only person on the planet with this then. That would be awesome!" Tabatha says with a little excitement in her face and body language.

"I can understand how that could excite you. I'm sure it gets pretty lonely being the only one who *actually* knows what it's like to be able to do the things you can do – see and hear the worst secrets anyone can imagine. I definitely feel for you."

"Yeah. I have gotten used to it, I suppose. Been dealing with it since I can remember. Thanks to my aunt and uncle for teaching me how to control it. Especially since they never knew how it worked either." Tabatha glances at Naomi smiling with feelings of thanksgiving for her god-mother and late god-father.

Naomi looks up and smiles back and goes back to reading.

"Well, thanks, doctor. Oh, and I see you gave me four bottles this time. Do I need to be given more if I have another episode or whatever?"

"No, just one. I had more made up for you since your episodes are becoming more frequent."

Tabatha has been mildly suspicious about where the medicine comes from, but her deep trust in the doctor and the fact the drug hasn't killed her alleviates the majority of her concerns related to the suspicion.

"Oh, since you're here, I would like to do another scan if I could."

"Dang it!!" Tabatha responds.

"I take that as a 'no' then," he surmises from her response.

"That's not it, my boss is calling me." Just then, her phone rings with a catchy rock melody.

"Yes, sir."

"Tabatha, a T.I.D. protocol was authorized. I need you here, A.S.A.P." the individual on the other line commands.

"Yes, sir." The phone disconnects.

"Have you always been able to know when someone's calling before they call?"

"Well, sort of. I can pick up on the signal just before it gets to my phone, but knowing who it is, well, that's slightly new. Maybe the signal carries the thought waves or something like that. I can't figure that one out either. But it comes in handy sometimes I have to admit," she explains.

"I see, that is interesting."

"Well, doctor, that scan is going to have to wait. I have to go interrogate a potential terrorist that was recently picked up," Tabatha says, enthusiastically, yet acting less than enthusiastic.

"Isn't that supposed to be classified information?" inquired the doctor.

"Yeah, but – so am I."

"Ha, right."

"Come on mom, let's go, I got to get you home super-fast." Tabatha helps Naomi up. Dr. Glessinjer opens the exam room door. Naomi puts the magazine down and walks out, followed by Tabatha and the doctor. Walking down the hall they continued talking about the appointment somewhat. David opens another door leading to the waiting room. "Remember to call and set up that appointment for that scan."

"I will. Thanks, doctor." Tabatha and Naomi walk out to the waiting room, toward the main facility exit. Upon leaving the office, a small end table was next to the door. On it stood a vase with flowers in it. "Those are pretty flowers." Naomi looked for the flowers but there was nothing on the table. They walk out the exit and *without* noticing that same guy from earlier who was still sitting in the waiting room, reading the home and garden magazine.

After leaving, the guy sitting in the waiting room looks beyond the magazine at the doctor who also glances back at him, gives a little nod then returns to the examination room. The guy puts the magazine down, gets up, and exits through the back door.

The Sentient

CHAPTER IV

THE INTERROGATION

A large truck pulls into a small parking garage, attached to a closed, run-down, and nearly dilapidated salon. An officer in a bulletproof vest stands next to a single, partially rusted metal door. He had a military haircut and wore dark glasses. He walked out into the parking lot with his hand signaling 'stop' to the truck pulling up.

The truck comes to a screeching halt just inches away from the guard. The door flies open and Tabatha jumps out holding out a badge. "Tabatha," the guard says, welcoming. The guard shines a small light on her badge which reveals the T.I.D. acronym over her picture, which in turn unlocks an old rusty door behind the guard with a 'buzz.'

"I'm in a hurry sweetie, can you park my truck for me please?" She requests, hopping on her toes to give him a thank you peck on the cheek, "Thanks Frank," she then speeds off toward the rusted door, shoving her badge in the back pocket of her jeans.

The door is pushed open by an African American man about 6'2", shaved head but had a goatee that attached to a thin mustache. He was wearing dark grey slacks, a white dress shirt with the cuffs slightly rolled up, a crimson-colored tie and black dress shoes. It was the director of T.I.D., Kurtis Jackson. He had a stern look on his face as usual.

"Well, if looks could kill…" Tabatha says sarcastically.

"I'm sure I don't have to tell you why I'm not in a good mood," director Jackson responds in his low and firm voice as they walk speedily down a narrow hallway.

"No, you don't," Tabatha confirms. They turn a corner heading down another hall that leads to a set of metal double doors at the end of it. Kurtis holds his badge over a box protruding from the wall, which unlocks and opens the doors automatically.

"There's a reason we issued you the other phone," Kurtis continues as they walk down several steps that lead into an atrium, which in turn branches into other offices and hallways.

To their left was a room separated from the atrium by panels of bulletproof glass. Several wall monitors were employing a multitude of satellite imagery and other surveillance feeds. One surveillance feed displayed the inside of the interrogation room. This was the intelligence and communications room. In the middle of the room was a long oval table with men and women around it. Some were sitting, some standing, some in military outfits, while others were in suits, with communication equipment on their heads. This underground facility was casually referred to by T.I.D. personnel as the *trench*.

"I know there's a reason. And it's a stupid reason." They make a right turn down another hallway opposite of the intelligence & communications room.

"It's an encrypted satellite phone. It can't be traced. And it's for your protection."

"*My* iPhone *has* encryption capabilities."

"It's never turned on, Tabatha."

"It limits my social media accessibility when it is," she says, shrugging her shoulder.

"You're our primary asset..."

"...You mean I'm your only asset." Tabatha corrects the director.

"Well, either way – we don't want to risk something happening to you." They stop in front of a large one-way window with a detainee sitting in front of a table with his hands cuffed and linked to the top of the table.

"True. The N.S.A. would *actually* have to start spying on our enemies and not our citizens, wouldn't they? Plus, you would have a hard time justifying the amount of taxpayer money that goes into running this *covert* operation without me. *Which*, by the way, *wasn't my* idea." Tabatha folds her arms. "The whole idea that 'we need to keep, *Tabatha the mind reader*, classified'...," she says in an imitating voice, throwing up quotation signs with her finger, "...is tantamount to prison in many ways," she complains. "Besides, you know very well that I can take care of myself." Kurtis simply stares at Tabatha allowing her to rattle off her grievances, as well as affirming her concerns with a partial grin.

Tabatha folds her arms and takes a breath – a sign that she has concluded her ranting. "So, I got here in fifteen minutes, you are very anxious. The situation is time-sensitive – though you don't know how time-sensitive it is," Tabatha retrieves information from the directors' memory.

The director opens his mouth, attempting to speak, but then closes it, allowing her to ramble off what he's already thinking.

"The capital building was targeted – again," Tabatha continues rattling off the information on the Director's mind; thus, he simply closes his mouth.

"You sent two response teams to evacuate congress from the capital – that's a good thing – although, just between you and me, you could leave a few of them in there, but I digress. Now you want me to locate whatever they are planning on doing, how many hostiles are involved, and their locations within the building," Tabatha takes a glance at the man in the interrogation room.

"Good plan...pretty standard...there's only one problem..."

"Which is?" the Director asks.

"It's not the capital building."

"He told homeland security interrogators it *was* the Capital. The evidence with him corroborated his statement." The director says.

"Yet you didn't trust that info; therefore, you want my professional opinion," she adds.

"The fact that this plan was so easily intercepted, didn't sit well with me," he admits.

"Definitely a good call. That evidence is a decoy; the memory feed of the capitol building I'm receiving is fabricated. I'm not sure what the target is, but it seems to be suppressed. Probably in order to get past your lie detectors. Which, apparently, he did."

"Yes, he did." The Director confirms.

"You know, if information from lie detectors are inadmissible in court, you definitely shouldn't rely on them in this department...Just a thought," Tabatha informs in a snarky tone. "I'll have to do a little digging." Tabatha begins entering the interrogation room, but the director stops her citing regulations.

"Wait, Tabatha, don't know the rules..." He reminds her, signaling to his administrative assistant further down the hall to bring a clipboard that has a piece of paper for Tabatha to sign.

"Oh-My-Goooosh!! This gets soooo ridiculous," Tabatha says, waiting to enter the room. She glances at the detainee again. "He's watching the clock." There was a digital clock on the wall across from where the detainee was sitting.   It was ten 'clock.

"Well, there's not much else to do in there," the Director wittily responds.

Suddenly Tabatha's demeanor instantly changed to very concerned.

"WHATEVER THEIR PLANNING, IS GOING DOWN IN THIRTY MINUTES!!" Tabatha informs.

The individual with the clipboard arrives and holds it up and Tabatha signs the paper giving her permission to interrogate the detainee telepathically.   Her signature was more like two squiggly lines.   "Get the *Seven* ready!   AND SOME TRIPPLE CHEESEBURGERS TO GO!!"   She exclaims, plowing through the door into the interrogation room, also referencing her bodies soon need for an excessive amount of calories to replenish the exponential amount of energy her brain consumes while she is in a hyperactive telepathic state, and usually for long periods during an assignment.

The *Seven* is a special unit Tabatha leads composed, of course, of seven individuals from different special local and national defense groups.   They are incredibly loyal to Tabatha, and likewise Tabatha's loyalty to them.   They consist of; Mitchell, the rookie, specializes in everything from mechanics to computer and software engineering. He was formerly employed by the air force.   Steve is a super sniper who was a former army ranger, as was Joe.   Mike was a navy seal and specialized in communications.   T.K. was a marine and specialized in multiple fighting techniques.   Diego is a former border patrol agent and Mexican cartel informant for the Houston Police Department.   And Samson, who goes by the nickname 'Hammer' which he got after single handedly taking out an entire terrorist hive with a sludge hammer after several I.E.D.'s had detonated, destroying the convoy he was a part of during a tour in the middle east, leaving him as the only survivor.

Director Kurtis Jackson sticks a small wireless Bluetooth device in his ear to communicate with T.I.D. protocol personnel.   Again, the Director is interrupted before saying a word, as Tabatha sticks her head out of the room and softly speaks so the detainee doesn't hear; "Oh, and let the F.B.I. go ahead and evacuate the capital.   I have a feeling that if you don't, the bad guys are going to think something is up and may prematurely deploy whatever terror act they have planned.   And ten-thirty is the climax of their attack, that much I know for sure."   She finishes and closes the door again. Director Jackson translates Tabatha's message in his own, more professional vernacular to an F.B.I. task force leader, coordinating the response to the capital building.

"Seryph, start a new E.D.T. (Estimated disaster threshold) to expire at ten-thirty eastern please." Seryph is the computer mainframe that runs the majority of the surveillance and communications protocols for T.I.D. Two high octave sounds back to back, followed by an automated computer voice is heard throughout the facility P.A. system.

"E.D.T. twenty-nine minutes and forty-five seconds," Seryph informs.

"And Tabatha's going to need fuel," the director adds, referring to Tabatha's request for triple cheese burgers – saying that Tabatha is going to need some triple cheeseburgers over a classified communications channel, just doesn't sound professional is his view.

The director pushes an intercom button on a small panel next to the door to the interrogation room. "Tabatha, we have about twenty-nine minutes," he encourages her to work quickly.

"Yes, I know. Please don't interrupt me."

"So, Adnan – or – Pleasure? That's what Adnan means, right?" Tabatha begins her interrogation walking up to the table.

"Yes, it does. You know Arabic," Adnan assumes, speaking with a Middle Eastern accent.

"No I don't really. Just a lucky guess, I suppose."

As Tabatha divulges Adnan's secrets telepathically, the Director writes the information down.

"Your father's name was Abd?" She asks, already knowing the answer. As Tabatha reveals some surface-level memories and Adnan freely confirms them, she can dig deeper without straining much of her ability, sparing her energy for use under more extreme circumstances.

"How do you know?" Adnan wonders.

"He was on the news about a year ago…the leader of an Al Qaeda cell based out of Afghanistan. He was killed by American led allies, wasn't he?" She asks, staring intently into his eyes.

"Why are you looking at me like that?" Adnan senses something is off.

"Twenty-seven minutes," Kurtis informs Tabatha, anxiously tapping his pen against his small pad of paper.

In the surveillance, intelligence, and communications room, all the individuals were watching a live feed from the interrogation room in suspense, as well as The *Seven* from their S.U.V., as they wait for Tabatha in the parking garage.

"Come on Tabatha...come on Tabatha..." was softly being repeated by some individuals watching the interrogation out of time crunching anxiety.

"So...Adnan...what is your target?" Tabatha continues to press for information.

"The Capital Building." He repeats his earlier statement.

"No, it's not." She pauses for a moment as she finds another piece of personal information in hopes of getting him to open up more. "I see. So *you...little* brother...want to be a big bad jihadist, in hopes of measuring up to your *older* brother Abd al-Hakim...or... 'Servant of the wise.'" Tabatha saw she was beginning to destabilize his emotions after that revelation. Adnan's face was slowly showing anger. "I have to say that he wasn't very wise, was he? And neither are you," she says, pushing him to become emotional.

Then with a quick outburst of anger, "WE ARE HERE TO BRING DOWN THE BIG SATAN AS IS THE WILL OF ALMIGHTY ALLAH...!! ALLAH..." Adnan attempts to stand up out of his chair in defiance, but his handcuffs bolted to the table, pulls him back down, embarrassingly "...Akbar."

"Thanks for the theatrics, but you didn't answer my question yet. What's your target?"

"Hehehehe...." he starts laughing, believing he has the upper hand by simply not answering her question. "You will soon suffer the wrath of Allah."

Adnan's emotions have become unstable which leaves his most recent memories vulnerable, so Tabatha seizes on her opportunity to find the location of the attack and hopefully other essential details. Tabatha slams her hands on the table to rattle him a little.

"Not today!" she says aggressively, then leans forward until her forehead is only inches away from Adnan's face. Adnan leans back slightly out of intimidation. Suddenly he feels something like a fluid running through his brain.

"What are you doing?" Adnan asks.

"What is your target?" She continues.

Tabatha moves her head slowly to one side, and Adnan's head moves with hers as if being pulled. His jaw drops, and memories start rising to the surface of his mind outside of his will. Images begin funneling into Tabatha like a montage of video clips recalling conversations, faces, names, and plans, anything Adnan has seen, heard, or memorized. Tabatha could have recited his whole life story if she wanted to at this point, and probably better than Adnan could.

"Got it!" Tabatha shouts so the Director could hear her.

The Director gets ready to write more information down.

"The Food & Drug Administration?!" Tabatha reveals.

"The headquarters in Chicago?" The Director asks.

"No, the little admin building not far from here," she answers.

"Hardly anyone even works there," The Director responds, questioning himself why a little place like that would be the interest of a terrorist attack. "Communications! Inform the D.C.P.D. of the current situation. But not to engage until we have a more Intel.

"Director, there are eleven that work there," Tabatha corrects the Director, "and there are fifteen terrorists in the building," Tabatha continues to absorb the information.

"E.D.T. Twenty minutes." Seryph continues to inform.

Tabatha leans in the opposite direction and again, Adnan follows as if something is pulling him.

"There are five armed men in the boiler room. I am creating a hive connection with them right now," Tabatha communicates to the director.

As time has allowed Tabatha to advance in her telepathic abilities, she's developed what she calls a '*hive mind connection.*' This expansion of her ability allows her to access all visual and audio perspectives as well as the independent memories of several hosts, simultaneously. This gives her an unprecedented amount of information for planning counteroffensives, mapping hostile environments, and stopping terrorist threats. In a physical confrontation, this ability also enables her to have, what seemingly is, an absurd amount of unpredictability against a multiple of aggressors and situations as well as an appearance of incredibly fast reaction time to counteract assaults and other aggression.

Unfortunately, on occasion, she concedes to the *delusion* that she's invincible, or even above protocol at times, while on assignment, as a result of her abilities. This sense of arrogance usually comes through in the form of brass cockiness and/or disregard for both – the seriousness of the task at hand, as well as for the potential fallout concluding the operation. Most likely the result of being on a manic high from feeling a sense of value and being dependent upon when she is called in on an assignment, compared to her usually melancholy and more isolated personal lifestyle.

"There are one, two, three, four, five...five barrels of butanetriol...whatever that is...apparently an incredibly explosive fuel...wired to a detonating ignition source. And we do have just under twenty minutes before it goes off. The laptop seems to be encrypted, and passcode protected. I'm not sure what I'm looking at, so it's pretty hard to describe what I'm looking at. Definitely above my pay grade. I hope Mitch has his game face on today!" she says loud enough that Mitchel could hear the statement through the directors' communication device.

"Just waiting on you, princess," Mitchell responds from the S.U.V. in the parking garage.

"Don't ever call me a princess," the Director responds to Mitchell.

"Uuhh...yes, sir," Mitchell replies with embarrassment. "Oops," he says to the humor of the rest of the team.

"One hostile has the passcode. He's in the boiler room. When we get there, we can't take that guy out."

"Why not?" The Director asks.

"Because the code isn't on his person, it's memorized."

"Can't you get them from his memory?" the Director assumes.

"I'm having trouble retrieving part of it. I'll need to be there to retrieve that information directly. Oh, and quit asking me questions – they're a distraction," Tabatha reminds the Director.

"Yes, ma'am," he responds sternly.

"Ok, there are ten more men on the main level. And, as I mentioned before, they're *babysitting* the eleven employees. I have created a hive mind connection with them now as well."

"Nineteen Minutes," the Director informs.

"Ok, I found where they entered the building from. It looks like they went down a man-hole, across the street from the building, and followed an underground utility tunnel that leads to the boiler room."

Tabatha blinks a couple of times, then shakes her head a little and stands back up. She severs the connection with Adnan.

Adnan was left in a state of cognitive disarray in the interrogation room attempting to process what just happened. He turned to look through the one-way window, but only saw his reflection.

Tabatha sprints down the hall toward the exit leading to the parking garage where the *Seven* were waiting for her in four S.U.V. The Director walks into the surveillance, intelligence, and communications room to direct the operation. Steve was waiting outside the S.U.V. for Tabatha and handed her a bulletproof vest and communication earpiece that she quickly places in her ear. She climbs inside, and another team member gives her a bag of cheeseburgers. Steve jumps in behind Tabatha and the S.U.V takes off screaming out of the parking garage toward the small F.D.A. facility.

The Sentient

CHAPTER V

THE ASSIGNMENT

"Fifteen minutes, ladies and gentlemen," the Director informs the team.

"Sounds like you've all been upgraded," Tabatha says through a mouth full of cheeseburger.

"Easy on the remarks Tabatha," the director attempts to keep her focused.

"Yes, sir – sorry, sir," Tabatha rhetorically responds rolling her eyes. She turns to the back seat and stares at her team with a disappointing glare. "Seriously, guys – no bacon?"

"Sorry. We were kind of in a hurry. But we're two blocks away princess, the buildings coming up on the left," Mitch communicates their approach.

Tabatha shoves her last wrapped sandwich in a vest pocket and snaps it shut. "Alright, in one block turn right then your first left – behind the series of strip malls. The utility maintenance hole is in the alleyway a block and a half down." Mitchell follows Tabatha's instructions and shortly pulls up to the entry point. He positions the SUV so that the rear of the vehicle is facing the maintenance hole.

"E.D.T. Twelve minutes," Seryph informs.

"You're cutting it extremely close," the Director lectures.

The Seven quickly exit the vehicle and assembles behind. Steve pulls the SUV's rear double doors open. He drags a hardcover case close to him, unlatches it and hands everyone a nine-millimeter sidearm, which they place in their holsters.

"Ok, princess," Mitchell directs the team's attention to Tabatha. "What's the plan?"

"Man! You keep calling her that, you're gonna get dropped, rookie!" Hammer threatens, to which Mitchell smiles and winks at him in response.

"Oh, she likes it," Mitchell responds in defense.

"Why? You don't think I could be a princess?" Tabatha says with a flirting look, to which Hammer attempts to ignore by *not* looking directly at her. He goes through great strides to maintain his tough-guy persona. However, he does look at her in her cute girlie pose and admits, "Maybe a little."

"Awe, you're just a great big teddy bear, Ham-Ham," Tabatha pats the side of his face.

"Ham-Ham? Really?" T.K. says with his slight Asian accent while the rest of them laugh.

"Dude, shut up!" Hammer responds. "She's the only one who can call me that."

"Be careful, Mitch, I could tell everyone why you're single." Mitchell shakes his head, not concerned about her threat.

"Ohhhh!!!" the others remark harmoniously. "Don't mess with the queen of blackmail," Mike adds.

"Tabatha!!!" The Director shouts in their ears. "Let's get moving!!"

"E.D.T. ten minutes," Seryph continues to inform.

"I know, Director. I have it all covered..." Her demeanor changes to *super serious mode.* "Alright, I've created a hive connection with the fifteen hostiles in the building along with the eleven hostages. I'll maintain this connection as long as possible. I may have to infiltrate suppressed memories of the terrorist who's in charge of making sure everything goes off with a *bang,* to get the rest of the deactivation code. Depending on how much digging I'll have to do, met get tired real quick." Tabatha pulls out her pouch holding two bottles of a liquid, and injection needle so her team knew where to find it in the event that she becomes too weak, or randomly gets stuck in a daydream again.

"It's always at the last second with her," the Director murmurs under his breath.

"It makes for better headlines, sir," Tabatha responds having heard him.

"So, that being said...." Tabatha begins communicating her plan. "Steve..." who is the sniper in the group, "...you're on this roof..." she points toward a maintenance ladder leading up to the roof of the strip mall, which the F.D.A. building was across the street from. The FDA building was reasonably inconspicuous. The only thing that made it stand out at all was that the front of the building had been constructed with polarized glass panels. Steve will have a clear view of the entire lobby as a result. "The leader is in the lobby behind the ladies at the front counter. Keep him in your sight. Take him out *only* if you're a hundred percent certain he's about to take a life. We need to be in the shadows as long as possible," Tabatha warns.

"Yes, boss!" Steve grabs a duffle bag carrying a DVL-10 M2 sniper rifle, a foldable stock, and ammunition throws it over his shoulder and takes off towards his position.

"Mike – keep Steve's exit clear..." Mike follows Steve to guard the maintenance ladder. "T.K. and Diego, you two hang tight here and watch the maintenance hole."

Diego reaches into a separate bag in the back of the SUV and grabs two circular electro-magnetics' with handles on one side of each. He hands one to T.K. They simultaneously attach the magnetic plates to opposite sides of the utility hole cover and lift it off the hole.

"Mitch, Hammer, Joe – down the hole with me." Tabatha tilts her head down and to the side as in deep thought for just a moment. "They set up cameras down there but they aren't infrared so as long as we keep it dark down there, we'll be good. Use your infrared shades." The four pull out what looks like sporty sunglasses from their cargo pockets and slide them on.

"What about you, princess?" Mitchell asks Tabatha.

"Those aren't quite my style," Tabatha responds, then jumps eight feet into the dark hole with her eyes shut and without the assistance of the underground maintenance ladder which the rest of the group uses.

"Holy..."

"*WATCH YOUR MOUTH MITCHELL*!!" Tabatha shouts back to the surface.

"...Shhhhhhhalom!" Mitchell quickly finds a replacement word to illustrate his disbelief that Tabatha just jumped several feet into an apparent black abyss with her eyes closed.

"Rookie," Hammer responds to Mitchell's shock as he maneuvers himself onto the ladder in the maintenance hole and climbs down to meet Tabatha in the dark utility tunnel.

"And, how does she know where she's going?" Mitchell asks T.K., Diego, and Joe before climbing into the hole.

"She uses her..." Joe taps his index finger on his temple, "...thing by tapping into their memory. At least that's the best way *I* can describe it." After quickly explaining in very layman's terms, he too climbs down the hole.

"It's all good, man. You'll get used it," Diego further explains.

"Ok, *Brainiac*..." T.K. adds, referencing Mitchells supposedly high I.Q. "This lid isn't getting any lighter and times a wasting...go...go...go."

"Right," Mitchell collects himself and climbs down with the rest of the team. T.K. and Diego place the lid back over the utility hole as Hammer, Joe, and Mitchell enables the infrared mechanism in their specs.

"Thought you weren't going to make it," Tabatha whispers to Mitchell.

Hammer laughs under his breath. "It's alright princess, I got your back," Hammer says to Mitchell in his low firm voice.

"I'm holding you to that, Ham-Ham."

"E.D.T. Eight minutes," Seryph continues to inform.

"Alright guys," she whispers, "there's a steel door at the end of the route; approximately a hundred and fifty feet down this tunnel. A key code is required to unlock it, which I already obtained from their leaders' memory. Two hostiles are guarding the door. Two others are guarding stairwell and the last one is monitoring the bomb behind the stairs – we can't take him out until I retrieve the rest of the deactivation code from his memory." Tabatha explains, though withholding her concern as to why she can only find part of the code telepathically. "When we get there, I'll line you up with your targets before unlocking the door. Once inside and after you have the *code holder* prepped or me, Hammer and Joe, you two head up and start relieving hostages. I'll stay in the dark since I'm prohibited by regulation, bla, bla, blah from being in a position to be identified. Once I have the code, Mitch, you can do your thing to shut down the bomb. So, that being said, follow me," Tabatha turns and begins running down the utility corridor with the others following.

Through their infrared glasses, they all appear as white silhouettes running through a black hole. Tabatha's shape, on the other hand, appears in various shades ranging from red to orange and then yellow towards the top of her body and head. A result of observing Tabatha's body exerting more energy, therefore, more body heat through infrared.

In the boiler room, behind the concrete staircase, which leads to the main floor of the small admin building, the *code holder* continuously monitored the bomb as well as the video feed of the utility tunnel. A laptop sitting on top one of the barrels of Butanetriol trinitrate displays encrypted information as to be remotely unaccessible. A digital timer was counting down. Then, the faint sound of footsteps coming from the surveillance monitor catches his attention. He studies the image on the monitor but sees only the dark passageway outside the boiler-room then disregards the sound.

"E.D.T. Six minutes," Seryph continues to inform.

As they approach the boiler rooms underground entrance, Tabatha signals with her hand to slow down and quietly approach the door. Tabatha shifts from viewing the memories of the terrorists to infiltrating their collective audio and visual senses, giving her a panoramic layout of the building and the present location of each one.

Tabatha lines all of their firearms in the direction of the first four hostiles on the opposite side of the door. "Don't move from these positions," she whispers.

"OOhhh crackers."

"What is it?" they ask.

"Steve!" Tabatha whispers. "The leader just spotted you!"

"He did?" Steve responded. The leader then begins acting irrationally and drags one of the clerks out into the center of the lobby with an assault rifle to her head for Steve to see. "Yeah, he apparently did. This guy must have eagle eyes. I'm going to take him out once I got a clear shot."

"We got to move now," Tabatha punches in the door code then positions herself for her target as well.

[Clank! Clank!] The door makes a mechanical sound as the magnetic seal is disengaged. It grabs the attention of the two hostiles on the other side of the door. The hostiles at the stairwell were about to ascend upon hearing commotion coming from the lobby, then reversed when they too heard the door unlock then aimed at the door.

All four hostiles were armed, and just as Tabatha had planned, one of them pushed the door open wide. Before they could even see into the dark corridor, all four terrorists were shot dead and simultaneously fell to the ground. Immediately, Hammer, Mitchell, and Joe rush into the boiler room with their firearms held high aligned with their eyesight, Hammer leading the way and Tabatha staying behind in the dark, temporarily. The silencers on the teams' firearms suppressed the sound of their shots; thus, their initial phase of the plan, excluding Steve having been spotted by the leader, was a relative success.

However, the code holder, behind the staircase, heard the sound of collapsing objects. Then, glancing at the surveillance monitor, which shows light in the feed, runs out from behind the stairs to find three individuals in black outfits' storm into the boiler-room and his co-conspirators dead on the ground. He quickly reversed course to ignite the explosives early, but a bullet entered the back of his thigh, and he collapses to the ground. Hammer and Mitchell then promptly rushed over and subdued him. Mitchell held him down while Hammer handcuffed, gagged, and blindfolds him. Joe guarded the stairs. Mitchell and Hammer sat the incapacitated terrorist on his knees as Tabatha walks into the boiler room. Joe closes the door behind her, re-engaging the lock.

"You got this?" Hammer asks Mitchell.

"I'm good from here, this guy isn't going anywhere," Mitchell replies with one arm around the terrorist's neck. He pulls his head back by his hair, so his face is tilted up, facing Tabatha.

Hammer meets up with Joe by the stairs and waits for Tabatha to give them more information.

Tabatha tilts her head slightly, the usual sign that she's processing telepathic information. Sweat begins lightly accumulating on her brow as her body temperature begins to rise a little due to the energy consumption her ability requires.

"Alright, these stairs lead to a hallway, which leads to the lobby of the building." She stops for a moment, distracted by the screaming women and Arabic rambling going on upstairs.

"Steve! You need to take that guy out," Tabatha says calmly.

"I'm working on it, he's using this woman as a human shield at the moment," Steve responds.

"Crackers!! This incident isn't secret anymore." Tabatha could see through the eyes of the leader a couple of bystanders walked in front of the building, which of course, consists of nothing but glass. The bystanders, spotting a man with a gun to a woman's head in the lobby, run to the side of the building and call 9-1-1.

"Ok, back to you two..." Tabatha continues her directions to Hammer and Joe. "The hallway is lined with offices. Faculty members are being held up in each office by the remaining nine terrorists in the building. You know what to do." Tabatha then turns her attention to hostile in Mitchel's arms as Hammer and Joe ascend the stairs. Tabatha reaches out with her hand as if reaching for something as she approaches the hostile.

"This is quickly getting out of hand, Tabatha," The director says their ears sternly.

"I'm retrieving the code to the bomb right now. I told you we would have five minutes to spare," Tabatha responds with her typical cocky and *over*confident attitude.

The director, continuing to monitor the incident from the surveillance room, looks down at the table and shakes his head.

"E.D.T. Five minutes," Seryph continues to inform.

"Ok, so maybe not quite five minutes but still...more than enough time..." Tabatha responds as she hovers her hand over the wounded terrorist, moving her head around as images start funneling into her mind. Soon she finds a memory of this same terrorist in a room with several other terrorists with him. He is inserting three numbers into a laptop. She knows it's the deactivation code.

"10-6-8...." She says to Mitch.

"Is that the whole thing?" He responds.

"No. There are three more digits. 10-6-8...," Tabatha replays the memory, "...He's only putting those three digits in."

"NO!!!" she exclaims out of frustration.

"What is it?" Mitchell inquires, getting a little apprehensive watching the timer continue to count down.

"He only types in three digits then backs away," she explains.

"Tabatha..." the Director speaks being cut off

"Shut up, Kurtis!!!!" She yells, starting to panic a little. She begins digging deeper into the facets of the terrorist mind. Additional images, higher in detail, shoot through her mind. The hostile starts squirming as he feels the sensation of fluid going through his head. Mitchell tries to hold him tight but feels a dense pressure pushing against him.

"Where's the rest of it!! She yells. That same pressure intensifies, pushing Mitchell away, slamming him against the floor as if an invisible lead weight landed on him. The blindfold partially falls off one of the hostile's eyes, allowing him to see Tabatha's hand directly in front of him, and between her fingers could see her face. Her eyes had a slight illumination to them. As she dug deeper into the orifices of his mind, the intensifying pressure also thrusts him into the ground, as the concrete cracks beneath. The handcuffs crumble, releasing his hands; however, he laid on the ground paralyzed.

Finally! She finds the memory she's been looking for as another man steps up to the laptop punching in the rest of the code. The code was not partially suppressed, it was split up between two hostiles to ensure its ultimate detonation. But, the code was necessary to activate the timing sequence – as well as to deactivate it. She recognized him as the lead hostile in the lobby.

Three gunshots were fired from upstairs as gunfire was exchanged between to more hostiles, though Hammer and Joe fired back successfully neutralizing them. A few hostages were relieved but told to stay put as Hammer and Joe continued to the next set of office doors. The sound of the gunfire drew the leaders' attention, and he turned with the woman he was using as a human shield to look down the hallway, exposing his back to Steve.

"STEVE!! WAIT!! DON'T...!"

"Bang!" "Crash!" "Splat!" "Tink!" The sound of Steve's gun reverberates through the air as the bullet is expelled from the barrel, crashing through one of the windows of the building, entering the base of the leaders' neck and exiting his trachea, before coming to rest in one of the floor tiles.

"Sorry, Tab," says Steve, locking the safety mechanism and quickly dismantling his rifle, then shoving it in the bag, throwing the bag over his shoulder and promptly exiting the roof.

The woman let out another high pitched scream when the bullet passed by her head falling on her butt as the leaders' grip on the woman was released, and he fell to the floor next to her. She pushed herself away with her feet and hands, backing up to the base of the front desk, exhaling slowly. The other clerk, also frightened, ran around the counter and embraced her before another set of hostiles rushed out of an office and grabbed them, both dragging them into the office.

"Not your fault Steve," Tabatha responds. The trauma to the leader's head had severed Tabatha's connection with him, making her unable to access his memory with her hive-mind connection effectively.

Since regions of the brain remain active moments immediately after death, Tabatha can still retrieve specific short term memories of the individual. However, her need to be extremely close to the cerebrum is essential, compelling her to make a B-line from the boiler room to the lobby. Thus, she jumps up and dashes up the stairs leaving the terrorist in the boiler room incapacitated and mentally disturbed.

"Tabatha!" Mitchell yells as she takes off upstairs. Trying to process what he saw Tabatha do for the first time, he then collects himself and finally can get up off the floor as the pressure alleviates.

Mitchell first checks the condition of the hostile sunk into the concrete floor. He's still alive, but unconscious. Mitchell then maneuvers to the laptop sitting on top of the barrels of explosives. He begins analyzing the mechanics of the setup: wires and cables leading in every direction. A small metal box sat on the middle barrel. Mitchel went to reach for it, then observes that it's on a pressure plate, thus if he moves it, it could set the bomb off. He, instead, pulls out a tablet from his backpack and begins attempting to remote access the laptop, while keeping an eye on the timer.

"Four minutes," Mitchel informs the team, watching the countdown on the computer screen. Realizing what he is dealing with, he too begins to sweat nervously.

Tabatha races up the stairs, and down the hall hallway lined with offices. Hammer and Joe had taken out four of the hostile's who had held up employees in the offices. Tabatha sprints past them, pulling her gun out of her holster.

"Tabatha!" Hammer shouts at her, "Wait! What are you..." he and Joe glance at each other, then begin following Tabatha down the hallway.

Tabatha targets the wall to her right and pulls the trigger to her nine-millimeter semiautomatic multiple times. The bullets pierce through the wall of an office, and into an un-expectant terrorist who's holding another woman hostage. He drops to the ground dead in front of the hostage, who initially screams at the unexpected intervention. Tabatha then points the gun to the opposite wall further down the hallway, behind which yet another hostile is holding another hostage. Again, she shoots at the wall as if having x-ray vision, emptying the clip with the same result as before.

Hammer and Joe follow up on the two offices across from each other that Tabatha fired into finding a dead terrorist and a shaken hostage in each room. After confirming the safety of the former hostages and the lack of a pulse on the bad guys, they meet back in the hallway to watch Tabatha run further down the hall, throwing her empty gun on the ground.

Upon hearing more gunshots in the hall-way, another two hostiles step out of the yet another office just as Tabatha leaps, headfirst into the air, inserting the crux of her arm around one of their necks then swinging around to catch the neck of the other with her upper legs. Then, with a twist of her lower body, she snaps his neck with her thighs – killing him. As his corpse collapses to the ground, Tabatha pulls the other, whose neck is still in her arm, over her shoulder and on top of the body of the deceased hostile, whose neck was still between Tabatha's thighs. She then grabbed a gun that had fallen from their hands during her acrobatic assault and hit him over the head with it, rendering him unconscious. She points the gun at the wall of the last office and fires, then as if nothing had slowed her down, continues her sprint into the lobby as the final hostile collapsed in the doorway.

"And the rest of us are here for – what purpose?" Joe asks Hammer, as they watch Tabatha take out five hostile's singlehandedly in less than a minute.

Tabatha makes it to the body of the leader in the lobby. She grabs the head of the corpse whose neck is still spewing blood out of the hole in his trachea where Steve's bullet exited. She pulls his lifeless head up, nearly touching her forehead and begins siphoning thru fragmented memories of the deceased leader. Each cognitive image seemed to dematerialize almost as fast as she finds them. However, she is also unaware of the side effect of pushing her ability passed her normal limit is manifesting in the physical destruction of her immediate surroundings.

"I guess we're just the spectators today," Hammer replies to Joe's comment.

"...Which seems to have become the norm as of the last few missions," Joe further comments, then the two of them continue down the hall, following up on Tabatha's onslaught, checking victims, as well as confirming the permanent incapacitation of the bad guys. The two of them collect the former hostages and guide them down the hall, through the lobby, while passing Tabatha on the way to the exit.

"Please don't pay any attention to her," Hammer tells the group assuming their curiosity of what she's doing holding a dead mans' head to her face. Hammer and Joe conclude leading the administrators out of the building to safety, where a crowd of police, E.M.T.'s, and a small multitude of bystanders had gathered to witness the incident. Several emergency medical technicians meet the former hostages at a police barricade, set up to keep people away from the building, and escort them to ambulances nearby.

The police captain stops Hammer momentarily to ask him about the situation.

"You're Director informed us of the incident after the prognosis of the situation appeared to be negative. Has it been resolved?"

"My opinion is to get these people out of here quick. The building *is* evacuated, except for my team, though there might be a detonation," Hammer answered quickly.

"Yeah, we tried to get rid of these people, but you know, this is entertainment for a lot of people any more...we had to run off some anarchists' who were chanting '*let it blow!*'" The captain further explained.

"Two minutes Tab," Mitchell informs from the boiler room. Sweat pours from his face and seemingly every other orifice on his body as he attempts to beat back the fear that he might be blown to bits in less than a minute if Tabatha doesn't find the rest of that code.

Tabatha continues pulling in memories as they continue to deteriorate. Then the floor tiling beneath her begins to crack and collapse underneath her. The flesh on the hostiles' forehead tears and coagulated blood bubbles to the surface. Finally, she finds the memory she's been looking for. The memory revealed the leader walking up to the laptop. Three digits remain to be input while at the same time this image, too, begins to deteriorate like watching a photograph being consumed from the edges inward.

"C'mon-c'mon-c'mon!" Tabatha impatiently mumbles to herself, watching the image play out like a movie. "Mitch!!" she shouts to prepare him for the information.

"Ready!" He responds with a tinge of momentary anxiety relief.

"4...!"

"4," he repeats pressing the key

"6...!"

"6."

"Oh, please, no, please, no please, please!" Tabatha pleads with the corpse as its mind becomes completely inactive and unable to give up any more of it's' secrets, permanently. "Come back..." She continues trying to get the memory back. As the image dissipates, the face of the dead man in her hands becomes visible to her again.

"Uhhh, Tab?" Mitchell's anxiety returns in full force

"NO!!!" Tabatha shouts, expressing her loss of control over the situation. Upon her brief outburst, the glass is blown out of the front of the building, exposing Tabatha to the crowd. Many of which begin recording the event with their cell phones. Having given up, Tabatha throws his head back to the ground in one more spat of anger. Simultaneously, a small, brief tremor was felt and rocked the building just enough to crack some of the foundation and walls.

Hammer and Joe, jump up and turn to the Police captain. "You got less than a minute to get these people out of here before this place is coming down," Hammer says to the captain, who picks up a megaphone and starts aggressively shouting at the crowd to disperse.

"Looks like Tabatha is going to have some new videos added to her anonymous website," Joe says to Hammer, referring to a YouTube channel that had been created by anonymous individuals who believe the government uses psychics, *or at least one*, in certain circumstances. They run back into the building to calm her down and to get her out of there.

"E.D.T – One Minute," Seryph continues to inform.

As they approach Tabatha, the dense pressure prevents them from getting to Tabatha. "Tabatha!" Hammer shouts, "We need to get out...it's too late." Hammers' calm firm voice gets her attention. She stands and turns to Hammer and Joe. The pressure is alleviated, allowing Hammer to run to her. Joe waits for them. Tabatha looks toward the crowd, watching some running away and others refusing to leave. The usual mess of psychic noise entering her mind disoriented her for a moment. She shakes her head, cognitively collecting herself, and getting back in control of her telepathy. She looks up at Hammer standing in front of her.

"I *really* screwed this one up, didn't I," she says with an embarrassed look on her face.

"It doesn't matter – let's go!" Hammer says, attempting to get Tabatha moving.

"Wait. Mitchell figured it out," She says confidently but out of energy. Hammer stares at her with a questioned look on his face.

In the boiler-room, Mitchell had input what he had of the deactivation code in his tablet, looking for a sequence, as well as repeating it to himself. "10-6-8-4-6…10-6-8-4-6…" Behind him, the hostile regains consciousness. He looks up and sees Mitchells back to him and over his shoulder can see the timer still counting down, then braces himself for death.

"E.D.T. ten seconds, nine seconds…" Seryph begins counting each second down.

"10-6-8-4-6…." Mitchell repeats.

"…Eight seconds, seven seconds…" it continues.

"10-6-8-4-6…."

"…Five seconds, four seconds…" The director lowers his head and closes his eyes, anticipating the worst.

"10-6-8-4-6….2?" Mitchell punches in a final digit based on an educated guess.

"Three seconds, two seconds, one second. Estimated disaster threshold has expired," Seryph concludes.

The Director glances up at Seryph, watching the number zero blinking. But no explosion is heard or seen on the video/audio feeds. Everyone in the surveillance room release sighs of relief.

Mitchell falls back on his butt and hands. He takes a couple of deep breaths as well while staring at the timer on the laptop, which had paused with three seconds remaining. However, the hostel, still on the floor behind him, was not so relieved. In silent anger, the terrorist stealthily gets up and quietly sneaks up on Mitchell. He pulls a utility knife out of his pocket and raises it above his head, *thinking* that he's going to plunge the blade into the side of Mitchell's neck to slay him.

"Mitch!" Tabatha picks up on the thought of the terrorist in the boiler room, arousing another emotion manifesting again destructively, completing the destabilization of the concrete floor underneath her and Hammer, sending the slab of concrete crashing into the boiler-room with the two of them on top. At the sound of the basement ceiling caving in, Mitchell instinctively roles himself out of the way as a chunk of basement ceiling and concrete flooring crash to the ground. Laying on his back, Mitchell grabs his sidearm from its' holster and points it toward the debris, waiting for the dust to settle. Then, seeing Hammer and Tabatha laying atop the pile of rubble, he relaxes.

Hammer sits up and lets out a cough then turns to see if Tabatha's ok. "Let's not do that again - *princess*," he says with a smile after seeing her move and cough a couple of times.

Joe ran to the hole in the floor. "Hammer! Tabatha! Are you guys, alright?"

"Yeah, Joe, we're good. Man – what a ride. Reminds me of the Tower of Terror. Only it was less painful," says Hammer.

"You know, I don't think she likes being called Princess," Mitchell says as he gets up off the floor and attempting to lighten the mood now that the danger is over, as well as referencing Hammers' dislike towards Mitchell's nickname for Tabatha. Hammer laughs with Mitchell at the comment before Mitchell turns to begins completely disabling the ignition mechanisms that could still set off the explosives.

Hammer notices the terrorists' hand, still holding the utility knife, was all that escaped the avalanche of concrete, drywall, and metal. "Oh, and apparently, you're welcome," Hammer points out to Mitchell.

"Whoa, where'd he come from?" Mitchell responds. "Definitely, thanks for that."

"Hey, girl. You don't look so good." Hammer observes Tabatha shaking and profusely sweating. He touches her face. "Whoa! Tabatha, you're burning!"

"I need...my...medi...cine..."

He unsnaps the pocket, pulls out the brown pouch, and opens it, revealing the twenty-seven gauge injection needle and two small bottles of liquid. Tabatha, with her metabolism, wiped out, instructs him on what to do with it. Hammer rolls up one of Tabatha's sleeves and injects the medicine in her arm. Within moments, Tabatha's body temperature begins dropping, and she starts moving then sits up. She takes the medication back from Hammer, disassembles it all places it back in the brown pouch, then slides it back in her vest pocket. She then reaches in the other pocket and pulls out a royally smashed cheeseburger leftover from the start of the mission and began eating it as if she hadn't eaten in a month.

Meanwhile, outside the building, the remaining public watched intently waiting to see what became of the individuals who fell through the floor. A figure appeared through some of the dust coming out from the hallway. It was Mitch, followed by Hammer, who was dragging the only two surviving terrorists out with him. Number Five from the boiler room who was still unconscious and barely alive, and number Twelve, whom Tabatha Jackie Chann'ed and knocked out with the handle of a gun during her hallway assault – He was barely conscious. Then finally, Tabatha emerged, still finishing the remainder of her cheeseburger.

The crowd became enthused at the reemergence of the team, indicating the elimination of the threat. Additional law enforcement officers rushed inside the building and took the two surviving hostiles off Hammer's hands and into police custody. The four of them maneuver through the crowd attempting to avoid eye contact with civilians, News cameras, and camera phones as they made their way back to their transportation.

A government I liaison for T.I.D. steps out of a vehicle behind the slowly dispersing crowd walks up to the police captain. The police captain introduces the liaison to the media as a T.I.D. (Terrorist Interceptor Division) official to explain the situation in a way as to cover up some of the more *seemingly supernatural* events that many witnessed.

Upon the teams' departure from the scene, Tabatha comments, "Well, the Director's super-mad."

"You can read his mind from here?" Mitchell inquires.

"I don't have to. He broke coms without saying '*well-done team*,'" she concludes.

"Out of how all of our assignments, has he ever said that?"

"Once."

"That must have been the *one* time you *didn't* make a public mess during an assignment," Hammer reminds her to which she shutters at the embarrassing truth of Hammer's statement.

"Well, I don't know about you all, but I'm ready to call it a day. Even if it *is* only eleven a.m.," Joe adds.

The Sentient

CHAPTER VI

PHILOSOPHIES

Tabatha and the *Seven* arrive back at the small inconspicuous parking garage. A couple of administrators with documents attached to clipboards in hand were waiting for them to exit the vehicle. As the team disbands from the S.U.V., each of them scribbles a signature on the paper attached to the clipboard. Rodney, the T.I.D. senior medical officer, shoots a steroid into each of their arms with an injection gun as they follow the admins back into the facility for a post-mission debriefing and medical examination. Tabatha was the last to get out and Rodney waited for her. She didn't need to sign anything since the document she signed earlier, allowing her to telepathically interrogate Adnan, covered all her activities for the assignment.

Formerly a chief army medic, Rodney currently practices medicine as the senior T.I.D. medical officer. During the Vietnam War, he saved nearly an entire platoon due to his quick thinking and medical expertise. Years later, he received the Purple Heart, alongside a few other military heroes, who never received recognition directly after the war. He was also involved in counter biological warfare operations for the military after the gulf war in the early 1990s due to his previous involvement in biotech engineering for pharmaceutical companies.

Tabatha slowly climbs out of the front passenger seat, still feeling rather slow and out of energy from over exhorting herself during the assignment – again. Sweat continued to accumulate on her flesh. Though her body temperature had dropped, it was still higher compared to an average individual. Rodney holds a large, thirty six-ounce glass of what looked like green slop with different color floaties in it, opposite the hand holding the injection gun. Tabatha glances at the glass and makes the usual '*I'm going to barf,*' face at Rodney.

"I hate that stuff," Tabatha complains as she usually does – and has ever since Rodney concocted the ten thousand calorie *energy drink,* of which nearly half of the ingredients in the glass are inconsumable by normal humans.

Rodney grins at her comment. "You always say that, but in about a minute, you'll ask me how you can make it at home."

"You're right...," she smiles, "...but I can't because the government regulates when I can even have it...like they do everything in my life." Tabatha takes the glass, pinches her nose, and begins to down the drink. She drinks about half of the glass. "Hmmm...it's not as nasty-tasting like it usually is." She drinks the rest of it and hands the glass back to Rodney after he puts his injection gun in a pouch and slides it in his pocket. "Strawberries, nice touch. It's more like fruity flavored toxic waste instead of just toxic waste this time. I still kinda wanna gag though."

Rodney chuckles and waits for Tabatha's posture to change – an indication that the concoction is stabilizing her metabolism. Rodney wipes her forehead with the sleeve of his shirt and notices the sweating has already stopped. She stands up straighter, another indication that her strength is returning rapidly.

"Feeling better?" He asks.

"Oh yeah...I'm ready for a marathon now," Tabatha replies.

"Unfortunately, you would get disqualified for doping after drinking this stuff," he responds in the same sarcastic manner but attached to some truth.

"I'm pretty sure I'd get disqualified for several reasons – *if* they knew about those reasons." They begin walking toward Frank and the rusted metal door.

"True. Oh, and sorry, the Director couldn't be here to greet you back," Rodney adds with some more sarcasm. "He's..."

"...In a meeting, I know."

"...With the secretary of defense, of all people," Rodney adds in a more serious tone as he holds out his badge for Frank, the guard, to scan and let them in the building.

The door buzzes. Rodney opens it and lets Tabatha walk in first.

"He must be in a lot of trouble," she remarks.

"Ha! Yeah. I don't think *he's* the one who's *really* in trouble," Rodney adds as they walk down the hall.

"Maybe I can get my report done and get out of here before he gets out of his *meeting*," Tabatha considers.

"Come on. You know the drill. I have to..."

"...Give me my post-mission examination first," Tabatha finishes his thought in an imitating squeaky voice, again illustrating her frustration over the rules associated with her occupation, but also fear that she's going to face the fury of the Director – again.

They continue down the stairs to the atrium. As they turn a corner and enter the hallway that leads to a medical lab, they can hear the secretary of defense yelling in the Director's office.

"That doesn't sound good," Rodney exclaims.

"No, it doesn't," Tabatha agrees. "However, this isn't the first time the Director's gotten mad at me for things not *quite* going as planned," Tabatha reminds Rodney, and herself as well.

"True, but it is the first time the secretary of defense has been here. I didn't even know he knew where to find this place," Rodney adds with a chuckle.

"Ha – true that. I'm surprised he remembers which house he leaves his pants in." They walk into the lab.

"What?" Rodney inquires of her statement.

Tabatha looks to the floor and shakes her head for a second. "Bad Tabatha," she lectures herself for partially revealing the secretaries' hidden immoral lifestyle that she picked up on as they walked passed the Director's office. "Oh, nothing. Don't worry about it. Some of my thoughts seem to enjoy bypassing the mental checkpoint on the way out of my mouth – *occasionally.*"

"Tell me something *none* of here know, would you. And I think it's a little more than *occasionally.*"

"Well, some people just need to keep their thoughts to themselves....or better yet just not think at all." Tabatha feels that she always has to get the last word in to validate her perspectives, no matter how farfetched they can be. She walks around the lab looking at monitors and medical equipment. She then heads toward the examination table anticipating Rodney's verbal command to do so.

"Alright, hop up on the examination table." Tabatha hops on the table while Rodney opens a cabinet door and moves things around on the counter. After putting examination gloves on, he grabs a twenty-one gauge needle and a few blood collection tubes. He walks up to the examination table and pulls over an aluminum tray. On it is a stethoscope, otoscope, and a little rubber mallet. He sets the needle and collection tubes on the tray with the other instruments.

Rodney pulls a tympanic thermometer out of his shirt pocket and sticks it in Tabatha's ear. "Ninety-nine degrees. You must be freezing," he sarcastically comments.

"Your green gook does the trick."

Rodney puts one hand on Tabatha's wrist and looks at his watch to check her pulse. "One-ten. Your pulse is normal – for you." Rodney then checks her lymph nodes.

"Cuz, I'm not *really* normal, *right?*" She responds, pretending to be slightly insulted.

"You know what I mean. I find you absolutely fascinating, honestly," Rodney attempts to correct his previous statement.

"Thanks, I think."

"You *should* be thankful – that your heart membrane and the elasticity of your arteries are twice as dense then everyone else's, or else your heart would have most likely exploded a long time ago once it reached your maximum heart rate," he reminds her.

"Right, something around three hundred beats per minute."

"Yeah. Something around there."

"Still, I'm not quite sure if I should be flattered or even more insulted that you get turned on by my vital statistics and not by my...." Tabatha looks down at her chest and tries to find a word that doesn't give off the impression that she believes her physical appearance to be, well, above average, "...more noticeable attributes," Tabatha finishes her statement attempting to sit in a mildly provocative manner for Rodney.

"Hahaha. You crack me up," Rodney responds to her attempt to hit on him – for the umpteenth time.

Tabatha falls back into her slouching position. "You know, any *normal* chick would think you're a Eunice."

"Maybe I am." He responds rhetorically. Tabatha glances at him with a raised eyebrow. "Haha," he just laughed at the idea. "Women are, well, trouble. No offense, by the way," Rodney begins explaining his reasons for avoiding any form of a romantic relationship. "Pregnancy...S.T.D.'s, etc., there are way more things I'd rather set my *mind* on in life than being concerned about possible consequences that can *ruin* my life. I suppose I'd just much rather become worm food naturally, having known that I've lived an exciting and fulfilled life is all." He picks up the rubber mallet and checks the reflexes of her legs and arms.

"You know, you have a pretty good life philosophy for someone who doesn't believe in God," Tabatha acknowledges, impressed, "minus the worm food perspective, of course," she adds.

"Well, there could be one. Or three hundred million – like what the Hindu's believe. Or there could be none. Who knows? Anyhow, the intention of my earlier statement, Tabatha, was to emphasize that what you can do challenges me intellectually and having the chance to study you, or your *gift*, I should say, is a privilege."

"So, I'm like a lab rat then, right?" Intentionally trying to make Rodney feel guilty.

"Aaaand, here we go again," he says to himself. "You know that's not what I mean. Say '*ah*,'" Rodney picks up the otoscope.

"*Ahhhhhh.*" Rodney looks at the back of her mouth with the tool. He then looks around her eyes with it and then her ears.

"Dirty girl," He blurts out with sarcasm.

"Yeah, you're funny," Tabatha rolls her eyes.

"You need to clean out your ears *big time*. They're disgusting." He sets the otoscope back down on the tray and grabs his stethoscope, placing the diaphragm on her back. "Deep breathe," he moves it over, "....again." He places it on her chest and listens to her heartbeat. He puts the stethoscope around his neck and then places a blood pressure cuff around her left upper arm and presses a button on a machine next to the examination table. The cuff tightens, then loosens slowly before revealing the systolic and diastolic readings on the monitor of the blood pressure machine.

"Well, you're pretty healthy, for just coming out of a firefight," Rodney informs her as he takes off the blood pressure cuff.

"You mean, healthy for – *me*, right?" Tabatha responds wittily with a smirk on her face.

"Right," Rodney simply agrees. "Alright, now for the fun poky stuff." Rodney grabs a rubber tourniquet and places it on Tabatha's upper arm. Then he picks up the needle and a blood collection tube. He pushes the needle into the artery in the crux of her right arm, attaches the blood collection tube to the end of a thin plastic transparent hose that connects to the needle, then removes the tourniquet.

"So, that was a pretty close call today, don't you think?" he recaps the days' events.

"That's for sure. For a moment, I really *did* believe that I wasn't walking away from this one. But, you know what Romans eight: twenty-eight says..."

"You know I don't." Rodney removes the first full blood-collection tube and replaces it with an empty one.

"Of course you don't, but it says: '*All things work together for good*, for those who love God and are called according to His purpose." Tabatha lowers her head. "I see that in so many circumstances anymore."

"Well, if this is your calling, I'd suggest following orders a little more closely and limit the messes during your assignments. I'm sure your *God*, doesn't look too highly on that."

"Yeah, admittedly, I'm *definitely* not the poster child of a church girl. And my aunt affirms that from time to time too," she responds.

"From what I know about your aunt, I believe it. But, I can see how that can be a comforting verse for some people. *I* would simply say that your one lucky weirdo," Rodney responds with humor. "You know I don't put stock in Biblical stuff. Don't get me wrong, I have a lot of respect for that book, especially regarding its historicity – the authors were undoubtedly literary geniuses." Rodney replaces another tube.

Tabatha rolls her eyes at the statement. He makes similar comments every time they have this conversation. A single memory from Rodney's past rises to the surface of his thoughts, and Tabatha catches it. "You might not now, but you used to," she reminds him to which Rodney stays silent.

"So, then why do you think I'm here?" Tabatha attempts to challenge Rodney's world view.

"Honestly, I am tempted to consider the possibility that you may be the first in a new stage of human evolution." He answers.

"Wow! You really know how to make *me* feel special. We're all a bunch of bagged cosmic goop, and I'm the first bag of new goop. If that's the case, then I have to admit, being the first, *sucks*," she replies with her interpretation of Rodney's ideas.

"Well, think about it. Even your ability is changing. In the last year, you have begun exhibiting what I believe are some telekinetic attributes alongside your telepathy. So maybe your *ability* is beginning to *evolve* as well," Rodney points out. "Besides, you really are special. I mean seriously, you are a hero. You've prevented how many attacks before they happened? Including your debut mission: stopping a nuclear missile launch that most likely would have had severe global ramifications. You set back Iran's nuclear program back, what, twenty years?" Rodney attempts to make Tabatha feel better about being, *supposedly*, a product of evolution.

"I mostly just remember the facility collapsing on me while I was attempting to retrieve the codes to stop the launch. Then waking up in a military hospital," she recalls.

"Yep, I was treating you."

Rodney pulls the last collection tube out, caps it, and sets it on the tray with the others. He grabs a cotton ball and places it over the area where the needle protrudes into her arm and pulls out the needle. Tabatha holds the cotton ball while Rodney gets a bandage and puts it over the cotton ball attaching it to her arm to absorb any extra blood.

"I think someone's read one too many comics in his lifetime." Rodney chuckles at Tabatha's comment. "I just better *never* come to work and see a skimpy skin-tight yellow and blue spandex outfit that I'm expected to wear. I *will* resign," she jokes but with some truth to it as well.

"Though, I find it interesting that you would classify me as a hero. But yet, Dostoevsky said, in the famous 'Grand Inquisitor' passage, that 'if there's no God, then there's no moral standard. Therefore everything is permissible.' *Therefore*, there's no reason for me to *save lives* or use my abilities to help anyone. In fact, if all this Darwinian nonsense is true, then survival is for the fittest and I *should* be using it to, *ultimately*, benefit myself."

Rodney picks up the blood collection tubes and carries them to the counter. He pulls a test tube rack out of a cabinet and places the collection tubes in the individual holes. He then turns to face Tabatha and leans back against the counter as they continue their conversation.

"Well, as far as the latex outfit idea, honestly, I think you would look pretty good, now that you got that idea in my head," Rodney replies with a grin to Tabatha's protest about wearing a skimpy uniform.

"Uhhh. I'm supposed to keep a *low* profile, remember?" She reminds Rodney.

"*Uhhh...*You don't try very hard to keep a *low* profile – even with something as *inconspicuously* average as what you're wearing now," Rodney reminds Tabatha.

"Hmmm...touché," Tabatha says, admitting defeat to that particular topic.

"By the way, when you said I was lucky earlier, would that be considered a *fact*?" Tabatha continues to attempt to dismantle Rodney's Godless existence perspective.

"Oh-my-goodness woman! So, considering the *fact* that every mission you've gone on within the last two years has been a *close call*, I'm tempted to answer in the affirmative. However, I do get your point. *Luck*, or *chance*, *isn't* a *thing*. Therefore it *can't*, nor *does it* affect the material universe. Therefore, it's not a *fact*," Rodney admits. "Though it does reference a coincidence."

"So was it a coincidence that stepped in and saved the day so many times?" Tabatha continues to ask with a smile and knowing full well that she's annoying him.

"Look, you got through every mission alive whether or not it was a close call. That is *the* fact," Rodney attempts to conclude the conversation, primarily due to the *fact* that Rodney's arguments are generally soundly defeated by Tabatha's simple philosophical questioning.

"It's ironic that you come off so *intellectually*, using '*fact* that' or '*fact* this,' however, you're not even entirely convinced that what's coming out of your mouth is a *fact*," she points out. "Just an observation."

"And this is why you're the *super* interrogator," Rodney compliments.

"There's a newly published article called 'Sweeping Gene Survey Reveals New Facets of Evolution.' You should look it up.

"I'll do that. Anyways, I do suppose that there's a certain amount of blind faith in whatever anyone believes in. Even for you, I'm sure, am I right? I mean, what makes *you* so sure that *you're* right about what you believe?" Rodney attempts to find an agreeable juncture in the conversation.

"Everything." She answers without hesitation, then glances at the floor as memories come to mind. "You know, when I was really little, I would have nightmares about horrible people doing horrible, *horrible* things." She takes a breath and continues. "And as I got older and understood that they weren't merely nightmares nor the product of my *overactive*, *lucid* imagination, but were, in fact, the product of *other* individuals' *lucid* and *overactive* imaginations. And I don't mean that someone was simply thinking lustfully of another person, or even the fantasies or wishful thinking of others – like one person *thinking* of shooting another person. I mean the most *morbid, disturbing* things you can imagine. Things that, *even now*, would cause me to want to vomit, just attempting to describe them. Some could have even made slasher movies look PG-13. But then, *later* discovering they weren't always just *thoughts* or *fantasies* of sick people, but some of these things were the *physical actions* of other people. I was *actually* watching it happen," she explains as her eyes begin to tear up. "That's when I discovered, with the help of my godparents, that I could access another persons' posterior occipital and superior temporal gyrus. Of course, it was by accident at that time. Then add to that; my telepathy has an approximate range of about a fifteen-mile radius, give or take, which tells me that there is a lot of evil in a relatively small area. So, all that to say – *yes* – I *know*, for a *fact*, that there *is* absolute evil. But, absolute evil cannot exist without absolute good. Fortunately, absolute good *can* exist without evil," she concludes.

"Oh goodness, I didn't mean to...."

"...Oh, it's ok. I honestly don't mind *occasionally* talking about those things. It's good to get some of these things off my chest every once in a while." She wipes her eyes and smiles. "Any more questions, hot stuff?" she asks trying to alleviate his guilt-ridden conscience by returning to her sarcastic self.

He cracks a smile and relaxes, "the disadvantage of debating a psychic, I suppose."

She winks at the comment. "Shouldn't you be, like, testing the stuff in my blood or something instead of standing there looking like you just lost a fistfight?"

"Yes. Later on." Rodney responds.

"What do you do with my blood samples anyways? Do you sell them on the black market somewhere?" Tabatha asks humorously while simultaneously probing Rodney's mind for the actual answer, but, instead, a more familiar and more aggressive thought pattern emerges.

"Oh, crackers!" she says.

"What is it now?"

"The *fact* that I'm about to get chewed up and spit out." Tabatha looks down the hall and sees the Director heading straight for the medical lab.

Rodney glances down the hall. "Well, good luck – again." Rodney sits the blood collection tube rack in a small Styrofoam lined box, then places it in a case along with some examination equipment and closes it. "I think I need to go check on the rest of your team."

"Thanks for the ditch, doc," Tabatha retorts.

Upon stepping out of the lab, the Director stops Rodney briefly. "Anything I need to know?" He asks.

"Nope, back to normal, and healthy as – Tabatha," Rodney answers.

"Alright, thank you, doctor." The Director walks into the lab and closes the door.

"I know *exactly* what you're going to say, and I'm..." Tabatha attempts to respond before the Director opens his mouth.

"I don't care if you know what I'm thinking or about to say or do. I don't even care if you know that the world is going to end in ten seconds. *You* are going to *listen* to what I *say*. Even if you have to hear it twice – via your head *and* your ears – Understood!?" The director sternly responds.

"Well, technically, my ears are a part of my head..."

"Shut it!"

"Yep, or'a...yessssir..."

"You are becoming more arrogant, cocky, reckless, and defiant by the day..."

"Technically, I'm not here every..."

"Shut it!"

"Mhmm...sorry sir,"

"You see this here? You *still* can't take *me* or *any* of this *seriously*, even now. Because, *technically*, you endangered your whole team today – again! Not to mention you were seen by dozens of bystanders – *again*!"

"But nothing happened to any of them – *again*. And everyone made it out without a scratch – I meant, very few scratches. And, the protocol was successfully completed. Besides, so what if anyone saw me. There are hundreds of women who work in the field for just about every law enforcement or national defense-related department in the country," Tabatha attempts to defend herself.

"None of whom can do what you can do, Tabatha."

"They don't know what I can do. It's not like I can move objects with my mind or spit fire or, whatever – something that would be *really* noticeable."

"Are you that oblivious to what you have been causing on most of your assignments?"

"I know I kinda put a hole in the floor today. I admit that when I'm concentrating heavily on something, I seem to block out the surrounding activities to an extent. So, I don't *explicitly* remember how that happened, but besides, a million things could have caused the floor to collapse I'm sure."

"You did far more than putting a hole in the floor of that building. Do you realize that the last five assignments you've been involved with, the property damage attributed to your *presence*, has cost our government over fifty billion dollars? Not to mention having to explain away what some witnesses have reported as – *supernatural activity*."

"Well, it worked to our benefit in the Iranian nuclear silo assignment," Tabatha manages to quickly think of one justifiable excuse for accidentally causing damage to an installation.

"Do you hear yourself? *Everything* is a joke to you."

"No! Not everything, at least."

"You can't even take *this* conversation seriously."

"I guess I *really* don't see *what* the problem is. *I* saved the day – again. And now *I'm* being lectured about *'being seen in public,'* doing my job, no less!"

"*You*?! *Saved* the Day?! *You* couldn't even find the entire passcode to stop the countdown that would have ignited the fuel *today* – Mitchel did that!! And without telepathy!!" The Director reminds Tabatha.

"Well, I picked him to be on the team," she mumbles.

"Tabatha! Your job, as described under section four of the T.I.D. program, says – and I quote, '...*the psychic interrogator also known as Tabatha Johnson, may, upon written approval, extract knowledge, Intel, and any information from an individual, which the joint Directors would believe to be critically valuable for the purposes relating to national security, but only when other natural interrogation practices fail to produce the information that the suspect is believed, beyond the shadow of any doubt, to have,*" the Director reminds her. "...And section six goes on to say, '...the psychic interrogator, also known as Tabatha Johnson, may proceed on an assignment only to direct appropriate personnel, equipped and trained for such assignments. But only in a manner that maintains her public invisibility for the duration of the assignment.' In other words, you tell the team what to do based on your Intel. Then you let them do it," the Director sternly adds.

"It's boring, though. Just sitting in a van telling them – wait, there's a guy with a gun around that corner, ok go ahead, it's clear in that room, blah-blah-blah...' I'm basically a surveillance camera..."

"Well, that's what you..."

"...A wireless surveillance camera..." she continues.

"But that's what you signed..."

"...The most sophisticated wireless..."

"Tell me when you're finished," the director says, but it translates more like 'shut up.'

"...Surveillance camera on the planet. Ok..."

"Thank you. Now..."

"...I'm finished now."

"TABATHA!! Do you have to act like a toddler every time you're in trouble!?"

"Do you really want me to answer that?"

"Please, Tabatha, I need you to listen," the director reverts to his calm demeanor.

"I'm sorry, I'm listening."

"Ok, what I'm trying to say is, did you not sign up for this job?! Because I can go get your file that you signed and initialed agreeing to all of this – if you need a reminder."

"Well, yeah, I signed up for it, but I didn't know it would mean a life of seclusion!"

"Tabatha! You seclude yourself. Just because the contract states that you're not supposed to do anything to draw attention to your telepathic abilities, doesn't mean you can't be out in public. You're the one who practically locks yourself up in your condo most of the time, except for what? Going to church or occasionally taking your aunt to the store?" the Director reminds her.

Tabatha's eyes widen as the Director reveals what she thought was a secret.

"...And of course, seeing Dr. Glessinjer from time to time?"

Mixed emotions stir up inside Tabatha at the revelation of the director's knowledge that she sees a private physician about her abilities. Knowing full well, that visiting any medical professional not specified by the government –to cover up her telepathic ability – is a direct violation of the agreement to the regulation that she agreed to. However, her personal search for answers as to why she can do what she can do as well as the apparent 'evolution' of her abilities over the past year, was what spurred her towards violating the regulation.

"I'm trying to understand what's going on with me," she attempts to explain her regulatory disobedience.

"I'm sure your excuse is...." The Director is interrupted again.

"...No, you don't understand. I know that I'm not supposed to do that, but no one in this stupid department or the whole government will do anything to help me figure this out. They want what I can do at their disposal, but yet, they won't do anything to help me understand any of it! Unless I volunteer myself to be dissected, of course." Tabatha elevates her voice. Out of a slight burst of anger, she hits the side of the examination table with the bottom of her fist. Simultaneously the aluminum tray table moves a few inches away from Tabatha and the Director takes a few steps back, catching his balance as if some lite pressure pushed him back.

"What was that?" The Director asks. Tabatha slightly crouches forward, placing her hand over her stomach and as a couple of drops of sweat run down the side of her face again.

"I don't know, but I'm really hungry."

The director says through his communication device, "I need Rodney to return to the main medical lab with some food, please."

"The secretary of defense wants to put you on an *extended vacation*," the Director continued

"You mean he wants to press charges on me for violating regulations," Tabatha responds, sitting upright again.

"Pretty much," he confirms.

"Just because some people saw me in a building next to a dead man? But for all they know, I was checking his vital signs or something." Tabatha hops off the examination table and begins walking around the lab.

"I would like to show you something." The Director pulls his iPhone out of his pocket and begins running his finger across the screen.

"Really? You're going to show me that *stupid* YouTube channel?"

The Director hands her his phone. The channel was created by someone anonymously who had somehow gathered video clips of seemingly supernatural events that occurred during supposed secret assignments in which Tabatha was present. The most recent upload to the channel was today's event at the F.D.A. admin building.

Tabatha takes the phone and watch's the video – sort of. She has never put a lot of stock into these videos as something that the majority of the public would have any inclination into believing. The video clip was a montage of four separate cell phone videos strung together, depicting the same event from different angles.

The video begins with Hammer and Joe emerging from the building, guiding the eleven hostages outside to safety, followed by Hammer talking to the police captain. The video draws attention to the individual in the lobby who can only be slightly seen through the glass that made up the doors and the rest of the front of the building. Then a sudden burst shatters the glass from the inside out, shaking the building as well as pushing several people closest to the police barricade to the ground. The footage of the incident is then replayed in slow motion. A voice was narrating what he thought was going on, based on his personal opinion. During the slow-motion replay of the incident, you can almost see a burst of energy come from the figure in the lobby that expands spherically blowing out the glass, rattling the building and pushing the crowd to the ground. The figure in the lobby is obviously Tabatha and is clearly noticeable after the glass is blown out of the building, and the image magnified.

"Yeah, computer graphics could have *totally* pulled that off," Tabatha critiques'. "Actually, computer graphics could have made it better in my opinion." She takes a closer look at the zoomed-in picture of her face in a freeze-frame. "Oh-my-gosh!"

"It's about time you took this seriously," the Director comments on her response.

"Look at my hair! And my face. Did I *really* look that horrible?" Tabatha responds to the image with her usual unconcerned attitude toward the situation. If the director could turn beet red, he would have at this point and hence the purpose for blood pressure medication – if he's on any of course. And if he is, it's probably classified anyways. But I digress.

"No worse than usual," Rodney interrupts, standing just inside the doorway holding a huge burrito.

"Thanks," Tabatha rolls her eyes at Rodney as he walks up to her and hands her the burrito, to which she devours it.

"By the way, we're in the news, again," Rodney informs, then walks to the T.V. monitor on the wall next to the lab entrance and turns it on.

"...It is confirmed that the Terrorist Interceptor Division arm of the F.B.I. and homeland security prevented yet another terrorist attack from unfolding today. Fifteen terrorists held up this small F.D.A. administration building this morning. Approximately forty minutes ago, the team responsible for disrupting the planned attack walked out of the building behind me. Two of the fifteen terrorists accountable for this plan were hauled off by the F.B.I. after T.I.D. personnel drug them out of the building. The remaining thirteen terrorists are deceased and their bodies are currently still in the building.

Ironically, however, this morning, the capital building was evacuated after evidence led to the arrest and interrogation of a Pakistani by Homeland Security yesterday morning then later substantiated by the F.B.I. exposing a potential terrorist threat to the Capital building. Though as for the moment, the F.B.I. has yet to find any sign of potential danger in, near, or around the capital building. However, compounded security measures at the capitol building are expected to be implemented for the near future as a result of the threat on the capital building, as well as the foiled attack on this F.D.A. admin building..."

"Ok, so that wasn't as bad as I thought it was going to be," Tabatha responds.

They continue watching. "Jeff Rhioner, T.I.D.s' public relations officer, made a public statement regarding T.I.D.'s role in the incident this morning shortly after the incident's resolution. According to Rhioner, the threat on the Capital building was most likely a distraction to throw off authorities from the real attack that should have taken place behind me, but thankfully was thwarted by T.I.D..."

"I was thinking the exact same thing earlier. Because I mean, what's the deal with this little dinky F.D.A. building. If they wanted to hurt the F.D.A, they should have gone to their headquarters in Chicago," Tabatha interjects.

"Agreed. It didn't make sense to me either," the director admits.

"...Now another interesting twist to this morning's incident involves the underground theory that T.I.D. was created for the purpose of allowing individuals with real-life superhuman abilities to be at the governments' disposal in times of crisis. Of course, there has been very little to substantiate such wild and fantastic ideas. However, an increasingly popular YouTube channel with only a few videos that at least reenact past potential terror attacks seems to be promoting the idea. These videos, by and large, focus on a particular woman who seems to be able to cause destruction supernaturally. Though the videos are vague at best..."

"Told you," Tabatha says, feeling affirmed in her belief that no one really takes those videos seriously.

"...However, today's incident may attract some real attention to the underground claim, as our own camera crew managed to catch this on video earlier..." the reporter pauses, and the news feed switches to a very clear recording of a burst of energy initiating from the individual in the lobby. The video is then freeze-framed at the point where Tabatha looked toward the crowd of people. The image of her face is zoomed in and clearly seen.

"Turn it off, Rodney," the Director orders. Rodney turns off the monitor and both the director and Rodney glare at Tabatha. "Rodney, go finish your examination of Tabatha's team."

"Yes, sir." Rodney doesn't hesitate to leave the lab. He also doesn't need to be a psychic to feel the tension rising in the lab.

Tabatha attempts to hide her head in between her shoulders and displays an anxious and apologetic look on her face. "You were soooo right, Director. I'm an idiot, and I don't think, and I get egotistical, and..."

"Tabatha," the Director interrupts her verbal self-assaulting binge.

"Yes, sir?"

"Go home."

"Okay? Don't I have to do my report?"

"No. I'll take care of it."

"Okay." Tabatha walks past the Director and out of the lab.

"And Tabatha!" Tabatha stops just outside of the lab, continuing facing the hallway. "You're not an idiot, I've seen your evals. You're incredibly intelligent. I just want you to know that" the Director tries to encourage her. Tabatha turns and smiles at him, "but I agree, you are very egotistical at times," he adds, to which she nods in agreement. "Why don't you go catch a movie or something? Clear your head. Well, if you can do that sort of thing. Anyways, I'll let you know what the secretary has to say about all of this." The Director concludes, and Tabatha leaves the trench.

The Sentient

CHAPTER VII

THE CONNECTION

Naomi rocks back and forth in her chair, crocheting, while listening to a Frank Sinatra vinyl playing softly from her bedroom, when she hears the deadbolt unlock and the condo door slowly open. "Tab? Is that you?" The door shuts softly, and the deadbolt is locked. Tabatha turns the corner and enters the living room.

"Yeah, it's me," she mumbles as she walks passed Naomi to the kitchen island. She empties her pockets, placing her keys, her medicine pouch, and billfold on the island.

"I take it you got in trouble again," Naomi predicts.

"Yeah. I seem to be unable to not get into trouble," Tabatha says, still trying to excuse herself to some degree from taking responsibility for her actions.

"Yeah, well, if you did what you were supposed to and follow the rules, you probably wouldn't be in trouble every time you go to work," Naomi says without lifting her eyes off her quilt – in progress.

"Really, mom? I don't even want to hear it right now," Tabatha responds.

"I know, but you need to. Besides, you know I'm right."

"Yes. I admit you're right. Like usual," Tabatha relinquishes some pride. Tabatha turns her cell phone on and sets it on the island, then opens the fridge and pulls out a container of French onion dip and grabs the bag of chips sitting on the counter next to the fridge. Her phone begins to vibrate and beep, indicating it received a text message and voice mail.

"I saw you on the news this morning," Naomi informs, still focusing on her crocheting. Tabatha heads to the couch with the chips, dip, and her phone. "I'm guessing that was Cindy."

"Yes. just Cindy." Tabatha plops down and sinks into the crux of the arm and back of the couch. She opens the dip and starts piling the chips in her mouth. "She *thinks* she saw me on the news today too."

Tabatha picks up her phone and responds to Cindy's text that she 'didn't know who the chick on the news was,' then sets the phone next to her on the couch. "If you and Cindy are the only two who saw me on the news, and that know me, I don't think there will be a problem."

"My phone has been going crazy since the news broadcast," Naomi informs Tabatha.

"Good for you," Tabatha says, attempting not to care.

"It seems everyone at church watches the news at the same time every day. Talk about a coincidence. But, they all think that *girl* in the video is you too."

"Really? What did you tell them?"

"Well, Tab, you can put me between a rock and a hard place at times. On the one hand, I hate lying, and on the other hand, I have to maintain your *confidentiality*," Naomi reminds Tabatha how much of pain in the butt she can be.

"Sorry about that."

"Yeah, well, I just acknowledged that the individual *looked* like you," Naomi pauses from her crocheting for a second to take a drink of her tea, sitting next to her on an end table lit up by a lamp, then begins crocheting again.

Tabatha doesn't say anything, only glancing up at Naomi admiring her wisdom and also the fact that she has the purest thoughts than almost anyone she knows – unless she's around a guy twenty plus years younger than her. "How do you have so many more friends than me anyway?" A random question proceeds from Tabatha's mind and out her mouth.

Naomi looks over at Tabatha with the look that shouts, 'why do you have to ask.' "How many friends do you have Tab? One? Cindy, right?" Naomi reminds her, then looks back down at her crocheting. "A rock has more friends than you."

Tabatha slightly smiles in agreement with Naomi then lays her head back on the back of the couch. "I'm such a loser," Tabatha says in self-pity.

"Yes, you are," Naomi affirms, not allowing herself to get sucked into Tabatha's 'poor me' attitude.

"Thanks, mom. Love you too," she says sarcastically. Tabatha shoves more chips with a mountain of dip on top of each one in her mouth. Then getting the impression that her phone is about to ring, she grabs it, and immediately the phone lights up, and before the catchy tune begins, she answers it.

"Yes, sir," she anxiously says.

"Tabatha, I just got out of a meeting with the T.I.D. oversight committee," director Jackson says. Tabatha closes her eyes and braces for worse news.   "You're being suspended,"

"Did you say at least one good thing about me?" Tabatha asks.

"Well, you are still getting paid, and you're not getting reprimanded."

"Wow. How did you..."

"...Pull that off?" the Director finishes her statement.   "On occasion, I can be – persuasive," the director adds.

"I don't know what to say."

"If only I could hear you say that more often. Also, you may be requested on a consultation basis only until we can put these PR fires out," the Director concludes.

"Ok, I understand. Thank you, sir." She replies, then hangs up.

"Ok, so what gives Tab? You've been in trouble many times, and I've never seen you cry over it. Did they fire you?" Naomi further inquired.

"Ha – no, they didn't, but almost," Tabatha explains. "I'm going to have more time to hang out with you, though," she adds, believing that will make Naomi happy.

Naomi pauses, both – her rocking and crocheting for a second – at Tabatha's revelation that she'll be home more, but keeps her mouth shut, but as usual, Tabatha hears what Naomi thinks of the idea.

"Seriously?   I thought you'd like having me around more," Tabatha says, slightly insulted.

Naomi puts her quilt down and looks at her sternly. "Tabatha, sweetheart, why do you want to hang out with your old aunt, seriously. You need to get a life. And as far as being home more often, you were already only having to work like three days a week unless there's some kind of 'secret mission' you were being sent on," she reminds Tabatha, emphasizing secret mission, since, by the time it was over, it was usually no longer a secret. "What you need to do is get out of the condo. Find something to do – like a hobby. And I don't mean walking around town and calling the police every time you pick up on someone about to commit a crime," Naomi takes another sip of her tea then goes back to her crocheting. "...Like you used to when you were a teenager," she concludes.

"Right. I remember those days. And the police captain finally came over to tell me that I can't keep doing that," Tabatha continues the recollection.

"I agreed with him."

"Then Mrs. Porter, who lived on the street behind us, was shot by her granddaughter's boyfriend. I remember practically watching the whole thing. It was torture not being able to do anything about that. Do you remember?" Tabatha concludes the memory.

Naomi stops crocheting and sets the quilt – in progress – along with her hooks and balls of yarn on her recliner. She stands up and chugs the rest of her tea before walking to her room, turning off the record player and putting on a light windbreaker, and grabbing her purse.

"You're going to the store now? We just went this weekend," Tabatha responds to Naomi's thoughts. "Well, I can take you," she adds about to get up.

"NO!! No, you don't have to take me to the store," Naomi quickly responds.

"It's no problem. Besides, it's..."

"It's only five blocks away. I can walk there and back. It's therapy for me anyway. Especially after some of our conversations," Naomi adds. Tabatha leans back on the couch, feeling deserted that her aunt doesn't want to hang around someone as full of joy and sunshine as Tabatha currently is-not. "Listen, if you want to sink into your little swamp of depression, go for it. You're not dragging me down with you," Naomi says firmly, pulling her key to the condo out of her purse.

"I'm not depressed," Tabatha mumbles, feeling insulted again, burying her chin into her chest and crossing her arms as if holding an invisible teddy bear.

"Oh good, then why don't you call Cindy. She called me this morning shortly after you dropped me off from the doctor's office. She's worried about you. Especially after your episode yesterday at church. That frightened everyone, honestly. Anyhow, I'll be back later. Hopefully, you won't be. Love you, sweetheart." Naomi says as she walks out the door and locks it behind her.

"Love you..." the door shuts, "...too." She then debates with herself whether or not to call Cindy as instructed by Naomi. After finding Cindy's name in her phone's contact list, then backing out about thirty times, as if anxious to ask out someone on a date for the first time – then this would be more understandable, but it's Tabatha – she finally hits the call button.

"Hello? Tabatha?" Cindy answers, enthusiastically.

"Hey, yeah, it's Tabatha. How's it going?"

"Did you see the news today? That was crazy. Do you believe all that stuff?" Cindy asks at a hundred miles an hour.

"I know that was pretty crazy, that's for..." Tabatha's interrupted.

"Right. Hey, you should come and check out these new clothes I bought last night. Hubs took me shopping and then to dinner. I think he was trying to get something last night, hahaha!" Cindy, like a water spout, opens her mouth, and everything comes out – somewhat nonsensically – other times without thinking what's coming out of the spout – no wonder these two get along so well.

"UUhhgg, Cindy, that's way too much infor...." Tabatha attempts to interject, too depressed to care about relationships.

"Oops!! Sorry, Tabatha. Sometimes I completely forget that you're single," Cindy kind of apologizes.

"That's ok. I haven't forgotten about..."

"...Which is really weird because you're sooo gorgeous. Buuut you're single. Gorgeous but single." Cindy repeats herself as if trying to make sense of something that has no basis for anything important.

"Yeah, well..." Tabatha barely gets two words out.

"And you don't have kids, and you make like, what, a hundred grand a year, working for the government – buuuut your single. You got Mula, a condo, and your gorgeous, but you're single..."

"*MAYBE I DON'T WANT ANY BAGGAGE, CINDY*!!!" Tabatha finally gets a full statement in that makes sense – even though it's a lie.

"Hahaha!! Tabatha, I don't have any baggage. Kyle's the one with the baggage, hahaha – me!" Cindy continues rambling.

"Cindy! You *totally* to lay off the espresso, big time!!" Tabatha shouts to get Cindy's attention.

"How'd you know I had an espresso?"

"Cindy, you own an espresso machine, remember?"

"Oh yeah, hahaha. I forgot I showed it to you. Kyle..." Cindy explains then is joined by Tabatha "got it for me/you for my/your anniversary," Tabatha cuts off, "last month," Cindy laughs at the fact they both said the same thing at the same time.

"Cindy!!"

"Hey, we should get some lunch tomorrow," Cindy spits out.

"Anything that gets you to calm down, girl!" Tabatha deals.

"Yeah. I am a little wound up. Sorry about that." Cindy admits. "How about the..."

"No coffee shops!" Tabatha continues to deal.

"Oh darn it. Okay, how about that new sandwich place a couple of blocks from the church?" Cindy capitulates.

"Sure, sounds great. Tomorrow at noon?" Tabatha compromises.

"Yes, noon is fine. Kyle will be working on his sermon for next week anyway."

"Alright, I'll see you then, girl."

"Alright, Tab, talk to you later now, bye." Cindy and Tabatha conclude their conversation, which seemed to lift Tabatha up. She silently says a short prayer, thanking her godmother for telling her to call her friend. She then grabs the T.V. remote and turns on the T.V. Tabatha's favorite channel plays old television shows which are typically in black and white. The Andy Griffith show rerun was on. Tabatha placed the remote back on the coffee table and, shortly after that, fell asleep.

....

"*T-T-Tabatha-tha-tha....F-F-Find....T-T-Tabatha...M-Me-me....T-T-Tabatha-tha...* [Tabatha! Wake Up...!] *T-T-Tabatha-tha...M-Me-me...F-F-Find-find...T-T-Tabatha...S-Save...T-Tabatha...H-H-HELP...T-T-Taba-* [TABATHA!! WAKE UP!!]"

"GUUGGGHHH...!! Whaaat!!" Tabatha wakes up both startled and angered to Naomi's frantic screaming for her to wake up.

"What?! Don't what me!! What you!!" Naomi frantically but nonsensically trying to communicate something serious.

"What??!!" Tabatha still tries making sense out of Naomi.

"What happened in here?!!" Naomi points around the living room.

"What happened where?!" Tabatha sits up and looks around the living room as well. "Oh-my-gosh!" she responds in just as much shock as Naomi.

"Please tell me you just had a bad temper tantrum after I left," Naomi hoping that the destruction of the living room was out of purely natural circumstances. The coffee table had been shoved into the base of the kitchen island and crushed. Naomi's rocking chair had been flattened like a folding chair, even though it wasn't a folding chair, and sunk into the wall behind it, along with the end table and lamp that was next to the chair. The T.V. had been shoved off its stand and into the corner and split in two with Naomi's crochet hooks protruding from one of the halves of the T.V. screen. The pictures hanging on the walls had all been burnt. The living rooms' scenic window was inundated with cracks. The bookshelf next to the window looked as though it had folded in on itself, like an accordion.

The two of them just stared and stared in awe of the devastation. "Tabatha! What is going on?!" Naomi says, somewhat frightened at the whole incident.

"I don't know..." Tabatha replies, basically speechless, before a random memory of what Rodney mentioned earlier that day came to mind. "But, this morning, when I had my medical exam after my assignment, Rodney, he's the medical guru where I work, but he thinks that I'm developing some telekinetic attributes," Tabatha explains, thinking that the living room assault may be an example of that *attribute*.

"Teleki-what?!" Naomi responds, having not the foggiest idea of what Tabatha's talking about.

"Telekinesis, mom. Basically, in the realm of science fiction and so forth, it's the supernatural ability to move objects with your mind – in a nutshell."

Naomi walks to what used to be her chair and touches it. It's warm to the touch. "Does it also involve burning things with your mind?" Naomi asks, noticing that just about all the objects were very warm, and others appeared to be charred, like the edges of her chair. "It feels like a sauna in here too."

"I can't tell. I'm always feeling hot," Tabatha responds.

"Yeah, you're covered in sweat again. Do you need your..."

"...No, I don't need my medicine. I'm super hungry, though." Tabatha walks over to the thermostat to see what the temperature on it is reading.

"Did you have another...?"

"...No mom, I didn't have another dream either," Tabatha answers Naomi's question again before she finishes asking. "However, now that I think about, I do remember hearing something. Like someone asking for my help or something. Then you were yelling at me to wake up." Tabatha touches the thermostat.

"Well, I figured this was pretty important. What are we going to do?" Naomi asks, regarding repairs, and replacing items.

"Well, I do have homeowners insurance. But, more importantly, if the government wants to hide what I can do, maybe they can provide some assistance," Tabatha responds, not necessarily as concerned about the destruction as how she managed to cause it all. "Well, the thermostat is saying over a hundred degrees in here," she adds.

"Sure feels like it," Naomi responds, then follows the hallway to the bedrooms.

"I'm not so sure it's accurate, though," Tabatha refers to the thermostat.

"Really?!" Naomi yells from her bedroom.

"It's smashed into the wall. Hmmm, it's three-thirty. I'm going to make a call." Tabatha Finds her cell phone on the couch, where she was sleeping, thankfully unharmed just like the sofa was.

"Nothing wrong in the bedrooms, or the hallway. It's just in the living room," Naomi informs, walking back into the living room. "I think I'm sweating more than you are at the moment," she adds, waving her hand at her face like a fan.

Tabatha scrolls down to a contact on her phone, and presses call then puts it to her ear. After a few rings, a low firm voice answers: "Hello."

"Hi, Director. I have to tell you about something I accidentally did this afternoon."

"Whaaat..." He responds, bracing for the information.

"Well......."

....

"So it appears that you *really* lucked out here. None of your neighbors were home. They must've all been all at work – like *normal* people. So, no one heard nor witnessed anything," the director explains to Tabatha and Naomi, both who were sitting on the couch – again, the only item in the living room not destroyed.

"Well, that's a good thing," Tabatha responds.

"For you, yes, it is. You've had enough publicity for one day." The director walks around the living room, looking at the damage.

"Director. Here's the information that you requested," one of the Directors officers hands him a piece of paper with notes on it.

"Thank you. You and the other officers can pack it up. I'll be down in a few minutes," the Director orders.

"Yes, sir," the officer turns and leaves the condo.

"I can't believe I'm agreeing to this," the Director says, shaking his head and looking out the cracked scenic window.

"Mom! Don't even think about it," Tabatha attempts to stop Naomi from requesting updated appliances.

"Too late, sweetie. So Kurtis, is there any way I could get my washer and dryer replaced? They are sooo old and don't work very well any more..."

"Mom, they work fine."

"Shush!"

The Director glances over at Naomi and smiles. "Mrs. Naomi, I can, *absolutely*, upgrade your washer and dryer," he answers without hesitation.

At that, Tabatha perks up thinking of an upgrade, "No!" The director answers Tabatha's request before she even makes one.

"What? What do you mean, no? I didn't even say anything yet," she says perplexed.

"I had a good guess what you were about to say."

"What? That's not fair. How come she can get her upgrade, and I can't?"

The Director leans close to Tabatha, "because she has to put up with you," he whispers.

Naomi laughs at the outcome, as Tabatha leans into the couch with her arms crossed like she's holding her imaginary teddy bear, or more like a *pity bear*, again. "Director, so how long will this take to fix the walls and replace the furniture?" Naomi asks.

"Let me see..." He looks at his watch. "...It's four-thirty. What time do you go to bed normally?"

Naomi's eyes light up. "Tabatha, you should have destroyed the condo a long time ago."

"Naomi, this, ultimately, is a one-time thing." The Director explains. "Let me go make some calls real quick." The Director walks into the hall and begins making his calls.

"Oh mom, I called Cindy after you left like you suggested," Tabatha informs as they wait for the Director to return.

"Oh, good. She's a nice young lady and a good influence on you. Both her and Kyle."

"Yeah. We're going to meet up for lunch tomorrow."

"Thank God. I knew she'd get you out of your funk."

After his phone calls, the director walked back into the living room and began recapping what Naomi said to him, which she confirmed. He then asked Tabatha, "And you don't remember any of this?" The director pries for more information.

"No, I don't," Tabatha responds.

"Oh wait, Tabatha. You told me you heard a voice calling for you or something like that," Naomi reminds her.

"Oh yeah, I forgot about that. I heard someone calling out for help – really strange. That's another first for me."

"Were there any images or visions associated with it?"

"Some vague, still frame images of sand, maybe? But nothing like the night terrors I've had."

"Could there be a connection to all this by chance, Director?" Naomi asks.

"I'm not sure. I'm not an expert in all this telepathic Naomi." He answers. Just then, Tabatha jumps off the couch.

"Who was that?" Tabatha shouts at Kurtis.

"Who was what?" he responds.

"You have been talking to someone – about me – about what I can do." She points out, having seen an image from the Director's memory appear then vanish.

"Tabatha, what are you talking about?"

"Tabatha! Watch your tone of voice." Naomi attempts to lecture Tabatha for talking disrespectfully to the Director."

"Mom, he's been talking to someone I just saw it." Tabatha defends herself.

"Tabatha, I haven't been..."

"...Are you suppressing something, *director?*" Tabatha asks, debating with herself whether or not to dig into the Directors' long term memories.

"Tabatha, don't do it. You have to trust me. I haven't been talking to anyone other than who I'm supposed to be talking to. I promise." The Director does his best to relieve Tabatha of any concerns that he may be hiding anything from her.

"Ok, Director. I do trust you. I just don't trust others." Tabatha sits back down. "And mom, I do respect the Director – a lot," she adds, correcting Naomi's assumption about Tabatha's apparent disrespect.

"You do, in your own way," he confirms. "Well, you are about to get a ton of visitors. Why don't you, Tabatha, take your godmother out, this evening. That way, you two are not having to tiptoe around a couple dozen men while they fix up your place," he suggests but in a slightly commanding way. He pulls out his wallet and takes three one hundred dollar bills out and hands them to Tabatha. "Here, it's on me. Go do whatever. Just stay out of trouble, please," he adds.

"Wait, did you say, dozens of *men?*" Naomi perks up with a smile and turns to Tabatha with her usual pseudo match making glee in her eyes.

"Oh gosh, mom, no, please don't try to set me up with anyone. As much as I don't like going out – we're going out," Tabatha makes clear. The two of them get up off of the couch. Tabatha grabs the cash from the Director while Naomi collects her purse from her room.

"Well, we could always sit around watching shirtless, sweaty, muscular hunks carry heavy objects around the house," Naomi resorts to plan 'B,' which involves indulging in her own fantasies as she watches decades younger attractive guys.

"Oh Lord," Tabatha responds, keeping to herself that Naomi's idea is slightly attractive. However, to avoid sinking into the mire of lustful transgressions, she continues hustling her godmother to get her things so they can leave.

"Ha-ha..." The Director laughs at the two of them. "I'll hold down your fort till everything's completed," he says, then opens the door for them. "You two have a good evening. And Tabatha, try to keep a low profile," the Director reiterates firmly, to which she agrees, then closes the door behind them.

The Director then walks back into the living room, standing in where he believes the singularity that destroyed the room originated from. He pulls out his phone and begins taking pictures as he turns three hundred and sixty degrees. He then finds a contact on his phone and puts it to his ear. "I'm sending you some new information." He says, then hangs up. He types a message, attaches the pictures he just took, and sends it to the same anonymous contact, then places the phone back in his pocket and sits down on the couch and begins waiting. "Man, it's hot in here..."

As they walk through the parking garage, Tabatha and Naomi consider their evening plans that have yet to be established.

"So, what to do first?" Tabatha asks.

"Well, it's about five-thirty, still light out. Let's go get some food. You're always hungry anyway," Naomi suggests.

"True. Sounds good to me. How about your favorite Italian restaurant?" They walk up to the truck, and Tabatha opens the door for Naomi and helps her up into it.

"Oh, yes. That sounds wonderful," Naomi responds, maneuvering herself comfortably in the passenger seat. Tabatha closes the door, circles the truck and jumps into the driver's side of the cab. "No wonder your calves are amazing, as much as you have to jump in and out of this thing..." Naomi comments about the truck again.

"Don't start on the truck now," she requests. She starts the truck and drives out of the garage.

On their way to the restaurant, they approached the cemetery where Tabatha's sister, Sara, and mother were buried. "You know, mom, we haven't visited their gravesites in almost two months. You want to stop by real quick?"

"You know, I'm trying *not* to be depressed today, right," Naomi responds.

"It was just a question," Tabatha explains.

"You're right. I'm sorry, we can stop by." Tabatha then pulls into the cemetery entrance and drives down a narrow dirt path passing several tombstones. Some small and seemingly insignificant, others too significant. After parking the truck, they walked several yards to the sites, reading a few epitaphs on the way. One read – *Here lies Fred, he was hit in the head* – an outline of a woman holding a frying pan was engraved underneath the statement. They laughed.

They approached the headstones of Tabatha's mother and sister and stood in front of them reading the narrowly engraved inscription that merely stated their names and the dates of their birth and death.

"You know mom, for as populated as this place is, it's pretty quiet," Tabatha says, slightly joking and referring to the fact that she can't hear the constant sound of people's thoughts since all the people around her were dead.

"That must feel refreshing, sweetheart."

"Yeah, it does. It reminds me of when we still lived on the farm back in Maryland." Tabatha sits down next to and places her hand on Sara's stone, that's about two feet tall and strokes the top of it as a mother would run her hand over the fragile head of a sick child in her arms. "Sara..." Tabatha begins talking to the stone as she usually does when they come here. Naomi stands next to her and places her hand on Tabatha's shoulder. "Sorry, it's been a while since I've visited you. I think two months now. A lot has gone on since then. First, I have to tell you about this..." Tabatha continues recapping the last two months to the stone.

Naomi just listens, occasionally thinking about *her* sister, Tabatha's mother. Tabatha rarely says much to her mother's stone. Yeah, she forgave her for the drug abuse and alcoholism she was engaged in while she was pregnant with her and Sara, thanks impart to their father who got her hooked on meth which eventually lead to other drugs including black ice and vodka before ultimately landing her in the hole she currently resides in, under the stone protruding from the ground.

No one ultimately knows for a fact what happened to her father outside of a few rumors. He took off like the yellow streaked chicken that he was after finding out Tabatha's mother, Martha, was pregnant and refused to get an abortion like he *demanded*, leaving her to fend for herself, including supporting her own severe drug habit. Sometimes in the worst ways imaginable. But this is supposed to a PG story so we won't go there. The most popular rumor about Tabatha's father, Rick, was that he had been gunned down during a drug heist with a few other buddies – good riddance as far as Tabatha was concerned. That was many years ago, and one of the reasons she got involved in the criminal justice field. Of course, that's in addition to the constant inundation of thoughts and images of people committing or plotting to commit crimes and not being able to do much about it. That is without becoming a masked vigilante. But she's probably way too Caucasian to become *Bat-Chick*, and even with her abilities, perhaps too distracted to be jumping off building tops in the middle of the night anyway.

About an hour goes by. Naomi had since begun walking around the nearby gravestones as Tabatha continued conversing with Sara's tombstone. Finally, Naomi sees that it's a quarter till seven.

"Tabatha, sweetheart, we should probably get going. It's getting close to seven, and it's getting dark out."

Tabatha looks up at Naomi, slightly shocked that over an hour has gone by so quickly. "Wow, I guess time flies when you're having a good discussion."

"Especially a discussion with a headstone."

"Really mom? You know how to ruin a moment sometimes." Tabatha responds, upset at being called out on reality.

"I'm sorry, dear. Sometimes it just seems...." Naomi begins to explain herself.

"...That I forget I can't communicate with her? Yes, I know she can't hear me. It's just the idea of it. And, it helps me feel better, I suppose." Tabatha faces the stone one last time, "well, Sis, I *gots* to run. But I'll be back in a few weeks. Love you." Tabatha concludes her conversation with Sara's headstone then stands up next to Naomi.

It has been customary for many years that before leaving the cemetery, a short prayer would be said, reminding them of their own mortality and that without the grace of God, creator of all things, there would be no hope for mankind. This tradition was started with Naomi's late husband thirty-six years ago, and Naomi has continued it since his passing.

"Heavenly Father. Creator of all things. We thank you for sending your Son Jesus, for reaping the punishment that we have sown, so that He may carry our burden during times of testing and trials so long as we put our faith in Him. Help us to love others no matter what and to discern how to use what you've given us for Your Glory. Put people in our lives that can help direct us during times of uncertainty. Help us, also, to forgive others regardless of what was done to us as well, whether intentionally or unintentionally, Lord. Continue to be with us as we leave this place and protect us and keep us steadfast on *your* foundation as we embark on unknown future challenges. We pray all this in your Holy name, Lord Jesus Christ, Amen."

"Amen. Good prayer mom," Tabatha compliments then quickly turns to head back to the truck, knowing part of the prayer was directed toward the fact that she blames her mother for the death of her younger twin sister due to the drug and alcohol abuse, therefore, struggles significantly with the forgiveness aspect of it.

"So, remind me why you never talk to your mother's *headstone* like you do your sisters?"

Tabatha turns back to her mother's headstone briefly, "Love you *mother*, thanks for *everything*," she says rhetorically, then continues toward the truck, Naomi following.

"You know, Tabatha, it's not like she meant to harm either of you." Naomi speed walks to catch up to her.

"Mom, you've told me this stuff a hundred times..."

"She was a more morally sound child than I was..."

"I know mom, she went to some bible summer camp, got saved, came back home, and lead you to Jesus..." Tabatha says, "I have that story memorized," she adds.

Naomi cuts in front of Tabatha. "Listen to me! It's time to get over it! They are in Heaven with God, and *you're* here. Why don't you impress them, and more importantly, God, by doing the most impossible task on the planet!! Actually enjoying life now and then!!" Naomi, shouts having had enough of Tabatha's 'pity me' attitude, then continues walking to the truck in front of Tabatha.

"Okay, you didn't have to yell at me," Tabatha responds softly, being somewhat intimidated by her godmother's discipline. "Just a quick question, though. Do you *really* believe my mother's in Heaven?" Naomi turns and gives Tabatha an evil look thinking that she's continuing to be vindictive. "No, mom, I'm being serious, really. In fact, whatever you say, I'll believe it," Tabatha confirms her sincere question.

"The last couple of years of her life, she royally screwed up. But, I *know* it was the drugs. It wasn't her. So yes, I believe she's in Heaven," Naomi concludes. "Now, let's go. It's passed seven, and I want to eat. And see what the condo looks like, and my new washer and dryer." Naomi changes the subject to which Tabatha welcomes with a smile.

"Tabatha…"

"What?" Tabatha responds to hearing her name called.

"Huh?" Naomi looks back at Tabatha. "Talking to me?"

"Uhhh…yeah, you just called my name," Tabatha reminds her.

"UUhh…Did I? Alright, sorry about that," Naomi replies. "It's about time I start going senile," she mumbles to herself.

"T-T-Tabatha!!"

"Mom, stop it, you're freaking me out."

Naomi turns, facing Tabatha once again. "Stop what! I didn't do anything," Naomi responds, frustrated.

"You just yelled my name," Tabatha informs firmly.

Naomi stands still mulling this incident over in her mind. "Sweetheart, I didn't say your name," Naomi affirms. "Are you feeling, ok?"

"Yeah, I think…."

"*TABATHA-THA!! F-F-FIND…T-T-TABA…HHHHEEEEELP ME-ME-ME!!*" The echoing voice shrieked through the ear of her mind so loud Tabatha was forced to place her hands on her head as if keeping from exploding.

"Tabatha! I heard that." Naomi says, slightly panicked, having never experienced anything like that before.

"You did? You heard that too??" Tabatha says excitedly that someone else experienced what she is always experiencing. Tabatha drops to her knees as she begins feeling weak once again and starting to sweat as it is custom for her body to do during an episode. She squints her face and grabs her forehead again, feeling another audible burst coming on.

"*AAAAAAUUUUGGGGGGHHHHH!!!*" The scream in her mind reflects that of someone experiencing extreme pain. Simultaneously, an invisible pressure shoots out from her in all directions, scorching the ground around her as well as the headstones. Naomi dives behind a large tombstone to avoid being hit by whatever was coming her way. Naomi rummages through her purse for her cell phone and quickly calls for help. After hanging up, she hears the sound of stillness, but the air smelled of smoke. She stands up from behind the tombstone she used for shelter and noticed the cross engraved on the top of it.

"Thank you." She said. She finds an approximate fifteen-foot diameter patch of ground had been completely charred, including along with the headstones within that circle. The only spot that wasn't charred was a small area of grass in which Tabatha's body was now laying in.

Naomi ran over to Tabatha still panicked. "Tabatha, Tabatha, can you hear me?" She frantically asked. Tabatha just mumbled incoherently. "Did you bring your medicine?" Naomi asked, but got no real response.

Naomi remembered that many times Tabatha keeps the pouch in her back pocket, so she tried rolling Tabatha over just enough to check. Sure enough, the pouch was in her pocket. Naomi complained about Tabatha's weight as she tried to get the pouch out of her back pocket. "You and you're big butt." Naomi opened the pouch and went through the routine of injecting the medicine into her arm. Within moments, once again, Tabatha's breathing slowed and she started sounding normal.

"Mom?" Tabatha mumbles before falling asleep

"Yeah, sweetheart, I'm right here," Naomi reassures her, holding her arm. Naomi's attention is shortly after that, drawn to two sets of headlights coming down the dirt path, pulling up next Tabatha's truck. Naomi squinted to see who it was through the lights beaming toward her. Two doors open then close and the silhouettes' of two individuals appear amidst the headlights and begin approaching Naomi and Tabatha, then one of them said:

"Naomi?"

The Sentient

CHAPTER VIII

EXPOSURE

"Where..." Tabatha mumbles as she grapples with waking up.

"You're ok now Tabatha, just relax." A familiar voice replies to her predictable question.

Tabatha slowly opens her eyes to blurry images at first. After a few blinks, she sees clearly. "David?" she responds, seeing the doctor looking down at her. "What happened?" Tabatha sits up in the bed and looks around the room.

"Naomi called me yesterday while you were, apparently, setting the cemetery on fire. I honestly don't know what happened, but I brought you here to take care of you.

"Mom? Thanks," Tabatha says, as she absorbs Naomi's memories of what happened the night before.

"You're welcome," she responds from a chair across the room from Tabatha. "You frightened me last night," she adds.

"Yeah, me too," Tabatha concurs. She looks down at her arm and observes an I.V. taped to her arm. She follows the tube up to an I.V. bag attached from a clothing hanger that hung from a curtain rod above the window next to the twin bed she was laying in. "Nice setup, doc," she critiques the jerry-rigged I.V. set.

"Well, I had to improvise," Dr. Glessinjer responds.

"So whatcha pump'n into me?"

"Nothing crazy this time, just saline. You were incredibly dehydrated."

"Hey, a woman's coming downstairs," Tabatha informs the doctor, concerned.

"It's alright, Tabatha, she knows," he responds.

"She does? I'm supposed to be a secret, remember," she reminds the doctor.

"Tabatha, you would be a secret even *if* you couldn't do what you do, as often as you leave the condo. Which is hardly ever," Naomi interjects. "By the way, remember, you have a lunch date with your best friend at noon today."

"Right," Tabatha remembers.

The woman that Tabatha was initially concerned about then enters the room. "Hey David, how's she...Oh good, she's awake now!" She says.

"Tabatha, this is..." the doctor begins to introduce his fiancé.

"...Jamie," Tabatha completes the doctor's introduction.

Jamie puts her hand over her mouth, attempting to contain her excitement. "I guess you *could* figure that out pretty easily, couldn't you," Jamie says, referring to the fact that Tabatha new her name without being told. Jamie walks around the doctor, who was sitting on a stool next to Tabatha's bed and held her hand out. "It's so awesome to meet you."

"Oh, yes, it's very nice to meet you as well finally," Tabatha shakes her hand.

"David, you told her about me?" Jamie says, smiling, flattered.

"Well, I – no, actually. She *intruded* on my memories about you yesterday morning."

"Well, she was the only thing on your mind. It was inescapable for me to see her," Tabatha recaps yesterday mornings' visit with him at his office.

Jamie smiles at David then gives him a big kiss on his cheek, flattered at the idea that she's always on his mind.

"Oh Tabatha, would you like some...?" Jamie attempts to be hospitable.

"Yeah, I'll take some tea, that would be great thanks," Tabatha answers.

"Ha-ha-that's so cool! Ok, I'll be right back," Jamie says, referencing Tabatha's telepathy.

"You think it's cool right now. Give it time. It will get annoying real fast," Naomi comments on Jaimie's idea that having her mind read is *cool.* To which Tabatha and the doctor chuckled.

"So, was I *really* thinking about Jamie the whole time yesterday?" the doctor asks Tabatha, questioning the validity of her claim.

"No. I just figured I'd help you earn some brownie points," Tabatha admits. "You two better sign that dotted line real soon though, that's all I have to say," she adds.

"Three weeks to go, Tabatha," he says.

"If she can last that long..."

"Tabatha, stop it. Get your head out of – everyone else's head," David lectures.

"Sorry about that. What time is it?" she asks.

"It's ten after eight in the morning."

"I need some breakfast. Like thirty pancakes and twenty eggs, lots of bacon. Actually, can we just go get a whole pig and throw it in the oven?" Tabatha acknowledges her bodies' biological signals indicating that she requires energy.

"Wow! Thaaaat's a lot of food," the doctor acknowledges.

"That's nothing, doctor – trust me," Naomi adds.

"I'd be three times as big if I ate nearly that much food. I'm jealous," Jamie adds to the conversation, walking back in the room. "Here's your tea, Ms. Johnson,"

"I'm Ms. Johnson too, you can just call her Tabatha," Naomi says rhetorically.

"Mom, you were married. You're a Mrs.," Tabatha corrects Naomi.

"Until death do us part – I'm *a-vai-la-ble*," Naomi continues, to which they all laugh.

"Well, Tabatha, I *totaly* know where you get your sarcasm from, ha-ha," Jamie acknowledges.

David stands up and turns the flow of the saline off. He sits back down and removes the I.V. from Tabatha's arm, placing a bandage over the area. He holds her arm and puts two fingers on her wrist and looks at his watch, checking her pulse, then takes her temperature.

"You appear to be back to your normal self. How about that breakfast. I'm starving myself since Jamie, and I didn't get to eat the dinner

95

we ordered last night," David briefly summarizes the night before when Naomi had called him from behind the safety of that tombstone. He and Jamie had just ordered dinner at a classy five-star gourmet restaurant that had been reserved weeks in advance.

"I'm sorry about all that," Tabatha says, feeling guilty about ruining their evening.

"Are you kidding me? Don't be sorry. Now, if it were any other emergency, like someone having just a regular heart attack or whatnot, then I would have protested leaving," Jamie explains, to which Tabatha, Naomi, and David all stare at her. "Ok, yeah, that was kind of harsh, but you get the idea," Jamie retracts her unintentionally cruel comment. "Point being, you're the secret government superhero – I can skip a fancy dinner for this," she reasons.

"Whoa! I'm not a superhero. Please don't put me on some pedestal like that. I break things." Tabatha corrects Jamie then stands up. "If I were to classify myself as anything, it would be the secret government screw up," Tabatha adds, admitting to the reality that she's made many mistakes in her appointed role. "Wait, your one of those YouTube channel groupies, are not you," Tabatha picks up on, holding back from laughing at the idea.

"No. I'm not a groupie, just a fan," Jamie attempts defends herself.

"No, babe..." David corrects Jamie, "...You're a groupie."

Jamie stares at the ceiling for a second before responding, pondering the accusation. "Yeah, I guess I am, aren't I," she then admits it to the laughter of the others.

"Well, let's go eat. Mom's anxious to see our newly renovated condo," Tabatha says, leading the small group out of the room.

"Actually, Tabatha, there's something I need to tell you real fast," doctor Glessinjer hesitantly says. Picking up on an anxious mind, Tabatha stops and turns toward the doctor, honing in on his thoughts.

"Yeah you do. Who did you tell about me? And why can't I see this individual? You're suppressing some information, aren't you?" She responds to the shadiness of the situation.

"Remember when I've told you to trust me?"

"Yes, and ironically, you haven't been the only one to tell me that in the last twenty-four hours. My trust for anyone is beginning to balance on a razors' edge right about now," Tabatha responds. Naomi and Jamie, in the dark about the whole conversation, keep quiet only listening to the situation. "So spill it...who is he/she, and what does he/she know?"

"Well, *he* knows you very well, and all I can say is that *he* has been looking out for you for a very long time. And, he wants to see you – today," the doctor concludes.

"This is like James Bond excitement!" Naomi perks up with an adventurous spirit.

"Mom, he's in New York," Tabatha explains, deducing the details, again, from the doctor.

"Yes, upstate New York, to be exact. He has a personal jet waiting for you this morning," David confirms.

"Ok, now I'm kinda geeking out. That's pretty cool," Tabatha admits.

"Wait, Tabatha, you have a lunch date with Cindy today, remember? You can't just up and leave to upstate New York," Naomi reminds Tabatha.

"Mom, this is *really* important, maybe this guy, whoever he is, can *actually* explain what's going on with me," Tabatha explains.

"Ms. Naomi, this is vitally important..." the doctor attempts to convince Naomi, but she cuts him off.

"...NO! Tabatha! She's your best friend, and you need that! You need her more than this secret stuff! This can wait!" Naomi shouts with passion, pulling seniority over the group, both because it just so happens that she's the senior in the group and she's Tabatha's mother-figure. Her concern for Tabatha has always been to have some semblance of a normal life, i.e., going on a simple lunch date with a friend. The group then grows quiet after Naomi's outburst of frustration.

"Well, I'm cool with anything, but since I have a feeling we're going to be here a while, I'll start breakfast," Jamie breaks the awkward silence and heads upstairs.

"Soooo, this afternoon, then?" Tabatha suggests an alternate flight itinerary.

"Looks like it," Dr. Glessinjer agrees.

"Three o'clockish?" Tabatha adds.

"I'm sure that will be fine. Ronald Reagan international. I'll text you the information later."

"Good, now let's go eat," Naomi says, satisfied that her point was taken, then ascended the stairs behind Jamie, followed by Dr. Glessinjer and Tabatha.

....

"That was a wonderful breakfast, Jamie, thank you. It's nice not to have to cook for once," Naomi compliments having finished her breakfast. Everyone had finished eating and sat with an empty plate in front of them. That is except for Tabatha, who was still shoving her last pancake in her mouth, while the rest of them just sat and watched with amazement. Well, Naomi wasn't amazed – that was normal for her to see.

"What?" Tabatha responds to their *amazed* looks at the four empty plates stacked on top of each other in front of her, and her last bite of pancake partially sticking out of her mouth.

"You know, Tabatha, I really thought you were kidding when you said how much food you wanted earlier," Jamie responds, laughing.

"I always wanted grandkids," Naomi begins randomly telling Jamie some of her life dreams. "...but I was diagnosed with polycystic ovarian syndrome after I first got married, so we couldn't have children."

"Oh my goodness, Naomi, I'm so sorry to hear that. That must have been hard." Jamie consoles.

"...Then my late husband and I were miraculously granted custody of Tabatha shortly after her birth. I thought, maybe I might see some grandkids after all. Well, basically grandkids – obviously, she's biologically my niece, but you get the idea," Naomi continues.

"Right, I understand."

"But then some days, I look at her..." Naomi was referring to Tabatha, who looked like someone who had just been picked up from living in a ditch for a month. Her cheeks were bulging with food to the point they could almost burst. And her hair – in a million different directions. "...and realize that those dreams are dead, murdered, ran over, buried...." Naomi elevates the emphasis of each verb higher than the previous one.

"Oh please, mom," Tabatha interrupts Naomi's sarcastically laced story after finally swallowing her last piece of pancake.

"What? I'm just telling the truth," Naomi defends herself, to which Tabatha rolls her eyes before standing up, anticipating Naomi's next command. "Well, we better get going."

Tabatha takes her four plates to the sink, and the rest of the group follow suit – only with one plate – each, then heading out the front door. "Oh, and thanks for not leaving my truck at the cemetery last night doctor," Tabatha says after spotting it parked in the driveway behind two other vehicles. They say their goodbyes as Naomi, and Tabatha get in the truck, pull out of the doctors' driveway, and speed off down the street.

Once Tabatha's truck was out of sight, David and Jamie turn to head inside, but standing on their porch was a young man in a white t-shirt and jeans. If Tabatha had seen him, she would have recognized him as the guy whom she met yesterday morning in the waiting room of the doctor's office.

"I'm looking forward to the day when she catches you, kid," David says.

"Can't wait," he replies, smiling then gets up and leaves in one of the other vehicles.

"Now, you cannot say anything about this to anyone, ok?" David informs Jamie, to which she nods. They smile, and he gives her a peck on the lips then they walk back inside.

"She is awesome, though," Jamie reiterates her excitement after having met Tabatha.

"Yeah, she's a good girl," the doctor agrees, "I just *hope* she stays *good*," he concludes.

....

Tabatha and Naomi return home to their condo. Upon entering, they see a nearly brand new home. The previously white walls were now in more elegant colors. The furniture had been replaced as well. The old couch that was the only survivor of the living room devastation was replaced by a leather sectional. Naomi's flattened rocking chair was also replaced by a reclining rocker with built-in massage settings. The recliner matched the couch in color, style, and material. Naomi's end table and lamp had also been replaced along with the bookshelf. However, most of the books were irreplaceable. The survivingl pictures were reframed and hung back in their original places, and the coffee table had also been replaced and matched Naomi's new end table.

The two of them were as giddy as little school girls. Tabatha, who *could* do cartwheels, nearly did several, and Naomi, who couldn't do cartwheels – wasn't going to do any anyways. But, she could clap, which is what she did. Tabatha did get her upgraded seventy-inch flat screen T.V. monitor in place of her older, crushed fifty-inch T.V. sitting on a new entertainment stand that was in the same likeness as the new bookshelf. I guess the director changed his mind about giving her an upgrade.

"Now, why do you need a T.V. that big?" Naomi begins her assault on the big T.V. in the same fashion she gets on Tabatha about her truck.

"You got to be kidding me," Tabatha says to herself. "Oh mom, why don't you go see if you got your washer and dryer," Tabatha attempts to divert Naomi's attention from the T.V.

"Oh! Right!!" Naomi perks up again with excitement, remembering the request for the new set. Naomi might not be able to do cartwheels, but she can walk *really* fast when she wants to. She bolts down the hallway like something that moves really slow but is moving really fast – like a snail being chased by a bird, or a turtle being chased by a flame (unless it's a ninja turtle, then the turtle would be chasing the flame), or a female sloth being pursued by a male sloth – wait, no – they still move slow, but you get the idea.

Tabatha smiles, sensing Naomi's excitement over her updated washer and dryer. Naomi then bolts to her bathroom and pulls out all the dirty clothes so she can use the set for the first time. "Tab! Bring me your dirty clothes!" Naomi shouts from down the hallway.

"All my clothes are clean! You just did laundry yesterday, remember?" Tabatha shouts back.

"Give me the clothes you have on. I'm sure you haven't changed in days anyway. And you smell like gun powder, smoke, oh and you either need to buy a new brand of deodorant, or you need to start using deodorant period, cuz your body order is nasty girl," Naomi divulges.

"You know mom, I could just drop you off under an overpass somewhere," Tabatha responds to Naomi's sarcastic insults.

"Yeah, well your uncle and I could have donated you as a lab rat for scientific research for a lot of money as a child," Naomi retaliates wittily.

"Touché," Tabatha responds admitting loss to that round of sarcasm smackdown. Tabatha walks over to the scenic living room window that was crystal clear now that it, too, had been replaced. She looks out across the city listening to all the psychic noise that continuously inundates her mind. "You know, sometimes I feel like a big lab rat in an even bigger test tube," she adds.

"Well, you sure smell like one most of the time," Naomi continues on her insult binge.

"Oh-my-gosh mom, fine. Let me go change into some new clothes, you sure don't want me walking around here naked," Tabatha responds walking back to her room.

"You're darn right about that. I'll drop *myself* off under an overpass," she says to herself.

"Well, in that case," Tabatha responds sarcastically, poking her head out her door winking at Naomi at the idea.

"Oh Lord Jesus, help my niece," Naomi says to herself.

"I heard that!!" Tabatha shouts from in her bedroom closet, pulling out new jeans and a t-shirt.

"Well, that's your problem!" Naomi shouts back. "Hey, you better take a shower first!" she adds. "I'm sure Cindy doesn't want to smell a lab rat either," Naomi concludes to herself.

"Hey! I heard…!"

"…I know you did!!!" Naomi quickly responds back to Tabatha before she had a chance to finish her statement.

Tabatha pops out of her room in a pair of jogging shorts and a tank top holding clean clothes in one arm and her dirties in the other. Tabatha sets the dirty clothes on the dryer for Naomi. Naomi notices the T-shirt that Tabatha picked out to wear. It's one she's seen a million times: white with loony toon characters. But what made repulsive to Naomi, is that, even when clean, looks like Tabatha picked up off the side of the road somewhere. Naomi quickly snatches the shirt out of her arm.

"Hey!"

"I have a better shirt. Just go take a shower," Naomi orders. "Can't believe I'm still teaching her about hygiene and how to dress in public," she says to herself again.

"Hey, I heard…."

"…I know you heard it! Shut up and take a shower," Naomi demands, then laughs to herself about the whole situation.

"Mom!! This is see-through!! I'm not wearing it!!" Tabatha shouts from inside the bathroom having finished her shower and observing the shirt Naomi set on the counter. It was a purple blouse. It really wasn't that see-through, but Tabatha has a belief that something is automatically see-through if it's under a certain thread count in thickness.

"It is not!!" Naomi shouts back reassuring her, while also still trying to turn on the new updated washing machine.

"See, you can see the outline of my bra," Tabatha tries to point out.

"Wait-a-second," Naomi notices Tabatha put a little too much lipstick on and grabs a piece of paper towel from the supply shelf above the washer and dryer, folds it and holds it up to Tabatha's mouth, an indication for her to blot, which she does. "There that looks better," Naomi says, trying to diverge from the ridiculous shirt topic.

"Thanks, mom, but the shirt, you can see..." Tabatha continues.

"Yeah, you can see your bra, with x-ray vision," Naomi says, walking back into her room. She pulls a black undershirt out of her dresser and hands it to Tabatha, "here. Put this on under it."

"That will definitely help," Tabatha says and goes back into the bathroom to change again, before returning back to Naomi for her dress approval.

"You look very nice sweetheart," Naomi compliments, while internally getting frustrated over failing to understand the washing machine. "I still think you looked fine before though too. You couldn't see anything Tabatha," she concludes.

"You only think that because there's not much to look at on you," Tabatha harshly responds sarcastically to Naomi.

"Why you little...!! Brat!! Get out'a here!!" Naomi shouts, chasing Tabatha down the hallway, who was laughing hysterically at the ordeal and out the door – like a ninja turtle chasing a flame.

"Oh Lord, what am I going to do with her," Naomi says, again to herself, insulted but humored at the same time. Her phone beeps, an indication that she got a text message. She walks back to the washer and dryer and pulls her cell phone out of her purse. '*I heard that*' was the text message from Tabatha, to which Naomi simply laughed at. She then, staring at the washer and dryer directions like a deer in headlights, decides to give up on them for the time being and walks into the living room. Naomi looks around the living room, continuing to admire the newly renovated condo, then seeing the remote laying on the coffee table to the new T.V., picks it up.

"Seventy inches huh. Let's see why you're such a big deal," Naomi says to herself and presses the power button.

"*POW – POW – BANG – BANG – THUD – THUD*!!"

"AAAAAAAHHHHH!!" Naomi falls over, terrified having been caught off guard by the sounds of guns blazing coming from the T.V. in which the volume was on maximum. When she came to her senses real quick and got the volume down, she saw that it was western and where Indians were riding through a town shooting sporadically. "Her and her *big, loud* stuff!"

....

Tabatha sat by herself at a small table under an awning outside a sandwich shop. She watches hundreds of people walk to and fro along the sidewalks lining either side of the four-lane street, which is also mildly busy with vehicles. She puts her earbuds in and cranks up the volume on her phone until the music drowns out the psychic noise. After a few songs, she begins picking up on a familiar bubbly telepathic pattern. She looks up and spots Cindy walking her way. Tabatha then pulls out her earbuds and stands up to greet her. They quickly embrace each other, then they step inside to order food.

"So, how're things going?" Tabatha starts off their conversation.

"Oh, it's been crazy – crazy good," Cindy replies. "I love your shirt."

"Oh, thanks. Mom, let me borrow it."

"Ha-ha, borrowing clothes still, huh?" Cindy laughs.

"Yeah, well, she doesn't necessarily agree with the way I dress most of the time."

"Can't blame her Tab. You do tend dress, super ultra-casual at times, I have to admit," Cindy continues. "It's a good thing you wore that undershirt though, just saying."

"I know, right?!" Tabatha says, feeling validated about her discussion in regards to the blouse with Naomi earlier.

"Oh,-my-goodness!" Tabatha begins to burst with excitement for Cindy, then catches herself before she divulges Cindy's secret that she and Pastor Reed just got the news that she was pregnant.

"What!!" Cindy responded.

"Oh, I just remembered that I have to – pick up – something – from the store – on my way back home – after lunch," Tabatha fibs a little to cover her knowledge up.

"Oh, wow! You must be getting something pretty exciting then," Cindy says. "Anything particular?" She continues.

"No, not really," Tabatha responds. They continue talking about random topics until they get up to the register and order their food, then after ordering, they continue ramblings.

"I can't believe you can eat all that food. I'm so jealous," Cindy says as they sit back down at the table under the awning outside the restaurant. "You have the highest metabolism I've ever seen."

"I know, what can I say, I'm blessed," Tabatha responds. "Actually, you should have half of this. You're the one eating for twooooo..." Tabatha accidentally lets out.

"WHAT!!" Cindy says with a glare.

"I meant, uh, you and, uhmm...." Tabatha stumbles over words, failing to get out of this one.

"I'm gonna kill him!!"

"I don't think that killing a pastor would be a good idea," Tabatha responds, trying to downplay the situation.

"I'm married to him. I don't care."

Out of the blue, Tabatha picks up on an echo of a couple of small children crying for their mother out of the vast ocean of psychic noise, which draws her attention away from Cindy momentarily. She looks down the walkway behind her, then behind Cindy, but sees nothing. The echo then vanishes.

"Tabatha? Are you ok?" Cindy inquires over Tabatha, seemingly to be distracted.

"Uhh yeah..." Tabatha regains her focus on the conversation. "Honestly, Cindy, Kyle didn't tell me anything," she admits, not wanting Kyle to get blamed.

"He didn't? So how..."

"Well, I mean, uh, look at you. I can just tell. It's obvious that you're pregnant," Tabatha doing the best she can to stumble her way out.

Cindy lowers her eyelids, not fully believing Tabatha. "Tabatha, I'm barely pregnant, I'm the same size I was two weeks ago," Cindy informs in a stern voice.

Tabatha quickly scans Cindy's recent memories looking for something to change the topic to, which will be of more interest than the one at present. "Oh, did you hear about someone torching the cemetery last night?" Tabatha blurts out snagging a memory that Cindy obtained from watching the news that morning, but then realizing that *she* caused the mess at the cemetery at first.

"Oh, right!! Kinda creepy. This morning the two caretakers of the cemetery found a whole section of the cemetery torched including several headstones," Cindy responds.

"Did they figure out who did it?" Tabatha asks, hoping it was something completely unrelated to anything that could lead to her, or draw the attention of the director Jackson.

"Well, remember a few years ago when they were having a big problem with satan worshipers and Wiccans and whatnot doing rituals and stuff at night?"

"Oh yeah, I remember about that."

"Well, now they think it's starting again," Cindy explained.

"I see." Tabatha quickly responded. Then, the sound of small children begins echoing in Tabatha's mind, which, again, draws her attention away from Cindy.

"Tabatha? What are you looking for?" Cindy asks, watching Tabatha turning her head back and forth.

"I know this is a stupid question, but you don't hear some little kids screaming, do you?".

"No, I don...." Cindy begins to say, then realizes she does hear a faint child's voice. "Actually, I do – sort of," Cindy affirms. "It's coming from down that way," Cindy points behind Tabatha toward the four-way crosswalk at the end of the row of storefronts. "What's the matter," Cindy then asks.

"I don't know. But, I will be right back," Tabatha gets up and starts walking toward the intersection guided more so by her gut than her telepathy. She then starts gaining speed until she was at a decent jog closing in on the crossing.

"Tabatha!! What are you...." Cindy not quite sure what the problem was, got up, and began following her.

As Tabatha neared the crowded four-way crosswalk, people began parting to let two very young children who were crying out for their mother walk passed them. No one even attempted to stop them from going out into the street where there was oncoming traffic. Tabatha realized what the danger was and picked up speed, noticing a public transportation bus heading straight to where the children were about to step out. Cindy, who had almost caught up to Tabatha then stopped and placed her hand over her mouth as she saw Tabatha grab the two kids, leap passed the bus and into the next lane. Tabatha looks up to see a dump truck heading right for them.

"This sucks..." was the only statement Tabatha could get out before the truck plowed into – nothing? The truck hit what seems to be an invisible barrier just inches in front of them, collapsing the front end of the truck and sending the entire rig into the air, rolling over the protective sphere before, finally, landing upside down on the opposite side of the Tabatha and the children.

The crowd looked in awe over the scene, and immediately, sirens were heard in the background. The children were scared and disoriented from the incident but were unscathed.

"My babies, where are my babies!" A woman shouts from the crowd. Looking out into the street, she sees her children and sprints out toward them. "GIVE ME MY CHILDREN – YOU FREAK!!" The woman shouts at Tabatha, as she was on all fours with blood mixed with sweat dripping from her nose and pores across her face due to multiple blood vessels erupting. She was dazed and confused, similar to someone being intoxicated.

Cindy, who had watched the incident along with hundreds of others, saw the young mother and heard what she said to Tabatha. She then ran with fury out to meet her. "SHE JUST SAVED YOUR KIDS LIFE. YOU DUMB NEGLIGENT, BIMBO!!" Cindy hauled off and decked across the face, to which she collapsed to the ground stunned. Then seeing the police vehicles show up, the young mother got off the ground, grabbed her two kids, and ran to them. Cindy watched the woman run off then observed all the people who had just watched the entire incident unfold but did nothing, to which Cindy went on an outburst towards them as well.

"YEAH!! TAKE YOUR PICTURES!! TAKE YOUR VIDEOS!! YET IF IT WASN'T FOR HER..!!" Cindy yells at the people, in which more had gathered to see what had happened, and pointing toward Tabatha, who was still trying to collect herself, "...THERE WOULD BE TWO DEAD KIDS

IN THE ROAD RIGHT NOW!!" Cindy continues her verbal assault on the crowd. "...YOU'RE AS CLOSE TO WORTHLESS AS HUMANLY POSSIBLE, EVERY ONE OF YOU!!" Cindy finally concludes then runs over to help Tabatha.

"Tabatha!! Are you ok?! What was that?! Do you have something you need to tell me? You're best friend?" Cindy frantically asks, trying to process everything she just saw. Cindy grabs Tabatha's arm and pulls her up off the ground, holding her steady. Her face still dripping with blood and sweat and once again, her body temperature was skyrocketing.

"Can you keep a – secret?" Tabatha says exhaling every word, attempting to be funny while incoherent.

"Excuse me, miss."

"WHAT!!" Cindy answers the voice from behind with another shout, thinking it's one of the *spectators*.

"Excuse me?" A police officer responds.

"Oh-my-goodness. I'm so sorry. I thought you were – someone else," Cindy apologizes.

"Well, be that it may, this woman said that you hit her," the officer responds. "Is that true?"

Cindy gathered her thoughts and contained her vitriol for the woman, who was standing behind the cop with a fowl gaze at Cindy, holding the hands of her children. "Sir, with all due respect, there is a dump truck upside down right next to us, and you're going to ask me that?"

"This woman said that woman over there, who I might add looks pretty drunk," the officer says referring to Tabatha, due to her attempt to keep her balance still, "for no reason snatched up these children, and when their mother saved them, you came out and punched her," the officer concluded the woman's story.

Cindy could have exploded at hearing this, but then the children spoke up, saying: "Mommy, mommy, lookit, lookit. That's the lady that saved us from the dup truck..." one said, "yeah, it is, is she ok?" the other said. The officer glanced down at the little children, then up at Cindy. Cindy smiled at the woman and said, "out of the mouth of babes. Next time, try keeping them a little closer to you." At that, the woman stormed off with her children and disappeared into the crowd.

The police officer tore the piece of paper off his small note pad that he wrote down the woman's details on, shredded it and dropped the pieces of paper on the ground. Then Cindy informed the officer what honestly happened. Midway through the story, Tabatha collapsed back onto the asphalt. Cindy and the officer rushed over to help Tabatha. When the officer tried to touch Tabatha to help her up, a dense pressure tossed him and Cindy back several feet plus shoving Tabatha in the opposite direction as well, scraping the side of her body upon the road. The officer's head slammed into the curb knocking him unconscious. This action reengaged the attention of the surrounding officers to which they all drew their sidearms, aiming them at Tabatha, who was trying to get up again.

"Get back on the ground and put your hands behind your back!" one of them shouted.

"I need – my medicine," Tabatha mumbled incoherently. And instead of getting back on the ground, she reaches to her back pocket for her medicine. However, one of the officers doesn't take it as she's reaching for some medicine pouch, and thinking she is, instead, reaching for a weapon, shoots Tabatha in her shoulder. The moment the bullet hits Tabatha, an enormous blast of pressure originating from Tabatha's body explodes through the streets sending people flying, pushing and overturning vehicles and blowing out the store front windows.

Cindy managed to get up, after also being tossed back by the explosion of pressure but was somewhat protected by the public transportation bus that had not moved since the children ran into the street. She ran over to Tabatha, who was unconscious but still alive. Though Cindy had never injected the medicine into Tabatha before, she had seen it done. After finding the pouch containing the medicine, she begins getting it ready.

"Lady!! Get away from her!!" Another officer shouts at Cindy, as several of them run up toward them, thinking Tabatha is a threat. "You don't know what she is capable of," the officer shouts again, approaching Cindy.

"NO!! YOU DON'T KNOW WHAT IM CAPABLE OF! YOU GUYS BACK OFF, OR YOU WILL FIND ME TO BE A BIGGER THREAT THAN HER!!" Cindy shouts, outraged about the whole ordeal. "Besides, this is Tabatha Johnson, and she's a secret government agent," she divulges to the officers, not exactly sure if that was true but hoping it would scare them into submission. "Easy on the *secret* part now, I have a feeling," she says to herself.

The officers stand around watching as Cindy injects the medicine into Tabatha's arm. After inserting the medication, Cindy pulls the needle out of Tabatha's arm and disassembles it. Tabatha's breathing begins to normalize again.

"Mom?" Tabatha says.

"It's me, Tabatha – Cindy. You're going to be ok. I'm here with you," Cindy consoles her.

"Cindy. Thanks," Tabatha responds, touching Cindy's arm then falling asleep in the middle of the road, which looks like it was now part of a war zone with hundreds of individuals combing through the devastation and getting a first look at the government's top-secret telepath.

The Sentient

CHAPTER IX

New Revelations

"...Several witnesses described the incident as something straight out of a movie..." News reporter.

"...An entire city block was devastated after an unknown explosion..." News reporter.

"...An explosion devastated this portion of downtown Tuesday afternoon. However, the F.B.I. have failed to find any trace of evidence of an actual explosion, such as residue, or pieces of an explosive device..." News reporter.

"...Many police officers who were on-site at the time of the explosion have *refused* to comment on what they saw, although police dispatch records report that multiple calls received by the police station noted a dump truck, apparently, *nearly* hit a woman protecting *two children*, but had stopped just inches away from them, rolling over them without touching them. It's really indescribable..." News reporter

"...One witness says it was the hand of God protecting them, another believes it was witchcraft, another believed it was an alien force-field, and a liberal bystander said it's a result of the newly passed Republican tax cut and jobs act – '*I really need to find a new line of work*'..."News reporter.

"...Attempts to obtain street cam footage of the incident was blocked by government authorities, stating 'they are reviewing the footage'..." News reporter.

"...Many were taken to nearby medical facilities. The driver of the dump trunk was one of the only two individuals who acquired life destabilizing injuries and is currently in critical condition — The second individual has been identified Tabatha Johnson and was escorted not only by medical personnel but also by several government officials as well as a woman who threatened to have her husband, who happens to be a preacher, call down fire and brimstone on the Pentagon if she wasn't allowed to ride with Tabatha on the ambulance. She described herself as the best friend of Tabatha Johnson..." News reporter.

....

"I think she's coming back around."

"Uhhh, yeah, I think I am too," Tabatha murmurs, regaining consciousness.

Her telepathy had been restored as the psychic noise funnels back into her mind from those around her and those outside her room. Guards surrounded the entrance to the hospital room, keeping the press and the many spectators, including groupies – at a distance. Sitting next to her on the edge of the hospital bed was Dr. Glessinjer. Standing behind, David was the Director. The combination of Dr. Glessinjer and the Director in the same room was an awkward sight for her.

"How are you feeling?" Cindy inquires, sitting next to her bed.

"Not sure," Tabatha answered, still facing the other way.

"Just so you know, I've known about Dr. Glessinjer for a long time," Kurtis reassures Tabatha.

"Yeah, I kinda picked up on that the last time you mentioned him," she responds. "How long have I been out?"

"Two days," another familiar voice answers.

"Rodney, what are you doing here?" Tabatha asks, excited that two separate worlds are coming together for the first time.

"Dr. Glessinjer and Rodney know you, medically, better than anyone else does, so I brought them both in," the Director answers for Rodney. "By the way, you missed your flight," the Director throws in to add a little humor.

"Right. To see this *mystery man*?" She responds, attempting to put the pieces together. "Whom I can't even see in any of your minds, because something is blocking that information, and I've noticed it for a while. Can it be time to explain *that*, at least?" Tabatha asks, confident that the answer is going to be no.

"We don't have any control over that. He prefers his anonymity," David explains.

"The way you guys seem to take orders from this *mystery-man*, makes me wonder if he isn't the King of the world," Tabatha divulges what is beginning to concern her, but in her usual sarcastic way.

"Not if I were married to him," Cindy quickly interjects her opinion on control freaks. Tabatha glances at her and nods in agreement.

"It's true that he does have an enormous amount of influence. Both politically and economically," Rodney says, understanding Tabatha's concern.

"Here in the U.S. and abroad as well, to a large degree," David adds. "However, this guy, well, has done more for you than you even know. He practically handpicked and placed us in your life to help you."

"Alright fella's, that's enough," the Director says.

"What? What do you mean enough? Help me do what?" Does mom know about all of this?" Tabatha prodding for answers with questions. However, the information she is looking for continues to be elusive.

"No, your god-mother doesn't know. But, this man did influence the system to help her, and your late uncle, receive guardianship of you, unbeknownst to them," David quickly adds despite the Directors order.

The Director walks over to Tabatha and places his hand on her arm. "Listen, I know that I've always been firm with you – that I've pushed you hard, especially to do what's right. I admit I've been harsh many times with you," the Director says with a soft, low voice, taking up the role as a close friend or even father than that of a boss, or Director of an entire governmental department. Tabatha can sense the emotion coming from the Director, and one tear falls from her eye. "And I also know you *hate* hearing this word, but I need you to *trust* me," he says, then looks toward David, still sitting on the edge of the bed and Rodney leaning against a wall next to the bathroom. "You need to trust all of us." He continues.

"And if it's any consolation to you, we have placed an incredible amount of trust into *this man*, that I, personally, have never met. Just one of his associates," Rodney says.

"I got a letter saying I was getting a new patient – with instructions," David adds.

"I've met him one time, a long time ago. Do you know what he told me? To trust him," the director admits. "And I have, sometimes hesitantly, but I knew the purpose behind it, and the purpose *was*, and *is*, worth it." The Director concludes. "At least to me it is."

"You guys know how to get me all emotional," Tabatha responds. "Kyle's here too?" Tabatha faces Cindy and randomly blurts out.

"Yeah, he went to get..." just then, a guard opens the door opens, and Kyle enters with a bag in one hand, and Styrofoam cup in the other.

"Kyle!" Tabatha exclaims. "You got me tea? That's a so...oh wait, never mind," Tabatha says, then picking up that it was for Cindy and not her.

"Tabatha! I didn't know you were awake. It's great to see you conscious again. Sorry, I would have if I would've known," Kyle says.

"Oh, that's ok, I need to quit jumping to conclusions all the time," Tabatha admits.

"Oh, but I did find *these*, downstairs, and thought I'd bring them with me," Kyle adds as the *Seven* walks in the room behind him.

"Boys! What are you doing here?!" Tabatha further exclaimed.

The Seven glanced at each perplexed for a moment. "Did she just call us – boys?" T.K. says to the others. "I don't know who she's talking about, buuut, I just see men in this room," Mitchell adds. "Yeah, I don't see any kids in here?" Joe continues in the same manner. Then they all stretch, revealing their manly physiques, as a protest to being called *boys*. Laughter fills the room.

"Mom would love to be here for this," Tabatha says, referring to her god-mothers lustful nature over younger guys.

"She was here until last night. Kurtis took her home to get some rest," David informs Tabatha.

"Yeah, I'm sure she needed it," Tabatha agrees.

"So, we were going to bring you flowers," one of the Seven says. "But we couldn't agree on which ones to get," another member adds. "So, we decided to take pictures of the flowers each of us were going to get you at the flower shop," another concludes. Diego brings his phone to Tabatha so she could look at the pictures of each of them next to the flowers of their particular choice.

"Uhhh, guys, why couldn't each of you bring the flower of your choosing?" Kurtis asks. They all gaze at the Seven as they look at each other, again perplexed – kind of like telling a dog how to take apart a car engine and put it back together as he sits and stares at you, only worse.

"I'm out on this one," Hammer says, leaving the lineup, refusing to be embarrassed any longer. He finds a chair and has a seat.

"Oh boys, you always crack me up," Tabatha says. The team begins looking around them for something they lost. Tabatha laughs.

"What are you doing?" Cindy asks them.

"We're still trying to find some little kids around here," they, again, respond.

"They have a point Tab," Cindy says, defending them. "There's nothing that *screams boy* about these hunks."

"Yeah, but you're married," Tabatha reminds Cindy,

"I know I am. I'm just stating a fact."

"So princess, how about some introductions here," says Mitchell.

"Right, so, this is my personal doctor, David Glessinjer. You all know Rodney. This here is my bestie, Cindy," Cindy smiles and leans in her chair toward Tabatha, tapping her shoulder to Tabatha's left, bullet wound free shoulder. "And this is Kyle, Cindy's husband, who is also a Pastor."

"You know, they wouldn't even let us in the building at first, till Kyle here recognized Hammer and Joe from Monday's newscast after the F.D.A. terror heist debacle," Mitchell says.

"*Only essential people* were allowed up here. At least that's what the guard downstairs said," Diego adds.

"Well, it's a good thing Pastors are essential people," Hammer responds.

"Yeah, or we would still be downstairs with fingers up our..." Michael adds but is interrupted.

"Language!!" Tabatha reminds.

"...Noses," Joe finishes Mitchells statement.

"Well, I just said that if they didn't let them in, I would call down fire and brimstone," Kyle says sarcastically, glancing at Cindy with a smile, about the *reported* statement she supposedly made to a member of the press.

"Hey, I didn't say it like that. They *totally* took that out of context. Besides, I was kinda ticked off, not to mention *freaked* out," Cindy attempts to correct the said statement. "None of the medics could even get close to you unless I held your hand and kept talking to you. Do you have any idea how hard it is to talk continuously?" Cindy explains.

"It's *totally* hard to talk that long," Tabatha agrees with Cindy as the rest of those in the room, all guys, stared at them, all having witnessed their fantastical ability for the two of them to talk for long periods continuously.

"What?" Both Tabatha and Cindy say in unison in response to their implied glares. Tabatha quickly picks up on their thoughts and rolls her eyes, saying, "whatever."

David, however, pondered on some of the details from Cindy's testimony, then glanced over at Rodney and said, "Almost sounds like whatever is going on inside of her is becoming more like a defensive mechanism. What do you think?"

Rodney runs his thumb and index finger along the ridge of his chin, pondering David's hypothesis. "I have been under the impression for a while that she is developing some telekinetic attributes. Since she is unlearned on how to operate that ability consciously, then it could very well be operating as a symbiotic relationship with her subconscious, therefore during instances of unconsciousness, due to something traumatic, this telekinetic attribute becomes conscious on her behalf." Rodney agrees.

"And because of Cindy's relationship with Tabatha, this attribute has a familiarity with Cindy and doesn't perceive her as a threat. That would further explain why there is a similar reaction when she loses control over her emotions, specifically anger. In psychology, many people who deal with anger issues have a hypersensitive fight or flight – I guess more fight than flight – trigger," David adds. Both doctors look around the room upon concluding their combined theory, at the glazed over looks on everyone's faces.

"Uhhh, translate, please?" Cindy breaks the silence.

"The only thing I got out of all that was that I have an anger problem," Tabatha says. "Which I don't!" she says slightly insulted.

"I wasn't saying you have an anger problem. I was using that as an illustration for..." David corrects her assumption.

"...Blah blah blah. Anyways!!" Cindy interrupts, trying to turn the conversation in a less confusing direction. "I'm just so glad that you're ok. You scared me to death," Cindy says to Tabatha. "Plus Finding out that my best friend is a..."

"Don't say it..." Tabatha, anticipating Cindy calling her a secret government superhero.

"Ok? Would you prefer, secret government freak of nature?" Cindy suggests sarcastically.

"That seems to fit my description anymore," Tabatha answers.

"Whatever," Cindy responds. "So, do you even remember anything that happened, though?"

"I remember a truck slamming into me," Tabatha responds. "After that, I felt like I was floating around in space or something. Lots' of vague imagery, though. And lots of noise. More noise than usual."

"Well, maybe you should watch some of this for a few minutes. It might get you caught up to speed," the Director turns on the T.V. mounted on the wall. Nearly every channel, even none news networks, were still talking about the event that took place, now two days ago.

The door to the room opens again by the same guard, and one of the Directors administrators walks in and whispers something into his ear.

"I'll be right back," the Director says and walks out of the room following the admin. Tabatha was too engaged in watching the different footage of the destruction that her untamed abilities once again caused, caught by cell phones and other privately-owned video cameras on the T.V. to prod the mind of the admin or what was being communicated to the Director. Though she did pick up on the fact that something terrible was brewing, most likely terror-related.

"Ok, someone can turn that off," Tabatha says, feeling awful over the scene. Hammer got out of his seat and turned the T.V. off per Tabatha's request. He saw that Tabatha was upset, so he went over and hugged her. "Oh, Ham-ham," she said. "Ouch!" She felt a sharp pain from the bullet wound in her shoulder upon placing her arm around Hammers' neck. She pushes on the wrapped up wound with her other hand.

"Oh, sorry about that," Hammer responds.

"Not your fault. It's mine. Like usual." She says then lays back into the propped-up bed.

"We're going to miss working with you, though," Hammer adds as he walks back to his chair.

"Miss me? What do you mean – Oh, no!! They're dismantling T.I.D.?" Tabatha responds to the Hammers' thoughts.

"Well, the senate T.I.D. oversite committee believes there has been too much attention drawn to the department at this point. So, thanks be to politics, we're officially out of a job," they explain.

"Not quite yet apparently," the Director responds, having shot back in the room in time to hear that last part of the conversation.

"What's going on?" Steve asks.

"Everyone, we're heading to Langley," the Director says.

"Everyone? Like in – Everyone in the room?!" Cindy blurts out, excited to be a part of something like this.

The Director's initial response was in the negative, having memorized the entire T.I.D. *C.F.R.* as well as developed a pattern of habitually executing the regulations, which include the restrictions of all, (especially non-governmental) civilians to be placed intentionally or unintentionally in a capacity to witness any aspect of a T.I.D. protocol. However, before his reactionary answer, he glances at Tabatha, who has a smile on her face. "Well, it sure wouldn't be the first time a member of T.I.D. was a little careless with the regulations. Right, Tabatha *Johnson*?" he continues. "What the heck, you can all come." He looks up at the spiritual behemoths in the room. "Besides, we could use a little more *Jesus* in the department anyways," the Director concludes, referring to Pastor Reed and his wife.

Tabatha picks up more psychic information on the situation as the Director turns his thoughts toward the unofficial assignment. "Looks like I'm going to have to do more digging," Tabatha responds to the information.

"Tabatha, I don't think you're going to have to do much *digging*," the Director says. "Not to say this isn't something we've dealt with before, though, far more disturbing," he continues as he hands Tabatha a tablet with an image on it.

"What is it?" David asks. The tension in the room rises over anticipation of bad news.

"Just your average picture of a terrorist being detained inside the C.I.A. headquarters."

"This individual just randomly wheeled himself right into H.S.D. headquarters yesterday, claiming that he was the terrorist leader Muhammad Ommar," the Director adds.

"Ok? And...?" One of the *Seven* responds, trying to grasp the relevancy for this to be T.I.D. protocol.

"Well, it looks like he was in an accident or an explosion at some point."

"And the C.I.A. can't get anything out of this guy?" One of the *Seven* responds, before Tabatha, shows the room the graphic image.

"Ohh-my-gosh!! That's an average terrorist photograph?" Cindy squirms out of her chair and into her husband's arms, burying her head into his chest over the grotesque image that also included writing on his forehead that read, '*Tabatha Johnson.*'

"According to a medical examination, he's missing his vocal cords," the Director explains.

The Sentient

CHAPTER X

THE MESSAGE

A caravan of black S.U.V.'s pulls up in a single file to a security checkpoint on the edge of the C.I.A. campus. A mechanical arm blocked their immediate entry. One of the many security guards stationed both inside and outside the guard shack walks up to the leading vehicle. The driver holds out an identification badge in which the guard matches the information to that on his clipboard. "Thank you, sir," the guard says to the driver, then signals to raise the arm and let the first vehicle through. The process is repeated for each vehicle.

A swarm of media and groupie spectators descends to the front of the C.I.A. checkpoint. Some of whom followed Tabatha directly from the D.C. hospital. A line of several armed guards gathered together between the checkpoint and crowd. Those who weren't part of the media were more boisterous with some chanting phrases indicative of excitement – if Jaimie weren't back in D.C., required to be in her accounting cubical, she surely would be in this group of individuals. Others threw out phrases of indignation toward the mere fact that someone like Tabatha exists to breathe the same air as them.

The caravan of S.U.V.'s then pulls up next to the primary entrance of the building. Waiting for the team, but mostly waiting for Tabatha, outside the entrance, was her *biggest fan*, Pat Thomas – the C.I.A. Director. He stood with his hands in his pocket. He was a stocky Caucasian somewhere in his late fifties. His head was almost bald but not completely. He was clean-shaven, which made the expressions on his face so clear that Tabatha really wouldn't need to invoke her telepathy to determine his mood.

Standing just a few feet away from Pat was the head of Home Land Security, Christopher Akins. He wore black slacks and a white dress shirt with a bulletproof vest over it, which had the Home Land Security initials on it. He had silver hair and some facial hair. He looked to be pretty athletic for someone in his early fifties. He didn't have the apparent disdain for Tabatha that Pat Thomas had. Christopher appreciated Tabatha and what she could do. When he was a police captain, and Tabatha was in her late teens, he unofficially enlisted her help, to take down an elaborate, but very elusive, regional criminal rink. Her involvement was kept hush-hush for many years for obvious reasons. And though Christopher was fond of Tabatha, he wasn't necessarily too fond of her taking rules and regulations as lightly as she does, however.

Kurtis, Tabatha, Cindy, Pastor Reed, David, and Rodney were all in one of the S.U.V.'s somewhere in the middle of the caravan. The *Seven* were in the vehicle directly behind them. The occupants of the S.U.V.'s then exit their vehicles. Tabatha makes a panoramic observation of the campus. She then starts exhaling heavily and slowly. She puts her hand on her chest. A tear falls from her eye. The Director puts his hand on her shoulder and turns her to face him.

"Tabatha, what's the matter?" The Director asks in a manner that emphasizes 'don't be crying here and now.' Cindy also notices a problem with her and leads Kyle, Rodney, and David over to Tabatha. The Seven also sense a problem and join the group.

"I just felt an intense emotion of anguish and despair," Tabatha responds.

"From you?" the Director further asks.

"No. But it's like someone is begging to...."

"...To what?" Cindy asks.

"...To die."

Tabatha regains her composure. Kyle puts a hand on her shoulder and prays to himself for her. "Director, are they sure this guy is a terrorist?"

"That's what was explained to me," Kurtis responds.

"What are they doing? Praying or something?" Pat Thomas asks Christopher, becoming impatient, watching Tabatha's inner circle huddled around her.

"Could be," Christopher responds.

"We don't have time for prayers right now," Pat complains.

"Sir, I agree with you on many things. But to that statement, I do not," Christopher firmly replies.

Pat glances at Christopher out of the corner of his eye. "Just don't let your past dealings with Tabatha cloud your judgments, Chris."

"They just took the word of note, and a partial facial scan comparing it to an old photograph of this Ommar guy?" Sometimes I think they should call this agency the Central Incompetence Agency, but I digress," Tabatha concludes then heads toward the steps to meet Pat and Chris.

"Took you long enough to walk twenty feet," Pat Thomas remarks to Tabatha as she approaches with her friends and team.

"Sorry, sir. We were, *praying,*" Tabatha responds to Pat, making it clear that she knew what he was thinking, to which Pat nodded, and Christopher chuckles silently.

"At least you confirmed that your, whatever it is, is still operational," Pat says. "Alright, let's get this over with." Pat turns and leads the way into the building.

"My 'whatever it is? Is that the technical term for what I have," Tabatha whispers.

"Tabatha. It's good to see you again," Christopher greets Tabatha.

"Likewise, Christopher," she replies, delighted to see an old friend.

"And since I didn't know you were bringing extra guests," Pat directs the statement to the T.I.D. Director, with a disapproving glare. "They will have to wait here in the lobby," Pat orders.

"What?! We can't go?" Cindy protests, to which Tabatha defends Pat's decision.

"Cindy, guys, just – wait here. We'll be back shortly. It's just a clearance thing." The group agrees, without a verbal protest, but Cindy still makes a disapproving smirk on her face and rolls her eyes.

"I'll hang out with the guests, while you three go do your thing," Christopher remarks, then turns and whispers to Tabatha's inner circle, "I can only tolerate being around that guy for so long," Christopher adds, referring to the C.I.A. director.

"There's a cafeteria down that hall," Pat tells the group pointing in the direction of the cafeteria.

"Hey!! You know, I'm kinda hungry myself," Tabatha divulges sporadically.

"Fortunately, I've been thoroughly briefed on your metabolic condition, requiring a large amount of – food. I took the liberty to have something brought to you. In fact, here it is," Pat informs as he spots an individual jogging down the hall with a paper bag to meet them.

"Pat," Tabatha says, surprised. "You shouldn't have."

"I know," he replies equally rhetorical.

"You're becoming a big ugly *softy* in your old age..." Tabatha continues her binge of mockery "...Instead of just big and ugly." She is handed the bag by the gentleman and quickly opens it. Chicken sandwiches with lots of extra horribly fattening and calorie-loaded ingredients filled the bag.

Kurtis leans over and whispers, "Tabatha, down girl."

"Yes sir," she responds as she begins tearing into her first sandwich like a prehistoric carnivore.

"Don't push it, Tabatha," Pat responds to her constant insults. "Your sarcasm is dripping from every orifice. If you don't watch it, one of these days your lack of discernment, will be the end of you," Pat explains, showing the absolute smallest indication that he *at least* cares for Tabatha's overall wellbeing.

"Maybe," Tabatha responds. "So, on the issue, how positive is the agency that this is this Mohammad Ommar guy?"

"On the record? One hundred percent positive."

"On, the Record?" Kurtis chimes in.

"That means off the record..." Tabatha adds.

"...It's not Ommar – at all," Pat finishes Tabatha's statement.

"He did possess some classified government information."

"Classified? Like what?" Tabatha asks.

"That's classified. This way." Pat guides them through the maze of hallways before leading them into a dark room with a large window as its centerpiece. The holding cell was brightly lit with a badly mangled looking individual in a wheelchair was in the center of the cell. But upon entering the darkroom, Tabatha's facial expression changes as to that of someone in some pain. She nearly collapses to the floor in agony, dropping her bag of chicken sandwiches.

"Tabatha!!" The Director shouts, concerned.

"What is this?" Pat says, just watching the show.

"Hold on, just a..." Tabatha responds, waiting for her telepathic equilibrium to adjust back into balance on its own. Analogically similar to that of blacking out and losing your balance, then regaining your balance again – only different. This occasionally happens when the psychic noise funneling into her mind is heavily inundated by physical and/or psychological emotions coming from another or several individuals. It doesn't often happen, however. "Whoa...I haven't felt that in a *very* long time. Ok, I'm good now. I'm good."

"Are you *sure?*" Pat asks, almost insultingly.

"Yes, I'm *sure*," Tabatha responds in like manner. "But this man is in serious, *excruciating* pain. Is there any way to get him some pain me-di-cine?" Tabatha interrupts herself as she picks up on a straightforward psychic voice. The clarity of the voice seemed to have been practiced.

"We don't have time..." the slurry almost automated sounding voice says.

Tabatha slowly turns and looks through the window at the individual in the cell. He is looking directly at her through the two-way mirror with his head tilted and laying slightly on his right shoulder. He indeed looked grotesque, much more so than the image on the tablet she viewed back in the D.C. hospital revealed.

"Can you read my thoughts?" Tabatha thought to herself, testing her assumption.

"I can read your thoughts – and you can read mine," he thinks to himself in like manner, confirming her assumption.

Tabatha takes a few deep breaths processing the overwhelming feeling that she's no longer the only one like herself.

"Now what?" Pat asks, observing Tabatha, acting oddly again. Tabatha holds her hand up toward Pat, signaling for him to be quiet, then slowly opens the door to the cell. She slips into the room quietly and slowly walks up in front of him, observing his physical condition while maintaining her composure. "Does she act like this all the time?" Pat asks the Kurtis.

"Ehh, more or less," Kurtis answers, shrugging his shoulders.

His head was still tilted as if he had no strength in his neck muscles to lift it up straight. His eyes followed her as she walked into the room. One eye was severely damaged as the pupil and retina were a milky grey color. The other eye looked to be normal. In fact, it was probably the only normal-looking part of his body. Tabatha noticed a scar on a portion of his throat that was sunk in. She remembered that the director said he had no vocal cords. However, it sparks a rather vague memory of someone else she recalled with a scar like that – herself, during some of her night terrors and daydreams.

One arm had a prosthetic limb. The other looked as though it needed one, but his hand still functioned slightly, enough to control his wheelchair via the joystick. Both legs had been amputated from just below the knee. His body had looked as though it had been badly burned. Other marks on his body indicated additional forms of injuries as well. He was filthy, and his clothing looked like old, worn, dirty rags that had been randomly placed on him. A stench seemed to follow the sweat out of his pores, though Tabatha wasn't even affected by the smell. Her preoccupation, with having for the first time met someone like her, overwhelmed any other sense.

"Tabatha," Director Kurtis speaks through the intercom. "Pull it together now. You got a job to do." Tabatha nods at the window, and a slight shift in her posture affirms that the same, as she collects her thoughts and begins asking questions.

"Are you Mohamed Ommar?"

"He is dead. His flesh, was surgically, grafted onto, my face to, resemble him."

"What's your name then?"

"I have, no name, only a number."

"Why was this done to you?"

"to get, your attention."

"I think you got a lot of people's attention."

"So have you."

Tabatha lightly nods in admission to the sudden onslaught of publicity she's gained the last couple of days. "Are there more like us?"

"I am, the last, but soon, you will be."

"What?!" Her response was laced with distraught.

Outside the cell Pat, having never witnessed Tabatha at work, aks Kurtis: "Is this normal?"

"Compared to what?" he replied.

"Please, I need, to give you, information, while there's, still time. He will soon, know you're, in my, presence. Then you will, see his, message."

"He? Who's he?"

"If there is, such a thing as, manifested evil, then he is, the creator, of it."

"Don't you mean *he* is manifested evil? I mean someone who could do something like this to you – is the evilest thing that I've encountered. And I've seen a lot of evil"

"No. He thinks he has, control of it." Images of a life filled with tortious experimental procedures played in his mind as he thought back on his existence. Tabatha watched the flashbacks like a time-lapse movie as his psychic voice narrated it. Many scenes contained images of death, while others were of machines and hardware.

"He in fact, controls it now, temporarily. When it's free, it will be, far worse than anything, conceivable."

"Does he know that you're giving me this information?"

"He has learned, how to manipulate, the telekinetic, component of, the psyche, because it interacts with, the material world, so it is, detectable. Thoughts transcend, the material, and so cannot be, manipulated, or detected, by machines."

"So, in other words, he doesn't know. "Ok, so now, what is *it?*"

"It is your, equal in power. The guns, won't stop it. Be ready for it. Thirty-six, years it has recorded, pain and hate. And it will use it, against everything, even you."

"Uhhh, I'm kinda feeling a little under pressure here," Tabatha responds, showing a slight sign of anxiousness and intimidation.

"When the message, is complete, I will be allowed, out of this, misery."

"What?! You mean you're going to die?" She shouts grievously.

"That doesn't sound good," Pat says to the Director.

"No, it doesn't," Kurtis agrees.

"Agony, has been everything, to me. I have been, kept alive, thirty-five years for use, of little more than, a lab rat. I...know nothing else, only pain, and suffering."

"No!! We can help you!!" Tabatha attempts to convince the poor man of an alternative but is unsuccessful.

"I agreed to, be the median for, his message, so I can finally rest, and..."

"No!! Please don't leave me!"

"...to save the world."

"Save the world? How are you supposed to do that when you're dead?" Tabatha says, still trying to convince him to let them help him.

"Information is like, a sword. I'm giving it, to you. Use it. Or don't. My hands, are clean, either way."

"What about..."

"SShhhh, he knows, you're here now, but one last thing, since he's learned, of your existence, he's wanted you. You will complete his work. Resist it."

"What? How did he..."

"...I told...him."

"Twenty four, are you broadcasting?" a new vivid image appears in *Not Ommar's* mind. It was a fabricated image being projected into his mind from an outside source. It was a familiar image of man – the man from her night terrors and days dreams.

"Ahhh, Tabatha, It's an honor to talk to you. You are an incredible individual." He begins his message with an accolade for Tabatha, but she doesn't accept it. "I'm sure *Twenty Three* gave you some information about me. Which was expected. He could never keep his mouth shut. So I took the liberty of making sure nothing could come out of it..."

"You son of a....."

"Tabatha!! Is everything alright?" Director Jackson asks through an intercom.

"Yes...Get ready to take down some information," Tabatha replies.

The shady individual inundating Twenty-Three's thoughts continued, "I'll make this quick for you. I've been eager to meet you after hearing about you. The fact that you are alive answers a plethora of questions for me. So thank you. You don't keep a shallow profile, that's for sure, hahaha. Which is ok, you shouldn't have to be forced to live in isolation, in fear of the world," as he continued, scenes of Tabatha's exploits and exposures over the last two years display in *Twenty Three's* mind for her to see. "But enough for now. I have someone incredibly important to introduce you to. Meet me here," an image of a dilapidated apartment complex appears. "Oh, and I'm a little temperamental, so, if you don't come within the next six hours, then I'll be forced to take my aggression out on these poor souls here." Images of random tied up and gaged individuals held up in separate, run-down apartment units within a dilapidated apartment complex by a multitude of hostiles – too many for her to get a count on through these images.

"Oh-my-goodness."

"Anytime now Tabatha," Pat shouts through the intercom as Director Jackson holds his small notebook and pen in hand, waiting for information from Tabatha.

"Oh, and one more thing, come alone. I would like our conversation to remain – confidential. I'm sure you understand what that means. If anyone else comes with you, you will be responsible for the consequences. *Twenty Three*, you are free to go," the message concludes, and the projected images disappear. Immediately *Twenty Three* begins shaking. His mouth opens as if attempting to scream. Steam rises off of his body.

"*Twenty Three*!?" Tabatha shouts.

Pat and the Director, both race inside the interrogation room, also observing the horrific scene. His skin begins bubbling as if being consumed by a flame.

"Do something!!!" Tabatha shouts, at both directors. Kurtis runs out of the room for help. Tabatha looks around the room and sees a fire sprinkler head on the ceiling and a small table in a corner. She races over, grabs the table, and slides it under the sprinkler head. She then reaches into Pats shirt, where she knew he had a cigarette lighter then jumped on the table, reaching up for sprinkler head.

"Tabatha, wait…!" Pat shouts, attempting to stop her, knowing that what she is about to do will be ineffective, but it was too late. She sparked the lighter under the sprinkler head, and immediately water gushed out. Simultaneously, the fire alarms around the whole building began screaming. Tabatha got off the table, and about the same time, Kurtis rushed back into the interrogation room, followed by two medics.

"What happened," Kurtis asks as water pours down on all of them.

Pat turns to Tabatha with a look of a rabid animal. "You incompetent woman!!!" He shouted as he was getting soaked. "You just set off the whole fire sprinkler system for nearly half of the entire building!!"

"Sorry. I was just – I thought..." Tabatha scrambles to string together an explanation of why she did what she did.

"Oh-my-gosh! Look," Director Jackson turns their attention to the charcoaled corpse in the electric wheelchair. Mostly scorched bone was all that was left of *Twenty Three*. Most of the water from the fire sprinkler instantly evaporated as it fell on his remains. The metal frame of the wheelchair had begun to melt as well.

"Mother of Jesus..." Pat responded to the morbid sight, astounded.

"How'd he spontaneously combust like that?" One of the two medics ask.

"I don't know. But his name was *Twenty Three*. And the man in his mind, well, I've seen him before," Tabatha answers, trying to wipe the water off her arms as it continues to pour on them.

"You have? Where?" asks Pat.

"My dreams?" Tabatha hesitantly answers, knowing how ridiculous it sounds to the C.I.A. director.

"You got to be kidding me," Pat responds, shaking his head. He turns his back toward Tabatha in disbelief and walks away from her talking to himself out of aggravation.

"Tabatha, what was this message? Did you get anything out of him?" Director Jackson asks, *believing* Tabatha.

Tabatha stares at the floor momentarily. She runs her fingers through her drenched hair then places her arms across her chest. "Yes..."

Lucas Gorton McIntire

CHAPTER XI

THE REUNION PART ONE

"Satellite infrared imaging confirms seventy-eight bodies in the complex, sir." An F.B.I. Terrorist task officer informs the head of the anti-terrorist division of the F.B.I. Brian Tamar.

Brian walks up the steel ramp and into the mobile com unit, followed by Director Jackson. The interior of the trailer was endowed with multiple computers and communications equipment. A different task officer manned each piece of equipment. A large monitor spanned the entire width of the trailer's back wall.

"Thank you, lieutenant. Push it thru to the big screen," Brian commands.

"That's a lot of bodies in that building," Kurtis comments on the images. "The question is, how we differentiate between the hostages and the terrorists," he asks.

"Captain Spencer's working on that. But my bigger question is – what's that?" Brian points to a heat signature that is far greater than any of the other independent heat signatures within the satellite image.

"Sirs, it seems to be a generator of some sort," the task officer guesses based on the coloration of the heat signature.

"I've never seen a generator move like this," director Jackson adds.

"Didn't you say Tabatha mentioned something about a machine that, that Twenty-Three character described as being pretty nasty?" Brian reminds Kurtis. Kurtis lightly nods. "You better go get your girl Director," Brian strongly suggests to Kurtis.

"She's in the second mobile unit changing and having new dressings placed on her wound by the two experts," Kurtis says referring to David and Rodney. Kyle, his wife Cindy, along with the *Seven,* was also in the second unit with Tabatha.

"Directors!!" another law enforcement official shouts from outside the mobile unit. "We may need some more officers to secure the blockades. The crowds are becoming more aggressive. More have been pelleted after jumping the barricade!!" He informs Brian and Kurtis.

"It took only three days for your girl to get the whole country into a frenzy since her public, mishaps went viral. That has to be a record." Brian remarks to Kurtis.

Kurtis and Brian walk out to observe the hundreds of people along the outside of the wooden barricades that circled the abandoned apartment complex. The decades-old towering complex sat in the center of an entire city block. Many of its windows had long since been busted out, and the front doors have been unsecured for years. The building could have very well been acquired for theatrical use in a horror movie. However, it did attract many of the cities' poverty-stricken citizens as an unofficial homeless shelter during the more extreme seasons – which was the main reason the city left it standing. However, the eyesore of the dilapidated building in the center of a busy metropolitan area has since lead the city council on agreeing to the demolition of the building to create a new future public park. If they're lucky, Tabatha will tear it down for free.

"Go get every available officer in riot control gear down here to reinforce for the blockade," Brian orders. Most of the spectators at the front of the blockade were half hanging over the wooden barricades. He pulls a two-way transceiver from his pocket. "Captain Spencer, come in," he calls.

"You think we might need the National Guard?" Kurtis asks Brian.

"I requested that as a last resort. I have to use all the district's law enforcement resources before the mayor okays that move. And hopefully, Captain Spencer should be about done getting his men in position," Brian answers.

"Spencer here," a voice comes through Brian's' transceiver.

"How're we looking on the breach?" Brian asks.

"We're just about set. The buildings surrounding the apartment complex have all been evacuated. I have forty snipers with thirty targets in sight – all on the top floor. It's a good thing our bad guys aren't keen on hiding." The directors glance at each with a concerned look after hearing that last statement.

"How about the hostage situation?" Brian again asks.

"Forty-eight hostages identified. They've been divided up into groups of four and being held in twelve separate units. Most of the units have two bad guys. Some have three."

"Ok. How about resistance and extraction contingencies?"

"I have fifteen angels on the roof," Spencer replies in reference to the part of his tactical team, currently positioned on the roof of the apartment complex. "Once the snipers let'm rip, the angels will repel into the units through the windows to isolate any additional threats and protect the hostages," he continues, "Then I'll lead my ground team up to extract the hostages. In fact, I'm heading your way right now to get them ready. These terrorists are about to get the parade of their lives."

"Famous last words of a trigger happy hothead," Kurtis comments. "How did he get to be captain of the SWAT again?"

"His uncle works for the Pentagon. Don't ask," Brian replies. "His only strategy – make lots of noise and overwhelm the target," he adds.

"Hmmm, I have to admit, the 'overwhelming' aspect of his strategy seems to be put together well."

"Spencer, And don't forget, Tabatha's going with you – to find out who this orchestrating mad man is," Brian reminds Captain Spencer, who has an irrational antipathy toward Tabatha that's spawned primarily from two facts, one of which is the not so subtle fact that he craves the spotlight, and feels now that he is competing with Tabatha for it, to which Tabatha could care less.

"Please don't remind me. I'm still in protest of – her existence," Spencer responds.

"Yeah, well, you'll get over it. Let's hurry it up now. It's getting close to seven pm, and we have about two hours remaining."

"Yes, sir. Over and out," Spencer concludes.

"At least it was nice of Virginia's governor to lend us some extra bodies for this," Kurtis adds, then turns and grabs the attention of another officer outside the mobile com unit. "Send someone to see if Tabatha's ready."

"Don't Bother!!" Tabatha informs while rounding the corner of the mobile unit then walking up the ramp. "I'm here." The *Seven* were behind her, and they stayed on the ground next to the com unit.

"Took you long enough. What in the world are you wearing," Kurtis asks, not sure whether to laugh or to compliment her ability to adapt to any type of clothing thrown at her.

"Love you too, Director. I mean, sirrrr," Tabatha sarcastically responds. "Oh, and this was the only thing anybody could find for me to wear. So, yeah, I know I look ridiculous," she agrees with the director.

Tabatha had changed from her water-saturated clothing into an extra-extra-large, grey, fire retardant, full-body jumpsuit, the only piece of clothing available in the unit. Though she was able to modify the oversized outfit applying a back brace around her torso and the use of long PVC gloves, tall boots and a looooooooot of black duct tape to keep the extra material of the outfit tucked in and close to her body as to not restrain her physical flexibility and agility – if the situation called for those attributes.

"Aaaactually," A lieutenant manning one of the communication terminals in the mobile com unit speaks up, "...I think you look really good – almost like a super...."

"...Don't you say it!!!" Tabatha interrupts the lieutenants having telepathically deducted his statement with a finger pointed at him like a mother lecturing a two-year-old. "You finish that statement, and I'll tell your kid that *you* were one the one dressed up as Santa Clause last Christmas," she threatens.

"Yes sir, or ma'am, or a – sorry," the lieutenant responds and quickly turns back to his work, slightly embarrassed.

"Santa Clause? That's the best you could come up with," director Jackson leans over and whispers to Tabatha.

"Ehhh, it was the first thing I could find that fast," she admits.

"Hmmm."

"Alright, Tabatha, what do you make of this?" Brian redirects the conversation back to the situation at hand. He points her to the infrared satellite feed on the monitor, and more directly to the high output infrared image, the directors were questioning.

"It looks like something that's consuming a lot of energy. But it's not radiating the energy it's consuming, like the other body heat signatures. It must be encased in something," she suggests

"We were thinking it may be that machine your Twenty-Three friend was describing," Brian also suggests.

"Right, Twenty-Three." Tabatha has a couple of split-second flashbacks of Twenty-Three, reminding her that she wasn't the only one like her for a moment. "Well, it could be." She looks at the image in question closer, watching the fluidity of its movements.

"What's your opinion of it?" director Jackson asks.

Tabatha takes a deep breath. "Honestly, I'm not a hundred percent sure that *It* is a machine," she answers, then turns to the directors. "Or at least all of it," she continues, to which the occupants of the mobile unit gaze at her confused and in need of some clarification. "Oh, come on. Haven't any of you watched Robocop? Only this would be like Robocop's evil cousin or something," she attempts to illustrate her ultra-vague theory.

"So you're saying you think it's a machine with the brain of a human?" Brian summarizes.

"Ha-ha, yeah, that does sound pretty nuts," Tabatha admits. "But you guys wanted to know what I think. And I have no clue what this is. But I guess I'll find out shortly," she adds. "Oh, and I have to say, I *really* don't feel comfortable doing this with so many people." Tabatha continues.

"Either do I!!" Captain Spencer shouts into the mobile unit.

Tabatha ignores Spencer and explains her position on the matter. "This, man, he specifically said he wanted to talk to me, alone. And that he set this whole elaborate scheme up so that I *would* come by myself." She explains.

"You got to be kidding me!!" Spencer jumps in. "I have nearly a hundred tactical officers ready to swarm all over these guys."

Tabatha continues to ignore the hot head and talks specifically to the directors. "Think about it. There's no threat of a bomb in this scenario. We don't even know where this man is in the building. And as far as this thing right here is concerned," she points to the high output infrared image that the current consensus is that it's a walking generator "...It could very well be a trap." The Directors begin considering Tabatha's position.

"You're not taking her seriously, are you?" Spencer exclaims, temperamentally.

"Furthermore, I can't even create a hive connection with anyone in that building. I've been attempting to over the last couple of hours. The best I can get are vague images. And they are not normal images either. No one holds on a single mental image, consistently, for hours like that. And they're all the same." Tabatha concludes her point, continuing to ignore Spencer.

"Or maybe your *stuff* just isn't working as it used. Retirements always an option," Spencer says, instigating Tabatha. "In fact, I vote to keep her pretty little face out of my way," Captain Spencer shouts into the mobile unit.

"Awe!! You think I'm pretty? That's so sweet of you," Tabatha, having had enough of Spencer's mouth, finally begins retaliating against his antagonistic comments.

"Alright, Captain Spencer, that's enough. How are things looking?" Brian asks the special weapons and tactics unit captain.

"Things would be looking better if I didn't have to concern my forces with babysitting,"

"Well, maybe you can stay out here and guard the coffee machine, then your team won't have to worry about babysitting anybody," she continues her witty verbal defense.

"OK, YOU TWO!! WE GOT IT!! You don't like each other!! But this is how it's going to go. Get over it!!" Brian demands.

"Sir," Spencer says softly, signaling for Brian to come down closer to him so Tabatha won't hear his explanation as to why he believes she shouldn't go into the building with him and his S.W.A.T. team. The *Seven*, still standing next to the mobile unit and within earshot of Spencer, eavesdrop on his insults of Tabatha, which start making their blood boil. "...And furthermore, she's done nothing but screw things up when she's out in the field..." Spencer is finally interrupted by Hammer, who had enough and walked up to the S.W.A.T. captain.

"Let me tell you something!! She has taken out more terrorists than any of us have in the last two years!!"

"Well, then I guess I'd be questioning how the T.I.D.s' *elite Seven* even got *on* the team if some *woman*, who spends most of her time cleaning up her own messes, has to take care of you all simultaneously!!" Spencer instigates.

"You little..." Hammer approaches the Captain with a righteous malice intent after those words. The other six also angered at the words, walked up behind Hammer. Spencer puffed his chest out and balled his fists.

"HAMMER!! STAND DOWN!!" director Jackson shouts, attempting to disarm the conflict.

"SPENCER!! YOU TOO!!" Brian commands, following Kurtis' lead.

"Ham-ham!! It's ok." Tabatha says from the top of the mobile units' ramp, calming Hammer down, and the rest of her team. She walks down the ramp in an almost provocative way. "Those are just empty words he's belligerently spewing." Spencer catches the outer rim of Tabatha's retina illuminate as she approaches him. Simultaneously, nobody notices the infrared image of the object previously being pondered on the monitor in the com unit was changing in intensity.

"Stay away from me!!" Spencer cautiously orders her, to which she ignores and moves closer. He takes a few steps backward as she approached him.

"Why?" Don't you like me?" She takes another step toward him. "You know what it really is? You're *afraid* – of me!!" She reveals his second irrational antipathy toward her, in an almost vicious voice. She sporadically raises her left arm, appearing at first as if she was going to strike him violently across his skull but instead softly places her index finger on his temple.

Meanwhile, the dramatic change in the infrared image, and that the video feed was becoming distorted with static as well.

"And you should be – so very afraid. Because I can get in here," Tabatha runs her finger slowly from Spencer's temple along the rim of his head and then down behind his ear. The feeling of something like a liquid begins following her finger within his skull. His jaw drops and eyes widen. His head tilts back almost like in pain, though he wasn't. His breathing becomes anxious.

"Tabatha, I think that's enough," Brian tries to get her attention. But his words don't make it to her ear.

"Oh, you do like me, and several others. Does your wife know about them?" Tabatha leans in and whispers his own dark secrets that he thought were hidden from the world.

"N-n-n-noooo," Spencer answers, struggling to get the word out. "P-p-pleeeasse."

"Oh, what's this?" Tabatha whispers in a slow and seductively becoming voice as she divulges more secrets. "You know, I could ruin your life. You're an evil person. But you know that already, don't you?"

"Yyyyeeessss."

"What do you have to say about your bad behavior?"

"I-I-I-I'mmmm....s-s-sssooorrryyy." Spencer backbends and his knees begin to buckle as if a heavy object was beginning to push him down. Tabatha leans forward mirroring his compressing body."

"I don't believe you." She continues whispering softly as Spencer collapses completely to his knees. "There, I think that's a better position to ask for forgiveness."

"Tabatha!! That's enough!!" Director Jackson shouts.

"Tabatha!!" Brian adds.

"Princess," Mitchell walks toward her and reaches her hand out to grab her shoulder and pull her hand off of Spencer. "Come on, girl, that's – Ooouuch!!" Before he could even touch her his hand was nearly burned.

"What happened?!" Kurtis exclaims.

"Something burnt my hand!" They looked at Mitchells' hand. It was red and some steam rose from it for a second, but he had pulled it back before it became a severe burn. The directors, the Seven, and many from the SWAT team began shouting at Tabatha, trying to get her attention and to let go of Spencer, but it was as if she couldn't hear them.

"Now, go ahead," Tabatha continues her mind torcher on Spencer with her provocative voice. "Repent, to, *Me*."

"H-h-h-hooowww?" He asks on his knees. She moves her finger to the top of his head and lays her hand flat over it.

"Start by...." She stands up straight with her hand on Spencer's head like a tyrant queen sentencing a peasant thief to a guillotine. Her voice then changes from the seductive and soft tone to a vicious scream that her face mirrors with the expression of aggression. "*BEGGING*!!" Her final word reverberated through the air with a blood-curdling echo that pierced the auditory senses of every mind within a block radius. Then there was a hush in the air. Even the spectators had quieted.

A voice manages to break through to her ear. She felt a hand on her left shoulder. Her surroundings became clear to her again. Shaking her head and blinking a couple of times brought her back to her normal senses. She pulled her hand off of Spencer and looked at the hand on her arm. It was red steaming and blistering.

She turned and saw that it was Kyle. After hearing the commotion outside the mobile unit that he, Cindy, and David were ordered to remain in, the spiritual leader surmised that something evil had taken her mind hostage. Therefore he had gone out to Tabatha, taking it upon himself to shake her out of whatever bondage she fell victim to. Which Pastor Reed believed could only be accomplished by injecting the name of God into the situation. So he suffered his hand to place it on her and pray for her to be released from whatever was causing her to act unlike herself.

"Kyle!! Oh-my-gosh!! Your hand! I'm so sorry!! I don't know what came over me," Tabatha exclaims, shocked at what she did.

"It's okay," Kyle responds, in pain. David then rushed out to tend to Kyle's hand.

"Tab, are you alright? Are you back to, you now??" Hammer asks.

"Uhhh, yeah. I think so," she answers.

Kurtis then approaches her to check on her. "Really director, I'm fine. I don't know what came over me. I just suddenly felt a sense of immense rage – out of nowhere," Tabatha explains to him.

Next, Rodney approaches Tabatha to check on her as well, concerned that she may be weak and out of energy. "How are you feeling?" He asks.

"Honestly? I feel amazing – physically. I feel like I could take on a triathlon – four times in a row."

Rodney checks her temperature, which was her normal ninety-nine point seven degrees. No sweat, no blood on her forehead from busted capillaries, completely alert – well, Tabatha's version of being alert.

"Well, normally I'd say this is a good thing, but under the circumstances, it's making me wonder a few things," Rodney says, concerned about one; what caused her to act as she did, and two; how her body remained functioning normally when these types of activities usually cause her to become weak and disoriented.

Tabatha made a three-sixty observation of her surroundings. The contour of her face shifted as she could pick up on the many thoughts surrounding her.

"What's the matter?" Rodney notices the shift.

"They're almost *all* afraid of me," she explains.

"Don't focus on them, here, can you feel what I'm feeling?" Rodney tries to be consoling.

"Ha-ha, yeah," Tabatha laughs softly.

"What's funny," Rodney asks, smiling, thinking he made her feel better.

"You're afraid of me too," she explains, then walks over to the *Seven*, leaving Rodney standing there contemplating what she said.

Captain Spencer was still on the ground in shock, dealing with the emotions of all the thoughts that Tabatha brought to the forefront of his mind. Brian ran over to get him on his feet.

"Captain Spencer, you alright?" Brian asks, not necessarily pitying him. Spencer comes back to his senses and gets back on his feet. A swell of anger over the incident crept upon him again and turned toward Tabatha.

"YOU CRAZY WOMAN!! STAY OUT OF MY HEAD!!" Spencer shouts toward Tabatha, followed by an immediate smack to his face from Brian.

"You know, hot head, I don't necessarily blame her for that. Now get your team together and get moving."

"Yes, sir!!" Spencer responds.

"I may have *slightly* deserved that," Tabatha admits. However, the Seven felt a little justification on Tabatha's behalf, watching Brian slap Spencer. "Besides, you guys think I'm crazy most of the time, too," she says.

"Well, that's a different type of crazy," they explain.

"Right," Tabatha says, then winking at them before walking back up into the mobile com unit. She finds and straps on a shoulder harness and places a nine millimeter in the holster under her left arm.

"Are you going to be ok using that? With your shoulder the way it is?" Kurtis asks.

"It honestly feels a lot better. Just a little sore still."

"You seem to be recovering from that faster than you normally would. Even with your super-molecular remedial capacity." Kurtis responds, referencing her above-average healing capability – an additional attribute her hypermetabolic condition enables. Not to be confused with the uncanny super healing features of a certain unnamed man, endowed with a metallic skeleton and adamantium claws – Tabatha wishes a gunshot wound would heal that fast.

"I'm sure there's an explanation for that too. But I better get going. Hothead is getting impatient," Tabatha agrees as she puts two magazines in her right pocket and a transceiver in her left. She then leaves the trailer to meet with Spencer and his S.W.A.T. team.

Walking down the ramp, she is met by an older man with white hair, a white mustache, and goatee and wearing a white suit at the bottom of the ramp. "Tabatha," he says. "I need to talk to you."

"Well, sir, if you haven't noticed, we're dealing with a slight crisis at the moment," she responds, not giving him much attention. She spots Spencer waiting for her. She points to her wrist, signaling to 'get on with it.' Spencer rolls his eyes then lifts up his transceiver to his mouth.

"Alright, take 'em out," Spencer orders. The snipers simultaneously take out their targets. Immediately after, the angels repel from the roof of the apartment complex and into the units. An eerie silence envelopes the area. "Ok, tell me something!" He exclaims through the device.

A few seconds pass then, "S-s-s-seec-c-currre." Brian, who was standing with Spencer, was unconvinced at the eerie response through the receiver, but Spencer didn't second guess.

"Tabatha!! Let's go!!" He shouts at her.

"Wait, Tabatha, don't go in there," the man in the white suit says to her again.

"Listen, you can send your hate mail to the FBI headquarters, attention Tabatha. I'm pretty sure you can google the address," she responds as she walks off.

"Tabatha!!" The man in the white suit again tries to get her attention. She turns around, glancing at him, frustrated. "Don't put all your trust in this," he concludes, pointing at his head, accepting the fact she's not going to listen to him at this particular moment.

"I'll keep that in mind," she says, contemplating the odd statement to herself,

"Tabatha!!! Hustle!!!" Spencer yells, grabbing her attention to which she runs toward the entrance of the apartment complex, disappearing into the building with Spencer and his S.W.A.T. team.

"Director Kurtis Jackson?"

The Director turns to find the man that attempted to convince Tabatha not to go into the building, and instantly recognized him. He immediately knew something was very wrong if this man was present. "If you're here, this can't be a good thing," Kurtis says, with an even more heightened sense of concern.

Mitchell, being a tech enthusiast, had made his way up into the mobile com unit to check out all the gadgets. He noticed the infrared images on the large monitor. The high output infrared image the point of discussion earlier was still there but struck him as slightly familiar.

"Hey!!!" Mitchell shouts, getting everyone's attention. "Has anyone ever looked at Tabatha through infrared lenses while she's using her – thing?" He asks.

The director rushed into the unit and looked at the image closely. "That's not a machine at all. Is that who I think it is?" The Director asks the man in the white suit.

"Yes."

Kurtis runs out to Brian. "Get everyone out of there double time!!"

"Why? What's wrong?"

"Just do it!!"

"Captain Spencer!!" Brian calls through the transceiver.

Inside the Complex – the rundown lobby was huge. To the left was what used to be a receptionist's desk. On the other side of the lobby, stairs led up to the housing unit levels. Toward the back of the lobby were three elevators. A light illuminated one set of buttons associated with the middle lift, which indicates that the elevator was operational. However, the other two elevators were not functional. The SWAT began slowly ascending the stairs. Tabatha, being impatient, walked toward the elevators.

"Tabatha!!!" Spencer softly yells at Tabatha.

"The elevator will be faster." She responds. "Oh, and why are you trying to whisper? As much noise as you've made putting this whole thing together, whoever is in this building, trust me, they know we're here. Excellent strategy."

"Tabatha, the elevator probably doesn't even work."

"Ding!" The middle elevator doors open seconds after Tabatha presses the illuminated 'up' button. It was dirty, but the interior light was on and looked intact. She looked around the elevator real quick then responded to Spencer.

"It looks ok." Then she walks in. "I'll see yawl up there, in, what, twenty minutes?" She says rhetorically.

"Tabatha!! Wait!!" He yells one last time, as he watches her blow him a kiss as the doors shut. "Ohh, I *hate* that woman!!" Spencer shouts.

Back outside, "I can't reach Spencer or Tabatha. Someone keeps repeating 'secure' after every time I speak into." Brian explains.

"Hammer, Mitchell, Steve and the rest of you, go get our girl out of there, I think she's way over her head," Kurtis orders.

"Are you serious?! When she's with like fifty members of the SWAT team," TK reminds him.

"I don't care. You seven are the top dogs in this arena. Now, get moving!!" Kurtis orders. The Seven run into the mobile com unit and collect all the ammo, guns, and equipment that they can find – which wasn't much. They rush out of the com unit and disappear into the building as the steel doors slam closed behind them.

"Ok, now, you…" Kurtis turns his attention to the man in the white suit. Brian Tamar was also eager for many explanations. "You have some explaining to do. Now, let's hear it."

Lucas Gorton McIntire

Chapter XII

THE REUNION PART TWO

"Ding!" The middle elevator stops at the top floor of the apartment complex. The doors open. Tabatha steps out of the elevator. Immediately the lights in the elevator flicker and go out, while the elevator doors remain open.

"Well, that's not at all creepy," Tabatha says to herself. She was at an intersection of two hallways that connected like a 'T.' She looks down the hall to her right, then to her left, then down the hallway directly in front of her. She tilts her head and stares into space, continuing in her attempt to receive telepathic information of the occupants in the building for a moment – but, still nothing.

"For over a hundred people in this building, it sure is quiet," Tabatha continues talking to herself, contemplating the possible reasoning behind the fact. The eeriness of the situation causes her to pull the gun out the holster under her left arm. She disengages the magazine, inspects it, then slaps it back in the gun and places it back in her holster.

"Ok, eenie, meanie, minie, moe…" Tabatha incorporates a highly sophisticated decision-making method – from her childhood – to help her decide which hall to go down first, which ends up being the hall straight in front of her. The moment of creepy elevator behavior had passed, so Tabatha started down the hall nonchalantly without a worry.

The carpet was destroyed, having stains and being ripped in many places exposing some of the floorboards. Old dolls, action figures, plastic golf balls, and other old toys along with torn up clothes and other miscellaneous objects scattered the hallways. Most of the faded paint on the walls had peeled off. Some of the hallway lights above the unit doorways were on but very were very dim. Some of the doors to the apartment units were open, which allowed some of what little daylight was left, coming into the units to shine into the hallway.

"Holy cow Spencer. I thought I was only joking when I said it would take you twenty minutes," Tabatha again says to herself, wondering why it's taking him and team so long to get up the top floor. She comes to the end of that hallway, which intersected with another hall. She again looks both ways, then sees a lit 'exit' sign at the end of one corridor and heads that direction.

Tabatha arrives at the exit sign. It's the staircase that Captain Spencer and his S.W.A.T. team should have ascended to. "YO!! HOT HEAD!!" Tabatha yells down the stairs." She waits a couple of seconds for a response, but nothing. She pulls her two-way transceiver out of her pocket. "Captain Spencer, this is your conscience speaking. Where are you?" Tabatha says with her usual sarcasm expecting an answer, which there was after several seconds passed.

"S-s-seeec-c-u-urrre…"

"Listen, I know you're all butt-hurt about what I did, I feel terrible, well, at least a little."

"S-s-seeec-c-u-urrre…" the same voice comes through the receiver a few seconds later.

"Come in, Director, it's Tabatha," she waits for an answer, and a few seconds later…

"S-s-seeec-c-u-urrre…"

"Brian??!!"

"S-s-seeec-c-u-urrre…"

"Santa Clause??!!" She rhetorically says out of frustration.

"S-s-seeec-c-u-urrre…"

"Bla-Bla-bla-bla – you're becoming a *secure* pain in my butt," she, again, says to herself then tosses her transceiver over her shoulder behind her. She then sensed something moving behind her and immediately drew her gun and turned around. She was shocked at the sight of objects floating around her. Pieces of torn up carpet, broken fragments of wood, etc. They seemed to have formed a circle around her. She reached out to grab an old plastic toy golf ball that was also floating around her. However, it repelled away from her while maintaining the same distance from her as she moved. All the objects acted in like manner.

"Oh-My. This is, uhhh, why do you keep talking to yourself, Tabatha?" She again says – to herself – as she slowly puts her gun back in her holster.

As she attempts to wrap her mind around what's going on, she recalls Rodney's theory, from a few days previous, about the possibility that her telepathy might be enhancing to incorporate telekinetic attributes.

"Telekinesis," she says. She moves her hands back and forth, up and down, moving the objects around in the air, without touching them.

Amid all the fun, a clear telepathic image forms in her mind from someone in the apartment unit behind her. Her attention is instantly drawn to it, and the objects around her fall to the ground. She notices the activity of the falling objects but pays little attention to it. She pulls her gun out and as quietly as possible and cocks it. The telepathic image depicted two hostiles holding four hostages, just as Spencer's intel had noted as well as the infrared images shown in the mobile communications.

She holds up the gun with both hands, looking through the site of the weapon. She positioned herself right outside the door of the unit, then kicks it open and runs into the apartment. But nobody was there, and the image was gone. She lowered the gun. A confused look broadcast across her face. Then she noticed an odor like burning meat. In the last bedroom, a window had been shattered from the outside. A black rope was hanging from the outside of the building, coming in through the window and fastened to a burned-up corpse under the window. The body was wearing SWAT gear. It was one of the fifteen 'angels.' The sight, which generally wouldn't have caused much alarm, having seen dead bodies numerous times in her life, however, since nothing was making sense at the moment, she was beginning to become anxious. She suddenly remembered the words of the man in the white suit just before she entered the building.

"Don't put all my trust in this." She closed her eyes and took a deep breath and said, "Lord, please give me strength." Then, with her gun still in hand, she swiftly leaves the bedroom. Since her telepathy at this point has become unreliable, she reverts to more natural tactics as she looks around corners. She exits the apartment unit and picks up the two-way transceiver that she tossed on the floor a little earlier.

"Somebody, anybody, can you hear me – please – this is Tabatha," she quietly says through the radio.

"S-s-seeec-c-u-urrre."

She puts the transceiver back in her pocket and on a hunch that the rest of the 'angels' suffered the same fate, went into the next apartment. After searching it, her suspicion was confirmed, as another burned up 'angel,' still attached to the rope he had swung in on, was lying on top of the broken glass – dead. She quickly left that apartment unit and went into the next to find the same thing. After that, there was no reason to go into each apartment unit; inevitably, they all met the same fate. At this point, Tabatha decides it's time to go. After exiting the third apartment unit, she placed the gun in her holster and sprints down the hall toward the intersection that led back to the elevators, of which she forgot didn't work. As she approached her turn, a voice on her transceiver came through.

"Tabatha! Tabatha! This is Director Jackson. If you can hear me, get out of the building immediately!!"

"No kidding," she says to herself as she turns the corner, but then stops immediately. "We think that this whole scheme is a set up to trap you!" the director concludes.

"Now, you tell me." She says to herself as she faces a figure at the other end of the hall.

The figure standing in front of the elevators was a woman. Her entire body was covered with a blue-tinted material in which the reflective sheen of the material gave her the appearance of being made of plastic – like that of a life-sized Barbie doll – except for a contraption over the lower half of her face, in which the shape somewhat resembled a respirator mask, hid nose, mouth, chin, and neck. She stood perfectly straight. Her eyes were wide opened, bloodshot, and glazed over, and they were intensely fixed on Tabatha. Her hair was matted as if it had never been brushed or maintained, let alone ever cut in her life. Her hair was as nearly as long as she was tall.

Strapped to her back, and mostly covered by her thick raggedy hair, was a small portable generator that, at first glance, could have potentially resembled that of an 'unlicensed nuclear accelerator,' designed to catch ghosts – if ghosts could be caught. Attached to both sides of the compact mobile generator were canisters filled with a yellow fluid. Tubes ran from the top of the canisters and into the mask she was wearing. A large power cable encased in an aluminum braided protectant ran from the top of the small generator to the base of her head.

The sensation of vulnerability arouses a shift in Tabatha's respiration, reflecting a new and profound feeling of anxiety that is foreign to her normal senses, as a result of her primary asset being compromised. "Ok, a woman in a latex suit means – what?" Tabatha says to herself contemplating the scene, as she is unable to get a telepathic reading from the mysterious individual.

"Hey! Are you alrig...!" Tabatha barely gets a few words out of her mouth, directed at the figure before a blast of intense heat barrels towards her. Visibly detectable only by the incandescence distorting the air. The unexpectant attack left Tabatha with just enough time to respond by which she merely, autonomously covering her face with her arms. She felt an initial blast of heat before a spectacular display of multi-colored flames circled her for a brief moment then vanishing.

She hesitantly lowers her arms, now even more anxious while continuing attempting to process what's going on while also being on guard. The heat blast left a trail of burnt residue consisting of hot ash embers in a straight line down the center of the hallway floor then dividing into two trails just inches away from Tabatha's position circling her. A steady current of steam rose from the charred floor and walls. Making a quick observation around her, she saw the walls next to her were also charred as well. Following the unexpected attack, she also observed the strange phenomena of floating objects once again revolving around her.

"Wait!! Who are you?!" Tabatha attempts to dialogue, taking a few steps closer before another attack in the same manner engages. This time two blasts back to back come at Tabatha, to which she tucks her head between her shoulders and crosses her arms in front of her face and torso again. Another spectacular light show circles her then vanishes. The trail of embers widened, and the walls next to her further burnt, revealing the studs behind the drywall. Her heart was beating heavily at this point and the floating objects seemed to vibrate with each beat of her heart, creating a lite ripple effect in the atmosphere directly around her.

"STOP!! I DON'T WANT TO DO THIS!!" She again shouts. But a third attack comes at Tabatha with even more ferocity, causing Tabatha to hide behind her arms yet again. This time an endless stream of smoldering heat and purple and blue flames were shooting up from the center of the floor and down from the center of the ceiling. Tabatha was encased in a brilliant circle of colors as the intense heat continually slammed into whatever was protecting Tabatha. As the relentless attack persisted against Tabatha, the ceiling, walls, doors, began bursting into flames. Tabatha, unable to get any response from the mysterious firewoman, starts becoming indignant of her current circumstances.

"EEEEEEHHHH!" Tabatha exhales, beginning to buckle under the pressure. An illumination circles the rim of her retina. "SSTOOOOOP!!" in a swell of rage, she thrusts her arms out. Immediately an intense pressure sends the spectacular light show around Tabatha along with every object in the path of the anomaly into the mysterious firewoman, in turn, sending her crashing into a section between two of the elevators behind her. The mystery woman drops to the ground on her bottom, her head fallen back against the wall and her arms rested, limping to her sides, with the appearance of full-body paralysis or even death.

Tabatha sprints down the hall toward the, now, disabled hostile. She pulls her gun out of the holster and cocks it and aims at the woman covered in charred and molten debris, and especially – hair - inspecting the scene on high alert. The elevator doors were violently inwards from supernatural retaliation, revealing elevator cables and shafts.

"Tabatha!" A deep, rugged voice invades Tabatha's auditory system, causing a chill to run down her spine. With her gun still in hand, she looks around and finds another mysterious figure at the other end of the hallway. She looked identical to the woman that Tabatha just subdued – or so she thought. Tabatha looked back at the wall between the elevators and saw only debris, pieces of wall, charred doors, but no mysterious woman. "You're an incredible creature. It's a shame they've had to hide you for so long." Tabatha turned back to the other end of the hall just as a towering man rounded the corner and stopping next to the mysterious woman. A towering man stood at the other end of the hallway, which she had come. His face, though not very clear, was familiar.

Getting control of her emotions, she points to where the mysterious woman standing next to this new figure is supposed to be. "How....?!" She then asks.

"Twenty-Four here, not unlike yourself, has an extraordinary gift!" he begins to explain. "She can access the visual and auditory system of the human brain and fabricate images and sounds. She can also implant thoughts and ideas into the mind as well. She's amplifying my voice into your head read now."

"Can you stop with the voice amplifying thing?"

He then bends over and whispers into the mystery woman's ear then responds to Tabatha - naturally, "Is this more tolerable for you?"

"Much more. Sooo, you're talking about mind control?" Tabatha interprets the man's previous statement.

"Ha-ha-ha!! It's impossible to override the freewill element of any person," he corrects Tabatha on her assumption.

"I don't know. If you can get into someone's head like that, it qualifies as mind control in my opinion," Tabatha explains her reasoning.

"Tell me, does a great orator not influence the mind through articulate words and impressive speech? Even that can be construed as a *psychic* gift to an extent. The human mind is highly suggestive," the man rebuttals.

"What I just saw was *far more* than *suggestive*," Tabatha rebuttals as she slowly walks back down the hallway toward the two individuals, focusing more on the mysterious woman standing in the same offensive stance Tabatha saw earlier. She still had a glazed look over her eyes as if she was zoned out.

"What just happened was real. I wasn't completely sure what you were capable of, so, to keep *her* safe, I instructed *her* to project herself into your mind. More specifically, your visual sensory system. However, the heat was real. And your retaliation was also real," he further explains.

"Hmmm, so, mind control." Tabatha doesn't budge from her interpretation.

The creepy man begins getting frustrated with Tabatha's resistance to see the situation from his perspective. "You have an amazing gift, Tabatha. Tell me, is it mind control when you reveal one's own hidden secrets in order to manipulate an individual's behavior?"

"First of all, that would be no worse than someone gaining tangible information about another individual to blackmail that person. Secondly, I *choose not* to use my telepathy for those purposes," she further articulates her perspective as she continues walking toward them, slowly.

"Unfortunately, you don't use your gift to its' full potential," the man manipulatively turns the conversation slightly.

"Maybe. But it's more important to me that *everyone* has the freedom to live to *their* full potential. Free from the fear of this kind of cognitive manipulation."

"Fear? Have you not heard the ranting about you since what you can do has become public? They are *afraid* – Of you."

Tabatha considers the truth in his last statement before responding. "Yes, they are. Right now. But I guess that provides me with an opportunity to give them a *reason* not to be afraid of me."

"Are you mad?! They're spitting at you, when they should be worshipping you, worshiping both of you!" He exclaims.

"What!!?" Tabatha says, almost wanting to laugh at his comment. "If anyone is mad in here, it's got to be you."

"Tabatha, the powerful are made to create order. Made to lead the weaker. Made to – dominate."

"That sounds like a pretty intimidating job honestly. I don't even have a degree in business administration, so I think I'm out on the whole *domination* thing," Tabatha says, injecting some sarcasm as the lengthy dialogue starts boring her. "Of course, your statement does prompt a rather significant question for me. If the powerful are made to *lead* and *dominate*, then who made the powerful?"

"That *is* the question. It would have to be someone with vision. Someone with the fortitude and relentless motivation to do whatever it takes to create order."

"Uh-hu. So, in other words, a few individuals create and control a small minority of powerful in order to subjugate the majority. Actually, it sounds like modern-day bad politics to be honest," Tabatha illustrates her interpretation of his message back to him. "In fact, by the looks of your relationship with *pyro-chick* there, it appears that you're the one pulling strings. I can tell from here, that she's under the influence of something heavy So your whole lecture referring to us as dominating leaders and being worshiped like gods, is pure bloviated hot air, and it's the really smelly, stinky kind of hot air too. It makes me want to vomit. It's just..."

"ENOUGH!!!" He shouts both verbally and psychically via the mystery woman as his temper wears thin. He again whispers something to the mystery woman. Tabatha's gun, which she was still holding, begins smoldering. She drops it just before completely burning through her glove. The gun landed on the floor, partially melted. The unanticipated event refueled her anxiety, awakening the eerie phenomena around her once more.

"It's incredible!!"

"Yeah, you said that before."

"You are more powerful than you can comprehend. Twenty-Four here can remotely interact with molecules in the air and inside objects causing them to vibrate and create heat at varying intensities instantaneously – as you have witnessed."

"Right," Tabatha acknowledging.

"I have a hunch you have a similar attribute – being able to manipulate atomic molecules."

"How would you know that?"

"Last time I checked, spoons, watches, wood, and pieces of drywall – those things don't float around on their own," he retorts. Tabatha looks around her at the floating objects again, at this point, she's becoming used to it, however. "It's also obvious to me that this additional attribute to your telepathic ability is reactionary at the moment. You don't quite know how to use it. I also presume that you don't know the limitations of it as well."

"Maybe I don't want to know its limitations. Maybe I don't want it at all. Honestly, it's caused me nothing but problems."

"You make it sound as though these gifts –"

"...Please don't call it a gift. I'm really starting not to like that term whatsoever!" Tabatha interrupts the man, expressing her disdain for that description of her abilities, but also because her patience is wearing thin on the whole conversation.

"Ha-ha-ha!! This is not like that gun down there," he points to Tabatha's half-melted nine-millimeter on the floor next to her. "Just like your own eyes, your hands and feet even, this is a part of you. This is – you. Consider this, your lack of knowledge – and willfully it seems – of how to operate your abilities is what has ultimately exposed you, and not very positively."

Tabatha's demeanor changes slightly, as she contemplates what the man is saying. She, on this point, could not disagree with him.

The man then takes a few steps forward and holds out his hand warmly as an invitation and says, "Come with me, Tabatha. I can help you learn how to control it and use it." However, Tabatha's five-year-old training on not going home with strangers kicks in, and thus, she responds: "You know, I read about someone like you once. And like you, he was a snake," she responds to his invitation, comparing him to the great deceiver of Genesis, to which the man retracts his hand.

"That explains a few things," he says, having understood the comment. "It seems those who have been *tasked* to influence you over the years had a concern about your future moral disposition," he acknowledges.

"I am aware of those facts. Thank you very much. Can we just get on with it? I mean, who are you? And who's this *pyro-chick* here? What are you doing here and what do you *really* want with me?"

"I'm, your father," he says confidently, to which Tabatha takes as a bad joke.

"You *have* to be kidding me. You're really going to use the *Star Wars* quote on me?" She reacts, placing her hands on her hips and shaking her head in disbelief. "You could have used any other line, and then I could have believed you at least this much," Tabatha says, using her thumb and index finger to illustrate how 'much' she would've believed him. "I mean, at least pyro-chick there, she's got the thing over her face, and, well – I guess that *is* all she has, huh," she finishes her sarcastic rebuttal.

"He sure wasn't kidding when he told me you were abnormally derisive," he responds, astounded at Tabatha's ability not to take things seriously just as he is at Tabatha's skills.

"He? Who's *he*?" Tabatha adds to her list of things she wants to know.

"Let's just say that not everyone who knows you has a limited imagination of what you can become. But my name..." he answers her first question.

"About time..."

"...Is...Sorvan."

Tabatha recognizes the name. "Sorvan? As in Ivan? Sorvan?" She clarifies.

"So, you have heard of me."

"Your name is secretly infamous within the ranks of the federal government for your *inhumane* human experimentations. But, you're supposed to be dead."

"Haha," he chuckles under his breath, "Not completely dead."

"That's obvious. And I presume your girl there, is an experiment of yours?" Tabatha determines. The realization of the monster in her midst was like injecting her with a gallon of pure adrenalin. A small concern of retaliation by pyro-chick, however, kept Tabatha in check.

"This is someone very special, even beyond her volatile attributes. And I've been eager to introduce her to you. This is – Twenty-Four." Hearing that triggers a few flashbacks to past night terrors and daydreams in which depicted herself being called 'Twenty-Four.' "but more than that, she is your – *sister*."

At first, it seemed not to register to Tabatha. "Wha – wha – wwwhat? No! No! My sister died when she was born. We were..."

"...Twins – I know."

"She's buried next to our mother."

"Are you sure?"

Tabatha then begins analyzing the woman in light of this information. The only noticeable feature on the woman that compared to her own was that the mystery woman's hair was the same coloration as hers – though incredibly longer and, of course, far more matted. She also seemed to be of the same height as Tabatha, but those two traits alone could hardly attribute to being twins. Still, Tabatha could feel something in her confirming that there was s deeper relationship between them, despite desperately not wanting to believe it. The mind-twisting idea that her sister's alive however causes a nauseating feeling to swell up in her, making her slightly dizzy to which she catches herself on a remaining piece of wall before she finally buckles over and vomits.

Sorvan carefully studied Tabatha's response to his information. "Hmmm. Admittedly, I wouldn't have thought this to be as big of a shock to you as it's proving to be. Have you never felt anything, a connection of some kind?" He says curiously, to which Tabatha, at this point, ignores him. "After twenty-three failed experiments and finally, number twenty-four. Her biology accepted the procedures and enhancements. I could never figure out why, until a couple of years ago, when your suppressed attributes began surfacing, slowly exposing you to the public."

Tabatha regains her strength and stands back up. Her face expressed hostility. Every word Sorvan spewed seemed to increase her aggression. However, she remained steadfast, not engaging for she still didn't know what he had up his sleeve. "What would I have felt??" She says through her teeth.

"I would have no idea. There is a transcendent connection, though, because if it weren't for either one of you being alive, most likely neither one of you would be by now. I took her because your condition at birth was more critical than hers. Where you thought Twenty-Four was..."

"SARAH!!! HER NAME IS SARAH!!! SARAH – JOHNSON," Tabatha corrects Sorvan, with a shout allowing her to dispel some of her pent up aggression.

"Ohhhh. She has a name," Sorvan affirms. "Well, as I was saying before you so *RUDELY* interrupted me, you thought – *Sarah* – died after birth, I was under the impression that you had seized shortly after," he continues his explanation with a small outburst of his own.

Tabatha continues her silent streak, for the most part, inching closer to the two of them.

"So, tell me, how do you feel? How's your bullet wound? Normally, doing things like this..." Sorvan alludes to the phenomena revolving around Tabatha, "...would have long since made you weak and incoherent, am I right?"

Tabatha considers what Sorvan is saying. She raises her left hand and puts pressure on her right shoulder – no pain.

"See? That's the connection. You need each other. To answer your question as to what I am doing here directly, I'm here to reunite you two," He finally concludes.

"Thanks for the reunion. I have a gut feeling the answer to my last question includes making me into another puppet!" she metaphorically implies.

"Ha-ha. No, no, not a puppet," he says dismissively, "...a weapon," Sorvan plainly and emphatically acknowledges.

"Sooo, you're the one who really wants to be a god," Tabatha determines, disgusted.

"I created you! Both of you! Should a creator not be able to do what he wants, with what he created!? The two of you will be an unstoppable force! Once I access the totality of your potential, Tabatha, the combination of you and – *Sarah* – will be incredible!" Sorvan reveals some of his intentions. "So now! I give you a choice! You can come by your own volition!" Sorvan pulls out a narrow black box. He flips open the lid and pulls out a transparent syringe filled with a yellow fluid. A long injection needle was attached to the end of it. "...Or....." he continues, holding up the syringe in front of his face, glancing at it as he turns it, making it clear that he would use it on Tabatha, "...I'll use *my type* of influence."

"I'm not afraid of you!!"

"You will be."

"SARAH!!" Tabatha shouts.

"Ha-ha-ha. She can't hear you right now!! And even if she could, she can't speak!!"

"What?!"

"At first, her emotions made her abilities erratic. Oh, the screaming – it burned. So I, took her voice," Sorvan admitted, then revealing why his face was unclear he took his right arm, wrapped it around the left side of his head grabbing an edge of what looked like a piece of hanging flesh from his neck then peeled off an entire layer of rubber covering his head and left side of his face. A combination of metal and bone made up the left half of his face as well as the entire crown of his head. Like Sarah, he too had an outlet at the base of his skull. His left eye was not a real eye. It was black and was also a recording device. "There was one benefit to this – I discovered away to keep her out of my head," referring to his metallic crown.

"YOU DID WHAT!!!" Tabatha could no longer restrain her aggression and she bolts down the hallway to engage Sorvan. Before long, however, the mysterious woman, now discovered to be Sarah, steps out in front of Sorvan. Again a blast of heat comes rushing at Tabatha. She braced herself as before deflecting a continuous stream of heat and energy.

"SARAH!! I'M YOUR SISTER!! Tabatha shouts over the sound of their individual potentials colliding with one another. Unwilling to possibly harm her sister, Tabatha restrains herself from using the same maneuver as she did earlier that destroyed the other half of the hallway and relies on trying to get thru to her verbally.

"Hahaha…" Sorvan laughs to himself with a grin on his face as he walks up next to Sarah. In Tabatha's determination to get through to Sarah, she leans forward with one arm maintaining the phenomena's ability to deflect the continuous attack and begins pushing herself forward like someone pushing something heavy.

Sorvan begins sweating as the sphere of fire comes closer. "Ok, Twenty-Four, subdue her," he tells her. However, a reformed reality strikes him as the command was not carried out. Sarah's attack on Tabatha continued at the same intensity. "TWENTY-FOUR!!" He yells insistently as the ball of heat is pushed closer and Tabatha gains ground while continuing to shout her sister's name and informing her they were sisters. Sorvan glances at Sarah's face and notices something he had never seen. Sarah's left eye swelled up with water and tears started running down her face.

A concerned impression takes over Sorvan's half robotic face. He reaches into his pocket and pulls out a small handheld computer. The device remotely monitors the activity and chemical levels in Sarah's brain and digitally displays it on the face of the device. The dopamine levels in Sarah's brain were rising as her body was beginning to reject the foreign chemicals in her body designed to keep her in a state of mental impairment, causing her to reestablish cognitive control over her own mind. Her glazed over eyes began moving, processing her physical environment.

Tabatha's voice finally gets thru to her sister. Comprehending the words, Sarah seizes her offensive. The two of them locked eyes momentarily before Sarah was thrown into what appeared to be an epileptic seizure, causing her to drop to her knees then buckle over catching herself on her forearms. Sorvan had remotely initiated a release of chemicals into Sarah's body causing her nervous system to shut down which also disabled her psychic and thermokinetic functions – a failsafe Sorvan developed to render her powerless in the case he lost control over her – as he currently had.

"SARAH!!" Tabatha yells, running toward her.

Sorvan shouts a foreign word in which a multitude of refugee looking men swarm around Sorvan and Sarah from the intersecting hallway, causing Tabatha to stop in her tracks. She watched as one large man picks up Sarah and throws her over his shoulder. "Do whatever you need to, I just need her alive," Sorvan orders the swarm of hostiles, then turning and walking away down the intersecting hallway, followed by the man carrying Sarah.

"SARAH!!" She yells again over the crowd of hostiles. She slowly raises her hands about chest high contemplating her move. "Lord, help me," she says to herself just before a new voice penetrates her auditory system – that didn't belong to Sorvan. "You have it back now." Then, immediately her mind is inundated with psychic noise as a massive amount of telepathic information resumes funneling into her cerebrum.

"God!?" Shocked at the idea, she may have just heard His voice.

"The elevators! Go! Now!" The voice directs her.

She quickly turns, then dashes back down the hall toward the elevators, and the hostiles start after her. With her telepathy back, her ability to predict oncoming offensives returns, coupled with her new, yet minimal knowledge of her telekinetic ability, gives a slightly higher chance of making it out of the building on her own volition without having to be drug out by Sorvan's pawns.

Perceiving additional hostiles approaching the upcoming intersecting hallway to attack, she picks up speed. As one hostile round the corner to cut her off, she thrusts a hand out in front of her, sending the individual backward where he's wedged in between the smashed elevator doors. Before reaching the elevator, another hostile comes around the corner, in which she grabs him by his shirt, then spins around and throws him into the group of hostiles gaining on her with the assistance of her telekinesis. She nearly makes it to the elevator when they catch up to her, and arms start wrapping around her neck and shoulders, bringing her to a halt. More hostiles begin piling on top of her, but refusing to be subdued she catapults herself off her feet, using the weight of her aggressors as leverage sustaining her balance, "IN YOUR DREAMS BASTARDS!!" she then lands pulling two of the men that had a hold of her over her shoulders, and upon slamming them on to the scorched floor, a dense pressure discharges from her body leveling everyone in the halls and further devastating the fifteenth floor of the apartment complex, as well as rattling the building itself.

After that round, she remained on her hands and one knee, breathing heavily again. Her energy was decreasing as she sensed that her sister was now far away, as Sorvan had escaped with Sarah. Tabatha knew it was a matter of time before her body would be incapacitated due to overexertion of her abilities. She could tell her body temperature was increasing rapidly. She could see drops of sweat and blood from her face drip on the floor.

"Tabatha!" The voice in her mind reveals itself again. "You got to get moving. Quickly to the elevator!" Tabatha sits up on her knees, attempting to collect herself, analyzing the psychic noise funneling through her cerebral faculties. The blast of telekinetic energy *did* permanently disable many of Sorvan's men, but not all. The ones that had survived it, however, were severely injured. One of whom begins lifting himself up reaching into one of his torn-up cargo pant pockets to dig out a remote detonator. Immediately Tabatha telepathically establishes the fact that dozens of jihadists surround her, therefore every body around her was technically a bomb.

The reality of the new realm of seriousness she was in the midst of was enough to start an adrenaline rush. She flies to her feet and runs to the elevator door where the body of the man she had telekinetically wedged in between the doors of was still trapped. She maneuvered her hand as she ran toward him, and a bomb strapped to the man flew out from under his shirt into the hallway. She jumped feet first into the trapped jihadist chest shoving him the rest of the way through the elevator doors, followed by herself. Simultaneously the trigger man had shouted "ALLAH AK...." pressing the detonator button before finishing his declaration. Tabatha grabbed the elevator cable with one hand to stabilize her freefall just feet above the also falling jihadist down the dark shaft at the same time as the entire floor lit up with explosions, sending a fireball into the elevator shaft not long after Tabatha begins her descent.

The explosions blow the top few floors clear off the apartment complex. The body of the jihadist had landed on the top of the elevator, which was stationary at about the fifth floor. Tabatha braced herself and landed on top of the jihadist. The compressed fireball in the shaft melted a section of the elevator cable snapping it, now sending the elevator freefalling toward the basement.

"Ok, a little help, God!" She says, still thinking she had heard His voice.

"Open the maintenance hatch," the voice responded in her mind. Tabatha released the lock, opened it, and jumped through it, all while the elevator continued its' fall. She braced herself for the immediate stop, but then the emergency brakes engaged on the elevator, slowing and stopping it at the basement level.

"Ok, I'm not SHERA here!" Tabatha shouts, unable to get the doors to open by her own physical strength, referencing a fictional female character who *would* have been able to open it. But, no answer to her implied statement requesting help to get out of the elevator came. Meanwhile, the fireball was still hurtling toward the top of the lift. Noticing the glass window with an elevator key in it. She rams her fist through it, grabs it, and inserts it in the keyhole below the panel of buttons. With a little pushing, the doors opened and she squeezed through them and into a concrete hallway.

"Go right!" the voice in her mind returned. Without hesitation, she obeyed and the fireball reached the top of the elevator funneling through the opened maintenance hatch and out the narrowly opened elevator doors, chasing her down the hallway.

"Where'd you go!?" She inquired while running for her life.

"Sorry, I got temporarily distracted by the thought of you dressed up like SHERA," the voice responded.

"What!!?? YOU ARE TOOOOTALLY NOT GOD!" Tabatha concludes, sprinting down the concrete corridors.

"The steel door coming up on the left, it's unlocked, quick, go in there." Again Tabatha obeys and slams into the door, throwing it opened then slamming it shut. Facing the door, she can hear the remnant of the explosion pass, rattling the door, as it finished dispersing down the hallway. Then, perceiving telepathically, someone directly behind her reaching for her shoulder, she, without analyzing the telepathic information or even turning around, grabs the individual's wrist and throws him up against the concrete wall, ready to go into full-blown Jackie Chan mode.

"ALRIGHT NINJA WARRIOR PRINCESS!! TIME OUT!! TIME OUT!!" He shouts, surrendering to Tabatha's Kung Fu grip around his neck and her other fist just inches from his face. "You're safe, princess." It was Mitchell.

"Mitchell?" she says, breathing heavily. Her face had layers of sweat mixed with trails of blood all across her face. Most of her hair was saturated, having absorbed much of her bodies' exudation. Backing up from Mitchel, she turns around to see Director Jackson, Dr. Glessinjer, Rodney, Hammer, the old man in a white suit that she briefly met prior to entering the apartment, and another currently unfamiliar individual wearing a white T-shirt and jeans. She had a violent infused and confused look on her face and, in a burst of pent of aggravation, yells at the group, "WHAAAAAT!!! JUST HAPPENED!!!" then continues breathing heavily through her teeth waiting for someone to answer.

"Tabatha, I'm Jason Penfield," says the old man in the white suit. "I can explain – everything. But first...."

"...You!" Tabatha cuts him off, "why is my SISTER alive!" she shouts through her teeth and stumbling toward him. She grabs the folded layers of his suit jacket with her fists and yanks him toward her.

"Tabatha, I tried to get here, but by the time I knew – I just didn't get here in time. You have questions. I know. And I have answers, but right is not the time, I need you to trust me," He responds, more concerned about her physical health than answering questions currently as her physical condition is noticeably in bad shape.

"Trust??!! I'm to the point that I'm gonna *vomit* every time I hear that word!" She continues.

"Tabatha, you're not looking good at all!" Hammer interjects. Everyone else moves in closer to Tabatha, fearing she's about to lose her balance and fall.

"Where's your medicine?" Kurtis asks.

Tabatha pats her backside feeling for her medicine pouch, having forgotten that she's not wearing her usual jeans with back pockets. She then starts sliding down the front Jason Penfield's suit, leaving a trail of blood and sweat on his white jacket. The group catches her then lays her on the floor. "I think I left them in my other superhero suit he-he," she responds incoherently. Her head falls back into Mitchell's hands and David spreads her eyelids to see her pupils, "she's going into shock!!" he shouts.

"Oh, man! She's burning up!" Mitchell interjects, feeling the heat radiate from her head on his hands.

"Christian! Do you have my equipment?" Christian, or the guy in the white t-shirt and jeans, hands Mr. Penfield a small case. He pulls out an injection gun, places it on the side of her neck, and pulls the trigger. The injection causes Tabatha's' body to jolt a little bit before her body relaxes.

"I'm just going to shut my eyes for a moment. Don't wait for me," she says, incoherently, before finally passing out on the cold concrete floor.

"Tabatha? Tabatha!!"

The Sentient

CHAPTER XIII

THE UPGRADE

"Her heart rate and blood pressure are finally stable," David informs. "That was nuts. I thought for sure we were going to lose her that time."

"She's always full of surprises," Rodney responds.

"There's truth to that. This is one surprise that I welcome," David adds.

"But her neuro-output readings appear to be conflicting. She appears to be in a coma in one cerebral region – here – and brain dead everywhere else," Rodney explains, pointing to the regions on a monitor. "Jason! Is she hooked up correctly? Or maybe I'm the confused one."

Penfield leaves his small desk and walks over to the column embedded with monitors. Next to the column was a transparent tank filled with a unique illuminating fluid. It was an electrolyte compound that Penfield had developed from vanadium and dissolved in a highly oxygenated liquid. It had vast metabolic regenerative properties, beneficial to Tabatha – who happened to be floating in the middle of the tank, still unconscious. Electronic monitoring equipment was wrapped around her arms, wrists, chest, and forehead, collecting different vital readings and sending the information up a mast of cables that also helped to suspender her in the liquid.

"Here, let me see," Penfield analyzes the readings for a moment. "What's going on is that her cortex is rewiring its' synaptic circuitry to compensate for the new load that's required to operate her telekinetic processes."

"That's amazing," Rodney comments.

"I see. So what you're saying is that her cerebrum is basically *upgrading* itself," David interprets Mr. Penfield's explanation.

"And, if you look at the image of her hypothalamus, there's a vast web of fairly new circuitry already in place, as well as throughout most of her limbic system," Mr. Penfield continues.

"That would explain some of her instinctual telekinetic *accidents* over the last couple of years. They seemed to happen during highly emotional or stressful situations," Rodney adds.

"Right, and the limbic system is theorized to be the coordinator of our emotions, and the hypothalamus is responsible for most of our autonomic processes," Mr. Penfield concludes.

"Do you think she's listening to us? Via her telepathy?" Rodney asks. The three of them analyze the real-time images coming in from the tank.

"Here's her telepathic antennae fila." Mr. Penfield points to an area in an image being displayed on another monitor recording her cerebral functions. "They don't seem to be active. However, her auditory region is receiving sound. But that's because Christian's projecting his voice into her auditory cortex telepathically. It doesn't appear that she is receiving any telepathic information at all, which *is* unusual. Her clairvoyant telepathic process is a neurological system associated with the frontal lobe, which continually processes information, so it's always on. Interesting."

"Maybe this is all part of her, quote 'mental upgrade," David suggests. "In the area of computer programing, many computer software upgrades require a reboot of some, if not the entire system, to completely sync the upgrade to the hard drive."

"The rest of her vitals read like she's asleep," Rodney adds.

"She is," Christian interjects, confirming Rodney's assessment. I couldn't derive much from her mind other than incredibly mentally and physically exhausted. And the thoughts I *could* comprehend seemed incoherent at the moment." The four of them turn their collective attention to Tabatha, floating in the tank, asleep.

"Well, Christian, this must make your day. How long have you been following her around for?" David comments on Christians' first forthright interaction with Tabatha.

"Yeah, kind of. I hate seeing her like this, though. It hurts my heart – a little," Christian admits to having a slightly different angle of feelings for Tabatha, than the others. The three doctors acknowledge Christian's romantic admiration for Tabatha with a smile Rodney adds a couple of eyebrow risers to the acknowledgment. "Yeah, whatever," Christian responds, rolling his eyes.

"You even roll your eyes and comment as she does," Rodney observes then chuckles. "I wonder what your guy's kids are going to end up like," Rodney continues his jokes to the humor of David and Mr. Penfield and to the embarrassment of Christian.

"The compound that helped create them also made them sterile. So, there won't be any kids," Penfield informed. "Just behave yourself, son," Mr. Penfield says to Christian. "No playing with her mind."

"You know I wouldn't do that." Christian defends himself, to which Mr. Penfield glances at him with a raised eyebrow. "Ok, let me rephrase – I wouldn't do that to *her*," he corrects his statement.

"I wonder what she's dreaming," David ponders out loud.

"Hopefully, something peaceful. I think she needs a break from the chaos of the real world. She's going to be out for several hours, more or less. We should probably get some sleep too," Mr. Penfield suggests, leading them toward the lab exit.

"Dad, I think I'm going to stay with her if that's ok. I just want to keep an eye on her vitals and such."

"Son, I might not be psychic, but I'm not an idiot. Yet, far be it for me to tell a thirty-seven year old whether or not he can be alone in the same room with a woman," Penfield responds in his usual dry, intellectual sense of humor.

"Well, there are such things as boundaries." Christian walks up to the glass tank, "And this..." he taps on the glass, "...is definitely a boundary," Christian wittily replies with his own sarcasm.

"I just figured out how to fix our society..." Rodney adds to the humor, "...we just need more glass tanks between teenage boys and girls."

"Hahaha. But, who goes in the tank?" David responds, jokingly.

"Well, in certain animal kinds, the female is more threatening than the male."

"Yeah, I'm sure that'll sell," David replies as they leave the room.

"Well, I guess it's just you and me now, Tab," Christian says as he turns to the tank. He walks up to it and stares at her peacefully resting face. Her hair slowly rises and falls as it floats around in the fluid.

A small desk diagonal, the tank had a laptop and a few pages of notes lying on it. Pushed under the desk was an office chair. Christian pulls the chair from the desk and maneuvers it to a seemingly comfortable position. He turns out the lights in the lab; thus, the only light then was emanating from the illuminating liquid in the tank. He plops down on the chair, places his hands behind his head and leans back, placing his feet on top of the desk.

After making himself comfortable in his chair, he continued observing Tabatha as her body gently floats in the tank, asleep. Other than the faint hum of oxygen pumps pushing air into the tank, creating millions of small bubbles that continually race from the bottom of the tank to the surface and the medical monitors receiving Tabatha's vital signs and neuro-outputs that lightly echoed in the background, the lab was quiet. After a few minutes of sitting in the silence, he begins a random conversation about life, feelings, events, etc., with – the tank – until he falls asleep in the office chair.

....

Hours pass by. Christian is still asleep when a new arrangement of sounds suddenly comes from the medical monitors, the result from a change in Tabatha's' vitals received. The disjointed melody wakens Christian. The lab was still dark except for the illuminating liquid in the tank. He turns his head to catch a glimpse of Tabatha, staring directly at him from inside the tank. The look on Tabatha's' face was eerie and startled him to which he fell out of his chair and onto the floor.

"Ouch!!" Christian says, lifting himself off the floor. "Tabatha, you sure startled me, ha." He stands up and stretches, making sure he didn't pull or break anything, then walks up to the glass tank. "How are you feeling?" He says to her telepathically. He doesn't get any response indicating whether or not she understood him. She follows him with her eyes and her head with a blank facial expression like she was automated. "Tabatha? You're kind of freaking me out looking at me like that. What's going on?" Still no answer. Christian walks over to the monitors. Tabatha slightly rotates her head, continuing to follow him with her eyes. After getting a good look at her neuro-output readings, he becomes very concerned and pulls his phone out of his pocket to call the doctors down to the lab.

"I hope you have an *incredible* reason for waking us up and dragging us down here at three A.M. Christian," Rodney blurts out after barging through the lab doors, followed by doctor Glessinjer then Mr. Penfield.

"Doctor, no joke, something odd is going on. She won't take her eyes off me..." Christian quickly explains.

"...And you're complaining about this?" Rodney adds.

"No, seriously, watch..." Christian demonstrates by walking back and forth and to and from the tank. Tabatha's' eyes did not leave Christian the entire time, not even to notice the doctors entering the lab. Mr. Penfield turned the lights on to the lab and walked over to view Tabatha's' vitals. The other two doctors followed him. Christian remained in front of the tank and continued projecting his voice into her mind attempting to get a response.

The doctors analyze the readings. "That's an interesting array of colors," Rodney comments on the abnormal coloration in Tabatha's cerebral output.

"I've seen something similar to this once before," David recollects. "When she was having one of her night terrors during an MRI."

"I've seen this before as well," Penfield added.

"Christian, have you tried communicating with her?" Rodney asked.

"Yeah, and I'm still trying, but no response."

"I don't mean with your projection telepathy, but your clairvoyant telepathy?" Rodney specifies his question.

"A little. The images are still incoherent. Like dreams."

"Wait!! Hold on a second," Mr. Penfield responds. He touches the monitor with a stylus and moves the images around. A file folder pops up, and he opens it, retrieving another set of brain images side by side with Tabatha's' real-time brain images. They look nearly identical to each other. He carefully compares the two.

"What are we looking at here? Another image of her brain?" David inquires.

"No," Mr. Penfield says decisively. "About eight years ago. I found the facility where Ivan Sorvan was working out of. It was in a small village near the northwest border in Pakistan. I was able to make some, how should I say – friends – that were more than happy to help me with an extraction attempt," Mr. Penfield explains.

"Friends?"

"Anyone will be your friend with enough incentives," Mr. Penfield continues.

"And you sure have a lot of *incentive's* don't you?" David infers that the friends were some mercenary group.

"One *old* friend from back in my naval days, who's ex-military – the man loves America, but hates what most of the taxes support, so he lives in Puerto Rico – he got me in touch with a group of mercenaries called task force sixty-one. I was able to hire them to scout out the village. Up until this point, I hadn't been certain that Sarah was alive. Once I confirmed that Sorvan was indeed working there, and Sarah was with him, we developed a plan to access the servers and extract Sarah remotely."

"It looks like you forgot something during the extraction," David adds, noting that Sarah is still obviously in Sorvan's custody.

"We were successful at retrieving approximately eighty-five percent of the server data," Penfield explains, with a slightly downcast face at the memory. David and Rodney got the hint that not everything went as planned in Mr. Penfield's scenario. "However, all that to say that this image on the left is an image of Sarah's cerebral output when her telepathic ability is active. The three of them then turn and look at Tabatha in the tank. Her eyes were still fixed on Christian. "That at the moment is not Tabatha, cognitively anyways." Mr. Penfield concludes.

"What do you think she's doing with Christian?" Rodney interjects. Mr. Penfield studies the images some more.

"Tabatha's' telepathy is still enactive at the moment. Her brain is still restructuring. I have to admit, this is incredibly fascinating. Look at all the new synaptic circuitry that's developed, and just in the last few hours. We see here in Sarah's images that the same synaptic restructuring that Tabatha's' going thru at the moment, is already in place," Mr. Penfield explains. "Anyways, even if Tabatha's' telepathy was active, I don't believe Sarah would be able to access Tabatha's' clairvoyant information. Looking again at Sarah's brain images, she doesn't have the fila that Tabatha does. Instead, there are millions of pinhole size gaps throughout her cerebellum, more specifically in her frontal lobe. All my research indicates that Sarah is the opposite of Tabatha in her telepathic ability. She's more similar to Christian in that she's a projector instead of clairvoyant as Tabatha is. However, observing the similar web of synaptic structuring that Sarah has and Tabatha's' gaining, my educated opinion is that they both have telekinetic capabilities. Although, how similar or dissimilar their individual telekinetic abilities are from each other, are yet to be known. But I can tell you that the combination of the two of them together can potentially be incredibly devastating," Mr. Penfield further explains.

"Incredibly devastating? How?" Rodney asks.

"From the data I've gathered from Tabatha's' *accidental* telekinetic mishaps and the footage I've gained from Sorvan's files on Sarah, they somehow interact with molecules at the atomic level."

"Ahhh, so they can split atoms. I suppose that could be just a little devastating," Rodney deducts.

"But doesn't appear that *that* particular capability exists, outside of a physical connection between the two of them. However, I have been able to deduct that Sarah can telekinetically manipulate atoms in a way that creates friction in molecular structures. But her limitation seems to be strictly thermo-kinetic. On the other hand, Tabatha's manipulation of atoms in molecules appears to extend to the reorganization of matter itself. By doing this, she, theoretically, could very easily be able to manipulate the density of molecules in the air..."

"...which would be incredibly helpful in creating invisible force fields..." David adds.

"...and, stop things like dump trucks..." Christian further adds.

"Precisely," Mr. Penfield confirms.

"Telekinesis! Ha! I knew it!" Rodney interjects, feeling proud of himself to which the others briefly glanced at his outburst. "Sorry, she and I had a discussion the other day and, well, never mind. Please, continue."

"This is incredible. How could they be able to do all this?" David asks.

"Well, doctor Glessinjer, that just so happens to be the billion-dollar question. All I can figure at this point is that their telepathic neurological systems which seem to be the material medium for sending or receiving particular patterns of transcendent information. And by information in this context, I'm referring to the waves or signals or whatever you want to call the information the mind emits. That same telepathic function I'm sure plays some role in their kinetic processes too."

"Well, that sounds like a pretty good intellectual answer...but it's still beyond me," Rodney admits.

"It's beyond all of us right now."

"Alright fellas, let's get off the; why this and that – and get back to; what's going on right now," Christian interjects, having not made any progress communicating with Tabatha, or whoever is in her brain at the moment.

"Wait, David, remember Tabatha and how she interacted with Spencer before they went into the building?" Rodney reminds them.

"Yes, I do. That was definitely not her normal self."

"And Jason, you said that the two of them together would be potentially problematic," Rodney continues.

"Yes, it has been obvious that there's a substantial symbiotic relationship between the two of them. I say it's obvious because they seem to stabilize one another when in close proximity to each other."

"Yeah yeah yeah, right. My point is that if Sarah's influence is over Tabatha's' mind right now, then Sarah must be relatively close, right? Not to mention that Christian is telepathic in both; projection and clairvoyance. Perhaps he could locate Sarah and by extension, Sorvan," Rodney explains.

"Hey! I heard that!! And that's a bad idea!" Christian responds. Rodney walks over to Christian.

"You think you could find out where Sarah's at?" Rodney asks.

"Doctor, the data suggests..." Mr. Penfield attempts to answer for Christian but is cut off by Rodney.

"Data, data, data. Listen, Jason, all I've heard is theoretical-medical propositions, where in reality, this is more in line with physics and quantum mechanics – which I took in college and failed miserably at, but I digress. Right now, the pressing question isn't '*how does someone interact with atoms and molecules and whatnot according to whatever data...*which is all speculative science for the most part at this point anyways."

"I have to agree with Rodney on this one, Jason," David adds. "We'll have plenty of time to discuss theories and to research all this stuff at another time."

"The overriding question right now is; where's this monster; Ivan Sorvan hiding," Rodney continues.

"Not to mention, how do you get over a hundred jihadists into Washington D.C. without tipping off some aspect of national defense, homeland security and so forth," David adds.

"Three words; Secretary of Defense. That's how," Christian responds.

"Are you serious? You really think the U.S. defense secretary is behind this?" David shockingly inquires.

"Director Jackson can tell you for certain that the secretary of defense does *not* like T.I.D. at all. And more specifically he can't stand

Tabatha – as a person. Especially after he failed to convince Congress to remove her classification as government asset a few years ago, which would have allowed for her to be researched a little more thoroughly – if you get my meaning," Rodney explains.

"But he could shut T.I.D. down in an instant, couldn't he?" David asks, not necessarily familiar with all the political workings of the supposed classified department.

"Not necessarily," Mr. Penfield interjects. "T.I.D.'s authority primarily derives from select senate intelligence committee members. They established the regulations and rules for selecting those who could be involved in the department. Secretary Terrence has minimal involvement in the department in that regard."

"I thought you wrote the regulations, dad."

"Maybe some," Penfield responds.

"I have to say, Jason, your level of influence is a little frightening," Rodney expresses.

"Say what you will, but I've devoted nearly half my life and invested billions over the years to ensure her safety and protect her wellbeing."

"I believe that," Rodney rhetorically concludes.

"Alright fellas, as far as Secretary Terrence is concerned, I've been keeping an eye on him for some time," Christian injects. "In recent years, interestingly, he's made some fairly frequent trips to the Middle East. Most have been to the northwest region of Pakistan, ironically."

"Really?" David responds, intrigued.

"And something else as well...there's been a lot of defense spending going toward, quote; *anti-Taliban operations in northwest Pakistan*," Christian continues, "However, I haven't been able to solidify any hardcore evidence linking him to Sorvan."

"And to add to all that, T.I.D. has been busier than usual the last two years. Especially on nonsensical terrorist targets," Rodney adds.

"Nonsensical?" Glessinjer says, needing clarification.

"Nonsensical as in the targets of these terrorists just don't make any sense. For example, the FDA building. Now, I understand that any terrorist threat no matter how small it appears needs to be taken seriously. However, for fifteen terrorists to take a practically empty building out, well, it's not logical. And the information surrounding these plots have also been very easily discovered. Almost like they want to be stopped and specifically by T.I.D," Rodney concludes.

"Which means specifically by Tabatha," Christian interprets.

"Right," Rodney confirms. "I'm betting someone's been attempting to get Tabatha to expose herself. We're all familiar with a certain infamous YouTube channel that's popped up in the last two years."

"I've wondered about that since its' inception," Mr. Penfield adds, to which Christian responds, "It's a good thing not many people believe that thing."

"I wouldn't be so sure of that, now that the media has been all over her lately," Rodney adds.

"And how many people believe the mainstream media?" Christian rhetorically asks, to which the others gesture, affirming Christians point.

"Anyways, we need to find this guy, that's task number one. Christian, right now, you're probably our best chance at finding him, considering Tabatha is, for all intents and purposes, currently out of commission. I know that Tabatha can create something called a hive mind connection, using one mind as a catalyst to another and so forth to retrieve telepathic information from great distances, I think that's how she put it."

"Yeah, I know that *she* can do that. Emphasis on; *she.* My projection is pretty advanced, however probably not even as powerful as Sarah's, but my clairvoyance is nothing compared to Shera here," Christian explains, out of apprehension to the suggested assignment.

"Well, lover boy, think of it this way, if you succeed, when Tabatha wakes up and finds out you know where her sister is, you'll be like He-Man to her," Rodney attempts to incentivize Christian.

"Uhhh, He-Man and Shera are cousins," Christian responds.

"Yeah, well, last time I checked, they were also fictional cartoon characters from the eighties," Rodney adds.

"Whew," Christian exhales with a little anxiousness. "Well, I'll give it my best shot. But I'm going to need a boost. Dad, I'm going to need some of Tabatha's medicine." Penfield heads to a cabinet filled with other medical equipment and retrieves a vial of the medicine created for Tabatha and an injection gun.

"I didn't know you could use that stuff. I mean, since you don't have the energy crisis issue that Tabatha does," David inquires.

"I thought it was radioactive?" Rodney adds.

"It is a little. That's the active substance that regenerates her metabolism, and which is why I don't need it. But I helped develop it, so I know its properties. It should give me an adrenaline rush like Tabatha, but the other aspect of it is that it's a pretty potent neuro-catalyst. It should stimulate the neurons in the regions of my brain where my telepathy fila are. Unlike Tabatha, where hers are all over and more densely populated near and around her frontal cortex, mine are concentrated around the back of my cerebrum. But, the plus side for me is, I don't have the continuous flow of noise coming in. I have complete control over its activation. The negative side is, it's not very powerful," Christian explains.

"Alright, Christian, I'm only giving you half the dose that Tabatha takes." Penfield loads the injection gun with the medicine and holds it o Christian's arm and pulls and holds the trigger until all the liquid is gone. Christian cringes at the burning sensation in his arm. Penfield then releases the trigger and removes the injection gun from his arm.

"How do you feel?" David asks.

"Well, the same so fa…wait, ok, now I feel it." Christians' hands begin shaking just slightly as if he just chugged a gallon of coffee in three seconds – caffeinated of course – "Just a little dizzy right now." Christian crouches down and holds himself stable by placing his hands on the outside of the glass tank. His muscles contract and veins puff out.

"You all right?" Rodney asks.

"Yeah, yeah. Wow, I should use that stuff when I work out. That's quite the rush," Christian adds. Then stands back up, his hands still on the glass. Then, he hears the voice. He lifted his face toward Tabatha's'. She was looking down toward him in the same blank stare.

"So? Anything?" Rodney says, feeling a little impatient.

"Yeah, I hear her."

"What's she saying?" David asks.

"Nothing really. Just muttering, like a little child."

"Ok, well, you're in contact with her, at least, that's good. Let us know what you find out."

"Dad, how long did you say this stimulant lasts?"

"I didn't say," Penfield replies.

"In other words, better get a move on it – He-Man," Rodney adds, then turns to Mr. Penfield and Dr. Glessinjer. "So, what do you guys think?"

"I want to take her to the island after all this. The isolation from all the psychic noise will be good for her for a while," Penfield responds. "I'll get the chopper ready. Rodney, I suggest you get a hold director Jackson. Have him and the rest of her team meet us there."

"You mean what's left of her team. You sure that's a good idea?" Rodney asks.

"Yes," Penfield stops halfway to the lab exit. "No more secrets," he adds then continues walking out of the lab.

"It's about time," Rodney agrees, then turns to David. "Well, doctor?"

"Doctor," David, likewise, responds. They grin at each other. "Go make your call. Oh, and tell him to bring Naomi too. She's a good stabilizing agent for Tabatha, ha."

"Ahh, the infamous godmother."

"Tabatha will never admit it, but Naomi's her rock," David admits.

"Tabatha will never admit a lot of things, Haha," Rodney adds.

"That's for sure," David agrees. "I'll keep an eye on Christian." Rodney then leaves the lab.

"Sarah" Christian continues his psychic communication efforts with Tabatha's sister, who has temporarily taken over Tabatha's mind, but with the mentality of a young child.

"Who's Sarah?"

"That's your name, isn't it?"

"I'm Twenty-Four," she corrects Christian.

"But that is just a number. Your name is Sarah,"

"I'M TWENTY-FOUR!!" Christian cringes at the piercing echo.

"Ok, ok. I'm sorry, Twenty-Four, I didn't mean to hurt your feelings," he says. "Twenty-Four, can you tell me where you are?"

"I'm in my other me,"

"Your other you?" Christian thought for a moment and realized she was referring to being inside Tabatha's mind. "Oh ok. Have you seen your – other you, before?"

"Yes. When I'm sleeping."

"Are you sleeping now?"

"Yeah."

"Can you show me where you're sleeping?"

"I don't like to go there. It hurts sometimes."

"Go where?"

"To my god body."

"Your god – body?" The statement sends a chill down his spine at the possibility of what that could mean.

"Uh-hu. He calls me a god. But I don't know what it means."

"I see. I would love to see your god body. Can you please show it to me? You can come right back here if you can take me to go see it."

"Well, ok." Then immediately, Christian feels a strain on his mind. David notices the change in Christian's demeanor.

"Christian!! Are you alright!!"

"Yeah, yeah. I don't think we're in Kansas anymore, though, or, New York, or, wherever we started." David watches Tabatha as her eyes closed again and her head floats back to her original sleeping position in the liquid. Christian became inundated with a plethora of emotions originating from Sarah– anger, grief, confusion, delirium as well as physical pain, panic, anxiety. It was dark. He couldn't see anything through Sarah's visual senses.

"I know you. What are you doing here?" Sarah's' voice came back, but not in the articulation of a child, but as a mature adult.

"Sarah? Or I mean, Twenty-Four?"

"Sarah? That's what she called me."

"Who called you that?"

"My other half. She said I was her sister. She called me Sarah."

"Yes. That was your sister Tabatha."

"I've needed her to find me and save me."

"I know. She did find you, though."

"She left me!! In that hallway!!" Sarah's' voice elevated and intensified with anger for a moment.

"She didn't mean to. She was attacked, and right now, she's asleep. That's why *I'm* here. I'm trying to find you so we can come to get you."

"Who are you?"

"My name's Christian. I'm a friend. Can you tell me where you are?"

"I don't know. I can never see. I can't feel anything anymore."

"Sarah, I need to know where you're at."

"They know."

"Who?"

"Outside of the dark."

Christian then telepathically senses many minds beyond the darkness and manages to retrieve several images from their memories. Images of mountains, canyons, valleys, and caves funnel into his mind. Then more disturbing memories of experimentations, machines, schematics, maps, and other plans. Beginning to have difficulty maintaining his psychic connections, he made one last comment to Sarah, "Sarah, we will come and get you. I promise. I have to go now though."

"Ok. My name is Sarah, and I have a sister."

"Yes, it is, and yes, you do." At that, Christian relinquishes his psychic connections and like a mental rubber band that had been stretched to its limit, snaps, severing the connection. He opens his eyes back in the lab. He was sitting on the floor leaning up against the tank. Dr. Glessinjer was wiping his face with a rag. Sweat and drops of blood had perspired from his forehead during his telepathic trip.

"Are you alright?" David asks.

"Yeah. What a trip!" Christian lays his head back against the tank. Shortly thereafter, Rodney and Penfield enter back into the lab. Another shift in the of the medical monitor's audio grabs the attention of Rodney and Penfield. To their pleasant surprise, they revealed that her telepathic processing system and her newly formed synaptic circuitry were now wholly functional. Though she still remained asleep.

"That's perfect timing if I say so myself," Penfield acknowledges.

"And I spoke with Kurtis, they're on their way," Rodney adds.

"Shall we get her out of the tank?" David interjects. Mr. Penfield taps a few buttons on a panel next to the tank, and the liquid begins funneling down a series of drains.

As the liquid levels drop, Tabatha's body is lowered to the floor. Once the fluid drained, they enter the tank through a door on the backside of the tank. She begins expelling the rest of the liquid out of her lungs through her mouth and nostrils, until she dry heaves, causing her to shake. Christian puts an arm under her legs an arm around her back and lifts her, pulling her close to his chest.

Rodney takes one of her arms and checks her pulse. David took a rubber suction ball and sucked out extra fluid from her nostrils. Tabatha reacted slightly to that. Penfield began unstrapping her from the maze of wires and harnesses before walking out of the tank and placing Tabatha on a small medical bed in the back of the lab, where David completes checking her vitals while the others begin discussing the information he obtained during his experience with Sarah.

"So did you locate them?" Rodney asks.

"Maybe. I'm still sorting out the information in my head."

"Well, so much for that idea," Rodney responds. "Did you find out anything?"

"Oh yeah," Christian replies emphatically. "Sorvan's using Sarah to develop an advanced military arsenal."

"For who?" Penfield asks, to which he responds, "everyone."

The Sentient

CHAPTER XIV

Ivan the Terrible

The concrete constructed room was dim, lit only by the enormous curved computer monitor mounted to the wall of which it spanned the length of. It tilted toward the ground at a forty-five-degree angle. Against that same wall protruded a lengthy metal desk populated by other electronic equipment on it with a chair in front of the desk. The monitor had multiple split screens that displayed various images, many of which were of Sarah in different visual formats. Some were inferred; others included analytical data next to the images. Others were of her brain also with analytical data. A hand, in a glove covered with small metal plates, reaches out and types on a keyboard, after which an electronic base next to the keyboard projects a large rotating holographic image of Sarah. After a few more keystrokes, the holographic image of Sarah then changed and included more analytical data around it. The chair was then pulled out from the desk and the individual sat down in it.

"Ivan?" A voice from the entryway, somewhat timidly says. The half-metallic/robotic face turned just slightly toward the direction of the voice. "I just received a communication from your resource." Ivan turned his head a little more, indicating that he was listening. "He's slightly upset that you were unsuccessful in capturing the government asset." Ivan slams his fist, like a gavel, onto the consul. Then relaxing his hand, a single stream of steam rose through his fingers. Then he turned his head again slightly, again indicating that he was listening. "I apologize for the failure. Their fanaticism over their religion causes a few wrinkles in some of the plans." The individual explained, referencing the hostiles who were supposed to *collect* Tabatha in the apartment complex, but chose instead to blow the building up along with themselves in the name of their religion.

Ivan turned around in his chair to face the other individual. He taped the tips of his fingers together, which made a dull metallic clanking sound. He stared at the man. "Anything else?" Ivan asked.

"Yes. He also made mention of some sort of Senate hearing he's putting together for Monday morning?" The man continued his message, but with a little confusion.

"Hehehe," Ivan chuckles, fully understanding the statement. "He thinks it's going to be that easy, does he?"

"Sorry, sir. I don't understand?"

"American politics," Ivan then stood up, towering over the consul, he looked closely at the data displayed on the monitors. "The less you understand, the less the burden." Ivan turned and noticed the man was still slightly curious about what he meant. "Well, if you're that interested," Ivan explained a crash summary of the senate and its committees and how they work.

"Ahh, I see."

"Do you?" Ivan asked rhetorically. Then he picked up and plugged a cable into the outlet at the base of his skull. More data began downloading onto the computer. Then, a second white humanoid image appeared above the holographic platform. The two humanoid images merged into one humanoid image. Analytical information appeared in different areas around the merged humanoid hologram. Shortly thereafter, a string of flashing alpha/numeric information followed by warnings: 'UNSTABLE – MOLECULAR INTEGRITY FAILURE – ATOMIC COLLAPSE IMMINENT – GLOBAL THERMOGENSIS' appeared in the hologram and over the information n the computer monitor.

"NOOOO!!" Ivan screams in a monstrous voice as he clenches his fists, attempting to hold himself back from destroying the monitors. Then another individual runs into the room, slightly anxious.

"Ivan!" he says, standing next to his counterpart in the entryway.

"WHHAAT!" Ivan turns and shouts. The reaction sent chills down both individuals' bodies.

The second individual gulps and then explains that "there's a problem with Twenty-Four." The statement caused Ivan's demeanor to change to that of a concerned father – the psychotically obsessive, abusive, narcissistic, type of concerned father. As he heads to the exit, he stops momentarily to briefly examine a piece of metal plated armor joined with mechanical and electronic components. A set of cables connected the armor to a towering computer server protruding from the concrete wall Sorvan then continued out of the room and into a maze of different corridors. These corridors were massive. Several feet high and wide. You could drive two tanks through them side by side.

He approached a door, but before entering it, he looked through the window next to it. Sarah, i.e., Twenty-Four, was standing as straight as a four by four, with her head tilted back as if staring directly at the ceiling.

Her mouth slightly hung open, and the plastic mouth cover was hanging off to the side revealing tubes protruding from her mouth and attached to the inside of the plastic covering. Five other individuals were in the room. Three were on the flour, having been burned alive. The other two were leaning up against the window with their hands and the sides of their faces pressed against the window. Their eyes wide open and looked as if in a trance. Their mouths were moving like they were saying something.

"Why isn't she sedated?" Sorvan asked the two with him.

"She is," one answered.

"Does it look like she's sedated?!" Ivan asks them in an elevated voice.

"What he means is, we gave her the medication."

"How much?"

"Three times normal."

There was a small intercom box between the door and the window. Ivan pressed it. The two men up against the glass on the inside of the room were speaking in unison, though not very harmoniously "My name is Sarah, and I have a sister – My name is Sarah, and I have a sister…" over and over again. The unequally yoked vocals made the statements sound eerie. Ivan then decided to enter the room. He pressed a few buttons on a keypad which unlocked the door then walked in. The two men against the window were still repeating the statement. The room was a little misty with the smell of burnt flesh.

"Twenty-Four?" Ivan says in his low voice but in a calm tone. Immediately Sarah's head dropped down, facing forward, almost like a zombie. Simultaneously the two men against the window stopped their chant. That grabbed Ivan's attention and he turned to look at the two men still up against the glass.

"Twenty-Four, how are you feeling?" There was no response. Ivan thought for a moment. "Sarah?" He said. She then turned her head toward him.

"I have a sister," Sarah mouthed but vocally came from the two men again against the window. Ivan turned and looked at the two men again, then turned back to Sarah.

"Yes. You do have a sister," Ivan confirmed.

"What's a sister?" Sarah, again mouthed, but vocally came from the two men.

Ivan thought for a moment. "A sister is someone who came from the same place you came from."

"Is she a god too?"

"Yes, very much so," Ivan continues his manipulation. Her eyes begin moving independently, as she begins to make personal observations. She raises her hands and looks at them. A concerning look comes over Ivan. "I took you to meet her." Then memories of Tabatha in the hallway of the apartment complex flash through her mind.

"She left me?" Sarah again said through the two men.

"Yes. She did." Ivan replies with a lie. Sarah's eyes look up at Ivan in sadness. Her eyes swell up with water. Then shortly thereafter, her eyebrows cross, her hands, which she had in front of her, began smoldering. Since she was not hooked up to her energy source, however, she begins to sweat. Ivan reached in his pocket and slowly pulled out a small device.

"Why am I?" Sarah said through the two men again.

"Why are you?" Ivan repeated the question, contemplating its meaning. Sarah's hand reached up to feel her throat. Then she looked at the two men against the window who were verbalizing what she was thinking and mouthing. She was becoming self-aware.

"Why am I?! Why am I?!" she kept repeating through the two men, mouthing the statement over and over. It was starting to dawn on her who was in front of her. Anger was gripping all of her senses. Ivan then quickly reached around Sarah's neck with the small device and shoved it into the outlet at the base of her skull. Instantly she collapsed along with the two men against the window. Ivan, however, caught her on the way down. "...Because," he replied.

Ivan then picked her up. Her arms dangled below her, and her head hung off his arm. She looked as though she was dead. Ivan carried her out of the room, down another corridor and into another room filled with medical equipment. He placed her on a contraption in which a plug protruded from one end. He lifted her head, pulled the plug out of the back of her head, to which she woke up temporarily but then her head was quickly reattached to the plug on the contraption.

"Sleep now," Ivan said softly, to which her eyes closed. She then appeared as though being in restful sleep. Ivan walked away from Sarah, thinking to himself. After a few seconds, he began laughing to himself.

"Ivan?" One of the two individuals who had been following Ivan asked. Ivan walked over to a table where a new type of gun was lying. He picked it up, and where a magazine would typically go, he inserted the device he had just pulled out of the back of Sarah's skull. He pointed the weapon at a concrete wall and pulled the trigger. A ball of intense heat, which was only distinguishable via the distortion in the air, completely evaporated a roughly ten-foot diameter section of the wall, which was several feet thick. The edges were red hot and smoldering. He then held the elongated gun up by his head. He then looked over at Sarah in her induced sleep.

"We have enough, with Twenty-Four, to start a new arms race. Tabatha has a unique, and unexpected-negative effect on Twenty-Four," Ivan says. "I think it's time to conclude thirty years of research and development," he says, stroking his weapon as a prize. Then he turns his attention to the two individuals. "...I don't need any more *resources* either."

"What do you want us to do," they ask, anticipating orders.

"Put all your men who've been through the procedure in the front of the building. The rest, well, since your guys love blowing things up. The hearing will draw a crowd. They'll need extra security. You know what to do."

The Sentient

CHAPTER XV

The Island

A calm feeling of peace revitalizes her senses. The imagery of nature enters Tabatha's mind, reinforced by the sound of chirping birds as well as a cool, gentle breeze kissing her cheek. The sounds of water gently stroking a shoreline as well as trees swaying in the soft wind gave her the impression that she, at least momentarily, was in paradise. She had no memory as to the events that had transpired since her encounter with Sorvan and her sister. A string of random sentences funneling into her mind turned her attention from the feeling of serenity.

"...During the intake cycle, the intake valve opens, and the piston moves down. This begins the cycle by bringing air and gas into the engine. The compression cycle begins when the piston moves up and pushes the air and gas into...."

"Mom?" Tabatha says, recognizing the psychic voice. "Are you reading a car magazine?" She speaks from under her blankets in a large king-size bed.

"Yes, I am sweetie. It's very enlightening. In fact, I think I know why your truck shimmies when you approach sixty-five miles per hour," Naomi says nonchalantly as if nothing ever happened to Tabatha. Naomi was sitting upright in the same bed against the headboard close to the edge so she could reach her coffee mug situated on the nightstand next to her. "Your suspension is misaligned."

"Does that mean you're going to fix it?" Tabatha asks sarcastically, also predicting the answer as she continued laying still with her hands under the giant pillow and the comforter pulled up to her neck.

"No, but I can walk you thru it," Naomi answers, having yet to lift her eyes from the magazine.

Tabatha laughs under her breath. She finally opens her eyes. Elegant white and purple drapes were pulled opened, outlining the edges of the open windows in the room and in between them, was a set of opened French doors partially revealing a concrete balcony. The tops of pine trees were visible outside the windows and beyond that a clear blue sky. Chirping birds were wrestling in the air above the treetops. Tabatha could have stayed right there forever. Most of all it was quiet. Very quiet. Actually, it was *too* quiet.

"Mom?"

"Yes, babe?"

"Where is everyone?" Tabatha asks.

"They're around here somewhere." Naomi answers. "Your doctors had to go back to the mainland for something. They'll be back shortly," she adds.

"The mainland?" Tabatha asks. She takes a quick peek at Naomi's most recent memories. A helicopter ride over an ocean with an island in the distance flashes in her mind. "We're on an island?!" she says excitedly. "I thought for a moment that my telepathy was broken."

"One could only wish," Naomi responds.

"This I got to see." She jumps out of bed but stops as she notices her body covered in thick bandages. "Oh great, now what'd I do?" Tabatha presses on the material. "It's squishy," she observes.

"That's good," Naomi answers, paying little attention to Tabatha.

"Hope whatever is it, isn't radioactive," Tabatha says jokingly

"Me too. Don't need you turning into some big green she-monster."

"Agreed." Tabatha makes a B-line to the balcony. "So pretty. I could *totally* live here."

"Good. Because apparently, this is your new home," Naomi informs.

Tabatha pauses in shock. "Get out! What do you mean, this is my *new home*?"

"I thought you could read my mind? Now I have to tell you everything?" Naomi responds in a way that indicates that Tabatha was interrupting her reading, to which Tabatha laughs.

"I thought you didn't like me reading your mind," Tabatha rhetorically replies.

"Touché."

The house was built on the side of a mountain overlooking a valley. A river ran through the valley and into the northern Atlantic Ocean which could be seen and heard from the balcony. Trees and other vegetation lined the river as well as the sloping mountainsides.

"By the way! I almost died the other day!" Tabatha says from the balcony. "Just to let you know!" attempting to guilt-trip Naomi for not consoling her upon waking up.

"It's not the first time. I'm beginning to think you're immortal. I knew you'd survive another building collapsing on you!" Naomi responds.

"What!? The building collapsed?"

"Well, it's hardly the first. But if it makes feel any better, the *whole* building didn't collapse. Maybe half of it," Naomi adds, trying to make Tabatha feel better.

"Oy vey!" Tabatha responds to the information by throwing her hands on her face and shaking her head out of a sense of guilt. Tabatha took a moment recapping the events that she last remembers. The serenity of her surroundings then took a back seat as she contemplated.

"Mom. Sarah's alive!" Tabatha reminds herself and informs her godmother. *That* statement did draw Naomi off the bed and to the balcony.

"I know," Naomi responds with a consoling look on her face. "I was told what happened when they picked me up," Naomi holds her arms out as they embrace each other.

"It's surreal – like a dream."

"I know, sweetheart. I feel the same way," Naomi empathizes with Tabatha over the somewhat disorientating thought of Sarah being alive.

"So," Tabatha changes the subject as not to get emotional, "how long have I been out this time?"

Just then, Kurtis enters the bedroom and having heard the question, answers for Naomi, "well, Today is Sunday...it's almost noon." Rodney walked in behind Kurtis with a metal case.

"Geeze, two and a half days," Tabatha says to herself. "So, what happened?"

"A lot," Kurtis replied. "After the doctors successfully stabilized and transported you to Mr. Penfield's Monticello lab, for your recovery, you were brought here to rest," the statement triggers Rodney to briefly recall memories of Tabatha submerged in a tank of liquid, to which Tabatha picks up on.

"Whoa! So that's what that funny taste in my mouth is," she comments, astonished at the vivid imagery.

Rodney chuckles at the comment. "And don't forget director, we had to bring Tabatha's *bodyguard*," Rodney adds.

"How can I?" and immediately Tabatha observes the memory Rodney is referencing involving a slight confrontation between Kurtis and Cindy;

"...I'm sorry, you just can't come right now..." – Director Jackson.

"Can't come? I'm her best friend!" – Cindy.

"Technically, this is all supposed to be a classified..." – Director Jackson.

"Classified? You can take your classified and shove it up your..." – Cindy.

"Cindy!" her husband interjects.

"Calm down, Cindy," – Hammer.

"Calm down? And who are you? Oh yeah, 'I'm HAMMER...I'm nicknamed after something you hit <u>nails</u> with,'" Cindy marches up to Hammer with her hands on her hips and looks up as his face, which was roughly a whole foot above her. "...Well, <u>HAMMER</u>, my nickname's <u>chainsaw</u> and I will <u>cut</u> <u>you</u> <u>down</u>..." – Cindy.

Intimidated by Cindy, Hammer leans over to Director Jackson. "We better take her with us, boss..."

"It's against protocol..." – Director Jackson.

"Protocol? I got something to (call) <u>you</u> – and it doesn't start with <u>pro-to</u>..." – Cindy.

Director Jackson looks at Cindy's husband, Kyle who raises his hands slightly – body language for – 'don't look at me.'

"HAHA-HA!! That's awesome..." Tabatha cracks up at the memory. "Well, Director, *Sir*, she *is* like a quarter Italian or something like that," Tabatha responds. "...Maybe it's an eighth or a sixteenth or..."

"Right. Oh, and please, don't call me *sir* anymore. Not that it meant much to you, to begin with. Your role under my authority is over," he informs. "But, for the better, I think. A lot fewer regulations for you to put up with here, I'd say. And more importantly, not a whole lot to destroy out in the middle of the ocean."

"I'm sure," Tabatha half grins.

"So, how are you feeling?" Rodney asks, setting the case down on the concrete balcony.

"Physically, pretty good to be honest. Emotionally? Kind of like a titer-totter. And what's the squishy stuff under the bandages? It feels like a rotating heating bad." Tabatha asks, pushing on the bandages as to demonstrate the squishiness.

"Yes, I'm sure it is – *squishy*," Kurtis begins vaguely explaining what she had undergone since she had been unconscious. "After your normal theatrical collapse in the basement of the apartment complex..." Tabatha rolls her eyes at the sarcastic comment. "...Luckily Mr. Penfield came prepared. He seemed to know almost everything that was going to happen before it happened." He walks out on the balcony, his hands in his pockets. "He was able to stabilize your body enough to get you to his Monticello lab, as I said before. You have, more or less, been in some kind of coma since then. My ability to adequately and coherently explain it all is, well, above my paygrade to say the least."

"David, Jason, and I..." Rodney adds his insights, "...concluded, on a theoretical basis, that your interaction with your sister stabilized the symbiotic nature of your telepathic process, which then triggered some kind of neuro – *upgrade* if you will. Your coma, we believe, was similar, though obviously thousand times more complex, to that of a computer hardware upgrade and reboot." Rodney further explains what Kurtis could not. Both Tabatha and Naomi just stared at Rodney with glazed over looks on their faces and their arms crossed. "Yeah, I thought you'd say that," Rodney comments sarcastically about their distinct 'lost in outer space' expressions.

"You were submerged in a tank of an electrolyte solution that Penfield had developed. That '*squishiness*' you're noticing? It's a gel made out of that same solution. I don't know how it all works, but apparently, the electrolyte is made from a mineral called vanadium. It's capable of holding a charge that your body can absorb to help stabilize your metabolism while you're applying your advanced telepathy and so forth."

"Hmmm, that sounds both interesting and super confusing, simultaneously. Did you get any of that mom?"

"What I heard was my grocery bill is going to be cheaper from now on."

"Right, even though I pay for the groceries, but I digress."

"Speaking of which," Rodney picks up the case and opens it toward Tabatha. "This was designed specifically for you. It allows you to..." Rodney begins explaining the item in the case, but Tabatha quickly walks up to the case and shuts it.

"Don't think so. Never wearing it," Tabatha firmly states.

"Haha. I tried to get a wager going as to how you would respond to this. Unfortunately, there were no takers that you would respond positively to it."

"Hope it wasn't expensive," Tabatha says sarcastically.

"Not really, just a couple of million. And only two years' worth of research, production, and fabrication went into it," Rodney informs antagonistically. "The tiara was way more expensive to produce. But there's a small problem with that one that we're still trying to work out."

Tabatha's eyes widened. "On second thought, maybe I will take it. Perhaps I can sell it on the black market."

"To who? I don't think there's a large demand for material that stabilizes the metabolism of telepaths," Rodney wittily interjects to which Tabatha again rolled her eyes. "Besides, it could've been a worthless yellow and blue spandex outfit instead," Rodney adds with a chuckle. Tabatha then sarcastically flicks her index finger at him, to which she inadvertently sent a pebble flying off the concrete balcony floor, striking him in the forehead.

"Ouch!! What the?" Rodney rubs his forehead where the pebble struck him.

"Oh-my-gosh!" Tabatha responds and places a hand over her mouth in shock.

"You might want to start getting that under control, and quickly," Kurtis advises, slightly stunned at the micro-incident, but not surprised at Tabatha accidentally doing abnormal things.

"Tabatha, you just keep getting weirder," Naomi responds, not surprised nor stunned.

"Love you too, mom," she responds. "Ok, *Kurtis*, so what's really going on? Mr. Penfield shows up seconds before I enter an apartment that *blows* up. Then I wake up days later in a house on an island. I kind'a feel like I'm in a James Bond movie."

"James Bond is hot," Naomi interjects.

"Which one?" Tabatha responds.

"All of them,"

"Alrighty-then, anyways."

"Well, Mr. Penfield has a belief that your *calling* is far greater than being some rogue character within some secret F.B.I. Department. Other than that, you should talk to him personally," Kurtis explains, then heads back into the room, followed by Rodney carrying the metal case, and Naomi. Tabatha slowly follows, contemplating all the information given to her.

"Mr. Penfield, or Jason – that must be the mystery man you all were telling me about, that you couldn't tell me about," Tabatha recalls.

"He wanted to maintain his anonymity from you until the right time."

"Right. But just an FYI, if he pulls out the Skywalker dysfunctional family drama script on me, I'm going be like Darth Vader vs. a Chihuahua. And I'm going to be Darth Vader," Tabatha warns.

Kurtis stops at hearing the random comment and turns, "What in the world are you talking about, woman?"

"Ohh yesterday, that metal head Sorvan freak made a comment that he created me," Tabatha explains.

"I see. I don't know anything about that, other than that was not yesterday, just an *F.Y.I.*" Kurtis corrects Tabatha.

"Right. I keep forgetting. No wonder I age so quickly, I'm spending three-quarters of my life unconscious."

"Well, you won't be destroying any Chihuahua's when you're unconscious. Besides, they bite, pesky little animals," Naomi interjects, announcing her dislike of the small annoying k-9.

"Well, then I'll be like the Death Star vs. a Chihuahua," Tabatha continues having got her mind stuck on the theme, which Kurtis and Rodney willfully ignore. "So mom, you didn't bring me any clothes by chance, did you? And no Rodney, that thing doesn't count."

"No, I didn't. That was the last thing on my mind," Naomi answers.

The Sentient

"The closet's over there. A couple of the guys bought you some clothes," the director points to the closet as he, Rodney, and Naomi exit the room.

"So, Director," Naomi whispers, since this is Tabatha's new house, can I have the condo in D.C. all to myself?"

"Hey, mom, you have to stay with me. I have to take care of you!!" Tabatha yells as she opens the closet door.

"Oh Lord, one of these days, *I'm* going to be like the death star and *she's* going to be like an *ant*."

"Hey!! I heard that!!" Tabatha shouts from the bedroom.

"I know you did!!" Naomi shouts back.

"Hey!! You should wait for me. I don't know my way around this place!!" Tabatha again shouts at Naomi sarcastically, instigating her.

"You'll be alright. Use your thing!!" Naomi responds.

Tabatha laughs to herself over the conversation, then pulls out the outfits and lays them side by side on the edge of the bed. After a quick observation, she bursts into a short hysterical laugh. "Yeah right! A *guy* definitely picked these out." She comments to herself. "Is this a costume?" she looks at the picture attached to one of the three outfits. "Seriously? Shera?" Tabatha considers that the costume was more than just a random or coincidental pick.

She laid the costume down and picked up a hanger holding a pair of polyester sports pants and a long-sleeved polyester-zipper-neck sport shirt. "Cindy, you are *thee* chick," she comments to herself again, referencing the only outfit that could completely cover her entire body. The outfit reminded her of when the two of them ran marathons together. She quickly threw the clothes on over her bandages. Then finding her tennis shoes in a corner next to the closet – the only piece of apparel familiar to her – slips them on, then leaves the room.

Tabatha wonders down the hall. The top floor, where her bedroom was located, was decorated luxuriously. Classical style paintings of nature scenes in fancy frames filled the hallway walls. Small, decorative chandeliers hung from the hallway ceiling every few feet. She peeked into the other rooms, which were designed similarly to the one she woke up in only without furniture, as she made her way to a staircase at the end of the hall.

Next to the staircase was a beautifully designed dark wood door with no doorknob. A small wooden panel with a similar decorative design stood out on the wall next to the knob-less door. It had a single dimly lit button that slightly protruded from the small panel. Caving to her curiosity, she presses the button, and the door slides open revealing a spherical elevator. She glances inside, then tests the stability of it by placing one foot on the floor and pushing down in a way that would suggest the development of a mental disorder – elevator-phobia (if there is such a thing).

"Seems safe," she said to herself out aloud.

"Voice identification recognized. Good afternoon Tabatha. Welcome home."

"Aaahh!" A familiar voice from the elevator startles Tabatha causing her to jump into a defensive fight position via reflex.

"Command not recognized."

"Uuuhhhhh...Seryph? Is that you?"

"Yes."

"How are you talking to me?"

"I've been programmed to respond to Tabatha Johnsons', Jason Penfield's', and Christian Argonias' voice patterns." Seryph answers.

"Ok. But *hoooowww* are you talking to me?" Tabatha's question prompts Seryph to begin explaining the fundamental principles of computer programing and electronics to which Tabatha stares into space over as if the information Seryph divulges is billions of light-years above her head, probably from the Klingon homeworld. "Ok, ok, ok...stop, stop, stop..."

"You do not want to be educated on the principals of algorithmic syntax?"

"Noooooooooooooooooo!!" Tabatha shouts as if she is under attack.

"What floor can I take you to?" Seryph asks.

"You know what Seryph, I think I'm just going to take the stairs today, thank you though."

"Are you sure? It will take you approximately forty-eight point two-three seconds to reach the first floor. By contrast, the elevator will only take seven point three seconds to take you to the first floor."

"Yeah, I'm pretty sure I broke the decent elevator record the other day," Tabatha recalls her trip down the elevator shaft in the apartment complex. "Of course I technically wasn't *in* the elevator, the whole time anyways," she says to herself.

"The fastest elevator on record is currently located inside the Guangzhou CTF Finance center. At an approximate forty-five miles an hour, the elevator can ascend from the first floor of the complex to the ninety-fifth floor in approximately forty-five seconds," Seryph informs Tabatha, having computed that Tabatha wanted the information.

"Oh-my-gosh – Seryph!!"

"Yes, Tabatha."

"For now on, when you *recognize my voice*, just say *hi Tabatha* or something. And, maybe a joke. Lord knows humor is about all that keeps me sane at times."

"Alright, Tabatha. New instructions accepted and saved to my mainframe."

"Ok, now that that nonsensical conversation – with an elevator no less – is over," Tabatha says to herself, descending the stairs.

She reaches the second floor and decides to explore it as well. The hall was designed in much of the same way as the top floor. However, the hall curved to her left as if circling a large structure in the center of the house. There was a single door to her right nearly halfway down the hall. She opens it and steps into a dimly lit room with the only light emanating from computers and other electronic equipment. It was a long and relatively narrow room that curved with the rest of the second floor. The walls were lined with monitors and control consoles.

She telepathically sensed that someone was coming, so she backed out of the room.

"Tabatha?" Someone says as she closes the door.

"Uh, yeah?" She turns to see the white-haired individual walking toward her.

"I heard you had woken up. I was beginning to wonder if you had gotten lost for a moment. Is everything alright?"

"I think so," she pinches her cheek, "Ouch, yes, definitely not dreaming. Sorry for my wandering around. I guess I get a little too nosey sometimes," she admits.

"You can wander around all you want. This is your home."

"Right. So I've been told," she says. "So, you're Mr. Penfield."

"I am, and Jason, please," he courteously responds.

"Ok, Jason. I have to say, you don't look *anything* like the *Jason Penfield* I've seen on the news."

"Ha – That's a given. *He* is an actor. I pay him to *perform* for the media on my behalf, to put it simply. However, he was doing such an awful job representing me every time a new acquisition of mine sent the anti-corporate media swarming, that I finally paid him to get a business degree *and* paid *for* his business degree."

"And he doesn't know anything about you beyond the C.E.O of a pharmaceutical juggernaut," Tabatha psychically derives.

Penfield smiles at the antagonistic comment. "He knows that I'm an incredibly busy individual, *working diligently for the greater good of mankind*," he smiles at his rhetorical statement. "However, the details of what all that entails is not necessary for him to know. Not to mention, he seems not to care. He gets his five million a year. His mansion, or *my mansion* – whichever way you want to look at it – is paid for – as long as he holds up his end of the contract. His cars, however – he has to pay for those himself," Jason explains, then re-opens the door that Tabatha just shut and walks in.

"Well, it's good to know that I'm not the only one on the planet kept in the dark about you," Tabatha follows Penfield back into the room. He simply smiles at the comment.

"This is the monitoring room. Many functions in this facility are automated. Ask for the lights," Penfield explains.

"Lights!!??" Tabatha says clearly to which the lights in the monitoring room come on, but with an unexpected side effect.

"**Hi, Tabatha...or something. Why did the physics teacher break up with the biology teacher?**" Seryph says enacting Tabatha's prior instructions –literally. "**There was no chemistry.**"

The two of them look at each other as if both of their I.Q.'s had just instantaneously dropped a hundred points. "Why do I have the feeling that's my fault?" Tabatha says.

"Well, we have been working out the bugs, but I have to say that one is most definitely new. You must have quite the influence on computer programs," Penfield says in his dry, sarcastic tone.

"Yeah. I may have accidentally programmed her to do that. She takes things awfully literally, doesn't she?" Tabatha says.

The Sentient

"Seryph *is* only a computer, and computers can *only* think logically," Penfield explains to Tabatha. "Seryph…"

"Yes, Jason."

"Initiate A.I. module shut down and reboot to original default settings, please."

"Yes, Jason. All facility automated functions will be inoperable for thirty minutes. Only manual operations will be functional," Seryph informs.

"Ok, what does that mean?" Tabatha asks, feeling the need for a translator.

"Basically that means, we'll have to use the light switch for the next half hour," Penfield translates for Tabatha and points to a simple light switch next to the door.

"So, *you* designed Seryph, huh," Tabatha discovers, telepathically.

"I did. Specifically for T.I.D. But it was more of Christians' idea to incorporate Seryph into this house and to program it to this degree. Christian has two master's degrees; one is in computer engineering…"

"…And the second is in psychology? That's an interesting combo," Tabatha adds.

"Yes. He graduated with both by the time he was eighteen."

"That's impressive," Tabatha acknowledges. "I thought I was going to spend four years in college just to complete math – and not get a math degree."

Penfield walks up to one of the consuls and turns on the monitors. The wall lights up with high definition images of the island.

"That's pretty," she responds. "So this is Belle Isle?" she again deducts from his recent memories

"Not quite. This island is about a hundred miles southeast of Belle Isle. I purchased it ten years ago. The Atlantic is littered with dozens of small islands. Most of which are inhabitable long term."

"I see. Well, honestly, I can't really blame the anti-corporate media for taking aim at you. You own four of the largest pharmaceutical companies in the world…"

"They're acquisitions…"

"...That was just sued in federal court for not following FDA regulations on the marketing and selling of opioids. How much was the settlement again?"

"...My CFO..."

"...Two *billion* dollars. Wow!" She continues to which Penfield closes his mouth and lets her rant over the information, much of which she already knew about via public records that had been reported all over the news in the past. "...That's a lot of money. But I guess you do have plenty of it. I mean you bought an island and built this house on it..." she says placing a hand on an area of a console that's clear of buttons and leans on it.

"...For you..."

"So I've been told. For the umpteenth time now. I'm still waiting for the catch."

"Are you done yet?" Mr. Penfield asks, starting to get a little impatient with her.

"Oh, I can keep going. But it would start getting a little uncomfortable for you – up here that is," she taps on the crown of her head as an illustration that her telepathy can be dangerous to the individuals' mind if she so chose to *rip* out thoughts that weren't willfully yielding to her.

"Go for it..." Penfield challenges her to get a glimpse of whether or not she had developed at least a nominal form of self-control as to when to dispense the use of her gift under temperamental situations, indicating a sense of moral discipline had *indeed* been embedded in her over the years. They stare at each other for a moment as if playing chicken – with their eyeballs. Finally, Tabatha rolls her eyes, turns her head, and looks at the scenery of the island through the monitors. Mr. Penfield smiles – pass.

"I see that you know about my continuous stream of telepathic noise I'm bombarded with every second of my life, so you constructed this place for me so I can get away from it all. I want to say that this is all sweet and nice – and I do, *mostly* mean that – this place is incredible – but how am I supposed to trust that you have my *well-being* in mind when I don't know anything about you – without having to rip the information out of your head. Yet, you know everything about me, not to mention most of those whom I'm close to, at least know *about* you," Tabatha explains her concerns. "...and who is this Christian individual? I have a sneaky suspicion that we have something in common."

The Sentient

"You're right to have all these questions. I always hoped that I was doing the right thing. Maybe not, but I suppose time will be the judge of all that. I've had your behavior monitored since you were a child. I kept my distance because."

"...Because I could discover all your little secrets..." Tabatha, again, antagonistically interjects.

"...Ha!" Penfield replies to her arrogant statement with a retaliatory laugh. "Most of my *secrets* would have most likely interfered with your maturity."

"Pfffff – maturity – I turned out just fine."

"You did, for the most part. Still fairly arrogant, though. When you were a child, one of the more prominent features of your behaviors I quickly noticed, was your slightly vengeful and highly temperamental attitude. I'm sure you can think of individuals who've committed terrible things. Now, just imagine what they could have accomplished if they had your potential."

She considers Penfield's perspective for a moment. "Ok. I see your point," she reluctantly admits that his logic is sound. "I guess I *was* pretty mean when I was little." A few memories of her younger, pre-teen, self of using her telepathy to humiliate and take advantage of some of her peers crept up on her.

"Yes, you were."

The memories re-induced a small sense of shame but then shook the feeling off and responded: "Listen, I know what I did when I was younger. But when my aunt and uncle lead me to the Lord in high school, I repented of all that, and haven't used my abilities in those ways, since – not intentionally at least. So you can't hang that over my head."

"Tabatha, I'm not telling you all this to guilt you, or make you feel bad. Overall, I've been impressed by how you've disciplined your handling of it," Penfield assures Tabatha that he is for her and not against her.

"That's why you created T.I.D.," Tabatha psychically deducts, just before he was going to reveal it to her.

"I did. It was ironic to discover that you had an interest in criminal law and the justice system as a young adult."

"Well, being able to see crimes before and during their commission, and not being able to do much about it without breaking the law myself, had a hand in that honestly," she explains.

"Indeed. And thanks to your aunt and uncle who helped you to develop a general, and moral handling of your telepathy, I felt it was time for you to learn how to maintain control of it during high stress and hostile environments. I was able to convince a few top-level government officials to create the secret department."

"I hate lobbyists," Tabatha says again antagonistically.

Penfield lightly smiles. "I know you do."

Tabatha stares at the pictures of the island through the monitors while analyzing what Penfield is currently thinking. "You know an awful lot about me, for someone who's kept their distance from me."

"And this brings us to Christian – my son. You're not wrong about him – he does have something in common with you. He's been keeping an eye on you for some time now."

"So I've heard. That's not creepy at all." She responds with light humor.

"Well, I felt it was the best way to keep you safe while simultaneously studying you without interfering with your life," he further explains.

"Right. Tabatha, the universal lab rat."

"Say what you want, but it's benefited you more than you know."

"Ahhh, the green goop super concoction and my medicine were also created by you," she again deducts psychically.

"Yes. And you're welcome."

"I was going to say thank you. Thank you."

"I know this is a whole lot to take in. I hope it's not too overwhelming."

"I've been in way more overwhelming situations than this. And regarding keeping secrets from me, I'll give you credit where credit is due. No better way to spy on someone with telepathy than to send someone whose mind is structured in a way that his brain waves can't be interpreted," she looks at him with a 'gotcha' glance. "Did you really think I couldn't figure out that someone was stalking me?" She laughs.

"Really. I have to say, I'm surprised. How long have you known?"

"Since I was a teenager," she replies. "In an endless ocean of psychic noise, often there was a stream that was absent of information. It took me a bit to figure out, but when I started seeing things like flowers that weren't really there, and hearing my favorite songs – without the radio on or headphones in open spaces – I began putting it all together. Honestly, I think he wanted me to know he was around. But I've never seen him," she continues. "I didn't know he was a – projector? That's what you call him?"

"Really? I was beginning to think you knew everything," Penfield responds to her *gotcha* comment. "A projector is simply the term I used to describe Christian's primary telepathic process. He can manipulate the active audio and visual regions of a persons' brain, projecting images primarily and sounds into the mind of another individual. He can induce thoughts to some degree, but that takes more effort and depends on how *logical* the mind of the individual is."

"That explains a little."

"He possesses some clairvoyant abilities as well, similar to you, only nowhere near as powerful as yours," he further explains.

"*Clairvoyant*. Now that sounds *fancy*."

"I apply the terms simply to differentiate between the two telepathic processes."

"That makes sense. Although, your description of a projector, sounds similar to how Sorvan was describing Sarah," Tabatha is reminded.

"Yes, your sister is a projector as well. And a very powerful one at that," he confirms.

"No, kidding! So what do you call her *heat blast attack* process?" She asks, partly sarcastic.

"Hmmm. How about a *heat blast attack*?" he replies with similar sarcasm. They look at each other for a moment, then laugh at the comment.

"I don't know, that seems a little too generic, don't you think?"

"Well, frankly, deducing terminology to apply to random abilities is hardly relative."

"Oh, is it now," Tabatha rhetorically responds.

"Listen, I know you have mounds of questions still, but I think you will enjoy being around more familiar faces. Besides – I need some coffee."

Lucas Gorton McIntire

CHAPTER XVI

Origins

"This is the study." Penfield led Tabatha into a room with a fireplace in between two windows on the north wall. A large Thomas Kinkaid painting hung above the fireplace. The east wall was primarily one enormous window divided into four panes. Digital numbers and other information regarding the weather and current temperature moved around in the window like a screen saver. Bookshelves, a table, and a desk lined the other walls around the room that were stocked full of reading material. Mostly philosophy, theology, history, politics, – all the kinds of content Tabatha enjoyed reading and studying herself incorporated the bookshelves. In the center of the room were some couches and a large coffee table

"Wow," Tabatha says, impressed. "That's a lot of books," she says softly. But more than the books were her friends that grabbed her attention. Cindy, Kyle, Naomi, Hammer, and Mitchell were sitting, randomly conversing amongst themselves. Kurtis was looking down at the valley through the east window. He didn't pay much attention to Tabatha walking in. But either did Naomi – she was playing solitaire on her phone.

"Tab!" Cindy shouts, jumps up and runs over to greet her best friend. "Welcome back from the dead – again!" Cindy exclaims, hugging Tabatha. "Girl, you need to quit almost dying on me!! That's twice in a week. You're going to make me miscarry or something. Not to mention, I'm still processing the fact that, you're – you," Cindy rambles. The rest of the group shares their enthusiasm as well, although less verbal, seeing Tabatha awake.

"Yeah, occupational hazard, I suppose," Tabatha responds.

"See Mitchell. I told you she wouldn't wear any of your outfits you bought her," Cindy informs, noticing Tabatha's sporty outfit.

"Of course not. I bought those for her to wear when she's out fighting bad guys," Mitchel remarks excusing Tabatha for not wearing one of his choices.

"Yeah, like that's ever going to happen," Tabatha says.

"What? Haven't you ever read comics?" Mitchel continues.

"Ha! P-lease! The day a female artist comes out with a comic series depicting all the *guys* half-naked and the girls fully clothed, then I'll read them," Tabatha explains.

"Amen girlfriend!! I'll be a subscriber," Cindy adds, then catching Kyle, her husband, and who, of course, is a pastor, glancing at her with a smirk on his face over the comment. "What? They may have good plots," she concludes, to which they all laugh.

"Alright, good point. Well, if you ever have a honeymoon, you're all set. You're welcome – in advance."

Tabatha walks over behind the couch where Mitchell was sitting. "Oh, you're so thoughtful. Who's the groom going to be? You?" Tabatha insultingly says while rubbing her knuckles on the top of his head.

"Like I'd be that lucky," Mitchell admits.

"You're right. You wouldn't be," Tabatha confirms harshly, to which the group responds with antagonistic laughter.

"Yeah, whatever," Mitchell responds with a bruised ego.

"However, Mitch, there's a receptionist who works at the front desk at Dr. Glessinjer's office that I should introduce you to,"

"Really?"

"Oh yeah. You two would get along – *perfectly*," Tabatha says confidently.

"Cool," Mitchell replies.

Tabatha then notices one of Hammer's arms is bandaged up. "Ham! You're arm!"

"Yeah, it's still attached. Just a minor wound, no big deal. You've seen me in worse conditions before," Hammer responds.

"True. Speaking of which, where's the rest of the team?" Immediately Hammer and Mitchell's thoughts turn to the events nearly four days earlier, which of course, Tabatha detects. "Oh-my-gosh! T.K., Diego, Michael, Steve, Joe..." She covers her mouth with her hands, and her eyes instantly swell up with tears. "Why did you guys even go in there??"

"Well..." Hammer begins to explain, but Kurtis cuts in to take on the responsibility for what happened.

"Tabatha, I sent them in after you," Kurtis admits, still looking out the window down at the valley. "When it came to my attention…" he turns around and walks to the group, "…that the whole scenario was a trap for you, my immediate priority was to get you and everyone else back out of the building. Brian radioed for you both but nothing except for some odd interference."

Mr. Penfield stood in the farthest corner of the room, disassociating himself from the discussion. He stared out the east window with his hands in his dress pant pockets glancing vaguely at the valley then the sky and the mountains and other objects on the island that caught his eye. But in reality, he was still evaluating Tabatha's behavior. Specifically, in this scenario – how will she respond to a heightened emotional state as she learns the fate of some of her friends?

Kurtis continued explaining. "So, I made the decision to send the Seven in to get you out."

"You did what!? Why!? You sent them to their death!" Tabatha lectures the director.

"Tabatha…" Mitchel attempt to defend the director. "…it's not his fault. He didn't know what was going on in there."

"None of us did. This wasn't something that we were ever equipped or ready for," Hammer added.

Tabatha walks around the couches and sits next to Hammer. "Can I see?" Tabatha asks him.

"You can," he says hesitantly. "…But It's not a pretty sight."

"I believe you," she then tilts her head toward Hammer and closes her eyes. "Ok, remember for me." Hammer then begins his recollection and, in the process, feels the slight sensation of fluid flowing through his head.

"We ran into the building…" Hammer then described the events that took place directly after entering the apartment complex. Mounds of dead, burnt bodies in SWAT uniforms covered the floor and stairs. And amid the hellish scene stood Sarah. He continued describing their confrontation with Tabatha's sister and the inferno she created around them. Their attempts to stop her failed and ended with the combustion of their teammates while Hammer and Mitchell narrowly escape through a series of hallways behind the old lobby front counter.

Both anger and grief swell up inside Tabatha as she watched Hammers recollections, unable to do anything – she was nothing more than a spectator. However, she used the opportunity to study her sister a little closer than what she was able to do during her previous telekinetic dual with her.

For Hammer, having little control over his own memory was a unique experience. The memory would occasionally pause, the image altered. She would also randomly fast-forward and even zoom in and out specific frames like that of a movie. However, she could only view details that had been within Hammer's line of sight at the time of the incident – if he didn't see a particular angle or perspective, he didn't have a memory of it. She, instead, lapsed back and forth through the recollection freezing the memory in specific frames where her sister was in different positions and studied her. It did, however, give Hammer a slightly different perspective of what he had already seen.

Some of the features Tabatha studied on her sister were her face, her laminate like suit, and what looked like a lubricant of some sort on her flesh beneath the outfit. She also noticed her glazed over eyes that made her appear to be zoned out. She also paid close attention to the electronic contraption she carried on her back that her head was plugged into by the protruding cable on the top of the contraption.

After expounding on Hammer's memories of the incident, Tabatha sits up and opens her eyes, shaking off the connection.

"That's always a trippy experience. I feel like I need to get drug tested now for some reason – ha-ha!" Hammer jokingly comments to lighten the mood, to which the others chuckle. The humor lasts, but a moment then silence overtakes the study as if they all just came back from a funeral.

"Seriously, guys? Stop worrying about me. I'm fine," Tabatha responds to the group, sensing their thoughts were of concern for her.

"I'm not worried about you," Naomi responds, who was playing solitaire on her smartphone still, not concerned at all.

"Of course, you weren't – you can move the king to the empty space, by the way."

"Hmmm, you're right, thanks."

"Any time, mom."

Tabatha bolts up off the couch, having switched to '*assignment*' mode and begins pacing around considering the current scenario. "Ok, so we have a twofold objective. Capturing Ivan and rescuing Sarah. That's a no brainer."

"Or visa-versa..." Naomi randomly interjects.

"Right."

"If he follows the same pattern as before, he'll most likely have a multitude of hostiles with him, *who* don't mind, blowing themselves up for his cause," Mitchell adds.

"Yeah, I don't think that his cause is necessarily their cause. During our lively discussion the other day, it seemed to be implied that Sorvan was utilizing their efforts to draw me out. In fact, he expected them to capture me alive. Yet they blew themselves up instead – along with half the building, under the guise of their religion," Tabatha explains.

"And you said before you went into the building, that you couldn't detect anyone telepathically. So you couldn't get any information from him, I'm assuming. Right?" Mitchel recollects.

"Right. Other than what he articulated to me. Sorvan said, and Penfield earlier confirmed this as well, that Sarah can fabricate images and scenarios, etc., Maybe that allows her to fabricate like an empty or blank space in the mind as well," Tabatha theorizes.

"There were, what? Seventy or so people in that building. You really think she could manipulate that many minds? Hammer asks. Tabatha slightly agreed that the idea might be a stretch to conceive, even in the world of telepathy. However she didn't like the only other available possibility that left her.

"Maybe she was in *your* head, suppressing the functionality of your telepathy," Mitchell alluded to what Tabatha didn't want to believe. She stared quietly into the air.

"Man, if she can get in *your* head and turn your psychic stuff off, to say you're going to be at a disadvantage, is a major understatement," Hammer adds.

"Seriously?! You know there *is* more to me than my brain, right?" Tabatha comments.

"She would say that. The brain is usually the *last* thing noticed on a normal chick," Cindy remarks. "Right, hunny?"

"I was attracted to your mind," Kyle responded.

"Uh-hu sure. You obviously don't remember the first comment you made when we first met. Let me give you a hint – It wasn't for help with your math homework. And you weren't *always* a preacher babe. Or do I need to remind you?" The threat of divulging the information in front of everyone jarred his memory.

"No! I remember," he then responded slightly embarrassed and to the humor of his wife, who kissed him on the cheek.

"Ha-ha! Kyle, you stud," Tabatha also responds.

"Keep that to yourself, Tabatha," Kyle quickly interjected.

"Having a husband you can blackmail is always a positive," Cindy continued.

"Blackmail? Girlfriend, you don't even know. I could retire right now."

"Yeah, well, you're disqualified – for enhanced grey matter," Cindy responds.

"Tabatha, your ability to rabbit trail a conversation is still unmatched," Kurtis interjects.

"Right. Regardless of any disadvantages, the bottom line is that he's manipulating Sarah as his personal weapon/bodyguard. Geez, seeing her like that – it makes me want to rip his metal face off his – face. So, Jason, would that fall under your *righteously moral anger* category?" she asks antagonistically.

"YES!" Naomi answers for Mr. Penfield.

"Mom overrules the billionaire CEO man." Mr. Penfield just shook his head and continued looking out the window.

"Well, I'm all in Tab," Hammer says, feeling pumped to get involved in another mission and potentially get some payback in for the deaths of his former team members. He stands up, walks around the couch, and sits on the back of it with his arms crossed. "But first things first..."

"I know. We need to find them. He seems to have a lot of advanced technology behind him. He's got to have a pretty secluded facility."

"During my interrogation with Twenty-Three, I saw a desert; mountains; a few references to the middle east. A possible base of operations in the region, maybe?"

"Maybe he went back there?" Cindy suggests.

"I'm not too sure about that. Many of the images I derived were from memories of his past. I'd say fabricated no sooner than a year and a half ago. What I *do* know is that Sorvan was pretty clear that his primary objective for coming here was to quote, *reunite my sister and me.*" Tabatha explains, using her fingers to illustrate '*quote*.' "We apparently have a unique connection to one another. It was a pretty intense feeling – like I was being pumped full of adrenaline and energy," Tabatha further explains. "He wants to, somehow, combine and weaponize our abilities."

"He might be able to do just that," Mr. Penfield finally speaks up.

"You know, you seem to know a whole lot about what's going on. Are you planning on sharing any time soon?" Tabatha frustratingly asks.

"I have been following his activities for some time now. A few years ago, I was able to locate a facility he was working out of, which happened to be in northern Pakistan. The attempt to take him out was unsuccessful. However, I did manage to get some information from his servers," Penfield explains.

"What kind of information?" Mitchell inquires.

"Military designs mainly. He was attempting to find a way to mechanically manipulate Sarah's thermal-kinetic capability to power new aged weapons. At the time, he hadn't yet been successful in elucidating the excessive amount of information required to discharge the type of energy Sarah's capable of generating. But he did discover a way to block telepathic information. In fact, I have been developing a little piece of equipment based on his technology in that area to assist your telepathy."

"Yeah, I can hardly wait, to see it," Tabatha rhetorically comments. "Wait. You said '*at the time*' he hadn't been successful. Is that statement current? I hope," Tabatha asks.

"I would love to say positively that it is. However, Christian was trying to obtain information about his location while you were unconscious, but instead, he primarily discovered more information relating to Sorvan's advancements than his whereabouts. Christian believes that Sorvan *may* have discovered how to catalyze the thermal-kinetic energy her brain produces and store it. He also mentioned a generator that may be associated with the catalyst, but it was a fairly vague recollection."

"Well, if your boy knows so much, where's he at?" Tabatha asks.

"He left last night. He tells me he's been following leads. Christian thinks that *Sorvan's* a puppet," Penfield answers.

"I would say that he's the puppet master."

"Either way, Sorvan is and has been a troubled individual for many years," Penfield explains as a memory from many years ago floats to the service. "He was a brilliant neurologist."

210

"Sooo, you two knew each other. And even worked together," Tabatha discovers.

"We did – for a time. I first met Sorvan at Oxford University. One afternoon, he got word that his mother had passed away. Out of the blue, he started telling me his life story." Mr. Penfield turned again to look out the window as he continued.

"His father was a military science officer under Stalin. His father was taken one day, and he never saw him again. After that, he and his mother were destitute. His mother became addicted to LSD leaving Sorvan to provide for the two of them by accepting odd jobs. Shortly after his mother became sick, he ran into a doctor who worked at a new rehabilitation and addiction research center. The researchers were all missionaries and took Sorvan and his mother in. That's where Sorvan took an interest in addiction research. He developed empathy toward addicts. He never blamed the individual addict but the substance. When I met him in Oxford, he was consumed with the idea that he could make mankind impervious to addictions. I thought it was a little farfetched, but his data was very impressive. After Oxford, He became an amazing neurologist and returned to the rehab facility in Russia to further his research. That is until the government discovered it was headed up by missionaries, so the government burnt the building to the ground. He wasn't in it at the time, but when he heard they were looking for him, he left Russia as a refugee and came to New York."

"Oh-my-goodness! Was there anyone in the building?" Cindy asks.

Penfield shrugs his shoulders. "I don't know. He never said. But he began working in a similar capacity in New York at a research hospital studying brain abnormalities. His research got national attention. He approached me one day. He said he did it."

"Did what?" Hammer asks.

"He had developed a chemical compound that strengthened the neurotransmitter receptors in the brain, which made them impervious to the neoplastic manipulation caused by addictive substances," Penfield continued as everyone listened intently. Except for Naomi, who was still playing on her phone.

"He wanted me to partner with him. After I saw the results from the chimps that he was allowed to test the compound on, I agreed. We were given the green light by the Food & Drug Administration in the late seventies to test it on humans. We got a pool of methamphetamine addicts.

Half were on a placebo, and the other half were given the chemical compound. The results were incredible – in the beginning. We gave each recipient a certain amount of meth every day. After *two days,* the group that took the compound had no desire for the drug. After one month, we released the volunteers."

"But it didn't work for long, obviously," Tabatha deducts.

"Five months later, the chimps went mad, developed a severely aggressive form of dementia. They had to be put to sleep. Oddly, however, the government wanted the chimps bodies, I couldn't figure out why at the time. I did a little digging and found that some key military personnel had been influential in getting the F.D.A. to fund Sorvan's research and group. I attempted to discuss this with Sorvan, but he was uneasy. He was under the impression that he and his research were being manipulated."

"Manipulated for what?" Kurtis asks.

"Biochemical warfare experiments."

"Oh-my-gosh!" Cindy exclaims.

"Sorvan's research got a top-secret classification, and I was no longer able to be a part of it. But I did have the records and names of the individuals who were given the compound. I discovered that twenty-five of the women in the group were pregnant at the time they received the compound. One of the rules was supposed to have been no pregnant women. The concern was obviously for any potential developing child. However, the compound actually enhanced the in-utero neurological development – which you Tabatha, your sister, and Christian are a testament to. All of the pregnant women except two had disappeared – Christian's mother, and your mother Tabatha."

Tabatha held in a mixed bag of emotions and stared at the ceiling, attempting to hide what she was feeling from the group. Penfield continued observing Tabatha's reaction to the information, then continued.

"Christians' mother began showing signs of rapid cognitive degeneration shortly before going into labor in her sixth month. Your mother, Tabatha, helped me deliver Christian. A month later, your mother suffered the same fate. However, your mothers' cognitive condition was much worse and had to be taken to the hospital, where I delivered both you and your sister. You two were taken immediately to the NICU but *you* weren't expected to make it all. Your mother's cognitive functions declined rapidly following the labor, and within hours, her autonomic system shut down.

Cindy and Naomi's' eyes were swelled up with tears as they listened. Tabatha's eyes were as well. However, she worked hard not to show it.

"I left the NICU for just a couple hours to rest after stabilizing you two. Again, you were in more critical condition, which is why I had a difficult time believing the staff when they attempted to explain to me – after I returned to find your sister gone – that she had simply stopped breathing. Concerned for you, I took you to your grandparents, where I provided them with all the medical equipment they needed for you. They understood full well what was going on, and took precautions. But they felt you would be safer with your aunt and uncle. I had some contacts in the judiciary and was able to fast track a petition for custody for your aunt and uncle."

Naomi had paused playing on her phone. She had never known the external circumstances behind Tabatha falling into their arms. She then added, "Your grandfather told me they felt they were too old to raise another child and asked if we would take you. We said, of course, we would. He said they would sign you over to us, and it was done – so fast. I thought we would have to go to court and file paperwork, but an envelope with everything we needed was on our door the next day." She then looked over at Jason, smiled, and said to him, "you did all that for us?" Jason responded with a simple nod. "Thank you so much."

"Yes! Thank you – for that history lesson," Tabatha then interjected harshly. It was intended to disguise her emotions however. "Now since you know so much about Sorvan, where is he?" Tabatha asks.

"He doesn't know," a new voice enters the conversation. It was a Christian. He was leaning against the doorway frame.

"Christian," Penfield acknowledges.

"Dad," Christian responds.

Tabatha quickly turns to the doorway, "Shera," Christian acknowledges Tabatha's presence as well, sarcastically.

Tabatha attempted to respond in like manner but finds herself frozen with her finger pointed toward him and her mouth half-open analyzing his athletic figure that filled out his simple black T-shirt. Though, she was also intrigued as to why she could not read his mind. The rest of the group waited for an additional response from the two of them, especially Tabatha, except Naomi as she went back to playing on her phone.

Tabatha's awkward silence prompted Cindy to whisper to her husband, "my goodness, girlfriend, do something." He silently laughed. "Within reason of course," Cindy adds.

Tabatha new what Cindy was thinking, so she rolled her eyes then quickly changed her demeanor by standing up straight, grabbing her hair and running her fingers through it.

"That's not quite what I was thinking," Cindy whispers again.

"So...*you* were the one inside my head the other day." Tabatha tilts her head a bit and takes a couple of steps toward him.

"Yes, I was. Aaaand – you're welcome," Christian responds.

"Tabatha, this is my son Christian," Penfield informs, a little late.

"Yeah, we've met, *I* just can't remember where..." Tabatha presses hard to remember.

"He was sitting by you in the waiting room at Dr. Glessinjer's' office last Monday." Naomi reminds Tabatha.

"Ooooh yeah! I remember now. Sooo, you're my stalker?"

"A hot stalker," Naomi interjects.

"Mom!" Tabatha retaliated.

"I was just tasked to monitor you and your behavior. Make sure you stayed out of trouble."

"Hmmm, sounds like a stalker," Tabatha repeated.

"A hot stalker."

"Mom! Seriously?"

"So, did I cross your mind at all this week?" Christian continued.

"Mmmm, no," Tabatha replied.

"And I even dressed up for you."

"You were wearing a white T-shirt and jeans."

"They were clean," he responded.

"This, coming from the chick that wore coveralls and a straw hat to the only date she ever went on," Cindy again whispers to her husband.

"You know I can hear you, right, Cindy?" Tabatha reminds her.

"Sucks, I can't even make fun of her anymore. I want my old Tabatha back," Cindy complains to herself, then snuggles between Kyle's arm and chest, to be consoled.

"I thought about you during the week," Naomi again interjects, though still fixed on her game.

"Oh, and moms' got a crush on you," Tabatha explains rhetorically, to which Christian responds un-flattered; "Oh, really?"

"I'm free tomorrow evening at seven. And I don't have a curfew. But, your shirt better be tucked in – I do have standards," Naomi continues.

"Though they're shallow standards," Tabatha adds.

"At least they're standards," Naomi admits.

"My standards are pretty low too, though," Christian says but directed the comment to antagonize Tabatha, playfully, to which Tabatha responds with an appalled look on her face, at which point Hammer cuts in, to bring the conversation back to the original intent.

"Not to interrupt you twos' form of flirting with each other – as embarrassing as it is for me to watch – but shouldn't we be discussing something a little more prevalent? Like, finding your sister and taking down Sorvan?" Hammer interjects.

"Right! I got it all figured out!" Tabatha says.

"Oh, this ought to be good," Kurtis says under his breath, familiar with Tabatha's' shoot from the hip plans that in the past landed her in trouble.

"Whatever, director. Oh, I mean *Kurtis*," Tabatha replies.

"Whatcha got Tab?" Hammer says to spur on the discussion.

"It's really pretty simple. Air for brains here..." Tabatha points to Christian, who smiles at the comment, "...knows where they are. Mitch, Hammer, and I will go in and..."

"...Save the day!! Right?" Christian, also clairvoyant, interjected his summary of what she was going to say next, but as to make her plan sound ridiculous.

"Awe. Does wittle chwistian want to go to?" Tabatha responds antagonistically to get a reaction out of him, but he continues leaning against the doorpost with his arms crossed, merely smiling. "You're so weird. Can you think something like everyone else?" Tabatha says frustrated that she can't hear his thoughts. Christian laughs.

"Princess, I have to tell you, normally, I'd be down with your plan, but, honestly, I'm a little hesitant to jump blindfolded into this particular scenario..." Mitchell admits.

"Seriously? You *are* still a rookie!" Tabatha retaliates against Mitchells' hesitance. Then picking up what Hammer was thinking, adds, "What?! Ham! Not you too..."

"Tab, you know I'd back you up. But I think we need a little more detailed of a plan. What are we going to do when we run into your sister again?" Hammer responds.

"When I confronted her last time, I..." Tabatha begins, but Christian cuts her off.

"...I saw *everything* up there. What you did was *purely* reflex. You had *no* idea what you were doing..."

"I was getting the hang of it," Tabatha responds.

"Oh, really? The book on the coffee table – move it."

Tabatha looks at the book intently and maneuvers her hand as she did in the apartment complex, which devastated the hallway. The group her watched just as intently to see whether or not she could perform. However, after staring at the object for about a minute, she finally shouts, "move!!" But nothing. "Ok, so I can't move a stupid book," she acknowledges. Then upon throwing her hands up – a sign of giving up – the book fly's off the table and through a window, barely missing Naomi's head in the process.

"TABATHA!!" Naomi shouts as she shoots out of her seat on the couch, shocked from the book buzzing past her head. "Can't you give me a heart attack after my date!?" She takes a deep breath and sits back down and resumes playing her solitaire game.

"Uhhh, I thought she was joking about that," Christian leans over and whispers to Tabatha.

"Yeah, sometimes it's hard to tell," Tabatha whispers back.

"Oh, and I'm sorry about the window Jason," Tabatha apologizes, embarrassed.

"You don't have to apologize to me, it's..."

"Right right right, it's my house. I keep forgetting," Tabatha says. "So Christian, what did you mean by '*you saw everything up there*'?"

"I could access the visual cortex of everyone in the building," Christian explains.

"How was that possible? I tried for an hour and couldn't pick up any telepathic information. She had everyone's' thoughts suppressed."

"No, she didn't. She was suppressing *your* telepathy, and projecting what she wanted you to see and hear," Christian corrects Tabatha's' assumptions.

"HA! I was right!" Mitchel interjected.

"Mitch! I will spill all your secrets," Tabatha threatens.

"Sorry," Mitchel responds.

"And how do you know for certain that she can do all this?"

"Well, first of all, I know, because *I* can do that too," Christian informed. Suddenly the psychic noise filtering into Tabatha's' mind began lessoning and lessoning. Finally, she couldn't receive any telepathic information at all. Her face lit up in amazement. She placed her hands on her head and glanced at everyone trying to read their thoughts, but was unable to.

"Oh-my-gosh! That's incredible. How long can you do that for?" She asks.

"Well, until I lose my focus more or less." Then the psychic noise began slowly funneling back into Tabatha's' mind, to which she responds, "Ahhh – pooo." Christian laughs, but everyone else glances at the two of them awkwardly.

"And secondly, I spent an hour trying to *get* her out of your head," Christian continued his explanation. "I'm sure everyone remembers your *queen Tabatha* moment, with Spencer," Christian reminds her, "That was Sarah. That's important to know because you might now have a better idea of what your sister is really like – just a thought." Christian concludes. Tabatha stood there silent, processing the information for a moment.

"Wait a sec.," Hammer interjects, "so you're saying that she can take over your whole mind and everything? Maybe you shouldn't be going after her then. If she can *control* you like that..."

Christian then further explained, "It's not really, mind control, in that sense. It's more suggestive. Though, incredibly powerful. Then combine *her* projection capability with *your* clairvoyance – that puts *you* at a disadvantage. However, I think it's something you can develop a resistance to," Christian further explains.

"How?" Tabatha asks.

"You're not going to like it, but if you were a little more emotionally balanced." Tabatha rolls her eyes at the statement feeling insulted. "Yeah, that's what I thought you'd say. Seriously though, it's the same principle as when you do your digging for information. It's easier for you to obtain telepathic information when your subject is emotionally unbalanced, right?" Tabatha softly nods, barely admitting that he's right.

"I know where she gets that from!" Naomi again interjects.

"Seriously? I'm nothing like my mother!" Tabatha aggressively responds.

"You wouldn't be saying that if you really did know her," Naomi continued.

"Just out of curiosity, Tabatha, what exactly do you know about your mother?" Penfield then asks.

"Here we go," Naomi says under her breath, expecting another verbal thrashing on her late sister.

"Let's see, oh yeah, she was promiscuous, a severe drug addict, and an alcoholic. And it apparently didn't even bother her that she was carrying us! What do you know about my mother?"

"*Apparently*, a lot more than you do," Penfield confidently responds.

"Why, because she was one of your Guinee pigs for a while?"

"She volunteered to be there."

"If she weren't strung out, she wouldn't have needed to be there!"

"She was there for you – you and Sarah."

"Well, it *obviously* didn't work for her, did it?"

"You know, when she was staying in my condo, we used to talk about random things. Sometimes just to pass the time. Usually, it was to divert from thinking about what she was going to be experiencing when the brain degeneration began. She was actually very funny. I see a lot of her sense of humor in you in fact – and wit as well. But, one evening, she told me that there was a point when she almost took her life due to the severity of her addiction. It was overwhelming to her. Yet, she didn't. What stopped her was you two. As fate would have it, she came across our ad looking for volunteers in a rundown apartment building where there happened to be a lot of drug use going on."

The story slightly took Tabatha. It was the first time she had heard about her mother ever caring about her or Sarah, other than times when Naomi would try to depict her in a positive light – usually in their childhood years. Tabatha remained silent with her arms crossed and stared at the floor as she evaluated her emotions.

"Tabatha," Kyle stood up and joined Hammer, sitting on the back of the couch to interject some words of wisdom into the tense atmosphere, "remember, bitterness is like a poison to the soul. I'm sure I don't need to remind *you* of bad choices *you've* made a time or two that resulted in some fairly significant consequences, right? And who knows, maybe you were placed here for such a time as this. Maybe all of the circumstances that transpired over the years that resulted in your abilities was to ensure you had the tools to confront something really evil," Kyle concludes his micro sermon. "Just something to think about."

"Aw sweetie, I love it when you adlib," Cindy responds.

Tabatha couldn't rebuttal Kyle's words. They did grow up together, so she kept silent.

Christian pulls out his phone and moves his finger around the screen. "Here, I think you should see this," he says. "I've been holding onto this for a long time." One of the east window panes dims until it was completely black. Then an uploading bar displays across the screen.

The video begins in the middle of a Thanksgiving family get together. The date stamp on the bottom of the video was nineteen-eighty. A shot of a much younger Naomi was included, briefly. Soon, Tabatha's' mother Martha came into the video. She was bragging about being off drugs for three months at that point. She also showed off her ultrasound photos of her unborn daughters. Tabatha glanced at Christian for a second then continued watching the video. She walked closer to the screen. Martha didn't look strung out or anything like the drug addict/alcoholic woman that Tabatha had created in her imagination. In fact, Martha looked very similar to Tabatha. Only her hair was redder than Tabatha's. And she looked very happy. Tabatha's grandparents were also in the video and they asked Martha what she was going to name them, to which she said, 'Tabatha, & Sarah.' Martha and her parents waved at the camera before turning it off.

Tabatha turned to the group. Cindy and Naomi were tearing up, even though Naomi wasn't watching the video – she remembered the event. Another video began playing shortly after the first. It was Martha again. Not quite as happy as she appeared in the first video. She was in a room talking directly into the video camera, addressing Tabatha and Sarah.

"Hey, girls. I don't know when you're seeing this. Jason is a really nice guy though. I don't blame him for anything. I hope you don't either. I'm so sorry I won't be there for you. I know Jason will take care of you. There's so much I want to say, but I can't seem to put the words together..." Tabatha slowly walks up to the screen and places her hand on it for a moment as if trying to touch her mothers' face for the first time. "I've made a mess out of my life. Now I get to face the consequences, right? I am always praying that my stupid choices haven't affected your development. I can already tell my mind is going. I'm starting to forget things already. I saw what is going to happen to me. I guess I'm primarily making this video to ask for your forgiveness." Martha begins uncontrollably crying in the video at this point. "Please forgive me, sweethearts. I'm so so sorry. I love you both more than anything. Bye, I love you..." Martha's hand covering the lens is the last thing Tabatha see's before the video ends.

Tabatha faces the group who empathetically stares at her. No one bothers to ask her if she's ok, or how she's feeling – it's obvious, though she tries hard to maintain her composure after seeing the videos of her mother.

"I – uh, need to go to the little girl's room," Tabatha fibs through a fake smile, then speed walks out of the room collapsing to the floor further down the hallway. No one initially follows her, allowing her time to process everything. Her sobbing got louder and louder. Soon her sobbing became hysterical. Shouts of, "Mom!! I need you!!!" & "I don't want this anymore!!!" accompanied her belligerent sobs. Sensing her excruciating anguish, Christian left in an attempt to comfort her some.

"Can I do anything for you?" Christian asks.

"Just leave me alone!" Tabatha says, embarrassed to be seen crying.

"I know how you feel, so if you want to talk, I'm here for you."

"You know!? How do you!?" Tabatha says, with a slightly aggressive tone.

"My mother went through the same thing. I was honestly a bit jealous when I found your mothers' videos. My mother didn't leave me anything like that."

"Oh, right. I'm sorry. I guess we do have a lot in common," she then remembers what Jason explained about Christian's mother. "So, you don't have anything from her?"

"I have a picture of her. With some friends at a club from years ago. I don't know what kind of club it was, nor do I want to."

"Oh, goodness. I'm so sorry. What about your father?"

"Yeah, I tracked him down about fifteen years ago. He's such a loser. He didn't care to meet me. He called my mother a few inflammatory names, that, regardless of my personal feelings about her, I reacted pretty negatively toward." The two of them then slowly walked down the hall as they talked.

"What did you do?"

"I gave him schizophrenia."

"You *gave* him schizophrenia? Oh-my-gosh! How did you do that?"

"Well, I gave him the idea that gremlins were after him. Then I had him admitted to a psychiatric ward. He's been there ever since."

"That's crazy, Christian! You really need to fix that," Tabatha says shocked at the statement.

"I know. Honestly, I feel guilty about it occasionally. I've even gone out to the hospital to fix it. But as soon as I would pull in the parking lot, the thoughts of what he said and who he is, comes back to mind and I get angry and think to myself – no, he deserves it. So I continue to leave him there."

"It almost sounds like your father has *you* locked up more than he is – in anger and bitterness."

"Yeah, I know. I can't seem to shake it."

Tabatha exhales and looks down at the floor and responds, "Of course, I'm the last person on the planet who should be lecturing anybody about bitterness, or forgiveness," she admits. "I spent nearly a lifetime *making* myself hate my mom. Thinking more clearly about it, it's apparent that I just wanted something, or someone, to blame for not being normal. And more so because for all these years, I thought my sister was dead as a result of her drug use and alcoholism. Now knowing that my sister's alive, I definitely have no excuse to hate her. Not that I really did before either." She stops walking and wraps her arms around her chest. A tear or two still fall randomly. "If only I could take back all the things I've said about her." Then a thought pops in her head. "How do you get off this island?" she asks. Christian smiles.

Shortly thereafter, Rodney and David left the lab in the belly of the island and entered the study with a new gadget.

"Well, Jason," Rodney says. "Got good news, bad news, and really bad news."

"Ok?" Penfield responds.

"The good news is we solved the equilibrium sensor problem in Tabatha's' tiara here..." Rodney explains, holding the devise up.

"What's the bad news?" Cindy asks.

"Tabatha and Christian left in one of the choppers," David answers.

"What? Where are they going?" Mitchell asks, both jealous and concerned.

"Awe! Maybe they're eloping," Cindy says excitedly.

"I wish. I've been trying to find a man to pawn her off on for a decade," Naomi says, jokingly of course. "I'm pretty sure I know where she's heading. She just needs some time alone. She'll be fine."

"She might not have much alone time."

Rodney and turns the screen over to a News channel in which Tabatha, once again is the subject of the News segment:

"...Friday, the D.O.J. issued a subpoena for Tabatha Johnson, a former lead member of T.I.D., ordering her to appear before the U.S. Senates' Armed Forces Committee Monday morning to answer questions regarding a suspected connection to the massive explosion of a building in the middle of D.C. on Thursday which left a multitude of dead bodies ranging from confirmed terrorists to an entire SWAT force. The attorney general stopped short of issuing an indictment since her status at the time of the incident was that of a "government-protected asset," which grants her immunity from state and federal prosecution while functioning in that capacity. Instead, he issued the subpoena after a meeting with the secretary of defense who reportedly produced documentation providing substantial evidence linking Tabatha to a string of apparently unexplainable incidents, whereas she was the focal point citing that she possesses a weapon of mass destruction..." the news castor informs. The group stood up in shock at hearing the accusations.

"That's the, really bad news..."

CHAPTER XVII

Dear Mother

It was approaching evening as Tabatha and Christian entered the cemetery in her truck. The section which Tabatha scorched was still noticeable, though some green grass made it's way back. The sight of the burnt area enticed Christian comment on the incident; "You're not going to barbeque us this evening, are you?" But Tabatha wasn't in a joking mood, especially over that incident. Thus she replied, "Seriously? That's not funny."

"Yeah, I guess you're right," he responded.

However, the inappropriate comment prompted a thought in Tabatha over the incident in question. "Wait a minute, how did you know about that? And be honest, please. I'm so tired of secrets and lies. Whether or not they were for *my benefit*," she adds firmly.

"I know you are. And, I am too, honestly. I've been tired of it for a long time. But, besides the fact it was on the news, and everyone around you knows about, I came with David after Naomi called him for help. I was always nearby when you were around someone who had details regarding things that dad believed you weren't ready to know. I telepathically blocked your psychic access to that information. That was my primary task. From time to time, though, I would lose focus and something would slip."

"Like director Jackson in the condo."

"Right."

"Well, that explains a lot. You know, I always thought someone like you was around. You're *illusions* kinda tipped it off. But then I sometimes thought that my telepathy was just acting up," she explained with a smile.

"Yeah, I got bored often. But, honestly, I didn't enjoy keeping those secrets from you," he admits.

"You could have said no."

"I guess. I did understand dad's reasoning behind it. I just didn't always agree with his approach. Plus I have a lot of respect for the man. He's done a lot for me – try raising a kid that when you're reading The Jungle Book to him, you're *in* the jungle. Though I didn't know what I was doing at the time. I guess you could say I had an overactive imagination – haha. When he figured out what was going on, he taught me how to control and develop my abilities," Christian explained as they continued walking. His short summary reminded Tabatha of her god-parents and how patient they were with her over the years as they helped her to develop and control *her* ability after discovering she had telepathy as a child.

"I guess I can't argue with that," she admits. Christian stops a few yards from Tabatha's destination in the cemetery.

"You go on and do what you got to do. I'll hang tight around here and keep these folks company," he says, referring to a couple of other large tombstones. "Besides, I don't want to be more of a distraction than I already am," he says sarcastically. She smiled and agreed then walked the rest of the way to her mother and sisters' tombstones.

As she approached the markers, the images and words of her mother from the videos replayed in her mind bringing back to the surface a few of her previous emotions. She stood about a foot or so in front of the marker. She read the marker:

'Martha Johnson

July 7, 1957 – January 20, 1981'

She had not stood directly in front of her mother's tombstone in years.

"Well, mom, I don't know what to say..." she begins rambling off unscripted words from the top of her head to her mother's tombstone. "I heard you, mom. And I forgive you. But I think I have more to apologize for than you. I know you didn't mean to get involved in all that stuff. I've done a lot of stupid things too mom – ha-ha – like now, I'm talking to a piece of molded concrete." Tabatha then collapsed to her knees and gazed into Heaven. "Lord, could you tell my mom thanks. Thanks for being my mom. Ha – I can do some pretty cool stuff now that I wouldn't be able to do if she hadn't been part of that test all those years ago," she continues speaking toward heaven with a mixture of grieving tears, and sarcastic humor. "Can you also tell her that I'm sorry too? For being such a jerk over the years. Jason's pretty much right. I am egotistical, temperamental, probably more self-absorbed than I should be. I'm not very wise in most instances, and ..."

"...And notoriously lacking in communication skills," a voice from behind her adds to her list. Tabatha drops her head and smiles, telepathically detecting Hammer, Mitchell, Rodney, and Kurtis.

"You guys are thoroughly persistent," Tabatha says.

"Well, we do work for the government – or at least did," Hammer says, sarcastically.

"Yeah, well, can't you *government workers* see I'm in the middle of a deep conversation?" Tabatha says, just slightly annoyed.

"Well, *us government workers* are trying to protect your bottom," Mitchell adds.

"I guess everyone else had enough fun for one day – except you all."

"Things just heated up," Kurtis explains.

"What's heating up?" she responds.

"Would you like us to tell you? Or *think it*, for you?" Rodney rhetorically asks.

"Ha, ha. Point taken, I'm all ears."

"Well..."

"...But skip past the part about taking away my protected asset classification..."

"No," Kurtis responds. "They want to take away your protected asset classification."

"Whatever," she responds, rolling her eyes.

"Why do they want to take that away?" Christian asks, not very educated on the topic.

"In summary, I can't be easily prosecuted for..."

"...screwing up? Lucky you," Christian finishes her statement.

"Ha! You're funny, Minor League," Tabatha responds antagonistically to Christian, referring to his telepathic ability being far less superior to Tabatha's.

"Anyways, children. They put together a hearing with some of the senators who were on the T.I.D. oversight committee. It's scheduled for tomorrow morning. Jason went to the capital to talk with one of the senators on that committee to get more information. He has a profound influence on a few of them," Kurtis adds.

"I love lobbyists," Tabatha wittily expresses her newfound gratitude for Mr. Penfield.

Christians' cell phone rings. "Hello?" Christian walks away from the group for a moment and takes the call.

"So, what exactly is this hearing all about? It's not the first time there was a petition to have my classification revoked. And there was certainly no hearing about it." Tabatha asks.

"Secretary Terrence did, once, try to convince the committee to dissolve T.I.D. so he could have you in his military research program," Kurtis reminds Tabatha.

"Ahhh, yes. I remember that. You think that's what this hearing's about?"

"Definitely a possibility."

"The oversight committee shut him down pretty hard back then. That's possibly why he's always hated my guts," Tabatha considers.

"Probably," Hammer confirms.

"Well, he didn't have much of a case back then, I'm sure he doesn't have much of one now either."

"Things are a little different now than they were back then," Hammer reminds Tabatha.

"Like what?"

"Now they're saying you possess a weapon of mass destruction," Hammer replies.

"What?! That's absurd! Where would I get something like that?!"

"I don't think it's a question of *where*, but *what* they're referring to as a weapon," Rodney explains.

"Come on. You all know I'm not a threat to anyone."

"Tabatha, we all know you. We all know that many of your mass destructo episodes were purely accidental. But the rest of the world doesn't know you as we do," Hammer explains. Tabatha silently validates Hammer's statement with a nod.

"Thanks," Christian ends his phone conversation and walks back to the group. "So that was Jason. He talked to a couple of senators. The issue seems to be spawning from the publics' apprehension of you and what *they* think you're capable of, more or less. There are some other details, but essentially it looks like the secretary of defense is using the publics' anxiety over you to his advantage."

Her face became downcast at the idea that she was intensely feared. Then she thought of her mother and sister, and a look of determination was expressed. "Ok. I will just have to show the world that I'm not worth fearing." The group smiled at her comment.

"And we got your back – like usual," Hammer responds.

"Just try not to drop a building on us," Mitchell adds sarcastically.

"I guess on the plus side; this will give me a chance to find out whether or not *Mr. Secretary of Defense* knows anything about my sisters and/or Sorvan's whereabouts."

"No, you won't," Christian responds.

"What do you mean? He'll be right there. I'll have direct access to his memories..."

"You won't be able to read his mind. I've been following him for the last two years. I can't project anything into his mind or detect even the simplest of thoughts he might be having. His thoughts are suppressed somehow," Christian explains.

"How can that be? I picked up on his perverted thoughts in the trench."

"If you're referring to the day the secretary was in my office blowing up at me – over your FDA debacle – his assistant was in there too," Kurtis revealed, to which Tabatha thought for a moment then responded, "huh. Oops. In that case, I got nothing – idea wise." The group was shocked to hear her admit that.

"However, Sorvan's been working that kind of technology for a long time. Which is why I'm almost a hundred percent certain he's been working with Sorvan," Christian continued.

"And you know this how?"

"It was in with the data Jason retrieved two years ago. In fact, we used that information to come up with a little something to help you control your telepathy."

"Just so you know, I'm not shaving my head, nor am I gonna wear a metal helmet in public."

Rodney then reaches into one of his cargo pockets and pulls out a small case and hands it to Christian, who opens it for Tabatha. An inconspicuous folded piece of metal laid in the case. Christian pulls it out and unfolds it. It appears as a simple black band formed to fit around the forehead. Tabatha takes it from Christian and looks at the front of it. In the center was an opening filled with glass that contained traces similar to that on a circuit board – that was equilibrium sensor.

"Well, it is cute. But it doesn't look all that gadgety," Tabatha responds.

"Well, looks aren't everything. It's made from a variety of rare metals. They give off low emissions of energy. Instead of your entire cerebrum receiving telepathic information, it funnels that information straight into your prefrontal cortex. You should have a greater sense of control over your telepathy," Christian explains.

Tabatha turns it around to place it on her forehead, but as she brought it close to her head and immense pain shot through her skull causing her to drop it and shrink to the ground.

"Tabatha!" They shout. They all rush to pull her off the ground.

"What in the world!?" Tabatha says. "Ok, that thing is my enemy now."

"That was the equilibrium sensor, it must have been set too high," Christian picked it up and pulled out a small device, pointed it at the front of the tiara, and pressed a button on it. "Sorry about that. All the psychic information was a little *too* focused," he explains, then hands it back to Tabatha.

"No way, Jose!" Tabatha said, now fearful of the tiara.

"Oh come on, I promise it won't hurt this time," Christian responds. Tabatha timidly takes it and slowly puts it on.

"Wow!! That's amazing! I can control the noise now," Tabatha says, astonished. "Hmmm, so how sure are you that the secretary is working with Sorvan?"

"I don't gamble, but I'm sure enough to place a wager on it," Christian replies.

"But, you don't know where Sorvan is?" Christian shakes his head.

"Tabatha, you said that Sorvan was trying to collect you. Now, there's a hearing four days later? Not much of a coincident to me," Rodney adds.

"Yeah, I was thinking the same thing," Tabatha agrees. "I have an idea." She then looks at Christian, who sees what she's thinking. "Are you tracking with me?" she asks him. The others were left out of the loop.

"Yeah, but I don't really like it."

"Like what?" the group responds, to which she responds, "Trust me." She then turns back to her mother's tombstone for a moment. "I love you, mom." Then to Sarah's' stone and adds, "Hold on sis, I'm coming." at that, Tabatha clenched a fist and half the tombstone broke off which then only read:

'Sara Johnson
Born January 20th. 1981 –

CHAPTER XVIII

The Hearing

The air was stale but with a hint of moisture. The faint scent of that of an un-sanitized morgue lingered in it. Tabatha slowly wandered down the dimly lit underground maze of tunnels, which seemed to be completely vacant of any occupants. The old brick laid constructed tunnel appeared to go on forever in many directions. The usual conglomerate flow of disorganized telepathic information that her mind usually is consistently inundated with was, again, absent, thrusting a dependence primarily onto her external senses. Her only guide through the maze was a single continuous echo in her mind for help.

After what seemed like wandering around for miles, she comes to a steel door with a small viewing window in it. She could see a figure suspended horizontally amid cryogenic liquid containers and compressed medical gas cylinders. She pulls on the door handle. It was unlocked so she creeps into the room. The sound of electrical equipment buzzing and medical equipment beeping was all that was audible.

She walked in, cautiously, toward the area where she had seen the suspended individual. After rounding the tall steel containers of medical gases, liquid containers, and monitors stationed on mobile racks, randomly situated like an obstacle course, she observed an arm outstretched and clamped at the wrist to a narrow metal platform. As Tabatha continued maneuvering past more equipment, a set of legs that, were restrained in the same manner, came into view. The figure's back rested on a similar platform, curving to the spine as if it had been molded explicitly for that purpose. The individuals' thick hair fell nearly to the floor and the head appeared to be resting on some electronic contraption in which the end was plugged into the base of the individual's skull. When Tabatha approached the body, she identified it as Sarah.

"Oh-my-gosh!! Sarah!! What did they do to you?!" Tabatha's heart sunk as she beheld her sister.

A paper gown, stained with blood and other dried fluids, draped over Sarah's body like a table cloth. The plastic covering that had hidden the majority of Sarah's' face and chin, the last time Tabatha saw her, was off, revealing tubes that had been inserted into her mouth and down her throat. Sarah's face looked identical to her own. A large scar on a portion of her neck was also observable — obviously, the remnant result of Sorvan having disabled Sarah's vocal cords many years ago. However, despite the tortured appearance of her sisters' body, Sarah's eyes were closed in a way that presented her as being in restful sleep.

"I'm going to get you out of here," she says, beginning to pull the tubes out of her sisters' mouth. Sarah's body convulsed slightly as her stomach spit up some fluid upon the removal of the tubes from her throat, then her body relaxed again. Tabatha then manages to release the clasp retaining one of her sisters' arms. Immediately Sarah's eyes open and zoom in on Tabatha. "Sarah! Are you ok? I've got you now," she says, excited to see her sister conscious, but then notices a sad expression enveloping her face.

"You were supposed to save me," Sarah says, beginning to cry. "Why didn't you save me!?" She continued in a grievous overtone.

"I'm saving you right now," Tabatha explains, not quite understanding Sarah's statement, as well as astonished to hear her speak without the functioning of her vocal cords. Then without warning, Sarah's free hand jumps to Tabatha's throat and clenches her windpipe. Sarah's appearance of grief morphs to a look of hostility.

"YOU LEFT ME IN THAT HALLWAY!!" Sarah scolds Tabatha, projecting her voice, piercingly into her mind. Her teeth clenched, her upper lip quivered like that of a rabid animal. She forcibly lifts her head, detaching it from the inserted device.

"Wait, what – are you – doing?" Tabatha struggles to speak through her clenched windpipe. She grabs Sarah's forearm, trying to remove it from her throat, but Sarah's arm begins burning her hands. In a panic, she manages to release a blood-curdling scream, "Aauugghhh!!"

"O-k, princess. You can – let me – down now – please," Mitchell says in a fractured statement as he struggles to breathe from being wedged between a wall and a fiercely dense pressure.

It was now Monday morning. The day of her spontaneous committee hearing at the capital. Tabatha had experienced another night terror and, upon waking up, mistook Mitchell for a hostile entity and telekinetically shot him across the room. It took her a moment to adjust to the reality that she was on Penfield's couch in the living room of his penthouse.

"Mitchell?!! Oh my goodness!!" she said, surprised at herself. She shook her head, which seems to be the only way she knows how to disengage any telepathic or telekinetic process. Mitchell then fell to the floor where he stayed for a moment before slowly getting back up. "I'm so sorry, Mitch!" Tabatha then leans back into the crux of the couch. She runs a hand over her face. Like usual, drenched in sweat.

"He'll be alright, it's what he signed up for," says Hammer as he and Rodney come into the living room after hearing the noise.

"Hey guys," Tabatha conjures enough energy to crack a smile.

"You don't look good, Tab," Rodney observes. "Do you have your medicine?"

"No, I don't. I was kind of hoping you might have something special for me," Tabatha says, referring to either a vile of medicine or the disgusting but very effective green super concoction.

"We do have something special for you," Rodney smiles.

"That's not what I meant," Tabatha responds, psychically deducting that Rodney was, again, referring to the suit, that she has thus far rejected.

"I know what you meant, Tabatha..."

"...Tabatha!" Penfield then walks in and cuts into the conversation firmly. "The outfit is not for fashion, but for function, you would do well to give it a shot." Penfield walks over with an injection gun and hands it to Tabatha then stands in front of the picture window looking out over the city. "Obviously the vanadium in your bandages has all been absorbed.

"Yeah, yeah. Ok, I'll think about it," Tabatha says, accepting the injection gun from Penfield and applying the medicine to her bloodstream. She sets the gun down on the coffee table and leans back into the couch. "So what does this suit do exactly? Does it make me invincible? And bulletproof? Can I fly in it?" Tabatha asks a series of rhetorical questions.

"The suit is insulated with that electrolyte compound. The inner lining is made from a conductive material that allows your body to absorb the energy stored in the compound within the suit. So you should be able to use your telepathic process to its full potential without draining your metabolism." Penfield explains. "However, the energy from the electrolyte will eventually be depleted and does not replenish itself."

"That does sound fascinating. You said I could use my telepathy in it, what about my telekinesis?" she inquires further.

"I'm not sure how much energy that process uses. Though, it is apparent that your metabolism exponentially increases while your telekinetic process is operating," Penfield suggested.

"Why do I feel like a robot when you're talking to me? Process *this*, operating *that*..."

"Well, if you don't like my terminology, you're definitely not going to appreciate the underground alias you've been subtly given."

"What alias?" Penfield tosses the newspaper on the coffee table. "After Tabatha Johnson devastated a portion of downtown and blowing up an abandoned apartment complex – supposedly with her mind – some are referring to her as the – Sentient?" she reads. "What's a sentient?"

"Something with a conscious, basically," Mitchell replies.

"Oh, well, that's redundant. They could have just called me *the Human* then." Rodney was about to interject his humanistic idea but before he got a word out, Tabatha responded, "Shut up Rodney!" He then closed his mouth. "Actually, I've been called worse. The Sentient – it's kinda cool sounding honestly. Better than *Process woman* or *operator chick* – right Jason?" Penfield glanced at her through the corner of her eye then went back to looking out the window.

"Speaking of your telekinetic stuff, you might want to work on getting that thing under control," Mitchell politely adds. "Especially since you have a hearing in about an hour, and you don't want to bring down the capital building on everyone accidentally – just saying."

"Oh quit being a baby, I got it under control," Tabatha replies.

About that time, Christian walks in the room, tossing a rubber ball in the air and catching it. "You think so, do you?" Then without warning, Christian chucks the ball towards Tabatha's head. Rodney ducked as he was nearly in the way.

"Dude!! Seriously?!" Rodney shouts at Christian.

"Sorry, Rodney, I'm just trying to make a point," Christian explains. Everyone looked at Tabatha. Her face was tilted and squinted, with her hands in front of her face as if attempting to deflect the rubber ball, but the ball was stationary just a few inches away from her hands. Christian took a seat on a stool sitting in the corner, then explained his hypothesis. "Well, the reflex aspect of your ability works, but that's not the same as having control over it. I've been thinking that it might operate similar to that of a phantom limb."

Tabatha looked at the ball for a moment, processing Christians' information. Then she drew her fingers in then snapped her hand opened which sent the ball immediately flying back towards Christian, hitting him square in the face and knocking him off his stool.

"Christian! Are you alright?" they asked – That is, everyone except Tabatha.

"Something tells me your right about that," Tabatha nonchalantly responds to Christian's assumption. Rodney helped him up, and blood was coming out of his nose.

"I'd say you deserved that," Rodney said to Christian with a chuckle.

"Probably," he admits.

"A little slow on the reflexes for someone supposedly telepathic I'd say," Hammer adds.

"The telepathic impression came a little late," he explained.

"Telepathic impression?" Rodney inquires.

"A telepathic impression happens before a physical *activity* occurs. If, for instance, you were going to draw a picture, the *thought* about drawing a picture would come across to me – or Tabatha – would appear fleeting. But, as you were about to engage in the action physically, the *thought* comes across clearer. Details are reinforced in the thought because you *are* going to do the activity," Christian explains. "Right Tab?"

"Whatever you say. I never got the *Telepathic Terminology for Dummies* handbook – you all have a word for everything."

"That's insightful," Rodney responds, intrigued.

Then Christian whispers to Rodney, "plus, in women, I've noticed there to be a narrower window between thinking about an action and the action itself."

"Or maybe it's because we want to get something done, and not stare at a wall for ten minutes before finally hanging up the picture. And I mean, what's the deal with five men needing to stare at an engine for twenty minutes before attempting to figure out what's wrong with it anyways. Talk about a gap between thinking and doing," Tabatha responds to Christian's whispered comment.

"Definitely a former government employee. You'd think she worked for the C.I.A." Rodney responds.

Tabatha narrows her eyes, then the rubber ball on the floor behind them flew up and smacked Rodney in the back of the head. Tabatha then held out her hand, and the ball came zooming toward her and into her hand.

"What was that for?" Rodney responded to being pelted in the back of the head with the rubber ball.

"Sorry about that, but you know, us women don't have much of a window between thinking and doing," she responded but directing the comment to Christian. "Anyways, I think I'm starting to get the hang of this."

"Just be careful, princess. You're starting to break blood vessels again," Mitchell responds, observing sweat drops of blood coming out of her forehead. A reminder of the enormous stress her telekinesis has on her body. She then wiped her brow.

"Well, Tabatha, if you're done playing around. You might want to start making yourself look presentable. Your hearing begins soon," Penfield interjects.

Tabatha nods, affirming Penfield's statement. She glances over at the case containing the special suit sitting on the floor under the window. "It's kind of exciting, honestly. My first public appearance – scheduled, public appearance that is. I suppose I better make a good first impression."

....

"We're here at the capitol building waiting to see whether or not Tabatha Johnson will indeed show up to today's' committee hearing..." – reporter.

"Recently released documents confirm Tabatha Johnson as the protected government asset responsible for the somewhat indescribable exploits during federal tactical operations in recent months. According to sources, due to the enormous cost of damages, her protected asset classification is being revoked. However, the context of the hearing itself, which was pushed for by defense secretary Allen Terrence, is highly classified," – reporter.

"As you can see behind me this morning, hundreds of protestors have gathered in front of the capitol building, which would explain the above-average number of security personnel present. Many protesters have been chanting slogans disapproving of the governments' involvement with an individual, who some define as superhuman. But others seem to be here in support of Tabatha. Rumor has it that she possesses some sort of mental powers – Hopefully, she's pro-limited government," – reporter.

Inside the chamber within the capital building in which the hearing was to be held, senators were walking in and out, talking on cell phones, and conversing about the hearing. Senator Pits had a close relationship with Penfield and new more than most about him, but of course, the relationship was reciprocal, i.e., Penfield was a big donner to Pits campaign in previous elections. Pits, was one of the senators who ran with Penfield's' blueprint for implementing the Telepathic Interrogation Division. He was also one of the senators on the phone.

"Ok, Penfield, I'll let them know," Senator Pits ends his phone call. "Secretary Terrence…" the secretary was finishing setting up a monitor for the hearing, then turned to the senator. "…They're here."

"They?" the Secretary inquires.

"Yes, *they*. Tabatha and the remainder of the T.I.D. protocol team," the Senator explains.

"Mr. Senator, the information in the hearing is classified. You know that."

"*Mr. Secretary*, these guys have top-secret clearance. They're part of T.I.D…"

"…Correction, they *were* part of T.I.D. Which has now been formally cast into the bureaucratic ash heap of legislative history," the Secretary firmly interjects, as well as making clear his opinion on the former T.I.D. project.

"Sir, we all know what you're trying to do. You might have some ally senators who get a wet pallet at the idea of dissecting Tabatha to figure her out, but the majority of us are going to give you the same answer as last time," the Senator firmly replies then walks out of the chambers and to the front of the building to greet Tabatha to the Capital.

The multitude outside the building was loud. But law enforcement kept the crowd at bay. Then a hush fell over the assemblage of people, and then the center of the crowd began to part, creating a path to the capital building. At the mouth of the opening in the crowd stood Tabatha. Several different reasons could have prompted the unusual silence, but it was probably brought on by her outfit.

The vague illumination from the vanadium electrolyte liquid within the interior of her suit was slightly observable through the suit's vents, and joints as the outer flesh of the outfit were mostly of a callous material. At least it wasn't a yellow and blue latex outfit. But she did have a tiara on her forehead, which was mostly covered by her hair. The glass piece in the center reflected the sunlight, thus appeared to be glowing to the crowd.

Tabatha looked around at the crowd for a moment. If there were a competition for being nervous, it would be a toss-up between the crowd and Tabatha. Mitchell and Hammer were on either side and a step or two behind her. They were in their T.I.D. gear – they obviously didn't get the directions to the trash heap the Secretary had mentioned earlier. Rodney was behind them as well as Christian and Penfield. Tabatha timidly smiled at the crowd barely waving "uh – hi," she softly said.

Penfield then walks out in front and says to her, "what's wrong with you? You act as you've never been in public before. Now, let's get this over with." Penfield then turns and heads to the capitol steps, not intimidated at all by the publicity with Christian and Rodney behind him and Tabatha, Mitchell, and Hammer following.

Tabatha made little eye contact with the people in the crowd. As Tabatha approached the capitol steps, a woman in the crowd started yelling for a child. A little girl, maybe three or four years old, attracted by the colorful illuminating suit, ran out past the police barricade toward Tabatha. But halfway to Tabatha, the child stopped at hearing her mother. Tabatha turned at hearing the commotion. She got a glimpse of an innocent thought from the child. She wanted to touch the glowing suit.

Tabatha walked toward the young girl who was now a little startled and bent down to her level. She smiled at the small child. "Hi, how are you?" Tabatha says. The young girl waved at Tabatha as the mother rushed in behind the little girl and swept her off the ground, followed by a police officer who was chasing after the mother.

"It's alright, officer," Tabatha said. The officer backed off and returned to his position. She then directed her attention to the mother. "She can touch it if she wants to. It's not going to hurt her," Tabatha affirms. The mother maintained her position with her child in her arms and hesitantly asked her little girl is she wanted to feel the glowing outfit. The child rapidly nodded her head. Tabatha walked up close and put her arm out toward the child. The child stroked the material of the suit a couple of times then seemed uninterested in it after that. "You can feel it too if you'd like Lori," Tabatha said to the mother, deducting that she was slightly curious about the suit also. Lori, still holding her child, smiled at the fact that Tabatha knew her name, then touched the material as well.

"Wow, that doesn't feel anything like it looks," Lori said.

"I know. It's, uh, it'ssssss..." Tabatha thinks for a moment, "...actually, I have no idea what this is made out of ha-ha," Tabatha explained, then the two of them laughed.

"You know, you don't seem anything like what's been described of you in the news," Lori informs Tabatha.

"Yeah, that's the mainstream media for you. A lot of exaggerated hype," Tabatha responds.

"Yeah, like the dump truck thing last week?" Lori asks.

Tabatha squinted half her face at that comment. "Weeeeeelll that one was fairly accurate, I suppose. It was a complete accident though," Tabatha admitted.

Meanwhile, as Tabatha was developing a new relationship, Senator Pits greeted Penfield and company at the bottom of the steps. "Penfield," he acknowledged and shook his hand.

"Senator," Penfield likewise responded. "This is Rodney. He's our – or should I say, he *was* head of the T.I.D. medical staff," Rodney then shook the senators' hand as well.

"You remember Christian, I'm sure."

"Yes, I do. Christian, it's good to see you again."

"Likewise Senator," Christian shook the senators' hand.

"And this is..."

"...Hammer, You're well known by army folk around here. Pleasures mine," the senator responded and shook Hammer's hand.

"Oh, really? I wasn't aware I had a reputation around here. I generally try to avoid politicians," Hammer responds.

"Yeah, I don't blame you. So do I," the Senator says, and they laugh. "So, I see Tabatha hasn't changed much. Still preoccupied until the last second," the Senator says referring to the fact that the hearing is going to start shortly and Tabatha is busy chattering with someone.

"I believe she's trying to make friends, sir," Penfield guesses.

"This will be a breakthrough," Rodney sarcastically interjects. They could hear Tabatha and the young mother, Lori laughing, while the crowd watched their interaction.

"Tabatha!!" Senator Pits shouted. "It's five minutes till eight," he informs her.

"Right!" she responds. "It was nice meeting you, Lori. And nice to meet you too, Kylie," Kylie's little hand. Then suddenly, Tabatha's demeanor again changed. At the same time, more commotion was coming from the crowd. Someone was screaming incoherently as he pushed himself to the front of the barricade. With the aid of her tiara, she was able to single out a hostile intention.

"Quick, get behind me," She says to Lori. Tabatha took a few steps toward the crowd, and when she was about fifteen feet from the barricade, a man broke through the crowd stopped by two police officers. The man pulled out a gun and pointed directly at Tabatha shouting profanity at her as well as his opinion that she wasn't human.

Then he fired several shots as Tabatha threw one hand out in front. Her suit lit several times brighter as the bullets began colliding with what appeared as an impenetrable glass shield. The concaved shells fell to the ground. Tabatha then lifted her other hand slightly and balled a fist as if clenching onto something, and simultaneously the barrel of the gun concaved. Then opening her hand, the gun flew out of the man's hand and stopped in mid-air in front of her. With a few maneuvers of her fingers, the magazine from the weapon uncoupled and ejected from the guns handle. She then walked toward the man, who was now on the ground being handcuffed by police. The gun and magazine followed her before landing in the hands of another officer as she passed him – he had an expression of shock at the scene. As soon as the gun and magazine were in the officer's hands, the brilliance of Tabatha's' suit faded back to its earlier illumination.

Tabatha knelt in front of the man who attempted to murder her. "What was that for?" She asked.

"For Breathing!!" he shouted at her in disdain.

"Yeah, sometimes I forget that I do that. It's an autonomic function. Sorry about that," she retorted.

"You're subhuman and a threat!!" he continued shouting nonsensical verbiage.

"Seriously? Do you even hear yourself? You're saying I'm less than human, *and* a threat," she rhetorically lectures him over his contradictory statement. The police get him up onto his feet, and Tabatha stood up, facing him as well. "I'm either sub-human *or* a threat. I can't be both. You have to pick one or the other," she continued. Then the man spits directly in Tabatha's' face, not listening to anything she said, but continuing to scream insulting language toward her. Some of the statements were directed at the crowd to get them to return to their earlier fear-induced behavior.

"Tabatha!!" Penfield yelled toward her. It was now eight o'clock. At hearing Penfield, she turned and rushed toward the capital building, slowing briefly to say goodbye to Lori and Kylie one last time.

"It was really great talking to you. We'll get together sometime for tea or something. Bye, Kylie," Tabatha said than continued off.

"We will?" Lori said to herself, shaken over the recent incident.

Penfield shook his head as she ran up the steps.

"Did you see what I did?" Tabatha said, totally proud of herself.

"Impressive princess. I didn't know you could do that," Mitchell said.

"Yeah, me neither," she responded.

"You mean you were just guessing," Rodney asked, shocked.

"Basically. One thing I've learned over the years is to, at least, *act* confident in public situations," she says.

"Right. And who taught you that?" Christian asks.

"I did, like – two minutes ago," Tabatha admitted. Then they all follow the senator inside. As they were entering the building, Tabatha glanced over at one of the security guards. "Peculiar," she said to herself.

"What is it?" Christian asked.

"One of the security guards. I wasn't receiving any psychic noise from him," she whispers. They were approaching a checkpoint with a few more security guards. "Ok, something's not right."

"I couldn't read them either. But, they look exhausted, maybe they're just tired," Christian theorizes.

"I'm a professional profiler, remember? Even without my telepathy, I can tell something's not right," Tabatha explains. "Hey, Senator Pits? Are *all* of the security guards new?" She asks as they continue walking down a hallway.

"Honestly, I couldn't tell you that for certain. But the majority of our security is contractual. Usually through the local police. In lieu of this mornings' hearing, I imagine they contacted extra security for obvious reasons," he explains. "Why do you ask?"

"Do you think it would be too much to ask your security…" they stopped just outside the doors leading to the chamber that the hearing was being held in, "…to check your security?" She asked the senator. He was about to answer her in the negative, thinking it was a silly question, but realizing who he was talking to, quickly considered that she might have a legitimate concern about something.

"Well, how about this. Mr. Penfield, unfortunately, you, Hammer, and the rest of your group here won't be able to sit in due to the classified nature of the hearing," Senator Pits reiterated.

"What?! But we're…" Hammer began to complain before Tabatha interjected.

"Calm down, Ham ham…"

"Ham-Ham?" Senator Pits questioned the nickname.

"DON'T ASK," the whole group said in unison.

"What the senator was about to suggest, was while this is going on in here, why don't you fella's check out security," Tabatha finishes the senator's suggestion.

"Yeah, I'm down with that," Hammer agrees.

They were told where the central security hub in the building was and headed that way.

"Hey, Christian?" She says. He turns around.

"Yeah?"

"Can you hear me?" she says in her mind. Christian nods. "Let's stay connected. Let me know if anything's wrong. And remember the plan," Tabatha concludes.

"You got it," Christian winks and heads to meet up with the others. Tabatha smiles. She turned to the senator, who had a questioning look on his face.

"Oh, sorry, they're coded winks. Three means I love you, two means you're getting a little chunky, and one means…." Tabatha's sense of humor was getting the best of her again but noticed that the look on the senators' face indicated that it was not getting the best of him. "…ok, I'm just kidding around."

"I see. My suggestion would be to keep the jokes until after the hearing. Preferably long after the hearing. And that's for your benefit more than mine," the senator explains, then opens the doors to the chamber.

The chamber was alive with conversations between the different senators and their opinions on this and that. But after Tabatha was observed entering, the level of conversations declined as many began clapping instead. But others just watched her walk down the aisle. Then Kurtis popped out of the group of senators.

"What are you doing here? I thought this was a super-secret hearing thing."

"I thought you could read my mind," Kurtis says sarcastically. Tabatha pointed to her tiara.

"I can turn it on and off now – kind of."

"Right. Well, you know I'm still under the F.B.I. so I have plenty of top-level security clearances available to me. Besides, your pal Pat..." Tabatha rolled her eyes at the statement, "...could go the rest of his life without being in the same room with you."

"Oh, how sweet."

"And I thought you needed someone by your side." She smiled at the comment. "I do have one piece of advice, however," he lowers his voice to a whisper. "Answer their questions *after* they ask them. If you get my meaning."

"Yeah yeah, I know."

"This way Tabatha," Senator Pits leads her and Kurtis to a table next facing the senators.

After the two were seated, Secretary Terrence walked up to them. "Tabatha, thank you for coming on such short notice," Secretary Terrance greeted, seemingly friendly. He was impressed by the outfit and commented, "That's quite the fancy get up you got on there. And you're..." he points to her tiara, "...that's neat too. Does it do anything? Or just something to make you look pretty? Not that you need any help with that of course," the secretary continues his casual and cordial conversation with her while the senators and other personnel in the chamber are taking their seats.

"It does do something. All this is an assist to my – superpowers," Tabatha sarcastically responds.

"Right. Interesting," the secretary responds.

"And, you're welcome."

"You're welcome?"

"For showing up on such short notice," Tabatha reminds him. She begins attempting to discern any thoughts from the secretary telepathically.

"Oh, right. Well, you know how it is, sometimes you just have to ask yourself – why wait?" the Secretary says, his demeanor becoming less cordial and friendly with each new statement.

"Wait for what? Exactly?" Tabatha asks.

The secretary looks at her with a puzzled face at the question glancing at Kurtis only on occasion. "Oh, I thought you could read my mind," he said slowly. A cynical smile then overcame his face. She smiled back at him. Then he leaned toward her ear and whispered, "Are you looking for something?" then he backed up and looked down at her.

"Actually, Mr. Secretary, I am looking for something."

"Oh, and what would that be?" Tabatha was about to answer, but a leading senator on the panel stood and spoke up. Tabatha then turned and whispered to Kurtis, "There may be a problem with the defense secretary and the security guards."

"What kind of problem?"

"I can't read their minds." Kurtis then enveloped a mild look of concern.

Meanwhile, as the hearing began, Tabatha's click was with the head of security going through security vendor records and looking over security video footage over the past several hours.

"Christian?" Tabatha says in her mind while the Secretary continues prompting the debate over topics regarding less about having the protected asset classification removed and more about how Tabatha would be a more significant asset in direct connection with military research.

"I hear you. What's up?" Christian answers in like manner.

"You're right, I can't pick up any cognitive transmissions from the defense secretary," she confirms.

"I told you."

"Yeah you did. Anyways, let me know if there's a problem on your end."

"Roger that," Christian sarcastically answers

"Oh, whatever," she accidentally verbalizes.

"Huh?" responds Kurtis.

"Oh, nothing, talking to Christian."

"Right."

The secretary had begun showing recorded video coverage of the missions she had been on and the damage she had caused in the process. The nuclear reactor centrifuges and missile silo in Iran; an airport in New York; a federal building in Michigan; and of course, the incidents that occurred in the last week which included; the F.D.A. building, the dump truck, and the apartment complex – all in D.C. Tabatha felt a sense of guilt for some of the mishaps but sensed the overall consensus from the senators was that she might have made mistakes that cost the government millions in property damage, she potentially saved thousands of lives in the process. A couple of senators, senator Pits was one, who stood up and declared that same thought verbally. However, others *did* have a concern that she was uncontrollable and a danger to the public. And yet others were neutral on the idea of whether she was a danger or not, but was more interested in her abilities in general and really really really wanted to find out how they operated.

"Mr. Secretary, with T.I.D. being dissolved, removing Tabatha's status as a protected government asset is acceptable for debate – no offense Tabatha – ..." one senator says.

"None taken," she responds.

"...Considering the publics' knowledge of her, but you're asking us to decide whether or not to lock her up in a lab. She's a citizen protected by the same constitutional rights as the rest of us. What you want to do is inhumane, Mr. Secretary."

"Oh, really? Inhumane is it? Using a remote the monitor then displays an image of a DNA strand. "You know what this is Senators?"

"It's a double helix," one senator said, unimpressed.

"I have a picture of that in my old college biology textbook," another Senator added, insultingly.

"Well then, senator, I'm sure you remember from your *college biology textbooks* that the DNA double helix consists of a string of *four* nucleotides linked together through phosphate groups. The *four* types of nucleotide units are characterized by the letters G, C, A, and T. Stay with me senators," The secretary continues. "This strand of DNA consists of *five* nucleotides." Curiosity then replaced the antagonistic attitude in a few of the senators. Tabatha stood up and walked up to the monitor.

"Look familiar, Tabatha?" the Secretary asks, with his cynical smile plastered across his face.

"That's mine?" she asks in return.

"Yes, it is."

Tabatha walked up to the secretary. "My DNA is off limits! Code of federal regulations under the T.I.D. protocol..."

"...T.I.D. is dead, that C.F.R. died with it when it was repealed last week. Or maybe you were too busy destroying buildings to have gotten the message. You, Tabatha, aren't one of us. You are chaos incarnate."

Tabatha held her tongue and walked back up to the monitor.

"Now listen!! She is NOT HUMAN!!" the secretary shouts out of frustration at the senators. "On her own, she's a potential threat to our democracy!! If she really wanted to be of ultimate value to *mankind*, she should be allowed to be thoroughly studied."

"Secretary Terrance, part of the reasoning behind her protected asset classification, is to avoid the potential unethical treatment that could arise by the scientific community," another senator.

"Senators, have you not seen the damage she's done? The government has spent billions to protect her and cover up her mistakes. And now the public knows of her existence, and they're afraid of her! What compelling interest does the government have in protecting her now? But there is a compelling interest in understanding her potential. If we're allowed to elucidate how she operates and apply...it...to..." the secretary continued his lecture but then became distracted at hearing giggles. Yes, giggles. Tabatha had started giggling after briefly studying the information on the monitor. Soon her giggling turned into full-blown laughter. The chamber was then filled with the sound of whispers.

"Tabatha?" One of the senators said.

"You know?" Tabatha interjected, "I literally just had an epiphany," she turned and faced the senators and Secretary Terrance. "Those *humans*, outside. Thousands of them. When I showed up, they backed away from me. They – hushed. One of my *gifts*, as my aunt would call it, is the ability to feel the emotions of others. They were, well, most were, afraid of me. For some time now, it would upset me when I felt that someone was afraid of me. In here, I don't feel fear," Tabatha walks back to the monitor and looks at the strand of DNA. "Everyone in here trusts me. I have five nucleotides, ' huh? Last I checked, five was greater than four…"

"Tabatha…" one of the senators said, getting a little nervous hearing what she was saying.

"…So maybe you're right – Mr. Secretary. Maybe I'm not human." She then turned to face the secretary with a scowl across her face, "…maybe…*I'm better than human.*" Tabatha swiftly raised her forearm and clenched her fingers together, and simultaneously her suit lit up as before. The secretary was then unable to move. As she walked toward him, he slowly rose off the ground. With a simple maneuver of her fingers, the secretary's body tilted diagonally toward her until his face was only a few inches from hers. As she glared at him intensely, he could make out the slight illumination of her irises. Then she added, "And that would make you – inferior to me."

Tabatha's sudden and unpredictable action immediately aroused a sense of anxiety in the senators. "Now I feel it," she said to the secretary. "I can feel fear in this room."

The senators ran to exit the chamber, however, maneuvering her other hand, Tabatha seeled the chamber doors, prohibiting the senators from escaping.

"Tabatha! What are you doing?" Kurtis stands up and exclaims. Tabatha then winked at the director, assuring him that she wasn't going to harm anyone, but was only attempting to make a point. He then sat back down and just watched the show.

"But you know the thing that *really* makes us human? Conscience." Tabatha lowers her arms, and the secretary drops to the floor and collapses to his knees, catching his breath. "My conscience directs me to do what's good and right. And standing for life is both. Where does your conscience lead you, *Mr. Defense secretary?*" He didn't say a word as the pressure holding him up also made it difficult for him to breath. "Secretary Terrance, you'll never experiment on me. You'll never use me for military research." Tabatha stepped away from the secretary for a moment and talked face to face with the senators who were all standing near the doors watching the scene.

"How are we supposed to trust you?" one of them asks.

"That's a good question. I've made a lot of mistakes. Many worthy of inciting fear. I suppose apologizing for my screw up would be a start, I hope. And I believe God holds me accountable for what I do just like anyone else. I'm learning to be more mindful of that. So trust me for those reasons, if you would." Her words seemed to relinquish many of the senator's worries as some smiled, and others nodded in accepting her statement. "Oh, and just one more thing no more of this *Tabatha's not human* junk. It certainly isn't the first time I've been told that, but it's getting a little old."

After talking with the Senators, Tabatha turned back to the secretary, who was still buckled over on the ground, collecting himself. His military background was pretty extensive, but that was the first time experiencing anything like that. "Mr. Secretary, are you alright?" she asks revealing her more compassionate side. But then she notices a small blinking light behind his ears. "What in the world?" she whispers to herself.

"Christian. Can you see what I'm seeing?" She asks.

"Yeah. That looks like an implant of some kind. That could be what's making it difficult to read his mind," Christian suggests.

"I highly doubt this is standard equipment for military personnel."

"Sorvan was doing research and development on something to suppress thought transmissions. That was part of the data dad was able to retrieve from Pakistan."

"So it looks like you were right, he *must* be working for Sorvan. Have you gotten a closer look at those security guards?"

"These so-called security guards are spread out through the entire building."

"No, kidding." Tabatha grabs the secretary and pulls him off the floor. "Ok big shot! You wanted to know what I was looking for earlier? Where's my sister?!" To which the senators look to one another and ask, "She has a sister?"

Meanwhile, in the security hub, Mitchell and Hammer had been watching time-lapsed video footage over the past twelve hours. Finally, something suspicious is noticed.

"Christian! I think we've found something," Mitchell said. He, Hammer, Rodney, and Penfield watched the recording from over the shoulder of the head of security who was sitting in front of the consul. Christian, who had been just outside the hub in order to concentrate communicating with Tabatha, rejoined the others huddled around the surveillance screens. The footage revealed dozens of individuals dressed in security outfits unusually walking in and out of the utility access door. The video feed then went black around three o'clock am then resumed at five o'clock am. The group looked at each and in unison shouted, "THE BASEMENT!!"

As they were heading to the basement, Christian pulled Penfield aside, "Jason, listen, Tabatha has a plan. But we will probably need back up if you know what I mean. You got the connections," Christian explained.

"Why do I have a feeling it's a plan I wouldn't approve," Penfield responds.

"You wouldn't, that's why I'm not telling you what it is yet," Christian further explains.

"Do you trust her plan?"

"It's risky, but it could work. We're keeping it close to the chest. I just feel that we might need some reinforcements when the time comes."

"I see. Rodney, come with me," Penfield called out.

"What do you need him for?"

"What do *you* need him for?" Penfield asked back.

"There's more of them then there is of us."

"I'm trusting you, you can trust me too. Come on, Rodney," Penfield again said, then he and Rodney left. "Oh, and if you get into a tight spot like Ms. Naomi says – just use your thing!"

"Right," Christian, he responds. "Tabatha, there's something in the basement. We're on our way down their now to check it out."

"It's probably anther bomb," she rhetorically replies. "Kurtis!! We should probably evacuate the Building. Get the senators out of here," she shouted with great concern. Kurtis, trusting Tabatha's' judgment, begins corralling the senators out of the chamber then pulls the fire alarm on the way out.

"Mr. Secretary, I'm still waiting for your answer, where's my sister. Don't make me get emotional..."

As Christian, Mitchell, and Hammer, make their way down to the basement, they're confronted by several more men in security outfits.

"You're not allowed down here," One of them said, attempting not to sound suspicious.

"Oh, well, you see, it's getting cold upstairs and, Uhm, we're part of the maintenance crew and just want to make sure the pilot's still lit in the furnace," Mitchell said off the cuff. Hammer and Christian glance at each in disapproval of Mitchell's noticeably fabricated statement. The *supposed* guards drew their sidearms and aimed at the group. The three of them slowly put their hands up.

"Now go," said one of the phony guards.

"I can read most of their thoughts," Christian said, then projected, "Don't move and whatever you do – don't freak out," into Mitchell and Hammers' minds. The guards then began acting incoherently and attacking each other shooting one another until only one was left standing. Mitchell quickly drew his gun and shot the remaining individual while he was distracted.

"Ok, what just happened?" Hammer asked.

"Gremlins," Christian answered.

"Gremlins?" Mitchell asks.

"Yeah. Giant gremlins," Christian added. Christian then inspected the deceased guards for the implants Tabatha had mentioned. The last guard he inspected indeed had Tabatha earlier described to him.

"Tabatha, one of your security guards down here had that same implant installed."

"I hate being right all the time," she responded.

"Has anyone ever told you that you're smarter than you look?"

"Yes."

"Of course." The three of them then rush through the doors and onto a metal-grated raised walkway. Grated steps lead down to the concrete floor. But they didn't have to go any further.

"No – way!" Hammer said anxiously.

"Tabatha. There are about a hundred barrels ready to blow down here!"

Hammer and Christian looked at Mitchell, the tech guru, who one of his specialties is the disarming of bombs. Mitchell made a quick, vast observation of the seen. Numerous metal barrels of high explosives filled the entire basement of the capitol building. Each barrel was wired to its own individual detonator and a timer counting down – they just passed the two-minute mark.

"I don't think so – not this time," Mitchell stated firmly before quickly turning and bolting back out of the doors and back up the stairs.

Mitchell immediately set his stopwatch on his wrist. "Christian, you better let your girlfriend know she's got about a minute and a half to get out of the building!" Mitchell advised as they ran up the stairs.

"Tabatha! You have a little over a minute! I hope your meeting's over!"

"Secretary Terrance, you're coming with me," Tabatha's' suit again lit up as she maneuvered her hand, and the secretary's body quickly sat up straight.

"What about getting the bomb squad down here?" Hammer suggested to Mitchell, as the three of them sprinted through the building. As they approached the building's exit, a number of bogus security guards blocked the exit.

"You gotta be kidding me!" Hammer shouts as the three of them duck behind two structural pillars just before the bogus security guards began shooting at them.

"Great! Now we're either going to get shot to death! Or die in an explosion!" Mitchell shouts. He looks at his watch – about thirty seconds till detonation.

"Hey, Christian! Can you do your illusion trick on them?!" Hammer shouts over the gunfire.

"I can't get into most of them. Plus, there's way too many this time!" Christian responds. Mitchell and Hammer returned fire every few seconds from behind the pillars.

"We only have twenty seconds, Hammer!" Mitchell informed.

"Tabatha! We could use your thing right about now. If you're available of course, no rush or anything like that,"

"My thing? Starting to sound like my aunt. Maybe you too *would* make a nice couple," she responds. Just then, the hostiles were tossed up in the air and held up to the ceiling, unable to move. Then Tabatha in her bright outfit, ran up from the protruding hallway with one hand held up in front of her holding the hostiles up against the ceiling. The secretary was following her in mid-air, horizontally frozen.

"Let's go!" Hammer shouts. They then sprint out of the building and down the steps followed by Tabatha – who was *technically* followed by Secretary Terrance. At the moment Tabatha exited the building, all the bogus security guards then fell from the ceiling, slamming into the ground. Mitchell looked at his watch as it flashed zero, and then – most anarchists' dream come true – the capital building explodes. With thousands of people outside the building, it was chaos as thousands of people were running around and screaming. Police and real security guards were trying to move, representatives, and other political officials out of the way. Tabatha dropped the secretary on the concrete and attempting to slow some of the large pieces of the dislodged building they came barreling to the ground. A large junk of the dome was hurdling to the ground where an individual was standing. Throwing a hand up in the air, the piece of dome stopped just above the person who just stood there in shock.

"Yeah, I'm thinking the same thing you are," she says to the person who was recording her with his phone. "Would you get out of the way?" She then shouted, then, with a maneuver of her other hand, the individual flew out from underneath the dome, and then she dropped the massive piece of metal and bronze.

"You're not looking so hot there, princess," Mitchell observed. Tabatha was beginning to sweat heavily, as the energy in her suit was depleted, which was evident by the loss of fluorescence emitted by the electrolyte liquid.

After the deluge of building pieces had ended, the secretary enraged began blaming Tabatha for the entire incident. "You did this!!" he shouts at her.

"You're out of your mind. I didn't cause this mess!" Tabatha shouted back at him. Of course, the media cameras were still rolling and the secretary knew it.

"You obviously wanted to disrupt the hearing and make yourself look like some hero to maintain your protected asset status!" the secretary continued.

"I don't even care about that," she responded.

"And you attacked me," the secretary added.

"I never attacked you!" She said. Then she changed her statement after thinking about it for a second. "Well, I wasn't attacking you – I was just proving a point. And really, I saved your life," she explained.

"To make yourself look like a hero when you're – dangerous. Like most animals." The statement riled her up and headed toward the secretary. But then Christian pulled out the device associated with Tabatha's Tiara and triggered the equilibrium sensor to increase in frequency immediately sending her to the ground in pain from the skull-splitting, ear-piercing noise. Once she appeared incapacitated, the head-splitting sound seized.

"Christian!" Hammer and Mitchell ran after Christian, having now believed that he turned on them. Christian turned toward them with a hostile expression on his face. He gazed at Hammer intensely, causing him to stop in his tracks. Collapsing to the ground, he placed his hands on his chest as it felt like it was going to explode.

"Christian! What are you doing?!" Mitchell shouted angered but cautious.

"I disrupted his autonomic memory that keeps his heart going – Just another little *gift* I have. You two just chill out. Oh and Hammer, if it's any consolation, I'm sure you'd whoop me in hand to hand combat," Christian answered then turned his attention back to Tabatha and the defense secretary. "Sorry, Tabatha. I really do like you. But I have to agree with Secretary Terrence. You are definitely dangerous."

He walks over and hands the secretary the device associated with Tabatha's' tiara. As Christian walked back from the secretary, Tabatha, full of rage, leaped to her feet and swung at Christian. The first fist was blocked, but the second lunged into his abdomen causing him to buckle over to which she then sent her previous fist back to his face with an uppercut, and with his head calked backward she sent a final blow to his lower jaw to which Christian fell to the ground feeling slightly disorientated from attack. The secretary then pointed the device at Tabatha again, and she fell to the ground in pain. He finally signaled for police to come and handcuff her.

Hammer, who was still recovering from the feeling of his chest concaving, was anxious to go after Tabatha seeing what they were doing to her. But Mitchell said to him, "Hey, man, I know what you're thinking, but we can't right now." Mitchell and Hammer glared at Christian on the ground, his face bloody from Tabatha's' blows. Christian glared back at them. Then he got up. A large armored S.U.V. pulled up and the police put Tabatha in the back in between more security. Christian got up and then crawled into the S.U.V., followed by the secretary and all Mitchell and Hammer could do was simply watch them disappear down the road.

Tabatha laid in the back of the S.U.V., barely conscience from the equilibrium sensor affecting her cognitive functions. Christian sat by himself in the seat in front of her while the defense secretary sat with his detail in the seat in front of him. Christian reached behind his seat for Tabatha's tiara, tampering with the equilibrium sensor. Shortly the S.U.V. pulls into a military airstrip and a modified C-17 was waiting for them with the cargo hatch open. A security officer opens the door and the secretary steps out, followed by his detail and lately, Christian. Then Tabatha was pulled out of the back. She didn't fight back. She looked worse than before. The secretary stood in front of the cargo door of the plane and Tabatha was brought in front of him. Blood and sweat poured from her forehead. Christian had a slight look of concern for her but then shook it off.

The secretary glanced over at Christian from over Tabatha's' shoulder. He saw the bruise on his face and a cut lip from Tabatha's' fists. Then without any notice, the secretary decked Tabatha, and she instantly fell – unconscious.

"Feel better?" he said to Christian. "Don't say I never did anything for you." Then he turned to his detail and ordered them to; "Put her in the plane." They obeyed. Christian began walking onto the plane, but the secretary stopped him. "Where do you think you're going?" he said.

"I thought I was coming with?" Christian replied.

"Hahaha!! You did well today. But you have a lot more to prove to me before I can trust you completely. Someone who can get into my head and make me see things? That just doesn't sit well with me." At that, Christian watched as the secretary turned and walked into the plane as the ramp closed.

CHAPTER XIX

The Operation Phase 1: Infiltration

The underground compound was an enormous facility with multiple levels. It was initially a covert military training complex, which was under the direction of the secretary of defense. Much of the material in the construction was fused with iridium – one of the densest minerals on the planet, which was useful for preventing the reception of thought wave transmissions. The vault was the heart of the underground compound. The vault was a dark dome-shaped structure. The only light in the vault came from the generator that spanned one entire wall. Condenser capacitor cartridges were designed to store the irreplicable energy Sarah's mind produced which was also the source of her thermal-kinesis. Hundreds of them were plugged into charging outlets in horizontal rows, lining the lower portion of the generator. These condenser capacitor cartridges are the lifeblood for the new age weapons Sorvan had developed.

Sarah was clamped onto a structure that held her body up at about a forty-five-degree angle just in front of the generator. The covering that hid the lower part of her face was removed, exposing tubes protruded from her mouth. Her long, tangled, and matted hair fell to the floor. Her head rested on a contraption that was plugged into the base of her skull. The underside of the contraption was an electrical box in which braided electrical conduits protruded from each side, falling to the ground and connected to an even larger electrical box protruding from the generator.

She, again, appeared to be in restful sleep as Sorvan approached her propping up a kinetic equalizer on one shoulder – the weapon was one of the many advanced armaments he had developed, powered by the condenser capacitors. Her chest slowly and lightly rose and fell with each breath. He leaned the equalizer against the structure Sarah was connected to, then began talking to her while stroking the side of her cheek.

"My precious thing, I almost feel grief, knowing I will never see you awake again." He then turns and pulls out one of the condenser capacitor cartridges and looks it over – admiring his invention. "But this – *This* is our only legacy now. I once thought if only your sister were a part of this work, we could reshape the world. Rip the corrupt weeds off every rock." A brief memory of his father being beat and drug out of his childhood home by Stalin's police flashed. He then places the device back into its' charging station, "but she would destroy you and everything we've achieved."

"Ivan," says a voice from a radio attached to his belt. Sorvan presses a button on the radio. "Sir, an aircraft is inbound with valid access codes. It's your resource."

"Let him in," Ivan orders then turns to the vault exit, leaving Sarah alone in the dark.

The hangar was cylindrical and spanned several hundred feet in diameter. It was lined with a multitude of elevator doors that lead to the lower levels of the underground compound. The hangar also contained his arsenal of thermal-kinetic weapons – from attack jets and tanks to drones, equalizers, and other handheld weapons. His exoskeletal weapons were his most impressive line of war machines. Standing ten feet tall, an individual would sit in the cockpit and whose movements would translate into the machine's actions. On each of the exoskeleton's robotic arms were attached thermal-kinetic canons. The aircraft entrance to the hangar was embedded into the hangar ceiling and consisted of three mechanical arms that opened vertically.

Sorvan entered the hangar with several of his armed men as the mechanical arms were rising out of the desert for the approaching C-17. The aircraft began slowing then descended vertically. From above ground, it appeared as if a giant desert mouth was consuming the aircraft as the arms closed over the C-17.

After the aircraft's descent, the cargo door opened, and the Defense Secretary walked down the ramp, followed by a small handful of soldiers – two of which were bringing Tabatha out on a medical bed. Before any words of pleasantries were exchanged, Ivan commented on the cargo, not knowing who it was at first. "Now you bring me your wounded?! I suppose you want me to turn him into some cybernetic soldier!" Ivan shouted.

"That's not a bad idea. Maybe that can be our next project," Secretary Terrence sarcastically responded.

"How was your *hearing*?" Ivan then asked rhetorically, not officially informed of the outcome, though the secretary's survival indicated to him it wasn't one hundred percent successful.

"Well, see for yourself," the secretary replies pointing at the medical bed.

Ivan approached the individual, and sure enough, it was Tabatha. Still unconscious, but alive. "YOU BROUGHT HER *HERE*?!!" Ivan shouts in anger, and with an ounce of trepidation. "YOU FOOL!!"

"You better realize who you're talking too – old man!" the secretary verbally lashes back. Both Sorvan's hostile forces as well as the secretary's soldiers, were slightly apprehensive as they watched the two of them verbally bash one another.

"SHE NEEDS TO BE *DESTROYED*!" Ivan marches toward Tabatha to do just that, but the secretary makes a gesture with his hand at his small band of soldiers. They immediately pull out their firearms and target Ivan. Ivan stops but not out of fear. He turns and glances at his men in the hangar then smiles at the secretary. The secretary looked around him and realized he and his soldiers were immensely outnumbered. Not to mention they were in a facility deep underground in the middle of a desert that Ivan controlled. Ivan's men responded by pulling out their own weapons and targeting the secretary and his few men.

"*I* supported your research! *I* gave you *purpose*!" the secretary shouts, then walks up close to Ivan. "We – had a deal."

"*I* had a deal with your *predecessors*," Ivan responded, then folded his hands behind him and turned his back to the secretary. "*You*...are just the latest in a line of U.S. military officials salivating over what these two women can do," Ivan turned back and stared at Tabatha lying asleep on the medical bed. "But only *I* know what they are truly capable of. And you should be terrified. If these two make physical contact – the collision of matter and antimatter would be a firecracker in comparison." Ivan glanced at his men and signaled for them to put down their weapons. Secretary Terrence did likewise then responded, "You don't know that definitely. Your models could be wrong."

"Alright, Mr. *Secretary of defense*..." Ivan says, insultingly. "Let's see how this plays out. Besides, technically, I'm already dead – aren't I?" Then he orders, "Take her to the lab." A few of his men guide the soldiers with Tabatha to his lab. "And whatever you do, do *not* unstrap her!" Ivan adds firmly.

A single brick pillar protruded from the desert ground — the only indication of possible life for miles. However, the pillar was the only entrance to the underground compound other than the aircraft hangar. The pillar led to the compound's central security hub. Inside the hub, additional hostiles intensely monitored video, audio, and other sensor data transmitting from satellites and other security instruments continuously monitoring the vast desert terrain which was under the guise of *government-controlled territory.* This territory also included several thousand feet of airspace.

"Sir, it looks like we have two jets passing overhead at thirty-eight thousand feet. United Airlines flight ten fifty-six and southwest flight twelve-fifteen," One of them informed their commanding officer.

"Those are no concern," the commanding officer responded.

"Sir, I'm getting a small seismic reading from the east," another one informed. He and the commanding officer analyze the data. "Other than an approaching electrical storm, I don't see anything."

"The storm's too far away to trip the sensors. Bring up the satellite feed. Zoom in one thousand feet from the surface," said the commanding officer.

"Alright, I see it. It's about a mile and half east of our location."

"Magnify," the commander orders. "You got to be kidding me. Another adrenaline junky out in the middle of no-where doing donuts. They'll pass by like the rest."

Unbeknownst to the commanding officer, that *adrenaline junky* was heading straight for the only protruding brick pillar in the desert. And after a few minutes, an alarm alerted the security personnel to a proximity violation. Surveillance cameras showed a truck in the background and an individual at the steel door on the side of the pillar. Then there was a pounding from outside the hub.

The commanding officer radioed two armed guards. "Check the shaft door," he ordered them. The alert drew the attention of most of the other security personnel in the hub.

"There's another plane at approximately twenty-eight thousand feet," another officer informed the commander.

"That's a little low. What is it?"

"It's a private Cessna. It will be out of the area in about a minute."

"That one's no concern either," again responds the commander for his attention was primarily on the person at the pillar.

The two armed guards responded to the pounding at the door. They opened it with their weapons held up.

"AAAHHHH!!" A woman shouts after seeing the armed guards. Their jaws dropped at the sight of the most beautiful woman either of them had ever seen. "I'm so sorry. I was on my way to my grandmother's house..." she continued her rambling as the two guards slowly put their guns down – not sensing any threat. "...And I must be like, you know, the biggest DITZZ, ha-ha, in the world because I think I took a wrong turn cuz, ha-ha, here I am in the middle of no-where," she continued. Her appearance so struck the two armed guards that almost everything she said went in one ear and out the other.

"I'm sorry, Ms., can we help you?" one of them asked her. With a perturbed look, she then replied, "I need a map."

"Oh, yes, of course. Why don't you step in here for a second while we get you that map," they respond.

"Oh, thanks. It is brutally hot out there today," she said. So is this, like, area fifty-one or something?" she asks, rhetorically. One of them laughed at the statement, but the other didn't find humor in it at all, to which the first guards' laugh quickly diminishes.

"We'll go get you a map. Just stay – here," they said. But before they took another step, however, both guards begin struggling to breathe and to speak.

"Are you guys, ok?" The woman asked, concerned, watching them grab their chests. The two guards collapse to the floor gasping for air. The woman kneels asking what she can do to help. One of the guards grabs his radio and hands it to her. "You need me to call for help?" They lightly nod but the woman just held onto the radio watching them suffocate to death. Her concerned expression then vanished before laying the radio on the ground, standing back up and walking off into the pillar, leaving the door cracked open.

After a few more moments, one of the two guards who met the woman walks into the security hub.

"What was that?" the commander asks.

"Oh, just some stupid ditzy chick got lost," the guard replied.

"Where's your other guy?"

"Well, I have to admit, she *was* a knockout. I think his heart stopped the second he saw her."

"Where is she now?" the commander further interrogated.

"Oh – she left." They looked for the evidence supporting the guards' statement.

"Sir, that truck is still there," an officer informed the commander, who then turns to the guard unconvinced and firmly inquired of him; "So – where's your ditzy chick at?!" All the security personnel in the hub then turn to the guard waiting for his answer, but instead, a suspicious grin enveloped his face, just before.

Meanwhile, on a private Cessna jet twenty-eight thousand feet above the surface of the desert…

"Alright, I'm receiving a transmission from the pillar. I stand corrected. It looks like your idea to send in a woman worked, after all, Mitch," Kurtis admitted, working on a laptop in one of Penfield's private planes.

"I told ya it would," Mitchell replied.

"Of course, I'm not sure what that says about some of our men in uniform," Penfield interjected from the open cockpit.

"If this is Sorvan's base, I doubt he has standard military personnel around," Hammer adds.

"There's got to be more to that base than that pillar. That's a fairly small compound if you ask me," Mitchell says, analyzing the pillar through binoculars. "That thing can't be much more than ten thousand square feet."

"The tracer in Tabatha's tiara indicates she's down there," Penfield adds.

"Mitchell, that's not the base," Kurtis responds. "This is," Kurtis turns his laptop so Mitchell, Hammer, and Rodney could see the diagram. The pillar was hardly a percentage of the entire compound. "Here's some more information. We can't drop below twenty thousand feet within a ten-mile radius of the pillar without triggering an alarm within the base. Also, there are seismic monitors around. So, you may want to try to land as close as you can to the pillar," Kurtis concludes.

"Shouldn't be a problem," Hammer says, slightly anxious to get the ball rolling. The three of them place communicators in their ears. "Testing – Channel two clear?"

"Channel two clear," Rodney and Mitchell confirm. They strapped on their parachutes and cargo bags – which contained mostly ammunition and firearms. Rodney carried a few pieces of medical equipment as well – then lastly, their helmets for the high altitude jump.

"Alright – boys," Kurtis says, using Tabatha's favorite vernacular to describe her teammates, "Get going." Hammer shook his head at Kurtis's statement and followed Mitchell to the emergency door – Rodney was last in line.

Kurtis pulled the latch and opened the door. Air immediately began sucking out of the plane. Mitchell, first in line, hesitated for a moment, saying, "I've never jumped out of a plane at this high an altitude before!" Hammer then shoved him out of the plane, then responded, "Now you have!" then jumps out shouting with excitement and full of adrenalin. "WOOO-HOOO! YEAH BABY!" Finally, Rodney jumps out with a summersault. Mitchell was falling slowly, with his hands and feet apart. Then Hammer buzzed by headfirst. "COME ON SLOWPOKE – LET'S GO GET OUR GIRL!"

"LAST ONE THERE IS BUYING DINNER!" Rodney adds as he also buzzes past Mitchell. Finally, Mitchell put his legs together and his arms to his side to catch up to the others.

Hammer, leading the way, counted down the distance to their target. "One thousand feet; eight hundred feet..." They waited for as long as they could before releasing their parachutes, as to not get picked up by the compounds' surveillance instruments.

Their chutes open, and they soon land near the pillar as planned. They quickly pull off their helmets, unstrap their cargo bags and pulling out their equipment. Along with firearms and ammunition, Hammer pulled out two hammerheads out of his bag followed by metal rods which he screwed into the hammerheads.

"You *actually* brought sludge hammers?" Mitchell rhetorically asked.

"Where do you think I got my name from?"

"Well, I guess I thought that was just a onetime event."

Hammer stood up and strapped an electro-magnetic metal panel to his back which held his hammers. "That's fancy," Mitchell added.

"Courtesy of Mr. Penfield. He thought it was cool," he responded. "I like that dude."

Rodney continued carrying one small duffle bag full of medical supplies. After they had all prepared themselves to the best of their ability, they walked up to the pillar, where the steel door was still cracked open.

"At least they left the door open for us. That was nice," Mitchell commented.

Two armed men laid on the ground just behind the steel door. Rodney checked for a pulse but they were both dead. Then they closed the door and stealthily moved on until finding the Security hub. They slowly, defensively crept into the room. They found that all of the security personnel were either lying on the floor or buckled over at their stations – all deceased. But there was one individual still sitting at a helm surrounded by monitors typing in commands on a keyboard. Some monitors displayed surveillance images of both the exterior and interior of the compound. Other's displayed schematic information of the underground facility.

"It's about time you guys showed up," said the individual at the helm – it was Christian. "Mitch, you're looking rather slim today."

"Excuse me?" Mitchell replies. Hammer and Rodney glance at Mitchell, but instead, they see the lost ditzy woman, only with Mitchells' uniform on and a gun in hand. Hammer and Rodney cracked up at the fabricated sight.

"Well played, Christian. Can we get our eyeballs back now," Hammer commented.

"Wait, what did he make you guys see?" Mitchell asks, having now gotten the joke, in part. "Guys seriously..." But they just ignored him.

"Afraid you'd have to save the day by yourself?" Rodney replied to Christian's first comment about how long it took them to get there.

"Trust me, I have come to the inescapable conclusion that Tabatha needs very little saving," he responds.

"How's that?"

Christian leaned back in the chair and looked up at Rodney, displaying the bruise on his cheek and the cut on his lip. "That chick hits *hard*," Christian answers and rubs the side of his face, then goes back to typing.

"Dude, you deserved that," Hammer interjected. "My chest still hurts from whatever you did to me."

"You're a big guy, I'm sure you can take it," Christian says snarky, but friendly at the same time. Hammer glances at him crossly for a second then ignores the comment, Mitchell laughed softly at the comment.

Mitchell studies the monitor showing the schematic and data related to the underground facility. "Wow, it looks like this underground base is sitting just above an underground natural gas pocket."

"You are correct. The pocket is roughly thirty-five hundred meters *below* the base," Christian confirms. He types in more commands. "That gas line connects to a cogeneration machine underneath the compound."

"A what machine?" Hammer asks, making clear his lack of engineering knowledge.

"It's fairly new technology. It burns natural gas which in turn heats water that then runs a turbine creating electricity. I saw one of these in Germany when I was stationed over there a few years back. This one looks way more efficient though," Mitchell explains.

"Check out the megawatts per hour being generated – over one million mwh," Christian adds.

"That's ridiculous. What would need that much power?" Mitchell asks.

Christian typed more commands bringing up more schematics and diagrams. One of which was of a particular dome vault. "Whatever's in that room apparently," Christian replies.

"What's in there?" Hammer asks, to which Christian types some more commands. 'ACCESS DENIED,' then flashed across the screens.

"Well, that's all I can get, but I have some sneaky suspicion that's Tab's sister's bedroom."

"That's all *you* can get," Mitchell interjects. "Move over. Let a professional do this." Christian gets out of the chair, and Mitchell takes it over. He opens a pouch and pulls out his tablet. He sets it up next to the keyboard on the consul and plugs it into an open USB port then begins typing commands of his own. 'DECRYPTING IN PROGRESS,' displays on the small tablet screen above the status bar.

"That's cheating," says Christian.

"Just the benefits of having classified clearance," Mitchell responds, "and being really smart," he adds then winks at Christian.

"Egotistical, much?" Christian whispers to Hammer.

"You have no idea. But, admittedly, he is really smart."

The decryption process is completed and all the monitors are then inundated with hundreds of desktop icons begin. Christian and Hammer lean in closer to see all the icons.

"Where do you want to start?" Hammer asks.

"Go to this one. Project twenty-four," Christian suggests.

"Project twenty four?" Mitchell questions.

"The night I was psychically dancing around in Tabatha's' head with Sarah, she called herself Twenty-Four," Christian replies. Mitchell clicked on the icon and more icons downloaded. Most were video links. Mitchell clicked on the first icon. A recording of an event dated from nearly two decades earlier began playing. The scene showed Sorvan medically experimenting on Sarah as a child.

"What the!" Hammer responds in shock at the video. Mitchell clicked on several and they watched a few moments of them in horror at the scenes.

"This is one screwed up jerk," Mitchell comments. He then finds and downloads the link that Christian was unable to access earlier. It detailed the generator Sarah was plugged into and the rows of the condenser capacitor cartridges being charged with Sarahs' unique power. Mitchell clicked on yet another link and more schematics detailing Sorvan's thermal-kinetic arsenal open.

"That's what I saw when I was communicating with Sarah that night, all kinds of advanced weapons like this," Christian explains. "Manifest?" Christian spots yet another link of interest. "Over here, click on this one." Mitchell clicks on it and several more icons appear.

"Iran? Pakistan? Turkey?" Hammer reads the title of some of them.

"Click on one," Christian again directs Mitchell. He randomly clicks one. An international freight carrier list displays. Mitchell scrolls down the list. Further down assembly instructions are also inserted as well as a diagram of what *is* to be assembled – one of the weapons they already saw.

"He's shipping these weapons all over the world." Mitchell clicks on another link at the end of the video document and another begins. This video documented the destructive power of one of the exoskeleton weapons as it decimated a town in the distance thermal-kinetic canons. The four of them glanced at each with vast concerns.

They continue opening and studying computer files after computer files as quickly as they can. "It looks like iridium was used in some of the construction of the lower levels. That vault, holding Sarah, is constructed entirely of the material," Christian adds.

"What's the purpose of iridium?" Rodney asks.

"Iridium is one of just a handful of rare elements that is completely corrosive resistant. Plus, it's one of the densest elements," Christian replied.

"Which means what?" Hammer then asks.

"The combination of its density and the type of radiation it gives off makes it ideal for interfering with things such as – telepathic communication," Christian explained.

"How do you know that? Hammer asks.

"There's iridium in Tabatha's Tiara," Rodney informs.

"But, how..."

"If we survive all this, I'll send you the manual to read," Christian deducts Hammer's further curiosity on the matter.

"Check this out," Mitchell interjects. "Ivan's skull, that Tab said was metal. It's completely made out of iridium too."

"The good news is that, since the twins telepathic and telekinetic attributes are two separate processes, it looks like their telekinetic processes won't be affected by the iridium radiation."

"Good news unless pyro-chick isn't convinced that we're here to help her," Mitchell adds. Hammer nodded in agreement.

"But this *quantum pulse* thing, says here it intercepts the telekinetic signal."

"Quantum, what?" Hammer asks.

"I'm not sure," Christian replies, attempting to understand the data that read more like mathematical formulas created for physics than anything. Christian glanced at Mitchell – the smart one – who looked just as confused.

"Alright, enough dilly-dallying in here. Mitchell, transmit all of this information to Kurtis," Hammer orders.

"Already on it," Mitchell begins typing on his tablet, then unplugs his tablet, and Rodney, Hammer, and Mitchell begin heading out of the surveillance room. But one more icon catches Christian's attention.

"Wait a second. I want to see one more thing," he says.

"Dude!! We got to go," Hammer responds. "SCNT? What's that?"

"It's an acronym for somatic cell nuclear transfer," Christian quickly responds, then clicks on the link in which seventeen more icons appear."

"Which means?" Mitchell asks.

"Cloning!" both Christian and Rodney reply in unison.

"They've cloned Sarah?" Mitchell asks with trepidation. Christian doesn't answer. He begins clicking on the first one labeled 'C-1.' Seventeen links later, each one said 'failure' in the description of the process.

"It looks like they were all unsuccessful," Christian informs.

"That's a blessing," Hammer exhales. At that, they finally exit the security hub and finding the elevator. They then begin their descent into the bowels of Sorvans' labyrinth.

CHAPTER XX

The Operation Phase 2: Sorvan's Labyrinth

The elevator doors open on the first level, which – according to the facility schematics – housed the vault where Sarah was believed to be held. The lower levels contained the living quarters for an unknown number of hostiles. The Four stealthily make their way down the concrete corridor, which was several feet wide and high. Mitchell, Hammer, and Rodney had their firearms at eye level, and Christian was attempting to telepathically discern their way through the maze of corridors – with some difficulty.

"You got anything, Christian?" Rodney asks. Christian closes his eyes and concentrates for a moment trying to obtain telepathic information.

"I can't pick up anything. It's like I have blinders on. It's a weird feeling honestly," Christian explains.

"Welcome to the human race," Mitchell whispers.

Meanwhile, Sorvan and Secretary Terrence were in the lab with Tabatha, along with the secretary's soldiers. Sorvan had begun preparing her for the sinister procedures that he had perfected after years of practicing on Sara – and twenty-three other unfortunate victims for a much shorter time span. Secretary Terrence was more or less a mere spectator – however, to Sorvan, he was more of a necessary annoyance that he simply tolerated.

Tabatha was still unconscious. Part of her suit was ripped up in order to place electrocardiogram electrode pads on her body to keep tabs on her vital signs during the process. Her arm was connected to a morphine I.V. drip. However, he was still uneasy having Tabatha in the same facility as her sister, certain of what they were capable of together.

"Isn't that too much morphine?" Secretary Terrence asked.

"Because of her high metabolism, her body cleans toxins out twice as fast as a normal person. So no, this isn't too much," Ivan explains. "In fact, one of the most beautiful attributes of their biology lies in their metabolism. So far, I have yet to find a virus or bacteria that can infect them," he further explained.

"Really?" the secretary remarks, highly impressed. "That could change the medical community forever. We should..."

"...It won't work," Sorvan responded before the secretary could finish his statement.

"How do you know?"

"You have access to all of your predecessors' records, yes?"

"Of course I do."

"Maybe if you actually studied them, you'd discover that *one* of your predecessors sent me some volunteers to attempt what you're thinking," Sorvan continued as he moved Tabatha's head from side to side marking areas on her neck with a marker – indicating where he would be making incisions.

"What happened?" the secretary continued to inquire.

"They were unable to return to their posts."

"Because?"

"They went mad. Not unlike my original experiments thirty six years ago," Sorvan continued. "The compound is deadly to humans. But these individuals developed *with* the compound as part of their genetic code. However, their DNA is laced with the compound, and any form of transfusion using the DNA of these two will still result in the death of any recipient," Sorvan concluded.

"That's too bad," the secretary responds. Sorvan had begun placing tubes down Tabatha's throat.

"Why do you put the feeding tubes in?" the secretary again asks.

"It helps to keep her under control. Her metabolism drains her. She needs a lot of calories to give her energy to use her abilities. This keeps her on the edge of starvation, but just enough nutrients to keep her alive," Sorvan further explains.

"I see. That sounds unpleasant – for her."

"Unfortunately, there's no guarantee that I will be able to manipulate her fully."

"You were able to with Twenty-Four, though."

"She's been in my custody since she was an infant. She has never had the chance to develop her free will."

"Free will?"

"Yes. That's why Tabatha needed to *volunteer*. An old friend strategically placed highly morally influential individuals around her all her life. She has a stringent moral code, believe it or not."

"I really don't care about her *upbringing*, just get rid of her morals," Secretary Terrence says, absolutely ignorant of morality in general.

"More people are willing to die than to give it up. Aren't you appointed to defend freedom?" Sorvan rhetorically asked.

"Freedom is an illusion, Ivan."

"So, you defend an illusion," Sorvan responds.

"Just enough of it to stabilize the majority of society." The secretary walks over next to Tabatha, looking down at her, almost resembling Sarah – minus the insanely long hair. "And sometimes that requires sacrificing freedom – forcibly."

....

As Tabatha's rescue party continued throughout the empty corridors, they came to a large opening – it was the hangar. They glanced inside to see an arsenal of weapons, unlike anything they've ever seen. The modified C-17 was in the center.

"I think that's going to be our ticket out of here," Mitchell whispers, referring to the C-17. Besides the arsenal, a handful of hostiles paced around the hangar conversing with one another – obviously not concerned about any potential threat. The Four quickly passed the hangar door without being noticed and kept on jogging down the curved corridor until it ended at a concrete wall with a mechanical double door. Next to the door was a handprint identification scanner. Mitchell gets on the floor, pulls out some small tools and starts dismantling the bottom of the scanner. Rodney and Hammer have their guns pointed back down the corridor watching for hostiles while Mitchell works. Shortly thereafter, they hear individuals walking toward them, talking casually in another language.

"Dude!" Hammer says in a firm whisper, "Hurry up!"

"I'm going as fast as I can. This is more sophisticated than it looks," Mitchell responds in like manner. Three of Sorvan's men walk around the bend, checking things out. All they see is the steel door and the hand scanner.

"I hope your close," Christian whispers to Mitchell. "I'm having difficulty with my projection. I don't know how long I can make us invisible to them." The guards walk up almost to the door, then turn around and begin walking back.

"Got it!" Mitchell whispers. The steel door opens, and Hammer, Rodney, and Mitchell bolt inside. Christian walked in backward concentrating heavily on making them invisible to the hostiles' senses. However, the fact that the door opened unexpectedly caught the guards' attention and walked back toward the door. The door then closed. They then noticed the handprint identification scanner had been dismantled so they reported the unusual incident on their radio.

"*This* is a big freaky room," Mitchell comments. They observe the vault. It was dark. The only light came from the enormous generator which was humming in the background. They could make out a diagonal structure in front of the base of the generator but couldn't tell what it was at first, but as they approached, they confirmed that it was Sarah.

"Alright, Rod-man," Mitchell said. "Ready to wake up Destructo-woman?"

"I think you mean inferno-woman," Hammer suggests.

"Either way, they'd both make awesome villain names."

"If we get out of here in one piece, you can maybe patent them," Christian adds.

"One thing at a time, kids," Rodney interjects. Rodney Digs through his duffle bag and pulls out some equipment and sets it aside. Rodney cuts a slit in Sarah's suit near the crux of her arm. He wipes off the oily substance on her skin. "What is this stuff?" he asks.

Mitchell wipes a little up with a finger. He sniffs it. "It smells like antifreeze. But feels like conduction grease." Rodney then sticks a needle in Sarah's arm and draws some blood. She didn't move an inch at the prick. Next, he placed the vials of blood inside a small device.

"What's that?" Hammer inquires of the device.

"It's an automatic nucleic acid-purification-sample-preparation-lab-ixer," Rodney answered.

"A what?" Mitchell and Hammer respond in unison.

"A blood mixer," Rodney repeated himself – in layman's terms.

"Why didn't you say that in the first place?" Mitchell asked.

"Because you guys make amazing deer in headlights expressions. It's actually quite impressive." Rodney then adds a few drops of a chemical to each vial of blood. He then caps the vials, closes the lid on the machine and presses a button which begins mixing Sarah's blood with the additive.

"Isn't that Tabatha's' medicine?" Mitchell asks.

"This is the active ingredient," Rodney replies. "Penfield and I were not completely sure that Tabatha's' medicine would react the same way with Sarah, so I'm hopefully making it more adaptable to her by using her own DNA."

"They're identical twins, though, so wouldn't their bodies accept the same thing?" Hammer asks.

"They are *physically* identical, but their abilities are not necessarily what we would consider physical. Jason's research indicates that Tabatha and Sarah are basically two separate polarities. Like the negative and positive on a car battery," Christian explains.

"So, what does *this* battery *power*?" Mitchell inquires.

"That's what makes me a little nervous," Christian admits.

"Ok, let's start figuring out how to unhook her. Christian, you've talked to her before, so when she wakes up, if she gets upset, maybe you can cool her off," Rodney suggests.

"Was that a literal statement," Christian asks, walking behind the structure, analyzing the mechanism that was plugged into her head. Hammer walked around to the other side of Sarah and began pulling out the tubes that were protruding from her mouth. Rodney was waiting for the blood mixer to complete its' cycle. Mitchell, on the other hand, was looking at the condenser capacitors plugged into the generator. The weapon that Sorvan had left in the chamber earlier was still leaning against the base of the structure that Sarah was attached to. Mitchell picked up the nearly two and a half foot long weapon and began analyzing it.

Hammer completed pulling the last of the feeding and nutrition tubes out of Sarah's mouth. A little vomit came up with it. The blood mixer finished its' mixing cycle. Rodney opened the machine and pulled out the vials and transferred them to an injection cartridge then placed the cartridge in an injection gun.

Mitchell was still being curious George over the futuristic weapon and the condenser capacitors. He pulled one cartridge out of the charging station and found where to insert it, then shoved it into the back of the gun. The equalizer lit up and made a sound that indicated it was ready for action. The sound of the gun caught the attention of the other three. They all temporarily stopped what they were doing and looked over at Mitchell.

"Dude! What are you doing?" Hammer sternly and nervously asked Mitchell.

"I'm just checking it out is all, I promise. Besides, it could come in handy down here," Mitchell responds.

Lastly, Christian pulled Sarah's head up with a slight jolt, which detached the base of her skull from the device and laid her head off to the side of it. A noticeable change in the generator was audible.

"Ok, Rodney, you're up," said Christian. Rodney placed the injection gun up to her arm and pulled the trigger. The others backed up a few feet from Sarah at this point. "Maybe it's a good thing you do hold on to that gun." The injection cartridge emptied and Rodney pulled the gun away from Sarah and backed up as well. Nothing happened at first. Then Sarahs' eyes immediately opened and her head raised quickly. She looked panicked. Her arms and legs were still strapped to the structure.

Christian could sense the panic and aggression in Sarah as she wanted off of the structure. Even with the interference from the metal in the chamber, Christian could still telepathically deduct that she was on the edge of becoming violent. Christian walked up to her and spoke to her in her mind.

"Remember me? I'm Christian. I'm your friend. I told you we were going to come and get you," he said.

"My friend?" Sarah responded positively, recalling the face, the voice, and the psychic conversation they had.

"Yes. Friend," Christian affirmed. Sarah then looked at the straps and became anxious again. But then Christian quickly began unstrapping her. He then picked her up and helped her on to her feet, a gesture of friendship. She then lifted her hands, and as if studying the material she was clothed in. Then she began running her fingers over her chest and her stomach like an animal attempting to remove something irritating from their body.

"What's she doing?" Mitchell asks.

"The suit or the stuff under it isn't comfortable to her," Christian again deducts psychically. Sarah then spots the weapon in Mitchells' possession, and an expression of anger envelopes her face.

"Woe woe woe!" Hammer says. "What's she getting mad about?"

Christian jumps in front of Sarah, trying to calm her down. "They are your friends too. We are all your friends. They helped me get to you. Your sister is here too."

"My name is Sarah, and I have a sister," she remembered.

"Your sister led us here. But now *she* needs our help." Discovering what was upsetting her, he said to Mitchell, "she thinks that part of her is in that gun," Christian informs. "That's what all these cartridges are. They're being charged with her thermal kinetic energy," Christian further explained. Sarah's intense gaze at the weapon caused it to heat up and in turn causing Mitchell to drop it. Upon the equalizer's contact with the ground, the gun discharged a sphere of thermal energy, disintegrated the totality of the vault wall leading out to the corridor.

"Woah!" Mitchell, Rodney, and Christian responded.

"Are you referring to the power of the gun? Or to the fact that all the bad guys *out there* can now see us *in here*!!? Hammer yells at Mitchell. The power of the weapon was breathtaking, but now they faced a small platoon of hostiles as they poured into the vault targeting their weapons at the rescue party while shouting in a foreign language.

"Any chance your girl's in the vicinity?" Hammer whispers to Christian.

"My telepathy is heavily distorted down here – but they know where she's at."

"What about your new friend here?" Mitchell suggests.

"She seems fairly oblivious to what's going on," Christian explains, "she's basically a toddler - mentally," Christian explains.

"Oh, this is exciting – surrounded by a bunch of Arab speaking gangsters while we have the equivalent of a little girl who can set you on fire just by thinking about it."

"Anyone understand what they're saying?" Hammer asks. About that moment, a leader in the group of Sorvan's men steps forward and, in a broken English accent, gives them orders to; "Move! Move!" he shouts, gesturing to them to put their guns down, and to go with them. The four of them slowly place their weapons on the ground. And while they were busy surrendering, Sarah lifted her face toward the dome ceiling with her eyes closed like someone absorbing sun rays.

"What's wrong with her now?" Mitchell whispered.

"I think she senses Tabatha," Christian replies. Then Sarah begins scrapping at her outfit again like before. Her erratic behavior quickly drew the attention of the hostiles, to which they target her directly.

"No! Wait!" Mitchell, more out of reflex, jumps in front of Sarah to protect her as a single bullet is fired and is lodged into Mitchells' arm. Mitchell dropped to the ground, instantly grabbing his wound and putting pressure on it while blood poured out. Christian and Rodney ignoring the leaders screaming at them and rushed to Mitchells' aid. Sarah looked at the scene – confused.

"They were going to shoot you. Mitchell protected you because he's your friend too," Christian explained to Sarah, to which she understood. Her face became hostile. Her breathing quickened. She looked up at the leader and all of Sorvan's men with horror in her eyes. Her body shook like a predator about to attack, then stepped out in front of *her new friends* and opened her mouth as if to scream at the top of her lungs. Then an ear collapsing skull-splitting scream pierced the minds of every individual in the base except for her rescuers.

In the lab, shortly after feeling a minor tremor, which, unbeknownst to him, was from Mitchell eliminating a chamber wall, Secretary Terrence, along with his soldiers, fell to the ground grappling their heads and squealing in pain from Sarah's psychic scream. It did not affect Sorvan however, due to his protective mechanical skull. The scream lasted just a fraction of a minute, long enough to let out a violent exhale.

Back in the Chamber, Sorvan's men got back on their feet, grabbed their weapons, and began shooting at her. Streaks of fumes shot out from their guns several feet before dissipating as each bullet evaporated upon exiting their barrels. At that many of Sorvan's men, knowing what they were up against turned and fled out of fear. Others didn't have much of a chance before the air in the chamber became so hot that the rest of Sorvan's men boiled to death. Though the attack was directed solely at the hostiles, Sarah's intensifying aggression began impacting those she was initially trying to protect. Christian attempted to calm Sarah down. Even the vault walls were starting to liquefy under the intense temperature. And though the remaining men under Sorvan who did not flee were now deceased, she had not stopped.

"Sarah! Sarah! You can stop now," Christian says from the floor. Sarah turned her face toward Christian in a way that appeared she was upset that he interrupted her. "You stopped the bad guys," Christian continued, "you can relax now."

"They hurt my friend!" She said psychically.

"I know, but now you're hurting us. You stopped the bad guys. You can relax now," Christian continued. He lifted his arm to show her that she was causing his arm to become red from the heat. Her demeanor then changed. Realizing what she was doing, her demeanor changed, which corresponded to an end of the offensive, and the four immediately felt relief. Rodney had extracted the bullet from Mitchell's arm and wrapped it up. Then he and Christian helped Mitchell up and leaned him against the structure that Sarah was earlier restrained to.

Sarah then walked over and stood next Mitchell while Hammer, Christian, and Rodney picked up their equipment and weapons.

"You are my friend," she said to Mitchell psychically while mouthing the words.

"Uhh, yeah. Yeah I'm your friend. Friends protect each other," Mitchell responds with a little trepidation. Sarah lightly smiled at him. Mitchell smiled back. However, even with Sarahs' smile, the manner of which her face protruded through her long matted hair that draped down both her back and her front was still eerie looking.

Having collected their individual hardware, Christian, Rodney, and Hammer turned around to witness Sarah rest her head on Mitchells' shoulder as she gazed back at them. The scene was an awkward one, illustrated by their expressions. Mitchell had a look of uncertainty about his predicament.

"Soooo – one down, one more to go," Hammer said, breaking the awkward silence. "Time to find *your* girl."

"Definitely," Christian responds. "And I really hope this burn turns into a tan," Christian adds as they turn and leave the Chamber. Sarah wouldn't let Mitchell move without whimpering. He finally picked her up in a way that allowed her to keep her head on his shoulder, placing his uninjured arm under her knees.

"I was *just* shot in the arm – just to let you know," Mitchell reminds her as if it mattered to her. "Thanks for taking that guy out, though," he continued, "And the tan too – hopefully."

...Meanwhile, Tabatha's vital signs began changing as heart rate steadily rose, and her brain activity increased. Sorvan was becoming more uneasy.

"What's happening?" Secretary Terrence asks, presuming there's an issue by Sorvan's expression. Just then, Sorvan's radio began flooding the lab with frantic voices, mostly in different languages. Sorvan looked even more cross at the secretary. "What are they saying!?" the secretary, becoming angry at Sorvan's lack of response to his questions. Sorvan immediately grabs a long knife off of a tray then walks to the side of the medical table. Sorvan lifts the knife above his head, ready to plunge it into Tabatha's body.

"Stop!! What are you *doing*!! We *need* her!!" the secretary shouts. "That's it!! *Stop him*!" he finally orders his four soldiers. They pull their guns out to shoot Sorvan, but he paid no attention to them as the soldiers themselves were too intimidated by the giant to pull their triggers. Sorvan hand came down with the knife tightly in his grip...

"*NO*!" the secretary shouts.

But the tip of the blade stopped only inches away from piercing Tabatha's' abdomen. At first, the secretary thought that Sorvan had stopped himself, but then Sorvan pushed harder, and the knife then got closer to Tabatha. As it did, the blade itself began curving upward until the blade broke in half sending the broken piece flying straight up inserting itself into the ceiling. Sorvan then pulled the knife away from Tabatha – the bottom three inches of the blade was all that was left of the knife. The soldiers were astonished at the sight. The Secretary was also impressed, but having seen similar, if not more spectacular events spawning from Tabatha in the past, he wasn't shocked.

"What was that?" the Secretary calmly asks.

"*That* is what you want out of her," Sorvan answered. He then turned his face toward the secretary.

"If we can weaponize it as we did with Twenty-Four..."

"...You mean if *I* can weaponize it. Like *I* weaponized Twenty-Four," Sorvan corrected the secretary.

"I gave you the resources to do this. All your men – all the cells I got in here for you – Do you have any idea how difficult it is to manipulate the refugee system?"

"You *gave* me nothing. I have *other* resources. And those cells you brought in? If memory serves, *you* orchestrated the events leading to *your* governments' most valuable, well-kept secret being unveiled to get around all their little regulations designed to keep her hidden and protected!" Sorvan reminds the secretary sternly.

"You have *other* resources?" the secretary was struck by the statement, but Sorvan ignored the question.

"So tell me, Mr. Secretary of *Defense*, how confident are you that you and your soldiers are the only ones here?" Sorvan rhetorically inquired, walking up the secretary and his soldiers.

"What? Of course, we're the only ones here!" he confidently asserted. Sorvan leaned over until his face was just inches from the secretary's face.

"Then how is it that *her* companions are escaping with *Twenty-Four*!!" he shouted. Then in anger and without warning, he thrust the remaining blade into the soldier next to the secretary. In a few quick offensive moves, Sorvan did the same to two more. The last soldier standing fired his gun at Sorvan. However, the bullet ricochets off his metal skull. Sorvan picked the soldier up by his uniform, tilted his head back, and then slams his metal forehead into the soldier's face. Sorvan then dropped him, and he collapsed to the floor, unconscious.

"Are you out of your mind!!" the Secretary shouts.

Sorvan turned to the secretary. Blood from the soldier had splattered across both his metallic and the fleshy part of his face. "He'll live," he continued. "At least *he* had the guts to pull the trigger. I feel your ineptitude to consider *any* consequence has severely jeopardized all of my research."

"If she would have accepted my offer to be a part of the program on her own accord, I wouldn't' have brought her here. I would have taken her to the mountain – to keep them separated. But she refused. I needed you to..." the secretary explained.

"*Exactly* how easy was it for you to obtain her in the first place?"

"She wanted to know where her sister was," he recollected out loud.

"How did she know that you knew that?"

The secretary pulled out the small device associated with Tabatha's tiara. He pointed it at her and pressed the button. But no reaction. He then dropped it on the floor and crushed it with his foot.

About that same time, Tabatha began making noises as she was attempting to regain consciousness. Her head began moving, and her hands clenched. Both Sorvan and the Secretary started to feel the pressure in the lab increase. At that point, Sorvan left the room. He grabbed the radio off his belt. He began speaking through it in a different language, instructing the rest of his men to find and destroy Tabatha's team. But not to harm Twenty – Four. Secretary Terrence followed Sorvan.

"What are you going to do with Tabatha?" the secretary asked, still desiring to elucidate and manipulate her and her abilities. However, Sorvan continued ignoring him. His primary concern was to recapture Sarah and destroy Tabatha's team – and Tabatha. However, he withheld that information from the secretary. Secretary Terrence's position as a cabinet-level official within the U.S. government has managed to keep Sorvan's overall disdain for him at bay – until now.

Shortly after leaving the lab, they entered Sorvan's computer room. All of his monitors and holographic projectors were displaying images, data, and other information. Against the wall just inside the room was his metal-plated suit weaved together with cables, one of which ran from a large modem on the floor next to his console, along the floor and plugged into the back of the suit. As he was putting it on, the secretary was browsing around Sorvan's computers.

"What are you wearing?" Secretary, hesitantly, asks, even more intimidated.

"A little something I designed for myself," he responds. Secretary Terrence decides not to question that any further, as a sense of vulnerability creates an uneasy feeling in his present location. However, one computer monitor, in particular, displayed decoded encrypted information from North Korea.

"What is this?" he asked in disbelief. "You *sold* these weapons to a *foreign* government!?" the secretary questions. Sorvan walks over and shuts off the monitor.

"I think it's time for you to go, *Mr. Secretary*. Don't want the administration to find you in unpleasant circumstances," Sorvan says then turns to exit the computer room.

"*Wait!*" the secretary yells and runs in front of Sorvan to confront him about the issue. "You're *selling* these weapons to our *enemies!*"

"I'm selling these weapons to *EVERYONE*!!!" Sorvan reveals, then shoving the secretary to the side and walking out of the room. The secretary stands there in disbelief with a frantic expression on his face.

Tabatha's team raced down the corridor toward the hanger – there planned escape route. On the way, Christian split off as to find Tabatha while Hammer, Rodney, and Mitchell – who was carrying Sarah, her head laying on his shoulder still, and her hair wrapped around the back of his neck and down the front of his chest – continued toward the hanger. The plan was to meet up with Christian and Tabatha at the C-17 – without getting caught in the process. However, as they turned a corner to enter the hanger, they found themselves confronted by a couple dozen more hostiles than they had planned on running into based on their earlier observation of the hangars occupants. The approximate two dozen armed hostiles quickly surrounded the three with their guns aimed at them. Hammer and Rodney put their hands up as Mitchell was unable too.

"Sorry fellas, my hands are a bit preoccupied at the moment," he explains with Sarah in his arms – but once again oblivious to what was going on.

Christian found the lab and Tabatha. He immediately began unhooking her from the medical equipment, pulling out the feeding tubes, and removing the morphine drip from her arm. He wiped off the remnant fluid that the feeding tube left behind. As he touched her lips and believing she was still unconscious, he decided to attempt to give her a little kiss on her lips. But when his lips were just about to touch her lips, his throat became clenched.

"Ok, sorry – sorry – sorry," Christian forced out of his windpipe. His head rose along with Tabatha's' hand around his throat but released it shortly after his face was clear of hers.

"You should be," She confirmed, then sat up. "Ewww, nice cheekbone there prince charming," Tabatha adds.

"Right? I thought you were supposed to pull your punches."

"I thought you were supposed to *pretend* to give me the mother of all migraines."

"You said you wanted it to look as real as possible," Christian reminded her.

"Within reason, *Jack*!" she corrected him. She then hopped off the medical bed. "Wow, I'm feeling the rush like I did last time. That must be my sister. What's the current situation?"

"Your guys' are in the hangar with your sister – prepping our evac. They're just waiting on us," Christian summarizes. Then Tabatha telepathically predicts a hostile approaching the lab hastily. She raised her hand right as the hostile was passing by the lab entrance. He instantly froze and rose off the ground.

"Let's see what's *really* going on," she says as she walks up to the suspended individual. She quickly began absorbing his recent memories through which she was able to promptly create a hive connection with several hostiles within the compound. "Well, Christian, some of your intel is slightly out of date. My boys are being held up in the hanger. And I just saw Secretary Terrence is heading that way as well. I still can't access his mind though."

"What about Ivan?" Christian asks.

"Don't see him yet. That's one elusive snake." She then releases the hostile, both from her telepathic connection and telekinetic hold. He drops to the ground in shock after having experienced his memories somewhat sucked out of him. "What happened to these guys?" she asks, regarding the soldiers on the ground?

"No clue," Christian responds.

"Well, let's get moving." Then they quickly exit the lab.

Back in the hanger, Rodney and Hammer had their hands behind their heads, as they were continuing to be yelled out by the surrounding hostiles. Hammer carefully studied their positions and body movement. One of them was yelling at Mitchell to hand over Sarah, but Sarah just clung tighter to Mitchell when he tried to let go of her.

"Hey, girl," Mitchell whispered to Sarah, "Your heat blast attack could be helpful right about now," but she seemed not to understand the statement and continued holding on tighter to Mitchell. "Or not," he added.

As Mitchell was being ordered to hand over Sarah, another was yelling at Hammer in such a heavy accent that Hammer couldn't understand him.

"I hope you have a fast draw," Hammer says, just barely loud enough for Rodney to hear.

"Are you talking to me?" Rodney replies.

"Yeah."

"I hope you know what you're doing."

"One thing I'm getting really tired of," Hammer says – then grabbing the handle of one of his sludge hammers, he hurls it toward the individual yelling at him. It connects with his face and he drops to the ground, the sludge hammer landing handle-up on the ground next to him. "...*You all not speaking any English*!!" Hammer concluded – then the fight was on as Rodney drew his firearm and began firing, Hammer grabbed his second hammer and retrieved the other one and began swinging them around like they were paperweights, slamming them into hostiles.

Mitchell, on the other hand, unable to use his firearm maneuvered in a way that put him (and Sarah) in between some of the hostiles and his teammates' blind spots, knowing now that they won't shoot Sarah. Within a short amount of time, the hostiles were incapacitated by either bullets or by broken bones via sludge hammers. Then they continued toward the C-17 and ran up the open ramp.

Hammer looked around the cockpit, confused then said, "Uhhh...I was in the army, not the Airforce." Rodney scratched his head as well. Then they looked at Mitchell – still carrying Sarah, who responds, "I'll walk you through it."

"We're not going to get very far with that ceiling door closed," Rodney added.

"First things first, let's get this thing fired up," Hammer said. Mitchell then began instructing Hammer and Rodney on how to start the aircraft. However, their sense of victory was short-lived as every elevator door in the hangar opened, and a flood of even more hostiles spilled into the hangar screaming and shooting as they entered. Rodney made a b-line to the cargo door control panel to close the ramp.

"Are you kidding me!!? How many of these crazies does he have down here?" Hammer exclaims.

"What do we do now?" said Rodney.

"Pray!" Hammer responds.

"This would be a good time to have Tabatha's' pastor friend here," Mitchell added.

"Speaking of Tabatha, where are they?" Rodney adds.

"I don't know, but right now would be a great time for some unexpected help," Hammer comment.

And as irony would have it, the entire hanger began to tremble. Loud 'booms' reverberated throughout the hangar. The gunfire seized as the seismic level pounding caught everyone's attention. Suddenly the three hanger door arms collapsed inward from the ceiling revealing several military helicopters and a multitude of soldiers descending into the underground hangar by ropes firing their weapons at the hostiles on their way down. The hostiles then turned their attention to the descending soldiers entering the hanger and began firing back.

"YEAH!!" Rodney, Hammer, and Mitchell all shout in unison at the sight of reinforcement.

"How's it going down there?" Kurtis said through their communicators.

"Kurtis, I love you!!" Mitchell randomly blurted out, to which Hammer and Rodney glanced at him awkwardly.

"Don't ever tell me you love me," Kurtis responds.

"Sorry about that."

"Let's get in this fight!!!" Hammer encourages his teammates then rushes to the back of the plane, followed by Rodney.

"I'm going to stay in here with Sarah – to keep her safe!" Mitchell responded to the others as they run down the ramp.

"Whatever Princess!!" Hammer shouts back.

"Girl, you're really making me look bad. Just saying," Mitchell says to Sarah.

While Hammer and Rodney were plowing down the hostiles with their fellow soldiers, Rodney spots a familiar face and points Hammer to him – Tabatha's' old friend Chris. Chris saw them as well, and they quickly took cover behind a large piece of machinery so they could dialogue about the situation.

"Great timing!" Hammer says over the noise.

"Yeah, well, technically, since the capital building was blown up this morning, this operation is still awaiting full authorization!" Christ responded.

"Not that an intact capital building would speed things up, but I digress!" Rodney interjects.

"Tabatha apparently has an old friend she's secretly kept in contact with from her old high school, some lady named Lindsey! She just so happens to work as a legal secretary in the defense department!"

"That's convenient for us!"

"Before the hearing, Tabatha contacted her and asked her to find anything on Secretary Terrence in connection with any research related to military experimentation on humans!" Chris continued.

"Did she?"

"Oh yeah. Billions of dollars for defense contracts going through multiple points of contact and winding up right here. And that's just in the last two years. Before that, it was going to some mountain town in Northern Pakistan. She also discovered plans for an underground bass that was drafted nearly fifteen years ago, when Trevor Kitten was the defense secretary!"

"He's the secretary of state now!" Rodney interjects.

"Right!" Chris confirms. "Top-level figures in the government have been in on some superhuman experimentation and cloning project for over three decades!"

"Christian found some files on cloning, but they were all failures!" Hammer added.

"That project was abandoned, but not because of the failures. One sample survived, but it had a major deformity!"

"What was the *major deformity*?!" Rodney inquired.

"It had a long drawn out scientific explanation describing what it was missing that I can't remember, but essentially – it had no soul!" Chris continued.

"That's a bad thing?!" responded Rodney – the agnostic, showing his lack of belief in the supernatural.

"Several scientists died once it became self-aware! They burned to death!" Chris continued.

"That sounds familiar!" Hammer responds.

"That's why they killed the project – literally!"

"Cuz, it couldn't be controlled, I suppose!" Rodney alluded.

"A new project replaced it – plans for a new, advanced military arsenal. The arsenal was initially being developed by D.A.R.P.A., but pulled from them when they failed to meet certain specifications! The technology for the weapon systems the defense department was wanting didn't exist!"

"Let me guess – they supposedly abandoned that project too," Rodney interjected.

"Supposedly being the keyword. It was never really abandoned, just moved."

"I guess we found where it was *moved* to!" Hammer interjects.

"Apparently so. That being said, where's *our* secret weapon?!" Chris asks about Tabatha.

"Christians' looking for her!"

"Christian!? Who's Christian!?"...

...Tabatha and Christian were continuing their way through the maze of corridors leading to the hanger. Christian had explained to her all the events that had transpired since her team got there, including all the data discovered and transmitted to Kurtis and Penfield. They could hear the commotion from the battle in the hanger as they approached it.

As the two of them rounded one more corner, closing in on the hanger entrance, a hostile in an exoskeleton came up behind them via the coinciding corridor, also on its way to the hanger. Sighting Tabatha and Christian, he targeted them with its arm cannons and discharged blasts of thermogenic energy at them. Tabatha anticipated the attack and, using her telekinetic potential, deflected the strike from her and Christian. The collision of the opposing forces, however, created a concussion burst fracturing the corridor and sending Tabatha hurdling further down the hall past the hanger entrance. Christian was sent crashing into the wall, where he hit his head causing blood to seep out and run down the side of his face. He fell to the ground temporarily knocked out. The exoskeleton, along with the pilot, was also knocked back several feet. The pilot, being somewhat protected within the cockpit, quickly got back up, entered the hanger and began discharging thermogenic energy around the hangar.

Observing the discharges from the single exoskeleton, the soldiers, who had just nearly subdued the entire army of hostiles within the hanger, began taking cover behind machines and other equipment in the hangar. One blast hit the tale of the C-17 that Mitchell and Sarah were in, sending it spinning around. Once the aircraft stopped, Mitchell glanced out of the back of the now damaged cargo door and saw a line of stationary exoskeletons minus any pilots.

"Sarah, you have to let me go, trust me," Mitchell says, attempting to get Sarah off of him.

Meanwhile, after Tabatha was sent flying further down the corridor, she had a rough landing on her backside. As she was about to get up, she was then grabbed by her hair and furiously dragged and then picked up and thrown into the vault. Tabatha regained her composure and got back on her feet. As she lifted her face, Sorvan greeted her with a rabidly evil expression. He grabbed her by her suit near her abdomen and lifted her above him. Tabatha kicked him in his face. Then he tossed her again. She braced herself for another impact, however, when she didn't hit the ground or anything else. When she opened her eyes, she saw that she was levitating.

"Still learning," Sorvan comments, interpreting her slightly confused expression. Tabatha makes her way back to the ground but doesn't respond to the comment. "That's what makes you so dangerous! Your lack of control!"

"You mean *your* lack of control – *over* me – and *now*, my sister!" She responds. She raises her forearm and the structure that earlier held Sarah broke free from the floor and rose off the ground. Tabatha then balled a fist and the structure folded in on itself like a piece of paper crumbling into a ball. Then springing her hand open, the ball of mangled steel shot off toward Sorvan. But a few feet before reaching him, the ball of metal collapsed to the floor. Tabatha attempted to hide being confused over that. So she then telekinetically picks up more debris, left from when Mitchell blew out the wall and started tossing them at Sorvan. Each piece landed just feet from him.

"You look confused, Tabatha," Sorvan infers from her expression as to why she can't hit him with anything. He walks over the metal debris maintaining his distance from her and slowly approaches the generator. "During our first encounter, I could tell that you were incredibly powerful. Far more than your sister even. All was not lost that night. The data I obtained from observing you lead me to discover the telekinetic signal that allows you dominance over the atomic domain. And by extension, unveiling a countermeasure." Sorvan points to the devices wrapped around his forearms. Digital lines fluctuated on the face of the devices. "This quantum pulse disrupts your telekinetic signal."

"Thanks for the science lesson, and showing me your new gadget," Tabatha responds rhetorically.

"Hmmm, but I suppose it was providence that I failed in obtaining you that night. That same information also revealed you to be that of an unstable element, and a physical connection between you and Twenty-Four..."

"*SARAH*!" Tabatha corrects Sorvan.

"...Sarah!" he corrected himself, "...would be a *global* catastrophe," Sorvan further explains.

"But isn't that what you want?!"

"After Hiroshima, *Hiroshima* was still there," Sorvan said, eluding to the fact that he believed she could destroy the planet if allowed to contact her sister physically. He pulls one of the device cartridges out of its' charging station.

"And if your *data's* wrong?" She responds, disbelieving his theory. Sorvan then plugs the cartridge into the bass of his skull, cringing initially, like someone momentarily suffering.

Steam, then began rising from around him. "Then – I'll destroy you for *entering my house and TAKING MY STUFF*!!" He viscerally shouts at the top of his lungs then sends a horizontal vortex of thermogenic energy towards her. She maneuvers to block the attack using her telekinesis, creating a spectacular light show in between them.

...In the hanger, the battle had intensified with the addition of an exoskeleton. Mitchell managed to get free from Sarah. She watched him climb into an exoskeleton with sorrowful eyes, breathing like she was on the fence of throwing a tantrum. Mitchell quickly studies the controls. After pressing random buttons and few unbalanced movements, he caught on how to operate the machine. However, he didn't have any firepower in the machine since that ran off of the condenser capacitors.

Two more hostile exoskeletons entered the hangar. Hammer was swinging his *hammers* around like a karate kid – with hammers – amid the hostiles. Spotting the two additional exoskeletons, Hammer drew his sludge hammers behind him and then with an outburst of adrenaline and a loud shout, he hurls his hammers which crash through one of the glass cockpits disabling the pilot which in turns collapses the exoskeleton. The remaining two hostile exoskeletons targeted hammer.

"Oh crackers," said Hammer, using Tabatha's vernacular. But then Mitchell in his exoskeleton sprinted toward the others, then tackling them both of them as they discharged their canons, sending both blasts upwards and out of the hanger into the atmosphere. One of which hit one of the military helicopters sending it crashing into the hangar with an explosion.

Mitchell wrestled with the two hostile exoskeletons before the two got the upper hand and pinned him to the ground. They lifted their canons and pointed them down at Mitchell and his exoskeleton. The hostile pilots then began struggling to breathe and grasping at their chest and throat.

They both fell over their controls dead and their exoskeletons fell over on either side of Mitchell revealing Christian behind them in the threshold of the hangar entrance. A clear expression of aggression consumed his face. Blood, some dried, covered one whole side of his face from injuring his head. With the hostile exoskeletons out of the way, the soldiers were able to overwhelm the remaining hostiles and incapacitate them finally. Then Hammer, Rodney, and Christian met back up with each other.

"It's about time you got here," Hammer says to Christian. "I'm never going to complain about your heart-attack-inducing mind assault ever again, man," he added. Mitchell got him in his exoskeleton off the ground and walked over to the group. He opened the transparent cockpit and leaned on the controls and said to hammer, "You're welcome too – Ham-Ham!"

"It's about time you got in this fight," Hammer responded. "Thanks for having my back, man." Mitchell smiled and nodded at him who gestured back in like manner.

"Wait, so if Mitchell's in there, where's Sarah?" Rodney interjects.

"I left her in the C – 17," Mitchell responded. They all rushed to the back of the aircraft. Chris joined them to discuss the situation but instead found himself looking into the plane, confused as to what they were looking for.

"Are you all expecting the plane to do a trick or what?" Chris inquired.

"I left her in here, I promise," Mitchell firmly asserted as they stared into the plane – absent of Sarah...

...Tabatha and Sorvan's battle lingered on with little progress by either one. Tabatha continued on the defensive, deflecting Sorvan's attacks with her forearm in front of her, leaning forward as pushing through high winds. Tabatha reached out toward the walls of the vault with the opposite hand, ripping out chunks of metal and rock telekinetically and hurled them toward Sorvan. They continued falling short of striking Sorvan, unable to get passed the invisible quantum pulse shielding him. However, her seemingly failing counter-offensive was merely a distraction. Simultaneously, she was concentrating heavily on the dome ceiling. Finally, the center of the dome began cracking and, along with tons of metal, rock, and sand, came crashing down on top of Sorvan, ending the dual.

It appeared that Sorvan was defeated. Then a stream of telepathic information from the pile of rubble was detectable. Predicting another offensive, she rushed at the mountain of debris as it blew apart, deflecting the debris as she sprinted to engage in hand to hand combat with him.

Sorvan's metallic, iridium laced skull was fractured by the mound of rock and metal that had landed on him, *now* allowing Tabatha with the advantage, being able to anticipate his moves. She hit him fast and hard in every open area on his body while dodging every counter-attack he attempted. Finally, with her legs, she swept Sorvan's legs out from under him, sending him to the ground on his back. She stood over him, sending blow after blow to his face. Sorvan became disoriented from the continuous on slot of punches to his face. Then Tabatha picked up a relatively large rock lying next to them with both hands. She lifted it above her head with the intent on smashing Sorvan's skull with it, but then lifted her eyes and saw Sarah entering the vault.

"Sarah!?" Tabatha shouted. Tabatha realized at that moment that she was inundated with Sorvan's primary emotion – Rage. She regained cognitive clarity, then dropped the rock to the side of Sorvan's head. His entire head was covered in his own blood. The blows to his head and body left him seemingly out cold. Tabatha got to her feet and headed toward her sister as Sarah, with her arms outstretched, was also heading toward Tabatha. As they neared each other, Sarah touched her face with one hand as to compare it with her sisters as she noticed the similarity in features. Tabatha smiled as Sarah's other hand, was held out to touch her face, but before Sarah's reached her sister, "*NOOOO*!!!" Sorvan belligerently and simultaneously released an uncontrollable projection of thermogenic energy. Tabatha attempted to deflect the discharge from her sister, and only partially from her. The collision of the two forces, however, propelled all three of them apart. Sorvan crashed into the generator then fell to the ground. The condenser capacitor in the base of his skull had overloaded from the untamed discharge of energy. He quickly reached behind his head and pulled it out. Steam followed the device out of the outlet in his skull. Sorvan slammed it down on the ground aggressively, where it busted into pieces sending the translucent core rolling away on the concrete. The black with a small amount of blue luminescence on the bottom – like an empty/full indicator. Sorvan expressed pain for a moment but quickly regained his composure.

Sorvan found where Tabatha's body was lying and walked toward her. Half of her body instantaneously sustained three-degree burns. Her exposed leg was black – the flesh charred. Sorvan kicked her leg. It wobbled like the limb of a fresh corpse. She appeared dead. Before he could verify the assumption, Sarah grabbed his attention with her heavy, anxiety-driven, frantic voiceless exhalations. The bond between the sisters was broken – a further indication of Tabatha's apparent mortality.

Sarah peered up at him from the floor through her hair. Tears streamed down her face. Her eyebrows sunk tightly and saliva ran down the sides of her quivering lips which revealed her clenched teeth like a predator about to attack a prey. Then, unexpectedly, she pounced on top of Sorvan like a vicious wild animal. Untrained in any form of physical combat, she clawed at his neck, and his face, and attempted to bite his metal skull. Sorvan peeled her off and held her out away from him by the crux of her shoulder. She began beating on the quantum pulse mechanism on that forearm. Then it cracked, disabling the device. His hand then began burning, causing him to drop her. Not being hooked up to the generator, and lacking the stabilizing connection she had with her sister, her ability was ineffective. Instead, she began sweating and becoming fatigued as blood droplets broke out of the poor's of her forehead. Sorvan shook his head, disappointed in her. "Pathetic!" he says to her. "You're a *goddess*! And you're acting like an *animal*!" he shouts at her. Her eyes roll upward as she then collapses to the ground. Sorvan reaches down and scoops her up into his arms and then exits the vault.

..."Mom!" a teenage Tabatha yells, running through the front door of the house, dropping her backpack on the floor then taking a seat at the kitchen table, laying her face on the table, and covering her head with her hands.

"Tabatha? What's the matter?" a much younger Naomi responds.

"Everything!"

"Can you be more specific?" Naomi again responds.

"I'm tired of hearing everyone's problems."

"Oh, sweetheart – sweetheart – sweetheart..." Naomi's response echoes as that memory fades and then finding herself alone in the study on the island in front of the video monitor.

"Mom – I'm tired of dealing with the world's problems."

"...I'm always praying for you..." her mother in the video responds.

"I feel so alone," Tabatha adds.

The video quickly backs up. "...I'm always praying for you two..."

"It's getting harder."

"...I'm always praying for you..."

"I wish you were here."

"I'm..." skip "...for you."

"What do I do?"

"...Always pray..." the video then skips to the end "...I love you," rewind, "...love you," rewind, "...love you..." The short phrase continued to echo as her surroundings fade away and her eyes slowly open to a piece of a blue sky observable through the hole in the dome ceiling. It wasn't long after becoming conscious that the severity of her current physical condition comes to light as her senses are consumed with excruciating pain.

She gazed intensely at the mall portion of the sky, and through the pain, said, "Help – please." Then a few small clouds began passing by as the electrical storm was nearing the area. She suddenly felt something familiar.

"Ssssarahh?" she squeezes out of her windpipe. Slowly and painfully, she turns her head anticipating Sarah's body to be next to hers but finds the core of the condenser capacitor instead. It was just within reach.

Slowly and painfully, she reached out for it. As her hand approached it, the tips of her fingers broke down into molecular particulates. The sight shook her and by reflex, jerked her hand away from the object. She was astonished when she looked at her hand – it was fully restored. She was starting to get an idea of what her and her sister's physical connection might result in. She reached for the object again and grabbed it. But nothing happened. The core was utterly black – empty. She then raised her eyes to the multitude of condenser capacitors plugged into the generator. And with a new determination, she suffered through the agony of dragging her burnt body along the rubble laced concrete toward the massive generator.

Meanwhile, back in the hangar, the remaining soldiers, having maintained the upper hand, had overwhelmed the hostiles and won the day. The surviving hostiles were forced into mobile containment units and lifted out of the hanger by the military helicopters. The electrical storm was closing in and thunder was now within earshot as lightning strikes were in the distance. The wind had picked up, a further indication of the storm's close proximity. Two helicopters remained awaiting to evacuate the soldiers. One of the pilots radioed Chris – as he was unofficially head of this particular operation – informing him of the lightning in the area. Chris responded affirming the pilots' concerns.

"Alright – storms coming!! Let's wrap it up!!" Chris shouts. The soldiers corral the last of the hostiles into the final container, then attached themselves to their lines and are pulled back up to the surface to which the area was then evacuated. Chris, however, stayed with Tabatha's team. "So what now?" he asks.

"My first inclination is to blow this place to kingdom come," Hammer replies.

"Got a plan for that?" Chris responds.

"I could use that exoskeleton to take out that generator," Mitchell replies.

"You think that will take out the whole compound?" Rodney questions.

"If that generator blows and ignites the gas in that main under the base –yeah – I'm fully confident it will blow this place to..."

"Language," Christian interjects, to which Mitchell rolls his eyes then continued, "...It will blow it wherever you want it."

"Hold up, we have to find Tab," Hammer reminds them.

"True. And Sarah – again," Mitchell adds.

"Where's Secretary Terrence? We need to get him out of here too," Chris also added, to which the others express zero concern over whether the defense secretary gets out alive or not.

"Chris is right. We need to get the secretary out too. Besides, I something special for him," Christian affirmed.

"You mean for his face?" Rodney predicts

"Exactly."

Having slightly higher respect for government authority, Chris inquired, "You're going to beat up the secretary of defense?"

"I had to take watching homeboy knockout punch, my girl."

"Your girl?"

"Christian has a death wish," Hammer rhetorically explained.

"Whatever dude," responds Christian.

"What about this Sorvan Character?" Chris further inquired as they head out of the hangar and into the maze of corridors.

"Don't know. We haven't run into him yet, and frankly, I don't necessarily want to. I'm good with blowing this joint with him in it," Hammer responds, and Mitchell confirms, "I second that."

"Alright. Mitch, get your toy over there, and head to the generator. Blow that thing when we give you the word," Chris orders.

"I'll go hunt down the secretary," Christian volunteers.

"Hunt?"

"Figure of speech buddy," he reassures Chris.

"The rest of us will look for Tabatha and Sarah," Hammer concludes.

...Meanwhile, after what seemed like an eon of crawling across the concrete to the generator in pain, Tabatha finally reaches the rows of capacitor cartridges plugged into their charging stations and pulls herself up off the floor cringing and grinding her teeth. Then with her good arm, she begins pulling the cartridges from their charging ports and slamming them on the floor, exposing their bright blue illuminating cores, grunting in pain each time. As more exposed cores pile up, a transparent emission begins radiating from the broken devices, noticeable only from the distortion in the air. The radiation seemed to be attracted to Tabatha and began engulfing her. As the emission consumed her, she witnessed as her body broke down into particulates then reassembled her. Once the restoration was complete, her body was in perfect physical condition – with an added visual effect, for millions of illuminating particulates were circulating around her analogous to protons and electrons orbiting the nucleus of an atom.

After a few moments of amazement, she then looked up at the generator, and the thought of her sister having been hooked up to this thing enticed her anger once again, and clasping her hands together, she held them over her head then slammed them into the generator. She was, again, astonished as she observed that her arms not only went through the metal skin of the generator but her arms had also changed in density to that of diamonds up to her elbows. After another round of amazement came and gone, she then continued fiercely attacking the massive machine. Sparks began flying as the charging ports and electrical components were being torn apart. A chain of explosions around the lower half of the generator started. She then raises herself into the air and slams the side of her body into the generator like a battering ram. Another chain of explosions begins as more sparks fly. Tabatha thrusts her hands into the generator in an attempt to pull the entire machine out. As the face of the machine separates from the hull in the rock, an additional explosion adds to the destructive scene.

Mitchell, in his exoskeleton, arrives at the vault as Tabatha is in mid-air, pulling the generator apart seemingly by hand. He was dumbfounded at the sight of Tabatha. He sat speechless in the exoskeleton, merely watching. Finally, he picked up his radio in an attempt to describe what he was witnessing. "Uhhh and by the way – Tabatha can fly now – and stuff. Out."

After a minute, he shook himself out of the shock and shouted at her, "Hey!! Need some help?! Or are you good?!!"

Tabatha had the generator at a near tipping point when Chris, Hammer, and Rodney, came running down the corridor stopping next to Mitchell to see what he was talking about.

Tabatha then let go of the generator, and as she descended in front of her team, the generator came crashing down revealing the guts of the machine in the rocky hull. Her physical structure was no longer in the crystallized form but the orbiting particulates circulating around her was still enough to prohibit them from verbalizing anything other than, "Woe!"

"I know, right! Isn't this like super awesome?" Tabatha says, excitedly.

"Definitely super-something," Chris responds. "You've for sure come a long way from a fifteen-year-old girl that used to call my police station every day."

"We haven't found Sarah, Sorvan, nor the Secretary," they finally inform.

Tabatha concentrates for a moment. "Sarah's with Sorvan, in the hangar. We need to stop them!" Tabatha says.

"I thought you couldn't read Sorvan's mind?" Hammer remembered.

"His iridium cased skull got damaged. Oddly, however, his thoughts are almost digital," Tabatha explained.

"Digital?"

"Like, computer-generated." she continued. "I'm not a hundred percent sure he's completely human."

"Let's get back to the hangar then," responded Chris.

"Right. Mitchell, if you would do the honors, and finish that up," Tabatha points to the remains of the generator.

"With pleasure!" Mitchell then aims the exoskeleton canons at the guts of the generator and discharges a few thermogenic rounds obliterating what was left of the machine. The discharges ignite a chain reaction of explosions leading down into the converter underneath the compound. As the converter exploded, it began shaking the compound as well as the earth around it.

While the Tabatha and her team headed back to the hangar, Christian found Secretary Terrence as he entered the elevator that leads to the pillar. Christian sprinted toward it and jumped in the elevator as the door closed and began rising. The elevator shook with the rest of the compound. The two men glared at each other for a moment, then disregarding any words, they immediately began violently clashing with each other. They continued battling physically until the elevator reached the surface. The doors opened and they both fell out. The secretary got on his feet first then ran toward the exit. Christian ran after him. They burst through the steel door into the hot desert, only cooled by the dense cloud cover and wind.

The others reached the hanger – again – just as Sorvan, carrying Sarah, entered into the back of the C-17 and fired up the engines.

"*IVAN*!!" Tabatha shouted. The plane began vertically lifting, heading toward the opening. They all ran toward the plane. Ivan then started firing the aircraft's exterior guns at them. She deflected the bullets then shouted to Mitchell, "Mitchell!! Shoot it down!!"

"But what about Sarah?!" Mitchell responded.

"JUST SHOOT IT!!" Tabatha ordered. Mitchell pointed the canons at the plane and pulled the trigger. The blasts took out the vertical thrusters on the aircraft, sending it back to the hanger floor. Once it was on the ground, they continued running toward the plane – Tabatha outrunning them all. Sorvan lowered the cargo door and walked down the ramp with Sarah, in his arms, she looked dead. "Sarah!! Wake up!!" Tabatha says in her mind. Just then, Sarah woke up in Sorvan's arms. Her eyes scowled at Sorvan and then began attacking him as she did earlier. In the process, she damaged the other quantum pulse device, cracking the glass, and rendering it useless.

Sorvan then dropped Sarah on the ground. He then rose his hands up, and his metal-plated armor began lighting up in rows of small LED lights. Simultaneously, the entire arsenal of weapons in the hanger woke up, obeying Sorvan's commands and began attacking Tabatha and her team. Even the exoskeleton that Mitchell was operating began leaving his control. Mitchell quickly opened a control panel on the floor and was able to disengage the A.I. signal giving him back control. He began firing at the other hostile weapons. Tabatha continued to deflect the intense on-slot from the robotic arsenal. Her team packed behind her – minus Mitchell who was in the exoskeleton.

"Can you do like a mind blast thing or something!?" Hammer suggests to Tabatha.

"A what!?" she responds.

"You know, like the comics…"

"Would you shut up!!? I got my mind on about ten things right now – *ELEVEN'S PUSHING IT!!*"

Sarah looked intently at Sorvan from the ground. Maintaining a semblance of self-control began attacking Sorvan with her potentiality. Sorvan felt his armor getting incredibly hot. Wires and electrical circuits started popping. He began screaming in pain as steam rose from the metallic flesh of his armor. Then looking down at Sarah, deciding between his life and hers, he pulled out a gun from his backside, aimed it at her, and then a bolt of lightning from the passing electrical storm shot down from the sky into the hangar and directly in Sorvan's body.

The arsenal disengaged, as Sorvan was being inundated with electricity. The lightning strike ended and Sorvan fell over onto his chest and face – dead. They all then rushed over to his body. Steam continued rising from Sorvan's corpse. His armor was black from the electric shock and a chunk of his metallic skull had blown off, revealing a glass casing protecting a compact array of wires and electronic components somehow attached to what was left of a brain. A mixture of bright and bluish fluid filled half of the glass casing. The rumbling under the compound was intensifying as the gas lines beneath the base were continuing to ignite. Finally, a massive explosion under the compound sent fire up into the facility.

"We need to get out of here – now!!" Chris shouts.

"How?! It's not like we can jump to the surface!!" Hammer responds. "The opening is over a hundred feet above us."

"Get on the plane!" Tabatha orders.

"It can't fly!" Rodney reminds her.

"GET IN THE PLANE!" Tabatha shouts. They all then hustle onto the plane as explosions get closer. Mitchell jumps out of the exoskeleton. Sarah lifts her arms toward him, wanting him to continue carrying her.

"You know my arm still hurts. But its ok," Mitchell says, sweeping her off the ground on the way onto the plane.

"Seriously?" Tabatha responds, watching Sarah wanting Mitchell. "I'm depressed now."

"Come on!" Hammer shouts at Tabatha from the ramp.

"Close it!!" Hammer, shaking his head, does what she says. Tabatha raises one arm and the plane slowly begins lifting off the ground. As the aircraft ascended toward the opening in the hangar ceiling, Tabatha followed rising herself up out of the hangar.

"Man, that exoskeleton thing was awesome. I was kinda hoping to take it with me," Mitchell says to himself, looking down at the machine on the ground next to Sorvan's body.

Finally, the energy converter underneath the compound fully explodes, igniting much of the gas destabilizing the sediment and rock around the base, causing the entire compound to implode in a brilliant explosion. Tabatha Securely lands the plane on the surface of the desert, following by herself. They all exit the plane then head toward the pillar, where Tabatha's truck was left not far from. The ground was still shaking as explosions continued beneath the surface.

As they approached the pillar, and the truck, they saw two men fighting. It was, of course, Christian and the secretary of defense. As they closed in on them, the two stopped for a moment.

"Please, continue. Don't mind us," Tabatha said. Then Christian laid another hook into the secretary's face, and they continued fighting.

"Can't read my mind, can't predict one I'm going to do next," the secretary said to Christian.

"You're not going to help him?" Hammer asked Tabatha.

"Nope," She replies.

"I can't believe we're standing here watching the secretary of defense get beat up," Chris says under his breath. Christian finally got the upper hand with a few good punches. Blood poured from both of their noses and lips. Christian had Secretary Terrence on the ground. He then grabbed the secretary's shirt, pulled him up and, with his other hand, calked ready to hit him again.

"That's enough, Christian," Tabatha said, feeling that Christian made his point to the secretary. Christian looked up at Tabatha, then withdrew his fist, letting go of the secretary's shirt. Christian walks up to Tabatha.

"It's good to see you safe and – sound..." he then notices the particles orbiting around her, "...and with little light things floating around you??" Christian says to Tabatha. She smiles and responds, "Pretty cool, isn't it?"

"It's different."

The ground them rumbles. "Let's get moving, I don't think this place is done blowing yet," Mitchell interjects. They all run to Tabatha's truck. Throwing the secretary in the bed, like a worthless inanimate object, then Chris and Christian jump in after him while the others cram into the cab. Tabatha throws it in gear and peels out.

"It's about time my truck got some dirt action!"

"Focus more on getting out of the blast range, and less on doing donuts please," Mitchell from the back, with Sarah hanging on him says.

"You woos," she responds.

"Whatever."

The desert heat rises as the clouds from the electrical storm clear out, but the ground continued rumbling until another explosion sends debris into the then falling to the surface. She swerves to miss some of the debris that lands in front of her. A large chunk of the generator crashes right in front of the truck and she slams on the breaks. And then another large piece of metallic debris falls a few feet from them. It's the exoskeleton that Mitchell had become attached to, slightly mangled up. That was the last of the falling debris.

"I think it's all finally over," they conclude as they look back at the remnant plume of smoke in the distance.

"Any chance you can fly us out of the desert?" Hammer asks.

"Dude, I am royally wiped out," Tabatha replies, placing the side of her head on the top of the steering wheel. They chuckle. They're relieved of the tension now that the mission is over. Tabatha glances back at her sister, curled up on Mitchell with her head on his shoulder and her hair wrapped around them like a cocoon. "How ya doing sis?" She then said, internally ecstatic to see her sister safe. She smiled back at Tabatha.

"Continue due east!" Chris shouts after getting off the radio. "Air transportation is heading our way to assist!"

"Good, cuz it is *hot* out here," Christian emphasizes. "And I still think we should leave the secretary in the middle of the desert."

"That wouldn't be very *Christian* of you, would it?" Chris says, laughing.

"You're a funny guy," Christian replies, finding the phrase overly redundant.

Tabatha puts her truck back in gear and circles around the debris, continuing due east toward a fleet of military helicopters – pulling a ball of mangled exoskeleton behind the truck.

CHAPTER XXI

Mission Complete

"What was initially reported as an extensive military exercise earlier this week in the Great Basin Desert on the northern border of Utah and Nevada – in an area designated a military arm's testing ground for nearly a decade – has now been confirmed as an actual military operation..." News reporter.

"Various high-level officials from the defense and state departments have been indicted after thousands of documents have been recovered that confirm the revelation of extra-human experimentation over three decades. Tabatha Johnson – who has gained quite the reputation recently after determining that she possesses some kind of extra-sensory capability – is found to have a *twin sister* who was among those being experimented on, and is the only living survivor of these experimentations..." Another News Reporter.

"I'm here in the Basin Desert. We were able to make our way to the site of this massive explosion. As you can see, the hole in the ground here is thousands of meters in diameter and recedes hundreds of feet into the ground. Mangled metal and debris litter the surrounding. Now, we have gotten word from the New York times that they have an anonymous source linking this to Russian collusion, and you know the New York times is super ultra-trust worthy..." CNN news anchor.

"Hey, you!!" An MP spots the anchor as he begins running as does the cameraman who happens to catch on camera the anchor falling over and five military police officers piling on top of him...

...At the Pentagon, the Joint Chiefs of Staff with the Chairman and vice chairman of the chiefs of staff, and state department officials were interviewing Tabatha with her team behind her. Sarah was also present but hid most of herself behind Mitchell with her exposed hand clenched to his wounded upper arm, suggesting that she was intimidated by those interviewing Tabatha.

"These are satellite photos of what *used* to be a secret research base and military satellite launch pad. Now it's a four hundred foot deep, and half-mile diameter hole in the desert ground," one of the officials narrates the photos on the monitor.

"*Secret* is an understatement general. I don't understand how you could have had a program like this directly under your noses and not know what was going on for so many years," Tabatha responds.

The officials glanced at each other in silence as they couldn't rebuttal her response. "Yeah. I'm having a hard time discerning how this wasn't caught myself," the general admitted.

"Oh, I do," Christian interjects. "Lack of oversight on defense appropriations. Not to mention severe holes in your immigration system..." he responded rhetorically, to which the joint chiefs quietly nodded to each other in agreement.

"Please wait until the question is directed to you, Mr. Argonia," the chairman replied. "Also, our new fleet of military hardware was lost in the desert event. What do you say about that?"

"I say; good! You are aware that my sister was being utilized as the source of your *hardware's* destructive capabilities, right? What do you say about that, general?" Tabatha again responded.

"I don't know how to respond to that," they again admitted.

"I'll accept that as an apology on behalf of *all* the monsters who were behind this," Tabatha calmly stated.

"*All* the monsters?"

"It wasn't just Ivan behind this."

"You're right. Speaking of Dr. Sorvan..."

"Doctor Sorvan?" Tabatha rhetorically repeated as the two words seemed to contradict one another.

"Your whistleblower friend in the defense department leaked these out to the public this week," he showed her the stack of paper equivalent to that of a novel. "These expose Ivan's involvement in anti-bio warfare research beginning in the nineteen eighties and culminating in his *apparent* death in nineteen ninety-three after an incident during an experiment damaged a large portion of his skull and right cerebral hemisphere. The information your team retrieved from one of Sorvan's servers adds an even more disturbing set of circumstances than what has been officially documented under the umbrella of the U.S. Defense Department."

"That's an understatement," Hammer interjected.

"Hold up. *One* of his servers?" Rodney inquired.

"Correct. This server is linked to a network of I.P. addresses positioned throughout the globe. Most are in hostile nations. The C.I.A. has been working on cracking the firewalls," the chairman continued. "Now it's quoted here; *Ivan's intellect is necessary for the continuation of the program and to ensure the success of project twenty-four.* Another communicate six months later, says; *Ivan's recovery, though, successful has resulted in unexpected shifts in his behavior. Insubordination and aggression are believed to be the result of; electro-engineered reconstruction of his brain, but his memory and intellect remain intact.* This is a year later; *"research on four of the psychic children; have surpassed all expectations. Number Twenty-Four proving to be the most valuable – though the reasoning continues to elude the Dr."*

"Mr. Chairman, we really don't need to hear it all word for word," Tabatha interjects, as the details cause her to swell with aggression.

"Understandable. In a nutshell, this report documents the gruesome experimentations, as well as their discovery of your existence and a detailed description of how to *persuade* you to be a part of their project," the general concludes.

"What about those who were apart of this?" Tabatha asks.

"So far, thirty individuals have been indicted for conspiracy. As you know, earlier this week, the president removed both the secretary of state and secretary of defense from their positions and are among those being indicted. Fifteen hundred hostiles are awaiting extradition as well."

"It sounds like a mission complete to me," Christopher responds.

"For now. I can see your sister has become somewhat attached to one of your – sidekicks," the chairman sarcastically noted.

"Sidekicks?" Hammer, Rodney, and Christian glance at each other insulted.

"Mitchell *did* take a bullet for her, and she is obviously very appreciative of that fact," Tabatha explained.

"I suppose I'd be appreciative too if someone took a bullet for me."

"And – my arm still hurts – but it's ok – it is alright," Mitchell adds under his breath from the pressure of Sarah's grip on his wound.

"On to you and your sister," they continue. "It's been explained, in very few details, that you and your sister possess some kind of metaphysical connection – or bond – that allows the two of you to do some interesting things. I don't know about the rest of this panel, but I, for one, am rather curious about what exactly you two are fully capable of?"

"Mr. Vice chairman, and chiefs," Kurtis chimes in. "Initial data aroused some concerns in regard to their opposing kinetic polarities. We have, however, over the last few days, been conducting additional studies in regard to this particular issue. What we *now* know, is that one; this metaphysical connection, to use your vernacular, is what we're currently referring to as *extrinsic D.N.A.*, due to the immense amount of information this *signal* consists of and is what allows them to do what they can do independently as long as they remain in relatively close proximity to each other."

"Which is what?"

"Interacting with matter, at the molecular and atomic level. I.e., Tabatha can move things, and Sarah can create friction in things," Kurtis simply put. "Now, a physical connection between them is something we're still determining. We have conflicting data on this currently, so they're keeping the affection to a minimum – so to speak – until we have more solid data. But essentially, the analogy being used is, they're opposing polarities."

"Do you know what the source of this is yet?"

"It's being speculated that their *immaterial* minds manage their *entire* physiology. But again, this is theoretical at the moment since we can't observe or study the mechanics of something metaphysical," Kurtis concludes his brief explanation.

"This sounds awfully dangerous to me," one of the officials comment. Tabatha could tell what he was thinking to which was explicit in her facial expression, but held her tongue until he finished.

"Your sister is suspected of having extensive psychological trauma…"

"Well, no, kidding. She's been isolated and experimented on for thirty-six years. What kind of psychological condition would you be in?"

"I'm not disagreeing with you, Ms. Johnson. Our primary concern here though is the documentation of apparent *disassociation personality disorder*, *SOA – or sudden onset aggression*, along with many other potential psychological problems," he continued reading from the report.

"As I said, what kind of condition do you expect her to be in?"

"Ms. Johnson," another official responds, "...I'm reading directly from Mr. Penfield's submission regarding what Sarah is capable of – *spontaneous thermal kinetic outbursts.* And *her ability to consciously control this attribute is currently minimal.* This is one of your allies saying this, not any of us. I don't know about you, Ms. Johnson, but I'd be really nervous around a toddler with a deadly weapon. And your sisters' mindset is similar to that *of* a child – only a child with an incredible built-in weapon."

"I know what you're thinking, and no, she's is not being put back in a box for therapy – or studying. She stays with me. I'll help her."

"How are you going to do that?"

"I've actually been putting quite a bit of thought into this, but I've decided that my sister and I will remain in seclusion to *not* interfere with the affairs of the world." Tabatha's statement drew both negative and positive responses from the officials.

"You're not going to stay here?" another general asks.

"Haven't I caused enough damage? There's a lot of fear over me, and frankly, I don't want to continue to contribute to public anxiety."

"Believe it or not, polling has you more favorable then congress."

"Is that hard to do?" she mumbles to herself. "But seriously, they probably like what I can do. Which is the other reason I want to get out of dodge – I don't want to be drug into fixing everyone's issues."

"Well, that's unfortunate. Prior to this hearing, the administration agreed to reinstate your protected asset classification, in hopes that we could utilize your kinetic abilities in certain cases."

"I defer to my previous statement," Tabatha responds. "Now, joint chiefs and generals, and sorry that I don't know the rest of your titles..." she then stands up from the table, "I have a very important function this evening, and we have one more stop. Thank you for not yelling at me this time." At that, she and her team – and sister – head to the conference room exit, but as she approaches the door, the chairman stands up for one more statement;

"Tabatha," he says, "Is your sister going to get a haircut?"

"After she gets over the fear of a pair of scissors approaching her, yes."

"Tabatha," he again says, "I hope you might take time to reconsider. And, well done – to all of you."

"Listen, if the moon starts falling – I'll see what I can do," Tabatha responds rhetorically, then turns and leaves with her team.

"You think you can really stop the moon from falling?" asks Rodney.

"Ha! I'm going to be on the first space shuttle off this rock," she responds.

"Some superhero you are," Hammer replied.

"Hey, I'm practical."

CHAPTER XXII

Reconciliations

"Are you ready?" Tabatha asks Christian as they sit in her truck in the parking lot of the psychiatric hospital.

"Yeah, I guess," he replies. "We better hurry before I change my mind again," he adds, as they both hop out of the truck and head into the hospital.

After signing in, they're then lead down a hallway lined with rooms passing a medication kiosk on their way. The doctor stops outside one of the many doors and opens it. "Charles," she says. "You have a visitor." A mixture of grey and white course hair made up his full mustache and beard. He obviously hadn't shaven in some time and he was partly balled. He was on his small metal frame twin bed pushed into the corner of the room, frantically staring at the edge of the bed.

"Stay back – back – get back..." Charles repeated at, what seemed like, the floor. Every so often, he would kick a leg out kicking something off the edge of the bed.

"Good luck with him, no one has ever been able to get through to him," she said, then walked away.

"You coming in?" Christian asks Tabatha before entering the room.

"No, no, no. This is all you," she replies. Then Christian entered the room.

Tabatha glanced at the doors down both ends of the hallway. A nurse in charge of the medications at the kiosk next to Tabatha noticed a single tear run down her face. Tabatha lightly shook her head, adjusting her mind to the inundation of emotions that were vibrant within the building.

"Are you ok?" the nurse asks.

"Oh, yeah. I'm fine. It's been a crazy busy week. And my allergies – man their bad today," she responded.

"Yeah, tell me about it. What do you think about all this superhero stuff all over the news lately? Pretty wild."

"Eh, I think it's fake."

The nurse looked a bit closer at Tabatha's face. Tabatha knew what she was thinking and avoided eye contact.

"Speaking of which, you look kind of like..."

"Oh, I just have one of those faces," Tabatha quickly replies before the nurse completed her statement.

"Yeah, I suppose so," concluded the nurse then went back to getting medication ready for the patients.

"Hey, Dad," Christian says. Charles looked up at him then back at the edge of the bed pointing at it. Christian intensely gazed at his father. From Charles's perspective, the edge of the bed was lined with ugly meat-eating little gremlins. Dozens of them were in the room. Every once in a while, one would crawl up on the bed, in which he would kick it off.

After a few moments, the nasty little creatures, one at a time, vanished. Charles then, anxiously, crawled off the bed and began looking around the room for them. Christian just watched. "Where'd they go?" Charles asked Christian.

"Dad, it was all an illusion. They weren't real," Christian explained.

"Dad?" Charles pondered the word, for having not been in his right mind for years, it was foreign to him. But, slowly, his normal cognitive functions began coming back to him. "You're my son?"

"Yeah. We talked once. A long time ago."

Charles stood in the middle of the floor, silent, contemplating. To Christian, he still looked crazy. "Well, I guess you're not much different then you were, after all," Christian commented before getting off the bed to leave. At least his conscience was now clear, having reversed what he did to his dad. Christian opened the door, but before leaving the room, Charles desperately, with a quiver in his voice, said, "Don't leave!"

Christian stopped and turned around. "I remember," Charles added. "I've missed you." That simple statement took Christian by surprise. Then the doctor walked by and observing Charles standing in the middle of the room, in awe, she said;

"Charles?" She then left quickly. Tabatha then stood in the doorway

"Who's that?" Charles asks about the woman in the door, watching them

"That's my, uhhh..."

"...Boss," Tabatha wittily inserts. Christian and Charles looked at each, then out of nowhere, Charles began laughing at the statement. Then Christian laughed with him. But Charles laughter soon turned to crying.

"Dad? Are you ok?" Christian asks, feeling a little concern for his father.

"I'm so sorry!!" Charles then said through his tears. He then threw his arms around Christian. Christian didn't know what to do and looked at Tabatha, who just smiled. "I said those things. I never meant it..." he then explained to Christian some of his past. "You're mother said she wanted to sew her oats and left. I never knew what happened to her. I got depressed and drank and drank. I never got over that." Charles's head was on his shoulder, and Christian's shirt soaked up the tears. "Can I have you," Charles whimpered. The question was an odd one, but Christian knew what it meant.

"Yes," Christian replied then threw his arms around his father's neck and began crying as well. The touching scene also triggered Tabatha to shed some tears.

Shortly thereafter the doctor came back to the room with two more psychiatrists. They watched in amazement of Charles's condition, and after the time of reconciliation between Charles and Christian, the doctors began asking Charles a series of questions to determine his mental state. His answers indicated that he was completely sane, just a little on the emotional side. During Charles's short eval, Christian discussed with the doctor about his father's release from the hospital.

"I'd like to get him discharged," he says to her.

"Well, I can understand that, but this is so sudden. What happened?" She asked.

"It's a long story. I needed to right some wrongs."

"It sure looks like you did something right. Would it be ok to keep him here for just a couple of days so we can make sure he's good to go? You have to understand, this type of turnaround is, well, not common, to put it mildly," the doctor requests with good intentions.

"Yeah, I understand. I guess that will give me a couple of days to get a place set up for him," Christian concurs. After that, he explained to his father the plan for discharging him. Then after some goodbyes, Tabatha and Christian left with the promise of coming back to get him in a few days.

....

"You may now kiss your bride," Pastor Reed says to, now, David and Jaimie Glessinjer, in front of a large leafy, flowery arbor, which was near the edge of the mountain that ran into the northern Atlantic sea.

"Tabatha!" Jaimie shouts and runs up to her in her white wedding dress. She plasters Tabatha with a hug. "Thank you so much!! I can't believe you let us have our wedding here on this island. It's so beautiful!"

"Haha, any time Jaimie," She responded. Music was playing that many were dancing to, including two unexpected individuals.

"Oh my goodness, that's your aunt and..."

"Jason Penfield, I know."

"That's both gross and romantic simultaneously."

"You're telling me. I've been seeing what my aunts been thinking for a week. Now I'm wishing she was still thinking of younger guys."

"Well, at least he's rich, right? Ha-ha!" Jaimie continues.

"Girl, go get your man and dance with him," Tabatha says.

"Oh wait, I have to toss my bouquet still," Jaimie remembers and runs off to get the ladies in a line.

"You're not going to go up there?" Christian says, walking up to Tabatha.

"No. I'm a freak. I don't know any guy that would be interested in me," she says flirtatiously, knowing full Christian's interest in her.

Christian, playing along, responded, "I know someone."

"Oh, you do, do you?" she sarcastically says. "Does he always wear T-Shirts?"

"He's not right now," Christian says, playing along, and referring to himself.

"True. You do look nice in that Dress shirt. Although the jeans don't really go with it."

"Coming from the woman who wore coveralls on her only..." Tabatha covers his mouth with her hand before he could complete his sentence with a, "Shhh. That was a one-time thing, and it was to get out of it."

Christian then softly took her hand off his mouth and held it. "I know," he responds, moving his face closer to hers.

"So, I guess I should confess – I did think about you a little since that day at the doctor's office."

"I know that too."

"One! Two! Three!!!" Jaimie shouts in the background then tosses her bouquet high in the air behind her. The line of girls was reaching out for it, each hoping to catch it. But then the bouquet suddenly stopped descending and flies into Tabatha's open hand, to a few 'no fair' cries in the background. Tabatha and Christians lips almost meet when;

"Seriously!!" They say in unison.

"Sorry to interrupt," Kyle was standing there, "Just wanted to let you know, I'm available if you want to tie the knot real quick," he offers, then walks away, revealing Cindy who was behind him.

"Cindy, what are you doing," Tabatha says.

"Nothing. Don't mind me. As your best friend, I should be the first person to see your first kiss," she says excitedly. Tabatha sends her a message with a raised eyebrow. "Oh fine," she too then walks away, mumbling, "Can't make fun of her or witness her first kiss," as she storms off. Then Naomi was next, holding a bag of salt and vinegar chips.

"Yes, Aunt Naomi?"

"Aunt Naomi," Naomi responds, for Tabatha changed her aunts' title since the revelation of her mother. "Well, it's about time. But, here are some coupons for hygiene products, sweetheart."

"Seriously, Aunt Naomi?" Christian laughed.

"Oh hush, you know you stink most of the time. Tabatha placed her hand over her face out of embarrassment. "Christian, thank you so much for taking her off my hands. Oh and congratulations on inheriting Penfield's corporate empire."

"Thanks, Ms. Johnson," Christian replied.

"You know, I almost died last week."

"You'll get over it, sweetheart," Naomi replies, then as turned to wander off, Tabatha, spitefully, snatched the bag of chips from Naomi's hands.

"You smell great, by the way," Christian says to Tabatha. "But you might want to take it easy on those salt and vinegar chips."

"You'll get over it," Tabatha responds as she puts some chips in her mouth.

Tabatha then spotted Mitchell walking toward the reception/wedding area. Tabatha headed toward him, leaving Christian without kissing him.

"How's she doing?" she asked Mitchell

"Well, I don't think she's ever eaten food in her life. She eats more than you!" Mitchell said sarcastically, but truthfully as well.

"Whatever. Did she watch the videos?"

"Yeah. I don't think she understood much of it. She kept running her fingers across the screen. I think she was trying to touch your guy's mother's face. But she's asleep now."

"That's good. Thanks for taking care of her like that. That means a lot."

"No problem."

"Oh, and speaking of taking care of things. As promised, I told you I'd in – tro – duce…" Tabatha was about to say that David's associate was there at the wedding, but sensed Mitchell's interests had changed. "No way!"

"What?" Mitchell responds to Tabatha's surprised expression

"You and my sister?"

"No! No! No!" he quickly responded. "Nothing like that."

"You're kind of taken by her," Tabatha deducted.

"Like a kid, you know? I don't know. A week and a half ago, I was scared to death of her. Even questioning the idea of saving her," Mitchell explained. "But, after all this, well, it's just really got me thinking about things besides myself, I suppose. I don't know. Maybe I have a purpose beyond my personal expectations."

"Mitchell, I know we get on you pretty hard sometimes, but let's face it, you usually deserve it," Tabatha said to which Mitchell reluctantly nodded in agreement. "Although I have to admit, this week has been an eye-opener for me too. But you, you are super smart. Intellect is a real gift. Just figure out where He wants you to use it. Me, sometimes I think I'm just a glorified accident," Tabatha concludes, to which Mitchell shakes his head.

"No, you're no accident. Neither is your sister. I'm fully confident of that," Mitchell responded. Then he began to turn to leave.

"You got a new job?" Tabatha psychically deducted.

"Can't hide anything from you," he replied. She smiled. "A private space exploration company in Texas needs a senior computer programing engineer. And I need a break from close calls."

"Yeah, no doubt. Well, good luck. I think Sarah will miss you." Tabatha said.

"I'll miss her too – as weird as that sounds. But I'm sure we'll visit again! Or at least I'll see you two on the news someday – ha-ha," he concluded then heads to the helipad.

"You liked him, didn't you?" he assumed.

"I did. He's a good guy. That's why I picked him to be on the team to begin with."

Then Hammer and Rodney joined Tabatha and Christian, also watching Mitchell leaving.

"Where's he going?" Hammer asked.

"He's got a new job in Texas."

"Texas? That's too bad. I liked him. He was funny," Hammer admitted.

"So, what happened to him?" Rodney asked.

"He lost his family in a fire five years ago," Tabatha replied.

"Oh, man!!"

"Yeah, but I think he's back on the right path now."

....

The wedding was now over, and everyone had left the island. Only Tabatha and Sarah occupied the rock. It was early morning, before daybreak. They were asleep in separate rooms. Sarah then woke up to hearing her experimental name in her head. The room was dark, lit only by the moonlight coming in through her bedroom window. She began following instructions indicative of a computer program in her mind.

She followed the audible instructions down the hall to the elevator and took it to the main floor. She then continued down the hall and entered the study. Shortly after entering the room, the windows changed to video mode and scenes of war and violence broadcast over the screens. The images of human brutality transported back in time when she was forced to watch brutality as a brainwashing mechanism. The digital voice in her head continued inciting her until an aggressive spirit took hold of her, and in a fury, the study was consumed in a flame.

POSTLUDE

A swarm of men in black T-Shirts, black slacks, and dark sunglasses combed the evening Great basin desert around the crater. Metal debris that scattered the perimeter of the crater was being picked up and thrown into black garbage trucks. One of the men stopped next to a transparent ball, half-covered with a partial metallic skull. A tight mesh of wiring and electronic components were inside. It was the last remaining evidence of Dr. Ivan Sorvan. The man knelt and opened an oversized briefcase that contained a small computer. He then connected the web of wires encased in the metal covered orb to the small computer. 'Communicating...' was displayed on the small monitor, followed by a blinking dot. Then a highly sophisticated computer code began streaming on the monitor. The man then stands up and speaks. "He's still with us." The front of the briefcase contained the acronym – U.N.

Halfway around the world in the bowels of the rugged mountains of Northern Pakistan, the short statement was received. An individual is handed a small Styrofoam box. He responds in a European accent, "It looks like our middle man came thru after all."

The lid was removed, revealing one vile of blood. Tabatha's name was written on it. It was then taken out and was injected into a tube of fluid that flowed into a glass chamber filled with a slightly milky liquid along with other cables and plastic tubes. Inside the chamber was the body of a woman floating around in somewhat of a fetal position. Her hair was red but almost resembled tentacles in which the strands appeared to follow the movements of the two men in the room as they paced and talked. As Tabatha's blood entered the chamber and was absorbed by the woman like creature and the body began twitching and particulates began circulating within its flesh.

"As you can see, Sorvan's fears were all for naught," the European comments. "She'll be the greatest weapon ever created."

"You think we can control her?" the other said.

"Not a problem."

"That's what Sorvan said. We need to be careful. The Americans have discovered many of our allies' networks. It won't take them long before they get in."

"Many of those *Americans* are still with us." The two of them stand in front of the glass chamber simply watching the body floating in the fluid.

A monitor recording creature's vital signs had a header; **C-117 – Status: Successful.**

Then, sensing their presence, her eyes open...

Made in the USA
Las Vegas, NV
31 August 2022

54459827R00187